# THE FORTUNATE SONS

A Novel of the 3d Alabama Volunteers

By
Booth Malone

# The Fort

unate
Sons

A Novel of the
3d Alabama Volunteers

Booth Malone

The Fortunate Sons

COPYRIGHT © 2020 by Booth Malone

All rights reserved under International and
Pan-American Copyright Convention.
Published in the United States by
ROBA Publishing Company

Jacket Design and Maps: Booth Malone
Book Design: Scott Sederstrom

ISBN: 978-1-7360143-0-1
MANUFACTURED IN THE UNITED STATES OF AMERICA

*For Frances*

'How now!' cried Zeus. 'Are you not now content? You have what you asked for.'

*Phaedrus*

TABLE OF CONTENTS

To the Reader
The Militias of the 3d Alabama Regiment
Some 3d Alabama Volunteers
List of Maps

## The Frogs:

1 Phelan • 2 Battle • 3 Hoyt
4 Best Laid Schemes • 5 Cecil • 6 Saint Nick
7 Charlie • 8 The Virginians • 9 The Roads
10 Doyle's Field

## The Swamp:

11 L'Commandant • 12 The Hornets
13 The Awkward Squad • 14 The English Opening
15 The Old Mulberry • 16 Princess Anne
17 Gracie and Hunter • 18 Dark Horse • 19 The Minstrels
20 Moseley's Church • 21 A Good Man
22 Hard Times • 23 Pig Point • 24 Lomax
25 On The Wing • 26 Drewry's Bluff

## King Log:

27 Gillies Creek • 28 Frogs
29 Casey's Redoubt • 30 Nine Mile
31 Seven Pines
32 Cowards • 33 Foolscap

## King Stork:

34 Brass • 35 Red Tape • 36 Cold Harbor
37 Savages • 38 Willis Church
39 The High Ground • 40 Private Quarters
41 Malvern Hill
42 Ravens • 43 Balaclava
44 Les Moutons • 45 Les Miserables

## Post Script:

Afterword and Acknowledgments
Chapter Notes
Appendix A: Seniority

# TO THE READER

I thought a preface would be easier than this.

My idea was simple, really. To relate the stories of an elite Civil War regiment through the eyes of its soldiers, not its commanders. Who knew our country's history would catch up to us before I could get that done?

Each time I try to put down a few thoughts, the world goes up the spout. A fresh spout every week.

Okay, so some of us suspected *some* of this was going to happen; but Pandemic? Economic shutdown? Rioting in the streets? "Dark Forces?" It makes you think, if not re-think.

And the trend of desperate times appears to have legs. I'm as curious as you are how all this will turn out; as curious as they must have been in 1861.

The story here, of the 3d Alabama Volunteers is true; a remarkable regiment, in a remarkable army, in a remarkable war. It is not another tale of Lee and McClellan, *et al.* and of this big battle, or that one, told from a slightly different angle. IMHO the generals have received more than their due. *Fortunate Sons* is a story of the volunteer militias: the planter's sons, the junior partners, the politically connected, the true believers, the 'gentlemen' soldiers, brought up to fight for 'The Cause.'

*'The Cause':* I have no desire to wave that particular flag. One may argue States' Rights, Slavery, the Constitution, Who's to Blame—have at it: "my country 'tis of thee," after all. What is beyond dispute is the side that lost, needed to lose; else we would find *Animal Farm* stocked with denizens from this side of the ocean.

Unless you are a descendant, it is likely you have never heard of this regiment, or even paused at its mention in accounts of the Seven Days, Chancellorsville, or Gettysburg. I had never heard of them before 2008, and I *am* a descendant (that's my great-uncle Nesbit on the cover). In histories of the war, they are usually relegated to a list of the "Also in attendance." Truly, it takes a keen eye to find them.

Yet, for all that, the Alabama Department of Archives and History, in Montgomery, holds more source material on this one regiment—'The Glorious Third'—than on all the others from that state, *combined*. That alone should make you curious.

I caution the reader (and I pray there is more than just the one of you) this narrative has an abundance of names and references. But you have survived *Game of Thrones* and *Lord of the Rings*—you'll survive this. You already know who Jeff Davis and Robert E. Lee, were; you have an inkling where Mobile is, and so forth—it's not like I'm dropping you in the middle of Mordor. Besides, *it's the Civil War:* the crowd will thin out. Only a handful of volunteers went through the entire war *viz.* beginning to end; another thing that should make you curious.

Maps, rosters, and chapter notes will help keep things straight and give the professionals something to harumph. Historical fiction it may be, but *Sons* is not balderdash. The effort has been made: no fact has been altered for the sake of plot, nothing of substance has been invented. Individuals conform to known events.

Other than that, you know about as much as they did at the time.

Projected as a trilogy. *The Fortunate Sons* is a work in progress. If you are a descendant of the regiment, I encourage your participation in their story, with whatever letters and diaries, family lore and photographs, may have come down to you. I am not hard to find.

Booth Malone
Midland, Georgia
Summer 2020

Col. Tennent Lomax, LTC Cullen Battle, commanding
# The Militias of the 3d Alabama
Their first Captains:

Co A: *The Mobile Cadets*
Robert Sands (36) to 6-1-62, then Thomas Brown (28)

Co B: *The Gulf City Guards (Mobile)*
William Hartwell (41) to 4-26-62, then John Simpson (28)

Co C: *The Tuskegee Light Infantry*
William Swanson (45) to 5-1-62, then Robert Mayes (33)

Co D: *The Southern Rifles aka 'Bald Hornets' (Union Springs)*
Richard Holmes Powell (39)

Co E: *The Washington Light Infantry (Mobile)*
Archibald Gracie (28) to 7-31-61, then John Chester (29)

Co F: *The Metropolitan Guards (Montgomery)*
F. Winston Hunter (42) to 10-31-61, then Wat Phelan (23)

Co G: *The Montgomery True Blues (Detached Feb. 17, 1862)*
William Andrews (35)

New
Co G: *The Lomax Sharpshooters (Formed May 2, 1862)*
M. Ford Bonham (33)

Co H: *The Beauregard-Lowndes*
M. Ford Bonham (33) to 5-1-62, then Neal Robinson (25)

Co I: *The Wetumpka Light Guards*
Edward Sims Ready (27)

Co K: *The Mobile Rifles*
Lewis Woodruff (45) to 5-18-62, then John Hoyt (21)

Co L: *The Dixie Eagles (Union Springs; formed April 1862)*
Joseph Jelks (42) to 6-27-62, then Richard Kennon (36)

Staff Officers:
Adjutants: 2LT Chas. Forsyth (25) then 1LT Isaac Wilson (24),
then 2LT Sam Johnston (22);
Surgeons: E. Semple (41), then Paul Lee (26); Quartermasters:
Capt. John Sanford (35), then 1LT Thos. Brown (28)
Sergeant Majors: Wm. Moreland (33), then Cecil Whitman (19)

(Approximate age in 1861)

# Other 3d Volunteers

*Mobile Cadets*
Robert Armistead • LT James H. Broun • Cecil Carter
John Chighizola • Jack Goulet • Wm. 'Zou Zou' Hartman
Nick Weeks • SGT Bruno Yniestra

*The Gulf City Guards*
James Hunt

*The Tuskegee Light Infantry*
Nesbit 'Neb' Battle • 'Cotton-Eyed Joe' Fort • Edmund Fowler
Henry 'Hal' Martin • SGT James 'Preacher' Tate • John Pride

*The Southern Rifles aka 'The Bald Hornets'*
SGT Jean Beaumont • James Branscomb • Lewis Branscomb
Micajah 'Boss' Cargill • Jas. 'Rafe' Herrin • Thomas Johnson
Amos Powell • LT E. Troup Randle • Henry Smith
Alonzo Stinson • Micajah 'Old Dick' Stinson

*The Washington Light Infantry*
Milton Boullemet • George Ellison • John Gilmore
Harvey Ellis Jones • Jas. 'Jester' Simon

*The Metropolitan Guards*
LT John McAnerney

*The Montgomery True Blues*
James Roach

*The Lomax Sharpshooters*

*The Beauregard-Lowndes*
Wm. R. 'Bob' Hardy

*The Wetumpka Light Guards*
LT Henry Storrs • James Stamp

*The Mobile Rifles*
'Little Joe' Baumer • Henry 'Shanghai' Donaldson • Jimmie Howard
Corbet Ryder • William Treat

## Maps

MOBILE, AL & ROUTES NORTH  27
NORFOLK, VA & HAMPTON ROADS  56-57
THEATRE EAST & SOUTH OF RICHMOND  178
SEVEN PINES, June 1, 1862  214-215
MALVERN HILL, July 1, 1862, Afternoon  299
MALVERN HILL, July 1, 1862, Evening  305

# The Frogs

*"Gentlemans, be seated."*

Cullen Battle, Esq.
Maj., 3d Alabama Volunteers

# CHAPTER 1 — PHELAN
December 31, 1860

PHELAN WORKED the reflection suspended in the lead panes. His creation appearing by turns puzzled or wild-eyed, even one-eyed; the slightest shift transforming the beast.

Oblivious to such moonshine, the creature would, from time to time utter a few grunts, mumbles wholly unintelligible to his secretary. Gazing outward from his vantage, the dear old thing seemed a thousand miles away.

Puzzlement, rage, concern, back to puzzlement, Phelan put the beast through its paces. With a start he realized the governor's eyes had turned upon him. A quizzical look it was, lingering long enough to become uncomfortable before turning back to its view: the sentries on the grounds below, smoke curling up from their fire. "The time has come," he said.

"Sir?" Phelan sat up straight.

"These sentries I see. I take it they are Battle's boys?"

"Yes, sir—the Tuskegee Lights. They arrived a few days ago."

A grunt. "We taking care of them?"

"Yes, sir. The Exchange has put them up, ten or so the room."

Another grunt. A pause. The plunge: "Phelan, how good is your geography?"

"I can name the capitals of all the states."

The response to this was so long in coming, the secretary (unsure whether his facetiousness had even registered), returned his attention to organizing the executive correspondence. When the Governor did speak, his voice sounded flat and as lifeless as the sky. "Can you? Bully." Over his shoulder: "When you can name all the county seats in Alabama you may have a future in this town."

"Yes, sir."

Despite its disjointed nature, Phelan knew this give and take was not idle chatter.

Governor Moore turned back to view Market Street, the beautiful tree-lined boulevard running from the capitol down to the artesian spring at the city's crossroads; the secretary looking now, too. It was a grand vista: Montgomery was new and vibrant. Phelan saw only a boundless future ahead—for the place, for himself, for all his brothers. On a clear day one could see for miles from this office, spot the steeples—way off there, in Lowndesboro. Though not this particular evening, the dull red glow of sunset was a grimace through the overcast.

"I see carriages arriving for the Blues' banquet; their New Year's, I suppose. Are you a member of the Blues?"

"No, sir. The Metropolitans; Captain—"

"Fine group," the governor cut him off, leaving him free to speculate.

"I helped build this State. Do you know it, Phelan? When you and your brothers were small—helped build this town. Your father played his part too, of course, but they never would have gotten the capitol out of Tuskaloosa without me."

"No, sir."

"Planted the first elm on Market, down yonder, by the Exchange. Can't see it. . . . "

The thought becoming an effort, his words petered out.

Phelan had never heard the governor sound so weary; a reflection of the man's state of mind, perhaps. The legislative session just ended, more than enough to wear down a man, make him pine for yesterdays, yesterdays before John Brown. Harpers Ferry had kicked open the ant pile, sure, and with it, the last bulwarks of rational discourse; the dream of Jefferson and Adams brought low by that lone murderous zealot.

The raid had changed everything, including the governor's thinking. Elected as an anti-secessionist reformer, the scales had at last fallen from Moore's eyes. For John Brown to hatch his scheme, to contract and transport his thousand pikes, it was plain as day he'd had help. Substantial help. From whence it came was the question.

In his desk, Moore kept a newspaper containing an interview with Brown recorded soon after his capture. As occasion demanded, he would brandish it for the edification of his audience. One passage, repeated so often, was committed to memory:

> "You had better—you people of the South—prepare yourselves for a settlement of this question—that must come up for settlement sooner than you are prepared for it. The sooner you are prepared the better. You may dispose of me very easily . . . but this question is still to be settled—this Negro question I mean; the end of that is not yet."[1]

The madman *was* disposed of easily: at the end of a rope, two months after his raid. But the Negro question remained. 'The sooner you are prepared,' the man had said.

"Time never lasts."

"Sir?"

"Days were longer when I was a boy."

Phelan took the governor's meaning, while pretending otherwise. "Winter has come."

Turning, Moore matched his secretary's wan smile: "You will see what I mean one day, young man. Mark my words."

"Yes, sir."

"But you are right: does one no good to wallow in this sort of thinking. 'Tis the season, nothing more, the end of a long and wearisome year." Heaving a heavy sigh: "Pay no mind to the mutterings of the old."

Taking his cue, Phelan straightened in his chair. With Moore warming to his subject, his speech returned to its usual fire. Ten days ago—the day following South Carolina's secession—he had given a stirring speech before a secret session of the legislature, vowing, this time, the Palmetto State would not stand alone.

"Tell me, Phelan: Do you know where Fort Morgan is?"

"Yes, sir. It commands the entrance to Mobile Bay."

"Good. And Fort Gaines?"

---

[1] *New York Herald,* October 21, 1859

"Across from Morgan, on Dauphin Island."

"And Barrancas? Fort Pickens?"

Phelan hesitated only a beat. "Those are Pensacola forts, I believe."

"Four for four. Sleepy little garrisons all, where daily, civilians come and go just as they please. Now then," the governor said, his eyes narrowing, "Ever hear of Mount Vernon?"

"Yes, sir, of course. Though I take it you mean the state arsenal: Mount Vernon *Arsenal*. It is north of Mobile, twenty-mile or so. At the old fort?"

"Not quite. On a hill west of there, three miles from the river, on the military road. A Captain Reno commands the garrison."

Phelan was still. He had no idea where this was going.

Lifting a letter from off his desk, the governor passed it across. "Tell me what you make of this here—from our friend, Mister Clopton, of Tuskegee."

The letter was a copy of correspondence between one of Alabama's congressmen and the President's Secretary of War, written on Christmas Day, seven days back. On the face of it the letter was a mere formality, an innocuous request between two branches of government. Nevertheless, Phelan's eyes widened as he scanned the contents.

Lowering it, the young man offered his summary:

"Five days after South Carolina votes to secede from the Union, and just *one day* after we elect our own delegates for a secession convention, a representative from Alabama asks the United States' Secretary of War for 'the plat and plan of the powder magazines at Mount Vernon Arsenal'?"

"Correct."

"Did—Pardon me—Sir, may I ask: did the Clopton request originate from this office?"

"It did not."

"I take it the congressman—" Phelan caught himself.

"Is an imbecile?" The governor's eyes were bright. "Yes, sir, he surely is. Based on this, I'd say the gen-u-wine article."

"Then let me ask this: what has been the Secretary's reply?"

"Unknown. I received this copy of the inquiry but one hour ago. Though one may safely assume the Secretary's answer has been—or will be—not just 'No,' but 'Hell, No!' This Secretary of War is one of the staunchest of Union men in Ole Buck's cabinet."

"In that case, War will—*is*—taking immediate steps to reinforce Mount Vernon?"

"Yes," said Moore. "I believe one may draw that conclusion: 'Seize and hold the Arsenal. Confiscate their guns. Sever all intercourse between Mobile and Montgomery.' Deny us the means to defend our rights. It is what I would do were I in those shoes and, I need not remind, just as the British intended at Lexington and Concord."

"Unless we are there first?"

"Unless we get there first," he nodded. "The abolitionists have already tried to seize one arsenal, why should they stop with Harpers Ferry? Papers found on Brown's person reveal as much—a strike was planned for right here in Alabama." On his stump now, the governor continued, "I will tell you this, sir, Alabama will not place herself at their mercy, will not bide the time while they plot her destruction. Phelan, the Lincolnites mean to subjugate the South, make no mistake.

"Ole 'Honest Abe,' my foot. The man is a bumpkin. You wait and see: 'tis Seward and his gang, are the power. And mind you me, before they are done, they will have the Negros rise up and murder us in our beds. The massacres of the past will seem a tea party by comparison." Moore lowered his voice, his tone subdued. "You have heard the name Nat Turner I am sure. Up there in Virginia?"

"All my life."

"That 'rising.' . . ." His voice grew husky, "Well, let us just say, Mrs. Moore. . . ." He cleared his throat and, removing his glasses, pretended to clean them. Never before had Phelan heard Moore speak of his wife. No one in his circle had seen her in years. "She has lived in dread of that day, Phelan, that day of wanton slaughter: scores of men, women, children—babes in arms, some of them—hacked to pieces. And the reprisals—the reprisals just as merciless; a horrible, horrible episode, all round.

"The North has never understood this. 'It is your problem' they say. With their next breath they presume to tell us how to fix it. 'Fix us,' they mean. 'Free the slaves. Free the poor slaves.' As though it were so simple as that. As though none of us had ever had the thought ourselves. As though they had not sold them to us in the first place.

"If the Republicans want war, Phelan—by God we will hand them one, right off the top shelf. It is they who have thrown down the gauntlet. By rights, the choice of time and ground shall be ours. Let Posterity be our judge."

Phelan harbored doubts about the governor's logic, but none as to his rationale. Nothing, absolutely nothing, exceeded the South's fear of a slave uprising; at some point in his upbringing, a part of 'the talk' every father had with his son.

"By God's right hand, sir," said the governor rising to his feet, pounding his fist: "The time has come. The abolitionists have had their boots on our neck long enough. Mount Vernon Arsenal is where our guns are. *Our* guns, I say. And I Will Have Them. I will have them, Phelan. Ere four days' time, Alabama takes her stand—come what may: Mount Vernon is where it starts."

## CHAPTER 2 — BATTLE
January 1, 1861

IT WAS past midnight before the operator finished transmitting the governor's orders. Standing back from his table he stretched, shaking out his hand. Phelan, half-way out the door, mouthing his thanks, so as not to disturb the boys sound asleep on their bench. The runners had been busy, too. Let them be. Nothing now that couldn't wait.

But one last duty remained. On the street he turned and faced the home of Colonel Lomax. From his corner he could see any number of carriages and drivers over there. The house was still up, its windows ablaze with light. Phelan was acquainted with the colonel. As part of the state's Second Regiment the Metropolitans were under his command, though he thought it unlikely Lomax would recollect his name. Over the walk, he rehearsed several introductions; an awkward situation, interrupting a family's New Year's Eve. He felt unstrung by the events of the day, by the jarring immediacy of secession. States' Rights had been so much hot air for so long.

Passing the dozing coachmen and servants, he opened the gate and started up the front steps. From behind a column a sentry appeared, stopping him at the point of his bayonet. The man wore the garb of the True Blues; their gaudy parade uniform at that. A fresh recruit, Phelan surmised.

"Halt right there," the man ordered. Looking him over, he judged the stranger's attire short of the occasion: "This is a private affair, mister. State your business or be on your way."

Before Phelan could answer, the front door flew open. A large man strode forth, looming over them both, his frock coat and his beard outlined by the light.

"Stand down, soldier," he ordered. The sentry obeyed. The big man held out his hand and gave Phelan the quick, firm handshake of a politician.

"You must be Judge Phelan's son. Lieutenant Colonel Battle at your service. Please: come in, come in. The colonel has been expecting you."

The butler took his hat, cloak, and gloves, and Battle led him into the parlor. The room was filled with familiar faces, prominent men of the city, most far too important to pay him heed, though conversations did slow while he passed their inspection. The captain and first lieutenant of the Blues, each gave him a nod before returning to their discussion. Colonel Siebels gave him a friendly wink. A fine portrait of Mrs. Lomax presided over the room, otherwise it was a stag affair. Phelan suspected many regrets had gone out, and many a New Year's gathering dampened thereby. His host, he did not see.

Reading his mind, Battle explained, "The colonel is upstairs, reading his children to sleep. Till he comes, let us find a corner where we may talk."

Entering the colonel's study, Battle took a chair facing the door, offering the seat opposite to the secretary.

"What news do you bring, sir? I beg your pardon, you *are* Justice Phelan's son, are you not? Please say yes. I will be mortified if you are not. Thomas, I know, is the eldest, but I do not know which one you are."

"I am Watkins, my father's second. There is Tom and me, then Jack and Ellis; the older boys."

"Splendid," said Battle, "I have it. Now what may I call you, sir? Do you prefer Mister Phelan?"

"Wat, Watkins, or Mister Phelan, as you please. Anything but 'felon'."

The remark took Battle by surprise and produced a loud, good-natured bark of a laugh. The ice was broken. "Indeed. Ha-hah. Very well, 'Wat' it is. Speak to me, Wat."

"This night we have conveyed the governor's orders to certain parties in Mobile, authorizing them to mobilize the local companies, to take and hold Forts—rather, to hold positions—at various points about the bay." Still feeling a little off, he added, "Forthwith," to make it sound official.

His hand dipping into a box of their host's cigars, Battle offered his guest an 'Habana'.

Phelan declined.

"Good for you," he said, nipping the end. "Filthy habit. Never start." Striking a match, he held it under the roll. "These local militias you mention are captained by Sands, Woodruff, and Gracie. You will find no better line officers in the South. Go on." Between his words he lit the smoke, rotating it slowly before the flame, the first quick draws enveloping him in a cloud.

"Yes, sir. The governor did mention those captains. The governor has a copy of a letter from Representative—"

"Yes, yes, I know all about the Clopton letter; I forwarded it. I'll wager the War Department jumped ten feet when they saw that one. What else?"

"Just that the governor has it on good authority *Harriet Lane* has sailed, bound, we believe, for Mobile Bay and her forts, with supplies and reinforcements. *Crusader* has been sighted as well. Governor Moore feels there is the risk the Black Republicans are behind this. Those ships could sever Mobile from the rest of the state."

"I agree. Though *Harriet* is just a revenue cutter and, if memory serves, lightly armed. *Crusader*, on the other hand, would command the bay. The governor is right to be prudent, better to be safe than sorry. Others should take heed."

"Yes, sir."

"And you are with the Metropolitans I believe?"

"Yes, sir. On detached service to the governor."

"Has he shared his plans—his plans for the Metros—with you? Do you know what we are about, here, tonight?" Peering over his smoke, Battle waving his hand vaguely.

"Colonel, I am not at liberty to speak to that subject before I see Colonel Lomax."

"I see." Battle shot him a mischievous look, of a type familiar to Phelan: a look those 'in the know' display, to be certain their opposites know it; one, all clever lawyers cultivate. Recently admitted to the bar himself, Wat knew Battle to be a highly regarded attorney out of Macon County, a land rolling in cotton money. Battle was kin to the Barbour County Shorters; John Gill Shorter (a shoo-in to be the next governor) was married to Battle's sister. Such was common knowledge, just as he knew the present Mrs. Lomax was the widow of John Gill's eldest brother.

"I'm sorry, sir, you have me at a disadvantage," said Phelan, to counter Battle's lengthy silence.

Battle chuckled, silence not being his strong suit. "All right, young man, you win. You have broken me. I will tell you what you surely know already: Colonel Lomax and I are to take an expeditionary force into Florida to seize the forts at Pensacola. A 'Fort Sumter-on-the-Gulf,' if you will. Men (those men in the library, there) are drawing up the plans right this minute, drafting orders that will call up all the militias within fifty miles of this place. Including the Blues, of course, and your own Metropolitans." Battle obviously expected this intelligence to elicit some sort of response. When Phelan failed to react, he prompted, "What do you think of that?"

"As you say."

Battle belched a hearty laugh, one ending in a spate of coughing. "By God, Phelan, I do like that! I do indeed. You are a cool one, I declare. I tell you—No: I tell you *all*, yet you give me nothing in return. Discretion. You and I shall get on famously."

"Nothing would suit me better, sir."

"Are you a college man, Wat?"

"Yes, sir: The Military Institute at Nashville."

"Tuskaloosa, myself," said Battle.

"Mm. A fine school, I am told. Frequently."

The conversation progressed to the relative merits of their alma maters, an exchange dominated by Battle. From there, the topic migrated to Tennessee's prospects for secession and the different factions holding forth around that state. There were strong Union men in east Tennessee, said Phelan; Senator Johnson and Preacher Brownlow not the least of them.

Battle and Phelan could agree on one point: as important as Tennessee was, success would hinge on Virginia. Virginia was all. And Virginia was still a long ways from leaving the Union, let alone joining a confederacy of disaffected states.

If she did *not* act, the rebellion would be confined to the Gulf States—plus Georgia and South Carolina—too weak to be sustained. Men like Moore and Lomax would be imprisoned; possibly, shot.

Battle turned the subject once again.

"I shall make no further attempts to draw you out before you speak with the colonel. Yet I will share this with you: The expeditionary force is to be a shakeout towards the eventuality of sending a regiment of volunteers to Virginia. In Florida we shall see which companies are ready, and which are not. War is coming, Wat, mind you well. And coming fast. Virginia will not be allowed to sit the fence for long. She will either be with us or against us. And, after the John Brown affair, I do not see her against us. Mister Brown's detestable pikes have been sent all over the South, as mementos: 'Lest We Forget.' Mine own Tuskegees have one for their flagstaff.

"When war comes, we (meaning Colonel Lomax and myself), and many of those whom you saw at work in the parlor, aim to be part of Alabama's Expeditionary Brigade, the first to go to Virginia."

"Then best we get off to a good start."

Battle smiled broadly. "There you go. Yes. Young man, *that* is what I want to hear.

"The powder kegs of Fort Morgan, Mount Vernon Arsenal, and the forts at Pensacola will be just a taste of what is to come. Those militia who best answer the call there, will be the first chosen for Virginia. I suspect Woodruff's Rifles will give good account, as will the Cadets, most assuredly." Halting in mid-speech, Battle stood. "Good morning, colonel," he said.

From behind, Wat heard: "It *is* morning, isn't it? . . . "

The voice was an orator's voice, as sonorous as any Wat had ever heard from podium or pulpit. Wat rose from his seat and turned.

"The year of Our Lord, eighteen hundred, sixty-one," the voice continued. "My, my, how time flies. Dear Cullen, have you been drumming the Blues and Metros into your army? Your Tuskegees may be raring to go, but we can't expect them alone to win the war for us."

Looking up, Wat had the ludicrous sensation of a sapling beneath an oak. The oak looked kindly upon him, and held out his hand:

"Tennent Lomax, Mister Phelan: at your service. It is good to see you again. Shall we get started?"

An hour later, Battle and Lomax were alone in the study.

"What do you make of our young friend?" Battle inquired.

Lomax inspected the ash of his cigar. "If events play out, he will be an officer by spring. He is ambitious and bright, and his patron, the governor, will be exiting the stage ere long. For such young men, the opportunities lie within the military. These days, at any rate. And he is very bright."

"Bright enough to nod pleasantly while I waxed on about Tuskaloosa," said Battle.

Lomax sighed. "Have you been hazing the lad, Cullen?"

"Well, a tad, perhaps."

"Tuskaloosa is, however, no Randolph College, you will readily admit."

"Yes, sir, I do readily admit it, colonel."

Both men laughing. Battle was glad to see his friend relax, if just for one night. He stole a glance over to a miniature on the table, where a beautiful young woman gazed back at him. The likeness was skillfully done, but no painter could ever do justice by Sophia Shorter. Sweet Sophie: Sophia Shorter Lomax.

Battle was no more than fifteen when Sophie introduced him to her beloved. Any boyish jealousy he may have felt on that occasion, evaporated under the bonhomie of the genial Captain Lomax. Two kind and generous souls, Sophie and Tennent were meant for one another. Upon the hero's return from Mexico, their wedding was the most glorious affair ever held in Barbour County. Cullen's sister, Mary Jane, having seen to that.

Sophie's death ripped the heart from out of the town.

For a time, Battle lost sight of the captain. Finishing his

studies at Tuskaloosa, he read law in Montgomery, passed the bar, married, and settled in Tuskegee.

Lomax made a fresh start, up the river, at Columbus; Mary Jane kept up with his doings, writing Cullen of Tennent's successes: captain of the Columbus Lights; editor for one of John Forsyth's newspapers, making the case for State's Rights, the Tenth Amendment, and Nullification; his views dovetailing with her husband's and those of like-mind back in Eufaula, the powerful 'Barbour County Regency.'

When the eldest Shorter, Reuben, passed away in Fifty-seven, Lomax came to Montgomery to pay his respects. It was here that Cullen and Tennent renewed their friendship.

Lomax also renewed his acquaintance with Reuben's widow. Closing his affairs in Columbus, he moved to Montgomery and he and Carrie wed the following year; the captain once again within the family fold.

Battle's thoughts returned to the present. "What do you make of events in Tallahassee?"

"We will have to push Florida to make some hard decisions. We are getting down to brass tacks, Cullen. Governor Perry wants the Yankees out of Pensacola, but I do not see that he is prepared to pay the price. Florida has a lot of territory to protect, and not much of an army with which to do it. I think Perry stands pat until he sees how things go at Mobile Bay. May be he hopes his Yankees just melt away. It is hard to say."

"Regardless," said Battle, lighting a fresh cigar, "We shall all wait upon our friends in Mobile."

## CHAPTER 3 — HOYT
January 4, 1861

LOOKING OVER the battle line, Captain Woodruff awaited the signal to advance, confident his men were up to the task. The Mobile Rifles were the best-trained militia in the entire AVC, the only one ('twas said) could pass muster with the French Army. In all, eight militias were in motion, each assigned to one of two battalions. The Rifles had landed in the Second under Colonel Leadbetter. His orders were straightforward: take and hold Mount Vernon Arsenal.

* * *

The officers and men had been forbidden to inform family or friends of the mission; not even a whisper to the servants. It was an overnight exercise, nothing more. Furthermore, on this occasion only officers would be allowed to bring servants.

Second Battalion had gathered at Armory Hall the evening last. Drawing their arms, the Rifles assembled for roll call and inspection; serious affairs, with fines levied for the smallest infractions. On this occasion there were none.

Beneath their greatcoats and shakos, the Rifles wore their fatigues: grey coatees and trousers. "Save your dress greens for the victory parade," drawled Lieutenant Marrast.

Their sister militias: The Infantry, The Fusiliers, *Les Gardes* Lafayette, went through similar (if less stringent), inspections, only the *Gardes* looking out of place. Their flashy Zouave-style uniforms could not conceal their ranks were filled with many well-fed, middle-aged, merchants—the bourgeoisie of old Mobile.

From the armory the battalion marched to the waterfront, where they boarded a side-wheeler. By eleven, they were steaming up the bay, to a landing well below the arsenal. Under a crescent moon local guides brought them safely through the woods.

Familiar with Mount Vernon from the regular maneuvers held there, Leadbetter and his captains did not know what new defenses might be in place. A large compound, the arsenal's walls enclosed sixty acres, its perimeter resembling the stamp of a horse's hoof. Though the garrison was reported to be small, even a skeleton force, forewarned, could defend the site—at least long enough to destroy its inventory. And it was the inventory they were after: rifles, cannon, bayonets, mercury caps and powder; everything a small army could want. Within its walls were barracks enough for a regiment, though most of the buildings had stood empty since the end of the last war.

\* \* \*

The Rifles waited in the damp chill of the surrounding woods, impatient for first-light to strike the watchtower. As they watched, the whitewashed walls began to brighten.

Sergeant Hoyt met the gaze of Henry Donaldson, who, widening his eyes comically, mouthed his stock greeting—an owl's hoot—Marrast's head whipping around to spot the culprit. Hoyt looked away before he laughed out loud and gave his friend away.

Further down, the ranks became an undulating line, the men shifting from foot to foot, blowing into their hands for warmth, tucking them under their arms. Woodruff forbade the use of mittens. Standing in the drainage off the hill, chattering teeth provided both amusement and apologetic looks. Hoyt was a North Carolinian, so too Donaldson; to them this chill was of no account. In truth, everyone's blood was up and all were eager to go.

Looking for sentinels, Hoyt scanned the walls through his glass. The ramparts were bare. *Never mind*, he thought, *the walls will be formidable enough*, brick and mortar ten feet high and two feet thick. The Rifles were to storm the walls, with Hoyt's squad (the ladder-men) given the honor of leading the charge. On the right, Gracie's Washington Light Infantry would crash the front gates, while the less experienced *Gardes* were to breach the far side. The Dutchmen (Emerich's Fusiliers) were in reserve, should they be needed to cover a retreat.

Thoughts of failure were few, however. Stalking the lines, Marrast paused here and there, to repeat: "Load. No prime." The men performed the procedure in silence as they had practiced. Hoyt's fellow non-coms were signaled to fix bayonets, and they did so, quietly. The officers and the orderly pulled their sidearms, mindful of Captain Woodruff's orders, not to fire unless fired upon. Given all the different militia uniforms present, there must be no error.

Dawn lit the tower's rim, the moment Leadbetter had proposed to signal the attack. Woodruff had, however, pointed out the sun would be most blinding to the defenders if the battalion waited for it to fully rise. Now, all watched the rosy light crawl down the turret, growing brighter with agonizing slowness, even stopping once—to make the leap to the outer stockade, before resuming its course. Nearing the ground, it appeared to pick up speed.

Striding forward, Woodruff came clear of the tree line and halted. The Rifles' color guard joined him, unfurling their splendid green banner and the newer one of blue. Sunlight finally touching down, Woodruff nodded to Marrast. Hoyt and his ladder-men came forward.

On the drill field the captain was a stickler of the first order. Here, he was aghast to see Hoyt, by parade ground habit, begin to dress his squad's line. Woodruff's gestures got his attention, fairly shouting: *get going*. Praying the gaffe might pass unnoticed by the ranks, Hoyt set off. Woodruff allowed them a fair start, before following at the double-quick, with the company.

Hoyt's embarrassment evaporated. To be part of this moment, a page in history, alongside the likes of Decatur and Houston and Travis. But the hill was steep and long before they reached the wall, he was hearing plenty of un-heroic gasping and blowing. Hoyt passed two teams of ladders, but the others kept a good pace. Gaining the wall, he saw that Gracie's boys had reached the gate. The Infantry raised a shout.

The Rifles were up the ladders in an instant. Someone's plan had thought ten-foot ladders would scale ten-foot walls, but by draping himself across the parapet, Donaldson showed how to pull everyone up and over. As Hoyt clambered over, he felt the night's chill captured in the masonry.

Inside, all was bedlam, men running every which way, the garrison taken completely by surprise. On the right, Gracie pounded on the gates. Hoyt spotted a solitary sentry race from the main building to open them, seized as soon as he did so (saying later, he had opened them to "see what was going on"). The commotion was its own alarm, however, and the garrison spilled from its barrack. A large body of armed men were seen forming to the rear of the buildings, an area still in half-light. Hoyt dropped inside the compound to alert Marrast, racing past federal soldiers, still hopping into their pants.

Swarming the grounds, the Mobilians squashed any thought of resistance. One squad nearly fired a volley into the ranks of the men Hoyt had spotted, before realizing they were no danger: it was only the Frenchies; no mistaking the Turkey-red trousers of their drummer, Zou Zou Hartman, and the small lad by his side. The two began to drum *Jefferson and Liberty*, the tour de force reassuring to all (with the exception of a dog, who, somewhere on the grounds, had set up an incessant, and defiant, barking).

The garrison commander made his appearance, a stocky little fellow, rushing about in utter bewilderment, *sans* jacket, boots, or hat. As he pulled his sabre free, Hoyt leveled his Colt. Colonel Leadbetter stepped into his line of fire, demanding the other's sword and the garrison's surrender "in the name of the Governor of Alabama." Leadbetter's manner (perhaps his Maine accent) seemed to settle the officer and, with dawning comprehension, he twisted his mouth into a smile and offered an exaggerated salute.

"Captain Reno, at your service, sir. I regret exceedingly, you did not advise me of your coming. I would have extended a *warmer* welcome."

"Ayah," replied the colonel.

With order restored, guards were detailed to the prisoners. The rest formed ranks to attend the raising of the state flag. On its blue field, beneath the golden star, someone had painted: 'The Time Has Come.' The three militias (allowed to prime their weapons) fired: the first salute to the new republic.

Arms were soon stacked and the arsenal storerooms thrown open. The militiamen had had no rations since yesterday and they badgered the Federal commissary sergeant to heat up a kettle of porridge. A bonfire was soon blazing.

Whistling a tune, Henry Donaldson went poking about the buildings to see what he could liberate. From time to time he would stop his whistling, to holler: *"Who will feed me next, I won–der-r-r,"* the line from a popular minstrel song.

Food was also foremost on the minds of the prisoners. All tolled, the garrison amounted to only eighteen soldiers, plus wives, servants, and civilian artificers. Reviewing the morning's events, Sergeant Hoyt thought it had the look of comic opera.

Captain Reno, dispensing courtesies like trinkets, took Colonel Leadbetter, *et al*, for a tour of the grounds. At the landing, the Fusiliers located wagons to bring the men's knapsacks and greatcoats up to them.

Donaldson's foraging was a success. Picking up an extra blanket, he also appropriated a banjo, and freed a skinny cur (the barking dog), discovered shivering atop the garrison trash heap—a female, about six months old. Wrapped in his blanket she still trembled, but her eyes were bright and fearless, and round with curiosity. Set down near the bonfire she circled her patron in a crouch, hindquarters all a-jitter in cautious optimism while he waited-out her inspection. Finding no fault, she stopped and, sitting at his feet, burrowed her head between his knees.

Taking up his new-found banjo, Donaldson regaled the soldiers with the tune he'd been whistling:

> The Shanghai is a pretty bird,
> That wakes us in the morning
> With dulcet sweetness long drawn out,
> To tell us day is dawning.

The men were happy to wile away the time before breakfast and joined in the familiar chorus:

> Oh! There's many a way to start mankind,
> To tell them day is dawning,
> But worse of all is Shanghai's *crowww*:
> *Get up! I tell you it's morning!*
>
> In Army and in Navy too,
> The reveille is sounded,
> And always in a good hotel,
> A Chinese Gong is pounded.

The lyrics, in this vein, till Donaldson, adding verses of his own, completed the saga of Shanghai the rooster, and his escapades at Mount Vernon. Slowing the tempo of the final verse, he set up the final line, belted out by every man familiar with the joke.

> Yes, the Shanghai beats them all for noise,
> And in his tones of thunder,
> Cries forty thousand times a day:
>   'Who–will–feed–me–next–I–won–der-r-r!'

Hoyt caught up with Donaldson back of the bonfire, sharing rations with his new companion.

"Well, well, well, who have we here? No 'dog of war,' I'm bound. Cooing directly to her: "Too sweet a face. *Look at her.* She friendly?"

"Quite tame, Johnnie. Beggars can't be choosers, after all. And *very* smart. May I present our newest recruit. I predict a rapid rise through the ranks. She'll make fourth sergeant in no time."

"Hold on, now: *I am fourth sergeant,*" said Hoyt. Offering the dog his hand, she came squiggling over. "What is your name then, mademoiselle?"

"I believe it shall be 'Car'line,'" Donaldson yawned. "For our old home state. A born retriever too, if I do say. She will make a splendid gun dog. Yes, you will: won't you girl?"

"Then welcome to the Rifles, Miss Caroline. I hope you can stand your Shanghai's crowing."

"Did we get what we came for, Johnnie?"

"How does a stand of twenty thousand sound? Muskets mostly, but two thousand Mississippis, plus a few Enfields, a couple of cannon lathes, and a great store of powder."

Donaldson whistled approvingly; Caroline pricked up her ears. "Well worth the trouble then, weren't it? I thought their captain took it well. Showed some paste once he got past the elephant."

"Well, West Pointers, what do you expect?" said Hoyt. "Him and Gracie and Colonel Leadbetter are already thick as thieves. Such as them take these things in stride."

"All of 'em Yankee, too."

"For that matter so is Captain Woodruff; though Reno sounds like a Virginian."

Shanghai considered. "War makes for strange bedfellows, at that. I 'spect none of 'em gets much 'Welcome Home' after this."

## CHAPTER 4 — BEST LAID SCHEMES
January 5 — April 22, 1861

PHELAN CARRIED the communiqué to the Old Man:

MV OURS SUPPLIES INTACT NO CASUALTIES.

The governor's reaction was hard to read: was it relief or disappointment?

"Should Mount Vernon refuse us *casus belli*, we will affirm our independence down the bay at Fort Morgan," said Moore. "Failing *that*, orders will be cut for Lomax to invest Fort Barrancas, at Pensacola. Phelan, we must not allow them a port a mere fifty miles from Mobile."

Wat delivered the orders to Lomax personally, who reacted much like the governor. He knew success at Mount Vernon had come at an unavoidable cost; the Federal garrisons around the Gulf were now on guard. *So be it. Blood shed at any one of these will suffice to cast the die.*

Returning to the capitol, the secretary helped Moore word a telegram to President Buchanan. In it, Moore vowed the measures taken were purely precautionary, intended solely to preserve the freedoms and safety of Alabama's citizens. Wat imagined that sentence alone would make Ole Buck spit his soup.

\* \* \*

Leaving *Les Gardes* to defend the arsenal, Leadbetter returned with the others to Mobile, where they learned the assault on Fort Morgan had also been successful, seizing nearly one hundred naval cannon—again, without bloodshed. The governor's hopes for a second 'shot heard round the world,' would be pushed onto the Florida Expedition.

The assaults made headlines across the country. Half of official Washington was outraged, the remainder delighted. Federal troops were ordered home from the frontiers and the navy began to outfit sloops of war.

In the North, the attacks swiftly eroded support for the Southern argument. Moore's actions were widely condemned as precipitous (*Harriet Lane* and *Crusader* having never appeared). Yet Mobile and Montgomery remained defiant: "The Rubicon has been crossed—let them come."

Given the nudge, many expected Maryland to join the Cause (at minimum, Baltimore and the eastern shore), making Washington City untenable. The new administration and congress (and their various departments) would be forced to relocate to Pennsylvania; the federal government in disarray before Lincoln could be sworn in.

* * *

Lomax focused his efforts on the expeditionary force proceeding smoothly. It did not.

His command (2d Regiment) was no more than a small battalion, much smaller than those forces sent against Mount Vernon and Fort Morgan. Regardless, his officers were capable, his volunteers well-trained and equipped. The day of their departure Mississippi voted to secede. When they crossed into Florida (January 10) the date coincided with that state's secession. Alabama approved the measure the following day.

Should his intent remain unclear, Moore directed Colonel Siebels to wire Lomax:

> "The Governor desires me to say that he has full confidence in your prudence, judgment and courage. [. . .] Do not unnecessarily or uselessly expose the lives of your troops, but the importance of having in our possession every fortified place in the harbor of Pensacola, may render a sacrifice necessary . . . "

Lomax read 'unnecessarily or uselessly' to be the governor's fig leaf in the event of bloodshed, but took no issue with it: all of them would hang should they fail.

At Pensacola, the fly in the ointment proved to be the acting commander of Fort Barrancas. Loyal to the Union, this lieutenant took his small band across the bay in rowboats, to the sturdier (and more defensible) Fort Pickens.

Lomax meantime, came under the command of Florida's authorities. Tallahassee was in no hurry for war, so a stalemate quickly ensued. Unbeknownst to Moore and Lomax, Mississippi's Senator Jefferson Davis (hoping for a negotiated separation) was advising Florida's Governor Perry to avoid any assault: "Bloodshed now may be fatal to our cause." With strategic options thus compromised, an unofficial truce was observed. Ignoring the status quo, Federal troops were landed to reinforce Fort Pickens.

In early February, delegates convened in Montgomery to form a new government. Newly resigned from the U.S. Senate, Davis was elected president and inaugurated. His first act was to wrest the reins of war from the likes of Governor Moore.

\* \* \*

Alabama's volunteers were 'Sixty-days men.' By late February their enlistment was running out. With his assault on Fort Pickens scrubbed, Lomax petitioned Moore to let the Second Regiment come home. In March they were relieved and it was from home they awaited developments at Fort Sumter.

Being volunteers, all militiamen were free to resign, and during this interim many—realizing they were too old or unfit to withstand the rigors of campaigning—did so. Others were approached with offers of higher rank in new companies. Some militias voted to serve only within the State's borders—*their* dissenters resigning, to go with more daring captains. In the days following Mount Vernon, the Rifles lost nearly a third of its members (most, receiving commissions) and the Infantry, half. So many resigned from *Les Gardes*, fluency in French was dropped as a prerequisite.

Despite the Rifles' prestige (and their substantial waiting list) competition for new volunteers was fierce. Woodruff et al. hosted levees, to which the right sort of man could be invited: younger brothers, friends from church or business––'Meet and Greets' with shrimp boils and beer, where they also debuted the new fatigue uniforms. The old-style coatees had been discarded for shell jackets, the lacquered shakos for caps (called *kepis*) favored by the French. (Officers and non-coms could opt for 'Hardees'—black slouch hats, replete with plumes and upturned brims.)

After these socials the box was passed round, and the successful candidate tapped and informed of his good fortune. Fifty-five replacements joined the company before April, among them Joe Skinner, a transfer from Gracie's Infantry, and Jimmie Howard (Hoyt's best friend). With Woodruff's permission, Joe Baumer was allowed to join them from *Les Gardes*. Neither the first chosen, nor the last: a bookkeeper named Corbet Ryder—known to one and all as 'Scotty.'

Mobilization did not hinge upon the bombardment of Fort Sumter. Dramas of equal importance were playing-out elsewhere. Surprising all, Maryland remained tied to the Union and with it, Baltimore, the largest city in the South. Once South Carolina played her card, all eyes turned towards Virginia. Virginia overwhelmingly desired peace; neutrality, if she could not have peace. It would take more than the surrender of Fort Sumter to alter that. And the Lincoln administration knew just what would do.

The last straw for The Old Dominion turned on Washington's demand that federal troops be allowed to pass through the state in order to enforce its will on South Carolina, an act viewed as nothing less than 'submission.' Lincoln's edict united all Virginia factions east of the Alleghenies. On April 17, her legislature voted to secede. The remaining undecided states quickly followed suit. Virginia still had a statewide referendum to hold the next month, but Alabama's militias were now in play.

Five nights later, on April 23, Woodruff's Rifles boarded a side-wheeler bound for Montgomery.

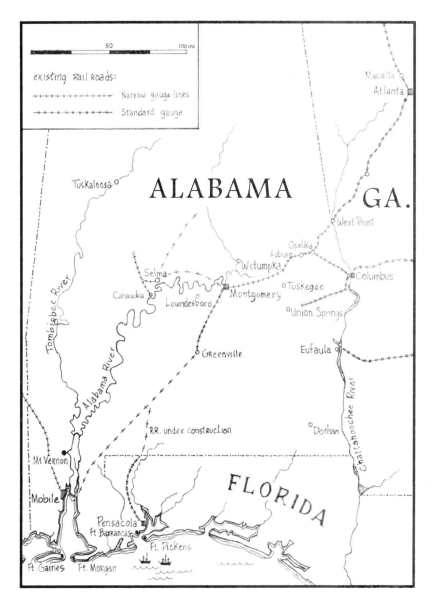

MOBILE, AL & ROUTES NORTH
April 1861

## CHAPTER 5 — CECIL
April 23, 1861


THE RAP upon the window caused Doctor Carter's youngest to look up from her breakfast. Already upset, she was startled to see a horrible face pressed flat against the glass. Though the features bore a grin from ear to ear, she reacted with a shriek, and bolted from the table in tears. Given the start, her mother clutched her chest, while her sisters (across from the now-empty chair), ignored the outburst and continued their reading; the Carters being a bookish lot.

Disrupting a peaceful setting was not the face's intent.

The doctor was nowhere to be seen, but son Cecil stood near, wearing a sheepish grin of his own. Taking delight in the caller's discomfort, his grin grew wider as the other's vanished altogether. Cecil waved his friend inside.

"Am I *that* shocking?" the visitor asked.

"Nick, Nick, Nick," Cecil intoned, mimicking his father. "I would not have 'par-tad' with farthing nor fig for the thought, ere now, no. But since the question has been raised, let us duly consider. . . ." Adding: "We have grown quite accustomed to your unfortunate looks."

"For *shame* Cecil Carter! Shame on you!" said his mother, recovering.

"Tis simply Floy playing the ninnie," said Cecil. "Her affliction: permanent; prognosis: hopeless. Come in, Nick, come in now and pull up a chair, won't you?"

"It was over this horrid dream he had last night. One he simply *had* to share," said his older sister, her nose still in her book.

The comment brokered an awkward silence and Nick knew better than to beggar the question.

"Good morning, Mrs. Carter, Miss Sue, Miss Mary. How do, Auntie, and, I suppose, *'mournin'* to the recently *departed* as well."

"Oh, don't mind her. Lately, Floy tears up twice a day,"

said Cecil. "She made her bee line because I said I had seen you in my dream. Yes, you. You needn't look so surprised. You appeared in it just long enough to announce: 'We are ordered off.'"

"As if that were all," said his mother. "Just the way you say it now makes poor Nick sound like Marley's ghost, *and,"* directing a menacing eye towards her son, "I do not wish to hear it retold, *s'il te plaît.*"

Turning her attention to their guest, she rose from the table. With her voice melting to honey, she said: "Now, Nick, Sugar: have you had anything yet this morning? Coffee? Biscuits? There's always plenty."

"Yes, ma'am. No thank you, but I do thank you kindly. My sergeant will have my hide if I tarry. I have a few more Cadets to find."

The sisters looked away from their books. Nick's words seemed to affect Mary especially. Sue maintained her composure.

"We *are* ordered off, then?" asked Cecil, his tone turning serious.

"Indeed. Your dream is fulfilled. Or soon will be. Two o'clock, at the armory—fatigues and gear. Stuff your haversack. They warn food may run scarce. They'll feed us in Montgomery (so they say), but yes, this is it." By the sideboard, Ann (the Carter's dinah), crossed herself.

A fresh wail came from down the hall. Mary's eyes began to well up, too. She closed her book. The cook, muttering a prayer, dabbed her eyes with her apron, while Sue heaved an impatient sigh. Mother Carter's face was ashen. "Montgomery?" she asked, with a flicker of hope.

"Yes, ma'am. Then, word has it, Virginia. We board the *Saint Nick* this evening. Captain Gracie's Infantry to go with us. The Rifles sailed yesterday, as you know. The plan is to put all of us together—the Cadets, Rifles, Infantry, and Guards, that is—into a new regiment: the 'Third'—filling it with some more boys from around Montgomery and Macon County. The vote of the Cadets (to go) was unanimous. Captain Sands expects a twelve-month service, says showing a strong hand now will demonstrate our resolve and save lives in the end." Seeing his words did little to assure his audience, he beat a retreat:

"Well, I have others in the neighborhood yet to find, so I best push on. Cecil, you see any of our people, pass the word."

"Yes, 'Corporal' Weeks. Can we swing by, give you a ride in?"

"That would be grand."

"Perfect. We will come for you at noon."

"Oh, one thing more: should you bring a hand, captain says there is no guarantee they get on board. They'll take a count and see how many we have. Officers first, naturally."

* * *

South Market, Mobile's newest and grandest commercial hub, was the site of the armory. Soldiers and their families had been gathering there all morning, traffic flowing in and out through clouds of dust and swarms of spectators. Porters, gathering up knapsacks, carpetbags, trunks and the like, skillfully trucked their loads to the staging area. Black women, about their chores, gliding through the crowds, baskets of produce or bundles of laundry perfectly balanced atop their heads; mothers and nannies exerted nominal control over the many children present—excited to fever pitch by the drummers, uniforms and flags. Unwilling to concede defeat, the women remanded their charges to the merciless eye of the family majordomo.

When the time came, Mother Carter embraced her son; standing back, she smoothed his jacket. "You look *so* handsome." She pressed a book into his hands, and another for Nick. "Here. Here is something to improve your minds. Now go on, before. I—and Cecil, you mind your. . . ."

The boys found the interior jammed with people. Working their way to the grand staircase, the sentry passed them to the first floor. There, the chaos was more organized. Sergeant

Huger, set up outside the Cadets' office, was going over bills of lading with the purser of *St Nicholas*.

"If the *Saint Nick* is required to record every item coming on board we will not sail before midnight," the clerk complained.

"Understood. You are accountable only for official inventory: horses, ordnance, commissary, quartermaster; plus: officers' and NCOs' baggage. Agreed? Good. Short of that, each Cadet stows his own gear. They have been told." In an undertone, the sergeant added: "The assets of the company are already on board and under guard." The clerk was visibly relieved.

Without looking up from his papers, Huger addressed the two. "Well? What are you two waiting for, an invitation?"

"We are reporting, First Sergeant," said Cecil.

"Then report! Find your squad sergeant. Who is that? Witherspoon? He is in the Gun Room. Go waste his time instead of mine."

"Yes, First Sergeant."

They found Witherspoon in the ordnance room. Each signed for a rifle.

Casey Witherspoon took a step back to appraise his recruit. "Cadet Weeks—my compliments. You do turn out well." He gave Nick's black satin cuff an admiring rub. "That is the best-looking uniform in the company, bar none. Take note of his buttons, Cecil, how they doth blind the eye."

"Hello, they are brand new."

"As *yours* should look: *pleasing* to the eye of one's sergeant."

Nick blushed. The youngest member of the company, he was the very last to be elected. The tailor had delivered the uniform only this morning.

"Assembly is three o'clock, boys. Sharp. Out front. We march down to *Saint Nick* at four. Horses, et cetera, board first. Then us. We have the port side. Infantry boards last, and has starboard. The lieutenants have worked everything out. Got it?"

*31*

"Yes, sergeant."

"Stay out of trouble. Be on time. Get out of here."

* * *

By half-past, the Cadets and Infantry had been counted off and inspected. Assembled in front of South Market, they heard remarks by Mayor Withers, praise from John Forsyth, a blessing by the bishop. Uncovering their colors, they got three cheers from the crowd. Striking up the band, they made column of fours on Royal; column right onto Conti.

As they boarded, the bells of Immaculate Conception rang out, and the salute guns boomed. The sun had dropped behind the city before *St Nicholas* let off her parting blast. With the multitudes waving (some singing), and all wishing them "Godspeed," the boat's great wheels began to back.

## CHAPTER 6 — THE SAINT NICK
April 23 — 26, 1861

BESIDES ITS militias, the *St Nicholas* had on board two young brides: Mrs. Daniel Huger and Mrs. Charles Forsyth—Captains Sands and Gracie having donated their staterooms to the honeymooners. Below, the main deck was jammed with horses and wagons, baggage and supplies. In the saloon, the volunteers were just beginning to settle when the ship's captain announced open bar. The carnage such a challenge would occasion, was, in this case, curtailed by the crush of bodies already in the room. Tumblers and tin cups, however, were soon passing overhead like ammunition to the front. With the rising of the moon, the steamer entered the switchbacks of the lower Alabama.

The 'tea-drinkers' resolved to a lengthy revel. The room growing loud, Cecil edged outside to the promenade. He found his crowd propped against the rail on the hurricane deck, Casey Witherspoon and his cousin, Henry Goldthwaite (a Cadet, newly returned from Princeton), Nick Weeks, and Nick's friend, George Ellison, of the Infantry. All of them were transfixed by a figure on the deck below, fumbling through close-order drill. The man, in civilian dress, would stop frequently to consult a manual (held open for him by a deckhand). His ineptness earning him catcalls from the many onlookers, barbs he was obliged to ignore.

Cecil wedged between his friends. Witherspoon, tapping his pipe out against the rail, greeted the newcomer.

"*Quand on parle du loup.* Nick, here, was just speaking of your dream."

The man on the deck dropped his bayonet, the clatter prompting a fresh round of jeers.

"Bob Armistead will never make a rifleman."

"That is Mister Armistead down there?" Cecil was genuinely surprised. "I didn't know he was on board. Isn't he a bit old?"

"Who else do we know has that shape?" said Goldthwaite.

"One which will look well enough on horseback," said Witherspoon. "He is a 'gentleman volunteer.' Here to learn the ropes. He plans to raise his own regiment."

"Don't we all," said the others in unison, the impromptu chorus, a cause for laughter.

"Speaking of, who is to be our colonel?" asked Nick.

His question stopped the small talk and the older men exchanged glances. "Montgomery wants Lomax," said Witherspoon at last.

"But do *we*?" Nick persisted. "My father expects me to vote for Mayor Withers. Says, as the greater part of the regiment, Mobile should stick together, have one of our own lead us in battle."

"I imagine Mayor Withers would agree with you," said Casey. "Cecil, I want to hear about your dream last night—sending poor little Floy away in tears; you heartless so–and–so, you."

"I *am* a beast. But it was only a dream. Foolishness, truly."

"We expect no less, but share it anyway. It was about today?"

"No. Much more than that, if I am bound to say, though, something less than a nightmare. It was perfectly vivid."

"Well, go on, then.

"Ya'll'll laugh."

They all laughed. "When has *that* ever stopped you?" said Casey.

"Hmm, well. All right. You have received fair warning.

"So: it is night. And I am waiting to receive word, right? Standing on a street: Saint Louis, I suppose; mine own. Alone. At a distance I perceive a tall figure. Dressed in black from head to toe, he starts towards me—slowly—his steps measured and confident. All is silent, save for the rhythmic crack of his boots upon the cobblestones. He nears. I cannot make out his face, so I ask his name. 'You know me,' he says. Then: 'We are ordered off.' ('twas here, dear Floy's screaming interrupted my first telling).

"I followed him to a place—a military encampment—where we stayed a very long while. All is well, there. Eventually, we are ordered away, and we are in a battle. My heart pounding as I tell you now. Death and destruction are everywhere, shells flying, 'bombs bursting in air,' confusion."

"Who was our colonel?" Nick asked.

"Aha! A good question; unfortunately one I cannot answer. We must have been in battalion. I did not see our colonel, nor anyone on horseback."

"Where were we?" Goldthwaite asked.

"*I don't know*. For heaven's sake, Goldie, Death and Destruction had my full attention. I was not looking for you. I will surely ask next time."

"And then?" Nick prodded.

"I barely escape with my life. But there is a *second* engagement: worse than the one before. A different landscape. I am on my back, gravely wounded; cold, and abandoned.

"I am brought off in some manner, and after, I am sent home with other wounded. A long and ghastly trip. Once home, I am there a long while, amongst my plants and books, nursed back to health by my loving sisters."

"Now it sounds more like wishful thinking. But you come back?"

"But I come back."

"You have always been a tenacious rascal," said Ellison.

"But here is the rub: *When* I rejoin the regiment, I am a stranger. You aren't there, Nick, nor you, nor you; I swim through a sea of unfamiliar faces. You know that queer feeling you have in dreams? Of being somehow out of step? You have missed something; you cannot find your place in line? The worry that you are not at all where you should be? It was like that.

"There then came a final battle, the greatest of the three. Smoke engulfing me like a shroud. Death is again nearby—"

"And destruction. Don't forget destruction," drawled Goldthwaite.

"Death," repeated Cecil, evenly. "Searching for me, calling for me. Again, and again. He asks: 'Where *are* you?' Where *are* you?'

"Let me add: mere words are inadequate to convey the manner of this question. My inquisitor did not use words, exactly, but I understood them; so near, his breath was hot upon my face." Cecil shivered, shaking off the thought. "The first time I heard this—this, *voice* (a voice like none of us has ever heard)—it was buried in the fog, in front of me, an impenetrable fog. In the blink of an eye, it is beside me, whispering into my ear, this shapeless thing repeating: 'Where *are* you?'

"Then he left me, flew down the wind."

"If you never saw him, how do you know he was Death?" Goldthwaite persisted.

"You may take my word for it."

"Fetid breath, I take it?"

"No. That would be Murray."

"Cecil: 'Is dat you dar, chile'?" mimicked Goldthwaite.

"What, then?"

"I think I must have been killed. It is all I remember: *Fini: 'Veni. Vidi. Vaki.'*"

"*'Vaki?'*" Goldthwaite arched a brow. Cecil ignored him.

"Jesus, Mary and Joseph. No wonder your mother did not want it repeated."

"It was just a dream."

The five were still. Ellison finally breaking the spell: "Nick, lets you and me go down there and help ole Mister Armistead get squared away."

Goldthwaite also left them, leaving Cecil and Casey alone, the former, over his elbows on the rail, trying to extract more details from his dream. Casey re-lit his pipe. Remembering the tomes his mother had given him, Cecil pulled one from his jacket.

"What is that one you are reading?

Cecil handed Casey the volume.

Examining the spine, Casey chuckled. "*The Virginians*. Very good."

"You've read it?

"Mmm."

The two fell into a long silence. Witherspoon spoke first. "Cecil?"

"Casey."

"You didn't tell us everything about your dream, did you?"

Pulling a hand across his face Cecil leaned further over the railing. Nick and George were demonstrating for Armistead. "No," he said. "No, Casey, I most assuredly did not. Not by a long shot."

\* \* \*

They drilled on the upper deck all the next day and the one after. Those in the Awkward Squad (and Casey made sure to enroll those who had jeered Armistead) came in for special attention.

*St Nicholas* ran faster than the Rifles' *Le Grande*. At Selma, they were barely four hours behind. Though all provisions on the boat had been consumed, Sands ordered the captain to press on. They would find food aplenty in Montgomery.

Arriving late at night, they tied up next to the Rifles' darkened boat. The city's welcoming crowds, expecting no more arrivals, had departed long before; her respectable citizens fast asleep. A party of one was at the landing: Wat Phelan, Third Lieutenant of the Metropolitan Guards. He had received a message to expect the arrival of *St Nicholas* and, being privy to its manifest, he felt honor-bound to represent Governor Moore, and the city. Coming aboard he reported to Captain Sands.

"Colonel Lomax sends his compliments and wishes me to convey Mister Forsyth has arranged rooms at the Exchange Hotel for the ladies in your party. Also, the colonel has placed his carriage at their disposal; the driver awaits their pleasure.

"Should it meet with your approval, I will escort your men to their quarters at the fairgrounds." At midnight, when all was ready, he led them up Commerce Street.

Skirting the spring at the city's center, Phelan pointed out the Exchange, and the Magnetic Telegraph Company, where the now famous order to fire on Sumter had originated. At the capitol the column turned north and continued towards the fairgrounds.

To the humiliation of their guide, the Cadets found no provisions. Sands received repeated assurances the army's commissary would arrive first thing in the morning. The Cadets and Infantry had trunks filled with meats, preserves, and other treats (packed by loving mothers), enough to feed a regiment, many times over, but these items were two miles back at the landing, and under guard till morning. Billeted in the fairgrounds' exhibit halls, the volunteers made the best of it and turned in.

Next morning, a lone commissary wagon arrived. When it was learned the delivery carried no rations, the teamsters exclaimed: "Nobody toe us 'bout no food, nah, Cap'n. *No suh.* All's we got is dissen' ra'chere."

'All's we got' was a box of soap bars. Fifty, by count—a requisition marked expressly for them.

## CHAPTER 7 — CHARLIE
April 26 — 29, 1861

THE RIFLES had encountered no such difficulties on their arrival. In fact, *Le Grande's* owners had arranged a farewell feast—with Captain Woodruff's blessing—to which the Rifles fell to with a will. Woodruff Wholesale had sold the bulk of the victuals to the owners in the first place; to spurn the offer would have been foolish.

Nevertheless, Woodruff himself had more pressing matters to attend. Leaving his junior officers in charge, he admonished them: "Off by seven-thirty, the men *sober*, the boat in one piece." With Marrast, Hoyt, and two others, he proceeded to the capitol.

At the Adjutant General's office, Woodruff reported the Mobile Rifles Volunteer Militia present for duty. In return, he was handed a packet with local contacts, a draw on Commissary and, directions to their billet. A man was sent back to the landing with these.

Down a hallway filled with sleeping militiamen, the party was led to the governor's office, where they found His Excellency with Colonel Seibels. Both greeted them warmly.

"Welcome to Montgomery. It is Captain Woodruff, I presume?"

Woodruff came to attention and saluted. "The Mobile Rifles Volunteer Mi—"

"Your subordinates may stay, Captain, I will not be long-winded. You have received your billet?"

"Yes, sir."

"Any immediate needs?"

"No, sir."

"How you fixed for food?"

Woodruff replied his men were well provided for.

Seibels got down to business. "Colonel Lomax sends his compliments and asks me to express his wish you be his guest at Lomax House, should that prove acceptable. I believe you know the colonel?"

"Yes, sir, we served together in Mexico."

"Splendid. Tonight, your men are at Estelle Hall; you passed it coming up here. Lomax has sent over a driver, and he is at your convenience. The colonel wishes to meet with you on certain matters of form. Tomorrow, he is hosting a meeting of those other captains who, it is felt, compliment the formation of a third volunteer regiment. As we have assured Mayor—ah, rather, *Colonel* Withers, and others—this *Third* Regiment will be first to deploy to Virginia."

The governor interrupted. "All right: That's that. Your people can work out the details. Now, so long as you are in Montgomery, the Rifles are assigned to me. If your lieutenant will be so kind as to talk further with Colonel Seibels, the colonel will tell you where your men are needed.

"Yes, sir."

"Well, captain—" the governor began, rubbing his hands together with childlike pleasure.

"Sir?"

"What do you wish for your company? Whatever is in my power to provide, shall be yours: our arsenal is at your disposal."

"Marching orders, your Excellency," said the captain.

"I beg your pardon?"

"Marching orders," Woodruff repeated.

"What? Do you want nothing in the way of arms, accoutrements, tents, mess kits?"

"Nothing but your marching orders, sir."

The governor was impressed, if a bit deflated.

"My compliments, sir. Would that all could say as much.

"I shouldn't want this repeated, mind, but I wish you could have seen this passel of Georgia boys, volunteers, who landed on our doorstep the other day. Their own governor didn't want 'em—turned 'em down flat, saying: 'this war won't last so long.' So, they show up here with their scatterguns, flintlocks, powder horns, and whatnot; coonskins for hats, no two alike—calling themselves the 'Rough Raccoons,' or some such." The governor chuckled, recalling the memory. "Colonel Lomax is very keen on their captain, however. Gordon, his name is.

"Joining them to the Third is out of the question, of course. And I imagine putting them in the Fourth would cause just as great a furor. I will find a place for them, however, have no worry; maybe in the Sixth, eh, Seibels? But 'Rough' don't hardly say it." Comically, he waggled an imaginary coon-tail behind his ear. Woodruff remained stone-faced.

It had been a long day, and, Moore, realizing he may have overstepped, cleared his throat.

Sergeant Hoyt, unable to contain a chortle, started everyone else (Woodruff excepted).

Wiping away tears, the governor regained his composure: "Well. Ahem—Captain, yes—you want your marching orders. You shall have them."

* * *

Next morning, Colonel and Mrs. Lomax provided their guests an abundant repast. After, work commenced on the organization of the regiment. The first order of business was to compile a seniority list. Lomax chaired this committee. Cullen Battle proposed a second group discuss the election of field officers and staff appointments. A junior lieutenant with the Mobile Cadets interrupted Battle's remarks. As the regiment was not yet formed, grades of rank were contingent, and, for the purposes of this meeting, the young man was on an equal footing with the other, older men, in the room.

He announced he had been elected spokesman for all of Mobile's volunteers, to petition criteria be followed in the selection of their colonel. The other line officers looked to one another, uncertain how to respond.

Murmurs informed Battle the lieutenant's father was none other than John Forsyth, publisher of the *Mobile Advertiser and Register,* among others—a most powerful voice in the state and throughout the South. 'Old Forsyth' was the son of former governor, senator, and Secretary of State John Forsyth. Lomax himself had worked under the younger Forsyth while in Columbus, where he had watched this son (Charles) grow and mature. His unmistakable voice came from the back of the room: "Let's have it then, Lieutenant Forsyth."

Like his father, Charles was a small man and, like him, carried himself with perfect assurance. *The pluck of a bantam rooster*, thought Battle, who held no fondness for roosters who interrupted him, bantam or otherwise. In a clear, bell-like voice, the lieutenant presented his petition:

"On this, the twenty-seventh day of April, eighteen hundred sixty-one; Be it Resolved: Whereas, this regiment—to be designated the Third Alabama Regiment of Volunteer Infantry—has been honored by the sovereign Republic of Alabama with the distinction of first regiment raised in the cause of States' Rights, the first chosen to defend the sacred soil of Virginia, birthplace of American liberty, and the first favored to offer its blood for our new nation; we, the undersigned volunteers of the City of Mobile, *viz*: the Mobile Cadets, the Mobile Rifles, the Gulf City Guards, and the Washington Light Infantry, do hereby petition that the colonel of said regiment possess such qualities of character, education, and leadership, as are commensurate with the distinction; to wit:

"The colonel of the Third Regiment shall be a gentleman of the highest moral rectitude and professional attainment; an officer formally trained, educated, and commissioned from a military academy; a leader practiced in the military arts; his valor demonstrated on the foughten field. . . ."

Battle ceased listening. *This was no rooster. This was a fox in the hen house*, and he and Lomax were the main course.

The merits of the proposal were undeniable, Battle even admired its craft: a first-rate politician lay behind these fine words. Whether their author was young Forsyth, or the father (or some other), was another matter; the intent was clear: to undercut all potential rivals outside of Mobile. Since neither he nor Lomax had attended a military academy, Forsyth's criteria dramatically reduced the field. In fact, only two candidates remained—the two West Pointers: Jones Withers (Mobile's Mayor), and Arch Gracie, Captain of the Washington Light Infantry (also Mobile). Given Gracie's youth, Withers would be the obvious candidate to put before the volunteers; any objections would appear self-serving.

Forsyth's petition sailed through.

Forsyth offered a second proposal: a gentleman's agreement, to unify the regiment. On the morrow, a single slate of candidates should be offered: Withers for colonel and, representing the other two voting blocs, Lomax for lieutenant colonel and Battle for major.

Lomax accepted the coup with grace; Battle less so. It was a demotion for them both, plain and simple. "We are wiser men by this day, dear Cullen," said Lomax. "You must not bother over it—all will come right in the end. Better to come second, than see Withers and Forsyth sweep Mobile's finest into another regiment. We will do the most good for our regiment, with Withers off hobnobbing at headquarters."

The committee report on seniority was accepted *in toto*. Captains Sands and Woodruff, the regiment's senior captains, were accorded the positions of honor, on the flanks. Sands' Cadets would be known as Company A, Woodruff's Rifles as Company K. The intervening letters assigned to each militia according to its captain's seniority.

The election next day, April 28, went as scripted: the slate received unanimous approval.

The following morning, the governor proved true to his word. Woodruff's Rifles were on the first train bound for Virginia. At the depot were one hundred new knapsacks, courtesy of the republic, neatly stenciled: '3d Ala. Vols. Co. K.'

Also scheduled to board were Captain Sands' Cadets. But they were nowhere to be found. "Blast!" said Woodruff. "Where the devil is he? Sands has never been late a day in his life." Woodruff's orderly could offer no help. Hoyt stepped in, "Shall I find him, sir?" The captain dismissed the offer. "No. *No, dammit!* Orders are orders. Signal the engineer."

Delighted by the mix-up, the Rifles stretched out. The journey would be tedious enough without their rivals. The freight cars were drafty and uncomfortable of course, and offered no amenities. Delays were to be expected; the boys did not have long to wait for the first.

The onset of mobilization put an enormous strain on the region's hodge-podge system. Georgia used wider-gauge rails—ones set further apart—than those under Alabama trains. Thus, at West Point, the Rifles were required to off-load all equipment and livestock for transfer onto a new line. Despite such things, nothing could dampen their spirits; the volunteers were thoroughly enjoying their celebrity. Telegraph wires broadcast their progress through the South, while newspapers heralded their arrivals. At crossings old men cheered, while girls and ladies tossed them bouquets, letters, and neatly wrapped delights. The train was mobbed at every stop.

At Marietta, a wedding party descended upon the train. One bridesmaid presented Sergeant Hoyt with a large bouquet and a beautiful cake—then boldly kissed him on the cheek. Little Joe Baumer caused an even greater furor. The Alsatian (who spoke English perfectly) offered nothing more than *"Merci—enchanté, Mademoiselle: merci beau coup,* ça *fait plaisir de te voir;"* his comrades gamely offering their services as translators.

Knoxville was a different story. The town displayed more Stars and Stripes than Stars and Bars. A pro-union mob turned out to impede their passage. Ready for any eventuality, Woodruff ordered the distribution of cartridges. The crowd grew to a threatening size, but in the end let them pass.

They arrived at Lynchburg on the fifth day; the town Virginia had designated as the rendezvous for all her allies.

## CHAPTER 8 — THE VIRGINIANS
April 29 — May 9, 1861

NESTLED IN the upper reaches of the James, Lynchburg was the 'City of Tobacco;' it's warehouses standing side by side along the river stocked to the rafters with the crop from which shallow-draft bateaux floated the cargos down to Richmond's tobacco factors. Perched high above the mercantile interests, Lynchburg's homes and churches attested to the prosperity of her people. On a bluff all its own was the estate called *Point of Honor.*

Several militias from Kentucky and Tennessee had already straggled into town, but Woodruff's Rifles were first to arrive fully armed, uniformed, and equipped. The sight of soldiers who looked the part was a welcome change, and cheering crowds lined the street. As they began their march, a telegraph runner, dashing through the column, shouted the breaking news: "Tennessee has voted to secede!" Huzzahs and hats filled the air. Taking their cue from the Alabama flag, the crowd began to chant: "The Time Has Come, The Time Has Come." Falling in behind, they climbed the steep cobblestone street up to city hall, and on out to the fairgrounds.

At the campsite, knowing the Virginians were getting their first good look at Alabama men, the Rifles fell to work. While one squad set out the teepee-like Sibleys (attaching the tents to the center poles), another swept the grounds; a third unloaded the baggage wagons. As these tasks neared completion Little Joe was ordered to beat the long roll. At the signal to cease, every man stood at attention by his station. The orderly sergeant surveyed the scene with a critical eye. All was square.

*"Raise!"* he shouted.

Sixteen tents shot skyward with such precision the effort garnered the applause of their audience, making an impression even on the Kentuckians and Tennesseans, whose campsites resembled shantytowns. A Kentucky colonel earned the lasting enmity of the Rifles' commissary sergeant, when it was learned the militia's cooking pots had been borrowed, not to cook with—but to soak that colonel's feet.

As Lynchburg's young men had already sprinted off to Richmond, their mothers, sisters, and sweethearts, were left to welcome the newcomers. Carriages began to arrive laden with food, tobacco, and wine. One of these came fashionably late: a four-in-hand bearing Colonel Langhorne's wife and beautiful daughters. Sergeant Hoyt was there to hand them down. Major Battle attended Mrs. Langhorne, freeing Hoyt to squire the sisters 'aboot.' That evening, his messmates lay in wait.

"Did you enjoy your stroll, Johnnie?" asked Shanghai Donaldson, all wide-eyed innocence.

"Most acceptable, I assure you," Hoyt smiled, "Did Caroline miss me?"

"You know who the Langhorne's *are*, er, don't you, Johnnie?" asked his friend.

"Not before today, no. Can't say's I do."

"Langhorne holds a fortune in tobacco," said Joe Skinner.

"I suspected the fellow had some means of support. His carriage says as much."

"And what did you learn of your companions today?" asked George Dunlap, turning up the lamp.

"It is their home, that fine one there on the bluff north of town, the one we saw when we arrived. 'Point of Honor' was a dueling ground, so they say."

"And the girls: have they names, too?"

"The older one's name is Anne—'Nannie' to her family and friends (among whom your humble servant is now counted). She is beautiful, intelligent, and charming. More than that a gentleman need not say."

His messmates exchanging glances, Shanghai finally took the bit.

"Darling John: Do you remember when Barbee's marbles came to Mobile, year 'fore last?"

"Yes. I saw that exhibition. Superb work. His sculpture, *Coquette,* was a *tour de force*."

Mess Number One fell silent remembering the show's

most popular piece: a life-size figure of a seated female, her beauty barely concealed beneath a diaphanous chemise.

"In hindsight, Johnnie, um, anything you might now find familiar?" Dunlap prompted.

Looking from Shanghai to George to Joe, then slowly back to Shanghai, the sergeant's eyes began to widen, as his face blushed two shades darker: "Noooo. No, *what are you saying*?"

"Miss Langhorne—ahem—'Nannie, to her friends'. . . ."

"No. It can't, *mm-mm* . . . not *she*. She has invited me to supper, and, and I am to sing with her in the choir on Sunday."

"You're complaining? 'Coquette' has asked you—you sap. We hope you were smart enough to be agreeable," said Dunlap.

"Yes, of course. Says all their boys have gone. That they need a baritone. And a tenor! Come with me George, I beg you."

George pulled a long face. "Well, 'a friend in need.' One must do what one can. I do humbly accept your gracious invitation."

\* \* \*

The Cadets and the Infantry arrived the next morning, as more and more troop trains began to stream into the railhead. Captain Sands was in a temper and in no mood to discuss his company's delayed departure from Montgomery. He suspected some saboteur of purloining the orders.

A pistol had been fired over the Knoxville rowdies, from the regiment's third (and last) train through there: the one carrying Captain Hunter's Metropolitans. The shot scattered the mob most effectively, but the Metros were remaining tight-lipped.

\* \* \*

On May 4, under lowering skies, the regiment formally mustered into the Confederate Army: eleven hundred-forty volunteers, committing to one year's service. Hunter objected to the twelve-month term starting now, pointing out it should have begun from the date they had all signed on, in Montgomery. The major in charge replied no one should feel any obligation to sign the muster roll. Virginia would muddle her way through the crisis, somehow. Common sentiment was to get on with it: what did a few extra days matter in defense of the Old Dominion? With a dismissive wave Hunter conceded. In witness thereof, the clouds opened up. For the next four days a freezing rain poured down upon all Virginia's patriots, great and small alike.

The new army restricted companies to one hundred-thirteen officers and men: one captain, three lieutenants, four sergeants, four corporals, one musician, and one hundred riflemen. Some militias had come with more. These supernumeraries were relegated to a list of 'gentlemen volunteers.'

Lomax established the regiment's routine. When the lieutenant colonel spied a civilian relieving himself behind a tent he addressed the issue:

*General Orders No. 1      Lynchburg May 5th 1861*
*I  Captains will instruct their commands to observe the following calls.*

| | | |
|---|---|---|
| *Reveille* | *5½* | *A.M.* |
| *Police Call* | *6* | |
| *Breakfast* | *7* | |
| *First Sergeants* | *7½* | |
| *Morning Drill* | *8* | |
| *Guard Mounting* | *9* | |
| *Surgeon's Call* | *9½* | |
| *Roast Beef*[2] | *1½* | *P.M.* |
| *Evening Drill* | *4½* | |
| *Retreat* | *5½* | |
| *Dress Parade* | *6* | |
| *Tattoo* | *9½* | |
| *Taps* | *10* | |

---

[2]'Roast Beef,' i.e. the call for mess leaders to receive rations from the Quarter Master.

II  *Assistant Surgeon Lee, having been ordered on duty with the 3rd Regt. with the rank of Captain will be respected accordingly.*
  III  *No drums to be beaten except under the direction of the acting adjutant.*
  IV  *Firing guns prohibited.*
   V  *Wearing side arms prohibited except sword and bayonets.*
  VI  *The Officer of the Day will cause the Sinks to be used exclusively.*

## CHAPTER 9 — HAMPTON ROADS
May 9, 1861


ACCORDING TO the grapevine, the Third would soon be sent to Harpers Ferry, or perhaps to Manassas Junction, to shore up Johnston's forces. In the event their enemies determined their destination: Hampton Roads. A raiding party off the *Cumberland* put the torch to Gosport Navy Yard, the greatest military facility still in the hands of the South. The raid had nearly destroyed the dry docks and other critical supplies. Third Alabama would head to the coast.

\* \* \*

At Lynchburg the rain showed no signs of letting up. Before dawn, the volunteers struck camp, completing the slippery march down to the terminus, simply to stand in ranks, drenched by the downpour for several more hours. There was little risk the sporting gals of the Buzzard's Roost would 'rally round' at this early hour, but taking no chances, the sergeants posted guards.

The arrival of the locomotive was another disappointment. The train consisted entirely of cattle cars—recently used cattle cars, at that. Its next occupants uttered the appropriate sounds as they boarded. Disgusted though they were with the accommodations, they were grateful to be out of the rain.

Hours later, at Petersburg, they were met by the usual well-meaning officials (speeches), lovely young ladies (bouquets), and complimentary 'feast' (sandwiches and beer). Of more appreciation, the cars were swept while they were being fed. It was night before they got back on board, with the ordnance sergeants issuing cartridges.

In the drafty cars, smoking was prohibited, so, rolling into their blankets, the men huddled together for warmth and tried to sleep, as the train rocked them onwards through the night.

\* \* \*

One of the great harbors on the Atlantic seaboard, Hampton Roads is formed by the confluence of the James and Elizabeth rivers, the gateway—historically and strategically—to Richmond and much of Virginia. Following the depredations of 1812, the government located Fortress Monroe on a small key to defend the harbor entrance. Its defenses received such improvements over the years that the fort was regarded as the Gibraltar of North America. A secondary fortification built in the middle of the shipping channel was known as the 'Rip Raps.'

As the national identity spiraled ever downward, Unionists in the War Department had the good sense to garrison Monroe with regulars, under the firm hand of Benjamin Butler. Butler was a hard-nosed Massachusetts democrat and a political appointee, but his loyalty to the Union was unquestioned. Any attempt to storm the fortress would be bloody in the extreme and, without the support of a navy, doomed to fail.

While the Federals maintained a footprint on the northern shore (where Newport News was the anchorage for the Union fleet), the south shore, encompassing Norfolk, Portsmouth, and Gosport Navy Yard, remained under Virginia's control. The yard was the focus of much intrigue in the months before the state's secession referendum. Until that vote (on May 24) should declare otherwise, Gosport resided in a state loyal to the republic.

The warships burned in the raid of April 20, had been in various stages of repair and refitting. Gosport's commander had colluded in the attack, to keep its vast stores of cannon and matériel from falling into secessionist hands. *Delaware* and *New York* were completely destroyed, and a third ship—a beautiful frigate named *Merrimac*—burned to its waterline. Only a clever ruse by the president of the Petersburg & Suffolk Railroad saved the yard from total destruction. Running his locomotives back and forth over nearby tracks, letting off steam and whistles, William 'Little Billy' Mahone created the

---

[3] In fact, only two militias companies were in the area: The Norfolk Blues and Petersburg Greys.

impression of multiple trains arriving, each filled with hordes of avenging rebels.[3] The sham so frightened the raiders, they retreated to Monroe before they could complete their mission. 'Little Billy' (not quite five feet tall) became the hero of the day. The South salvaged more than twelve hundred cannon from the yard, among them three hundred smoothbore Dahlgrens—huge guns that would defend southern coastlines for the next four years.

In the wake of this excitement, the arrival of another regiment, went largely unnoticed. Worse still (from their perspective) Yankees were found to be in short supply. By sun up, and, receiving no other guidance, Colonel Lomax ordered the regiment to stand down.

\* \* \*

Scotty Ryder liked Norfolk from the start. Its flat terrain and proximity to the ocean reminded him of Mobile, though the city was smaller, grittier, and older-seeming. The blustery climate and raucous gulls stirred his childhood memories. He had immigrated as a youth and now, at twenty-eight (thanks in part to King Cotton), he had gotten on in the world. Steady habits and well-placed friends had provided him a good start. A bookkeeper and draftsman, with a natural bent for details, Scotty had proved himself a useful member of the Rifles.

At Norfolk, he and Joe Skinner were detailed to staff. Battle ordered them to locate army headquarters and ascertain to whom the regiment should report. Headquarters would be found in the new Customs House, about a mile from the depot. There, they should ask for Colonel Huger.

On Main street the two paused at Market Square to look around. The ancient slave market was here, the newspapers *(The Examiner, The Norfolk Day Book),* and the better restaurants, bookshops, dry goods stores, bakers, tailors, and haberdashers. From the square, the waterfront could be glimpsed, and Scotty surmised the saloons, flops, and other lower-caste enterprises would be found there. Walking on, they came to the Customs House.

If they had expected to find headquarters abuzz with activity, they were disappointed. Ryder reported to the acting Officer of the Day, handing over the regiment's orders, rosters, and requisitions. Exhibiting minimal interest, the clerk took the dispatches and tossed them into a hamper marked 'Alabama,' mumbling they could wait there for the colonel or return at eleven, the usual time he appeared. Taking the hint, they went in search of breakfast.

At the Atlantic House their waiter was a helpful freedman. Between trips to the kitchen, the man provided useful information: where the best hardware and dry goods dealers were located; the most reliable food suppliers and druggists; where Negroes could be hired. "First things first," said Scotty: "Where is the nearest bath house?"

Over coffee and eggs, Scotty sketched out a rough map of the town, identifying the major roads, buildings, and businesses.

As they were leaving, a distinguished-looking gentleman entered, a mane of silver hair and impressive 'Imperial' covering the collar of his frockcoat. He had a military bearing: the air of the *ancien* régime. He was, in fact, conversing in French with his party, which included the Third's own Colonel Withers, and Withers' aide de camp, Sergeant Huger—both men escorting their spouses. Ryder caught the eye of the sergeant, who, evincing mild surprise, signaled them permission to approach.

Ryder, hoping his uniform had aired out sufficiently, saluted Colonel Withers and made a polite bow to the ladies. Withers, under no pretense of familiarity with enlisted men, turned to Sergeant Huger with a questioning look. The sergeant made hasty introductions. As Ryder suspected, the old gentleman was Colonel Huger (Sergeant Huger being his nephew, while Wither's daughter was married to the sergeant; all very cozy). The pleasantries were brief: Colonel Huger was delighted to meet them, welcomed them to Norfolk, expressing his hope their stay in Virginia would be of short duration. Ryder informed him they had been instructed to report, and to carry back any messages.

"Consider it done, young man! You see your regiment is well represented here already—ahem, well then—then, enjoy the rest of your morning. Yes. Explore the town a bit before you head back to your—to, eh, where are they, Daniel?"

The sergeant answered, "Third Alabama is at the depot, sir. Latterly, they will be at Doyle's Farm."

"Quite right—a marvelous field. Clover. Rode past there just the other day. You boys could not do better, eh?"

"Yes, sir. Thank you, sir."

With their own colonel staring blankly, the volunteers knew to take their leave. Ryder, as senior man, decided they should take the old colonel at his word and explore Norfolk. To remain under the aegis of military duty, he continued his map-making, plugging in whatever information might prove useful. Ever diligent, he explored the dockside neighborhood and Widewater street, on the riverfront. On a side street, was pointed out to them an establishment known as *The Forty Winks*. On their way back they stopped off at the bathhouse recommended to them.

Returning to the depot they found the regiment had indeed moved to Doyle's Farm. Happily, all the work of setting up had been done, the tents raised and pinned, the company streets neatly lain out. Reporting to the O.D.'s tent, Ryder handed his notes to Lieutenant Storrs, along with his map. Placing the papers to one side, Storrs dismissed the two, to finish his own worksheet for sentry postings.

Skinner and Ryder went their separate ways—the latter to find his mess. Ryder looked to locate the colors. The color company was always in the center, so the Rifles would be on the left. Near the banners stood two Cadet sergeants: Casey Witherspoon and Bruno Yniestra, 'the Spaniard,' both with folded arms, alert and observant.

Yniestra spotted him. Immediately suspicious he pulled out his watch to note the time. Scotty reckoned such a thing seldom bode well. The Spaniard's face was sharp as a raptor and twice as intimidating. He imagined those coal-black eyes burning under the kepi, holding him and all Celts to blame for the wreck of the Armada. He also feared Yniestra may have figured out who had scuttled the Cadets' breakfast rations back in Montgomery, or who had waylaid their travel orders. Ryder scurried away, trying his best to look as though he were under orders. He sought a quiet corner to re-draw his city map, while the details were still fresh, knowing there were those who would appreciate his efforts.

Following Ryder with his eyes, Yniestra formed the question: *Where has this majadero been all morning?* Ryder was not a Cadet, so, the man was of no immediate concern. He was one of Woodruff's new men and, according to some, a potential soldier. Witherspoon simply dismissed him for a gadabout. *Well and good, so long as he does his gadding far from me.* The sergeant was a meticulous soldier—a jeweler and watchmaker in civilian life—and, in the right setting agreeable as any man. He was a merchant, after all, and had learned to suffer fools, taking solace in his power to menace the likes of Ryder; the Ryders of this world were always guilty of something.

He and Casey had charge of the Cadets. Captain Sands and the first lieutenant were away at headquarters; the second lieutenant was seeing to provisions for the regiment, and Ensign Forsyth (with his armed guard) was at the Exchange Bank establishing the company's line of credit—accomplished by the deposit of six hundred pounds of gold. The same assets which had put *Le Grand's* purser in a sweat. The gold was purposed to cover any debt incurred by a Cadet. Soon, the brass 'MC' on their kepis would be synonymous with "Made of Cash."[4]

As each mess got their tents squared away, the sergeants granted them permission to head over to the creek for a swim. The water was brackish, but better than nothing. Officers and off-duty non-coms, could go into town for a proper bath.

---

[4] In the current market, using a conservative benchmark of $1250/oz., a pound of gold is worth $20,000. Six hundred lbs., therefore, would be worth $12,000,000 in today's money—or nearly $106,000 per Cadet.

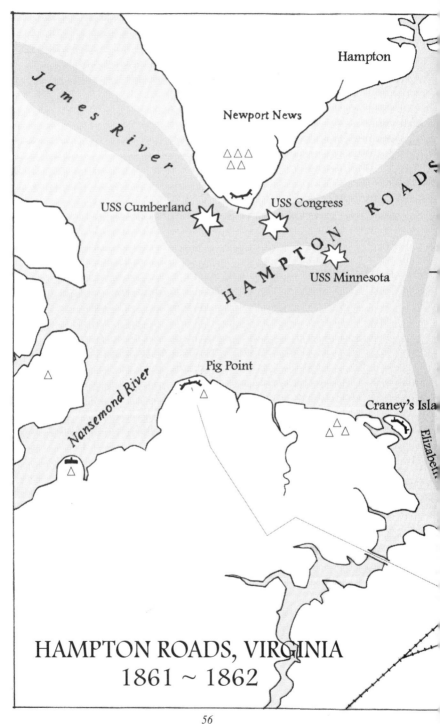

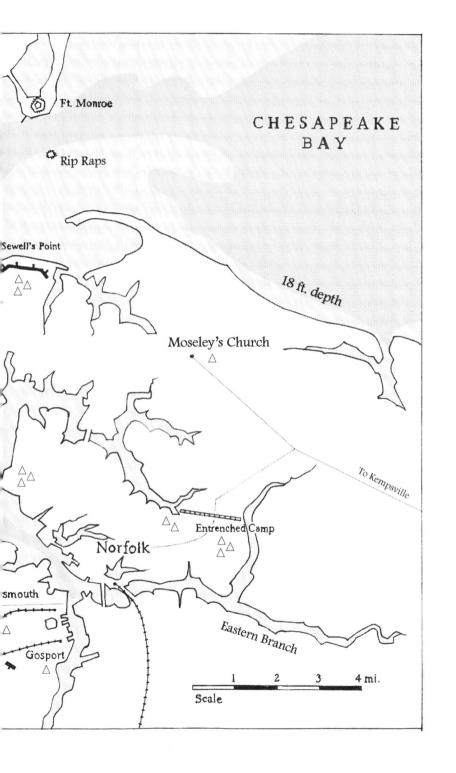

## CHAPTER 10 — DOYLE'S FIELD
May 12, 1861

Lieutenant Storrs thought nothing could be more gratifying at the end of a long day than a hot bath, even if it did require a hike into town. The locals were most obliging, quick to offer a lift to any soldier found on foot, but there were so many more soldiers than carriages. Still, the luxury of a good soak was worth the effort. The Scottish fellow's map had provided perfect directions.

The baths were clean and well-staffed. By the time his coat received its brushing, others of similar mind had formed a line outside the facility. To accommodate the soldiers, the city had allowed the owner to remain open past time. Storrs recognized many of the faces in line; officers and sergeants from the regiment. Soon, he would be able to put names to faces.

The moon was up and almost full, the night clear. So beautiful a night, in fact, the lieutenant, accompanied by his friend, Stamp, decided they should stretch their legs a bit and walk back.

They had not gone far when a liveried coach came barreling down the road from the direction of camp. Storrs posited this would be Laura Forsyth and Hattie Huger—the young brides—returning to town. The newlyweds had been honored with a dinner hosted by the Cadets. The champagne had flowed.

Sure enough, as the coach sped by, the girls playfully "hallooed" from the windows; one, tossing a flower from her bouquet. With neither man in uniform, the lieutenant supposed the girls took them for ordinary volunteers. Squeals and giggles swirled in the dust behind the retreating carriage. Picking up the flower and blowing the dust off, Storrs offered it to Stamp. When his friend declined, he adorned his own lapel.

Few would have picked Storrs out as an officer. To outward appearance, the lieutenant was just another slight, bespectacled scholar; his pale complexion earned at Charlottesville and Harvard Yard, where John Brown had put an end to his studies. There, the reaction of his fellow law students had come as a revelation—resoundingly pro-Brown—beyond all reason, precedent, or statute. He had always revered the law as the surest way to redress wrongs, so the epiphany was sobering: Law be damned; Might makes Right.

Coming home, he immediately joined the Wetumpka Light Guards and, soon, was serving in the ranks at Pensacola. There, among the sand fleas and sea grapes he earned the respect of his comrades, and departed Florida as a second lieutenant.

He thought it a shame, really, that the volunteers must be restricted to camp. They were not allowed through the lines without a pass or the countersign. And the countersign was given only to the officers and to the sentries. His hometown friends—Stamp included—complained bitterly of this loss of freedom (and of the privileges afforded officers). Something as simple as bathing for instance: the only recourse available to the volunteers was a dip in the brackish creek that bordered the camp. Fresh water was in short supply at this campsite. The regiment would soon be moving to greener pastures.

But this was no time to relax the rules. Officers were responsible for the men under their charge. Even his closest friends must learn to accept, and to be governed by, military rules. A sacrifice which fell harder on some more than others.

A half-hour's walk brought them back to camp and Storrs noted the sentinel stationed at the gate. The man appeared completely ignorant of his duties. *He could do no worse if he stood with his hands in his pockets, whistling 'Hey Diddle Diddle.'* By the trim on the sentry's uniform, the lieutenant judged the man to be one of the Gulf City Guards, his mind recalling: *Mobile—Captain Hartwell's Company B.* He waited to be challenged. The sentry offered only a vacuous stare.

"'A friend with the countersign'?" Storrs said, prompting.

"Come on, then," said the guard.

Storrs and Stamp looked at one another, the sentry holding his rifle by his side in an approximation of 'trail arms'. Regardless, protocol required the lieutenant to step forward and to give the countersign, leaning in so it could not be overheard, not even by Stamp. Quietly, Storrs said: "Fort Mims."

"'At's the one," confirmed the guard.

Exasperated, the lieutenant looked about for the Officers of the Guard. He had made out the schedule himself just the other day, so he knew Spaulding and Brown were on duty somewhere. His own Captain Ready was Officer of the Day, but captains were not expected to be physically present. So the responsibility here was his alone. To Stamp he said, 'Go on in, Jimmy, I'll catch up with you later."

To the sentry, he said, "Soldier: At-ten–*HUT.*"

Taken aback by the change in tone, the sentry slowly came to 'attention' while remaining alert to the chance this might be some prank. Storrs was accustomed to this reaction from men unfamiliar with him, could almost read the sentry's thoughts: *Friend, if you are a lieutenant you are way too small to be taken seriously, especially out of uniform.*

"What is your name, volunteer?"

"James Hunt," the man replied, his eyes darting around to find his true tormentors.

"*Volunteer: Look at me* when I am speaking to you."
Hunt focused.

The lieutenant sighed, continuing with a tone of calm instruction: "You should say 'Yes, sir' at this point."

"Okay."

"Yes—*sir.*"

"Oh. Yes, sir."

"Mister Hunt."

"Yes, sir?"

"Where are the Officers of the Guard?"

"Lieutenant Spaulding is making his rounds, Lieutenant Brown is—making water." His smirk fading when his jest did not elicit the response he expected. Stiffening a little, he added, "Lieutenant Brown should be back directly. *Sir.*"

"We are at war, Mister Hunt. It is not for you to make puns

while on duty. *Or,* to guard your post with 'Come on, then,' and 'That's the one.' Do you understand?"

"Yes, sir."

"I don't think you do. When I come out of the dark to your post, I am the *enemy* as far as you are concerned. Until I establish otherwise. Is this not so?"

"Yes, sir."

"And how do I establish that?"

"With the, um, countersign?"

"Exactly. With the countersign."

"'Fort Mims,'" the sentry offered.

"Yes. Fort Mims. So, whenever a stranger approaches your post—if it is dark, as soon as you hear a sound—you are to come to the alert, bring your rifle up in the 'low ready,' cocked to the safety position (as you have been shown), from whence you issue the challenge: 'Halt! Who comes there?' Remember it is not a question, per se, it is not a plea—*it is a challenge*—say it with strength, like you mean it. You are *challenging* them to identify themselves. Say it now."

"Sir?"

"Halt! Who comes there?"

Catching on, the sentry mumbled, "Halt who comes there."

"*Louder*, man! Let me hear you. Say it with me."

*"Halt! Who comes there!"* the two shouted.

"Better. The other side—me, in this case—says: 'Officer with the countersign,' or 'Friend, with the countersign.' Or they say nothing. At which point you say: 'Advance Friend, with the countersign,' or, 'Advance and be recognized.' If you face a group, you direct one only to advance. If he cannot give the countersign, or they appear to present a danger to the camp, you say: 'Stand clear,' and call for the Corporal of the Guard.

"You see, Hunt? *You* are the main defense of the camp—*this camp*. There are hordes of Yankees not ten miles from this very spot who would like nothing better than to do us grievous harm. This is no game we play."

"Yes, sir—*no, sir.*"

"When I approached just now I might have knocked you over with a peashooter; half asleep, dragging your rifle around behind you—easy to shoot yourself if you are not careful. Here comes one with a lantern; your officer Brown, no doubt. See here Hunt, there is no need to report all this to him. We are all newcomers to this strange business, I understand. However, 'a word to the wise.' Right?"

"Right—I mean, yes, sir."

"Good man, Hunt."

As the duty officer approached, the lieutenant introduced himself. "Is it Lieutenant Brown? Lieutenant Storrs at your service. Returning from town."

"Evening, lieutenant, I just passed your street, where you are asked for. I was requested to find you or Doc Lennard. You have a sick man needing assistance."

"I will attend to it. Thank you, sir."

Stamp, who had remained waiting at a discreet distance, now rejoined Storrs. Together they crossed the camp to the sick man's tent on 'Wetumpka Street.' On the way the lieutenant collared one of his Wetumpka Guards:

"Come with me, Butler. I will need you to find Doc Lennard. I saw him in town at the ablutionary. Tell him to come quickly.

"Here—wait a moment. I shall need to pass you through the sentry. A good fellow; means well. A little slow, I think."

Together they marched to the camp entrance.


The gunshot echoed throughout the camp shattering that peaceful night. All was stopped, till the cry was heard from Sentry Post One:

*"My God*—I am a dead man!"

# The Swamp

*"... I do not intend my men to learn that part of Hardee's Tactics"*

Charles Forsyth
Adjutant, 3d Alabama Regiment

## CHAPTER 11 — L' COMMANDANT
July 2, 1861

BY SUMMER, the cascade of national events had slowed and the regiment's routine become one of drills and instruction, parades, inspections, and courts martial. Colonel Huger was promoted brigadier in the Virginia State Militia—as distinct from the regular army—and given command of the Department of Norfolk. Among his first orders was one attaching the Alabamians to Mahone's Brigade,[5] encamped three miles east of the city—where several hundred hands were employed constructing a lengthy defensive palisade, called the Entrenchment—a check on any force coming overland from Fortress Monroe.

By dent of his commission date, Jones Withers became Mahone's senior colonel. Asserting his privilege, Withers demanded the Third be assigned *le place d'honneur*—on the right of the line. This required 12th Virginia to strike its camp and move to the opposite end; an imposition that did not sit well.

Making the switch, the Norfolk Juniors—Company H of the 12th—used the occasion to pepper their rivals: "Say, Mobile? How many officers have you bagged today? They still in season? Watch out fellows, it's de Turds: make *damn* sure you know their password—What is it tonight, boys: 'Don't shoot me?'" Being first to pass, the Cadets caught the brunt, but the Rifles, the Infantry, and the Guards, all came in for their share. Arriving at the 12th's vacated camp, the newcomers found their tent sites defiled in the common manner.

---

[5]Before this, Mahone's Brigade consisted of the 6th and 12th Virginia. With their smart uniforms and ancient bloodlines, the Virginia regiments were every bit the dandies 3d Alabama purported to be. The Juniors' uniform was a short blue jacket with red and white buttons; vest and pants. Their fur cap had a crest of bearskin bound in white cloth, a black cockade, and a liberty cap front-piece of tin.

* * *

Three more events significant to the regiment occurred in June.

The first was General Huger's promotion to brigadier in the *regular* army. At the time, the date on this commission (June 17) was nothing more than clerical detail.

In the second, Colonel Withers was promoted to a position at Army Headquarters.

The third event caused the most upset. Private Hunt was acquitted of the murder of Lieutenant Storrs. "To the satisfaction of the court" his rifle was shown to be defective and prone to slip out of safety.

'Not guilty' meant nothing to Storrs' friends. The Wetumpka volunteers made it known the Jonah would be shot on sight. Hunt was dismissed from the service. Henceforth, Lomax ordered all sentries to carry unloaded weapons.

* * *

*This will work out. These things always do.*

A natural optimist, Cullen Battle felt his credo confirmed by the departure of Withers. The move made him *de facto* lieutenant colonel (pending confirmation by vote of the volunteers). Storrs' death was a sad thing—most sad, indeed—but Battle favored the long view, perhaps it would help the soldiers more closely attend to their duty.

*Things are never so bad as they seem.*

*Nor so good, either.* Overall, however, the dictum had served him well as a successful lawyer and he trusted it would so continue in these turbulent times.

As the regiment's second-in-command, his concerns were many. Some flitted through his thoughts like hummingbirds, while others flocked like crows. The most worrisome circled like buzzards. At his table in the day room, Battle was lost in thought. His fingers twirled a steel-point pen back and forth, back and forth, rapping out a mindless tattoo. He could not shake this worry that things were not proceeding as well as they might, nor at the pace required. Everything seemed so—

so *improvised. Had Phelan been right, after all, that long-ago night in Montgomery? Have we jumped the gun? Here it is already July. Washington must soon move. We should have taken Washington the day after Fort Sumter.*

From what he had seen, Richmond was unprepared to receive the enemy. The Confederate government was a mess: filled with second-raters, more interested in their own advancement than in the fortunes of the country. Lacking Northern scoundrels to bait (or to obstruct), the Southern representatives seemed at a loss how to proceed. Davis's cabinet was questionable, too. Secretary of State Robert Toombs was a brilliant orator, but hardly a diplomat, and Leroy Walker was not the man to head the War Department, even if he was from Alabama.[6]

Battle was satisfied he could best serve his country in the military. He was fit as a fiddle, though a slight paunch betrayed his fondness for the sideboard. He was a frequent (if not necessarily invited) guest at many a mess table. This kept him well informed and attuned to the pulse of his battalions. Like all lawyers, he was happy to hear a good joke, and had a gift for the retelling.

Today, he pondered a knotty question—one of his larger buzzards. Withers' promotion had led to an opening at major. So who to fill it? The decision belonged to the volunteers; they would cast their ballots at the end of the month. He had no doubts as to the outcomes, at least where he and Lomax were concerned; seeing beyond that was difficult.

Bob Sands had declined to stand for major, owing to his strong attachment to the Cadets. While laudable in many respects, the decision was problematic. As senior captain, Sands had been everyone's first choice for major. Coupled with Gracie's resignation (everyone's second choice) the door was now flung open. Gracie's leaving was no surprise—everyone knew he was destined for field command—but that wrinkle

---
[6] Toombs disagreed with the decision to attack Fort Sumter and resigned July 25, 1861. Walker was vilified for not ordering the army to Washington after the victory at Manassas; he would resign in September.

threw all previous handicapping into disarray.

*Who then: Swanson? Powell? Andrews? Hunter?*

Battle shuddered over the last two names. He went over it all again, dull as it was: *Swanson's unlikely—the men loathe him and obey him grudgingly. Besides, Bill is a Tuskegee—* another Macon County man—and that would not sit right. Unfortunately, it also worked against Captain Powell. The Mobile bloc would never suffer two Macons as battalion commanders: a question of pride if not political balance.

Mobile just might take a second Montgomery man (Lomax being the first), but he shuddered anew at the prospect of Andrews or Hunter. More likely, the Mobilians would fall in step behind one of their own; Woodruff filling the bill nicely were he younger. *But he is forty-six*, and like Gracie, slated at some point to command his own regiment.

Captain Hartwell of the Gulf City Guards was competent, and well-liked, but his health was fragile. *So, who? This was frustrating. Pick a name from a hat? Captain Ready? No. The Wetumpkees don't throw enough weight for me to like his chances. And Bonham's company is so divided they may disband. So, it might be Ready, yet; the dark horse.*

*If not Ready, the spot must surely go to one of the Mobile lieutenants. Young Forsyth can be trusted to orchestrate something there.* Battle paused. *Charlie himself may bear watching.* The fact that Forsyth had outmaneuvered them all back there in Montgomery, still rankled. *Tennent should have gotten the colonelcy then.*

*But ahh, if he had, we would have lost him to promotion instead of Withers.* Battle's Dictum held true.

He refocused on his work: filling out requisitions, reading directives, reviewing requests. At his elbow, two corporals were making duplicates and triplicates as fast as they could write. Tedious but necessary work: turning the wheels of the army.

A pleasant interruption had come at noon, in the form of the widow and her pretty daughter. They arrived with a bountiful basket: a ham, two roast hens, corndodgers and a rice casserole. And a pie! Despite sharing this largesse with the staff, the warm afternoon now stretched endlessly before him. The corporals did not help. Their steel nibs, skittering across army forms, provided the room a soft background buzz, punctuated by the occasional tap and a clink against the ink well; enervating sounds on a full stomach.

Battle's uniform had become snug. He suspected it may have shrunk. *My Land, but I eat too well, here.* The thought was a recurring one, though each time it came, it was with a little less dismay. *One of those two ladies must have a cook worth her weight—*

From his window, he spotted the Frenchman crossing the parade ground under guard, coming his way: Zou Zou, the guards, and a string of cats. It took him a moment to recall the circumstances. *Ah yes, poor old Zou's run-in with Charlie Forsyth.* Yesterday, while performing a purely ceremonial role for dress parade, the adjutant had had the poor man arrested for refusing to bang his drum during Pass in Review. *What could that be about? Lord.*

Battle fretted. *I have no peace; I grow old before my time. I am but thirty-two. No, thirty-three—I was thirty-two last month!* The Tuskegee Lights had serenaded him with 'Do They Miss Me At Home?'

*Tempus fugit, old boy: tem–pus–fu–git. Well and good, Youth be damned! Another birthday passed.* He recalled the old judge's lament: 'Now are we found, in the twilight of a mediocre career—'"

Still, he knew he should be grateful for Zou's predicament. It provided him excuse to evade this stack of paperwork: requests for furloughs (young Johnnie's twentieth birthday will be next week); letters of recommendations (please make private so-and-so a colonel, won't you?); of complaint (lieutenant such-and-such has not satisfied a debt); of advice (the regiment must attack Fortress Monroe on the next new moon). *Children, children.* ...

The detail arrived outside his door. Battle put on his lawyer face now, for the men expected it. With a knock, the guards entered, the senior man reporting his charge. Battle, pretending to be occupied, looked up from his papers impatiently. He ordered off his staff. Grateful for the break, the scribes gave Zou Zou a quick *bonne chance* as they weaved around his escort.

Zou delivered a smart, yet sheepish, open palm salute. Battle took note of the nuance—someday he might need to so instruct a client. He admired the Frenchman's guile: the moustaches brushed downward, in lieu of their usual jaunty points. *Bravo, Zou.* He dismissed the guards.

"Drum Major Hartman," he said, his voice stern (and loud enough to be heard through the door), "I understand you have disobeyed a direct order from Adjutant Forsyth." More quietly, he asked, "What have you to say for yourself?"

Circling his kepi through his hands, the Zouave cleared his throat:

"Monsieur *L'Commandant*, it eez theze: I am given permit to cross the lines, to buy food fer za mess. *C'est bon*: I buy *un petit cochon*. Zozat others will not see, I take the head uf—pardon, *off*, my drum, and put leetle peeg inside; I put head back on. Now am beck across za lines—parade she eez foaming—no time—I take my place. When zee drummers *passer en revue*, Monsieur Charles, he see me and make signal to me, to drum" (Zou pantomiming). "Theze I must not do, sir. Vor I beat zat drum, leetle peeg, she cry out and parade eez—eh, em—*fou*. Monsieur Charles, he place me—*Me*—under arrest!" Combining bewilderment with indignation, Zou concluded his account with a shrug, *"Bof, c'est normal."*

Two could play this game. Battle nodding, sniffed, frowned, ran his finger over his nose. He knew Hartman for a cagey veteran of '*La Grande Armeé.*' A favorite of the entire brigade; of his Alabama comrades, especially. He also brewed the best jim-crack around. His tales of derring-do in North Africa and Sevastopol embellished—no doubt—but the man was hardly an insubordinate soldier. Zou and Battle also shared a fondness for cats, Battle had noticed on more than one occasion his feeding scraps to the camp strays. An *ami-*

*ca curiae* jumped atop his desk now. "Shoo, cat. Get down." Gently brushing the cat aside.

"But tell me, Monsieur Zou, are not those of your, ahh—tribe, forbidden—um, that is, Leviticus: Eleven, for instance, cloven-footed . . ."

"Sir?"

"No, never mind. A trifle. All right, Monsieur. You may go. I will have a word with Mister Forsyth. Tomorrow I may not be so forgiving."

"Thank you, *Mon Commandant.*" Zou straightened up and appeared much relieved. Putting the kepi back on, he snapped a salute and made his about-face. Marching to the door he turned and, with a broad wink, added, "And sir, I send you some of ze leetle peeg, eh?"

Captain Swanson was standing just outside. Big Bill aimed a kick at the cat. He had arrived to take the provost detail into town—a duty shared by all Norfolk's regiments, to preserve the peace—to catch soldiers 'running the lines.'

Eluding the provost marshal's men was nearly as exciting as the other charms found near Widewater Street. Some soldiers were better at it than others, and nothing suited Swanson's temperament more, this game of cat-and-mouse. Other captains were only too happy to relegate the patrols to their lieutenants, but Swanson felt no such compunction.

Swanson had been 'Big Bill' as long as anyone could remember, the name carried as much for his personality as for his size—sometimes called 'Black Bill'—for his face was the color of mahogany, and his beard black as jet. Even his teeth were dark-stained from tobacco. Big Bill or Black Bill, he answered to both. The men had awarded him less-flattering names. Only one volunteer had ever dared to buck Swanson. George Ellison faced discipline for a minor infraction and was brought before Swanson's court. The outcomes of courts martial were preordained and Ellison's trial followed the pattern—except when the recorder asked the defendant, if, before starting the proceedings he had any objections to any member of the court; an obligatory, if pro forma question.

Ellison replied he did. He objected to Swanson.

Swanson gave Battle a careless salute. "Taking the provost to the Customs House," he announced.

"Very well, captain."

"Any 'instructions'?"

"Try to go easy on the Virginia boys. Remember it is their state."

"As long as they obey Virginia law."

"Right." Battle began to look through the papers on his desk.

"'Zou the Jew' seemed pleased—I take it you let him off."

"With a warning, Bill."

"I'm tellin' you, Cullen, they're getting out of hand."

"Our 'Jews,' or the Frenchmen?"

"That's not what I said. There's some bad apples in that Mobile bunch—"

"They're patriots, all. And good soldiers."

"Ryder: in the Rifles—he's a ringleader; so is that imbecile in Gracie's bunch: Simmons."

"Scotty Ryder doesn't 'lead' anybody. It's Shanghai they all listen to over there. And Simon—it's James *Simon*, Bill—he's just a boy. Archie doesn't run them hard enough."

"Gracie don't run 'em at all. He's up in Richmond half the time."

"I won't argue that point. Thank you, captain. If that is all, you are dismissed."

Battle felt spirits lift in camp whenever Swanson was away, and he would approve any request that got the captain out of his hair. He did not think Swanson was a poor officer, he simply disagreed with the man's fixation on punishment as a means to promote efficiency and discipline, the two having gone around and round on these things since the first organization of their militia. Battle had never made any headway against Swanson's reliance on brute force. Lieutenant Mayes, the junior officer in the original officer triad, saw things as Battle did, but once Swanson became captain there was no changing him.

And Battle could understand why Zou Zou would make an appeal to his *Commandant*. The guardhouse—'Swanson House'—was not a pleasant address. In his civilian life, Battle had some familiarity with prisons: incarceration bred its own peculiar *esprit de corps*.

The men would find their own strength, whichever weak vessels were placed over them. *Yea, in time, all things will work out as they should—Lord willing and the Creek. . . .*

Another knock upon the door interrupted his thoughts.

"Enter," he sighed.

## CHAPTER 12 — THE HORNETS
July 3 – 5, 1861


BATTLE'S HOME was Tuskegee, in Macon County, the heart of the Black Belt, the land so-named for the dark, rich, soil that wound through Georgia, Alabama, and Mississippi. Cotton sprang from the ground at four or five bales the acre; at auction bringing ten cents the pound.

He had been raised just outside the belt, in well-to-do Barbour County, below Columbus. Over the course of his youth, however, he had seen the rise of little Tuskegee; watched, as the village established two colleges, a military academy, and a girls' finishing school, while building and supported four large churches. With less than 400 white families, it now boasted the county seat, two newspapers, and a cadre of merchants and lawyers to handle the needs of the planters. Varners and Drakefords imported Italian artisans to build their magnificent homes—mansions—to rival those in Lowndesboro. Barbour County may have been more genteel, but Macon County was where the money was. Her planters summered in New York, shopped on Fifth Avenue, stayed with friends along the Hudson; raced their horses and took the waters at Saratoga.

When the railroads came, Tuskegee sniffed at the opportunity: 'Why ruin what we have? Trade our peace and quiet for the noise and filth of trains? Notasulga and Auburn are near enough for those who desire that sort of thing.' Just as intransigent when it came to politics, the planters wanted no part of Reconciliation. 'States' Rights: now and forever,' they declared. 'And the Devil take the hindmost.'

\* \* \*

Union Springs was also a part of Macon County. Smaller than Tuskegee, her boys didn't plan to settle for hindmost, either; their militia, the Southern Rifles, was nearly as well-trained and equipped as their neighbor up the road.

Jim Branscomb was proud to be a Rifle, though he was

required to be a reluctant one. Having met his obligations in the first call up, in January, he ignored the summons that came three months later. Spring was a critical time in a farming community. Yet, failure to 'fall in' was no small thing in a small town. People talked. Few wished to disappoint Captain Powell, or be on the short end of an argument with a Randle. The Powells and Randles represented the wealth of the community, and the planters living out on Chunnenuggee Ridge were accustomed to having their way.

But a volunteer was still a *volunteer,* and Branscomb held out—the crops were not going to walk themselves in. His older brothers were tanners and exempt from military service (along with overseers, public officials, teachers, riverboat and railroad men). Brother Lewis was just sixteen and his mother would not hear of his going. So, when the militia headed off, that April, not a single Branscomb marched with them.

It meant backbreaking work for those who stayed behind, the shortage of man-power demanding long days in the fields, and fielding the slurs about their manhood and patriotism and duty. But eventually the work got done and Jim made his decision. On a warm June evening, sitting on the porch with his folks, listening to the saw of cicadas, Jim stated: "I'll be heading off."

Pa drove him out to Suspension where he would take the cars. The trip proceeded in brittle silence until they came to the spur, where others were waiting. "Keep away from them sharps up there on the river," advised his father. "Hope you got ever'thin." He handed down the bags, sat back on the bench. "As fer this business. . . ." He gave the reins a slap and turned the mules for home.

\* \* \*

Three nights later, Jim stood on the platform at Norfolk, his eyes fixed on a spectacular comet suspended high over the city. He had never seen the like, the tail so long and so beautiful. He held his hand out: the light was so bright it cast shadows. The depot clerk, more than ready to turn in, pointed him towards the boarding house where the Third Alabama kept rooms. There, a servant girl lighted him up the stairs. "They's gentlemen sojers' already got the bed," she explained, but she had put out a blanket and palette for him.

He awoke to the sound of cannon fire; the Fourth of July still being cause for celebration. His roommates were up and gone—presumably to catch their train. Jim used his last day of freedom to explore the city.

Norfolk was draped in flags and bunting, soldiers everywhere—though (so it appeared to Jim) no two wore the same uniform. He began to feel quite invisible in his civilian clothes, folks hurtling past him without so much as a 'how do.' Like any good farmer he went to the market, where he noted the prices and quality of the produce. The land hereabout must be very poor, he thought. On Main Street he peered into the shops and, assuming an air, entered a few, his hands stuffed firmly into his pockets. Wandering down one street, he stopped at the water's edge, before several enormous ships, marveling at their complicated riggings. The river fed into the Roads, and he wondered if he would ever get a chance to see the great harbor. Reversing course, he took a ferry to Portsmouth, his first ride on a real boat. Walking down to the navy yard, he went on board one of the burned ships.

Back at the boarding house, he arranged to be taken out to the Entrenchment, next morning. After an early supper, he retired to his room and laid out his uniform. He had the bed all to himself.

\* \* \*

At the camp gate, he received the usual challenge.

"Volunteer James Branscomb of the Southern Rifles, reporting."

"Who is your captain?"

Jim was surprised the sentinel did not know this already. "Is this the—? Captain Richard Powell."

With a smirk, the sentry said: "Just joshin' ye. Here, watch this."

"Corporal of the Guard." the sentry cried. "Stranger at the gate!"

"But I'm—"

"Corporal of the Guard!" the sentry's shout was urgent.

From the guards' tent, an immense corporal emerged and waddled towards them, shooting the sentry an evil look. Branscomb came to attention, saluted and announced himself. The corporal included him in his scowl.

"If you are waiting for a corporal to return your salute, you may be out here a while. Or don't the Southern Rifles, 'Bald Hornets'—or whatever you're calling yourselves these days—teach that? Give me your papers, mister."

Embarrassed, Jim lowered his arm and took his transit orders from his jacket.

"Hurry up, I don't have all day."

The corporal looked them over.

"You will be escorted to Captain Powell. Later, you will report to Awkward Squad One. It meets by the A and P board at one o'clock. You *will* be in full rig. You *will* report to Sergeant Broun: B-R-O-U-N, if letters mean anything to you. All you 'sunshine patriots' belong to him, and you *will* be brought up to snuff before you are inflicted on the regiment at-large." With a trace of sarcasm he added, "Questions?"

"No, corporal."

The corporal instructed him to wait there for his sergeant to arrive and, without another word lumbered back to his tent.

The sentry offered Jim a sardonic look: 'Welcome to Norfolk," introducing himself: "I'm Ryder: Mobile Rifles—but everybody calls me Scotty. That one is Roach, of the Montgomery Blues—'Roach' being about the nicest thing anybody calls him. I didn't need to call him over. I just like to make him get off his arse. Pleasures are few, here."

Nearby, a soldier marched in place—under full arms and gear—perspiring heavily, his face beet-red; with every step helping hollow a bowl-like depression in the earth that was his station. Branscomb whispered to Scotty:

"What did *he* do?"

"Ah. Our Mister Ingraham. Last night at tattoo, Sergeant Yniestra politely inquired would the young gentleman refrain from conversing in the ranks. Or words to that effect. Mister Ingraham, just as politely, answered, 'Make me.' Or words to that effect."

"Aha," said Branscomb. "Well."

The prisoner glared at the two.

"It eeze two 'ourze on, two 'ourze off. From nine thez morn, till seven thez evening, as Monsieur Scotty, he says."

The voice was instantly familiar and Jim turned to see his Sergeant Beaumont coming towards them; with another man, and behind them, a servant.

Beaumont was 'Chef' to all the boys from Union Springs, but he offered Jim no further greeting. Pointing to Branscomb's bags, the servant took them up and hurried off. A second signal instructed Branscomb to follow.

Beaumont led Jim to Battalion Headquarters. Passing an active camp, Jim took in the sights and sounds: dogs were everywhere, especially around the mess kitchens; washerwomen making their pick-ups and deliveries, truck farmers offering their produce; a row of Negro barbers were set up under a shade tree; youngsters of both races playing tag through the tents.

They stopped before a large wall tent. Under its fly was a lady Jim knew from home and church: 'Miss Mary,' *viz.* Mrs. Richard Powell, wife of the Captain.

Miss Mary greeted the sergeant: *"Bonjour Monsieur Beaumont. C'est qui là? Il ressemble à l'un des fils Branscomb de chez nous à Union Springs."*

*"Bon jour, Madame.* Indeed. May I present Volunteer James Branscomb."

"Lan' sakes, Jimmy," she exclaimed, "I should have known *you*. You are the spirit and image of your father. We are so *pleased* you are here. And what handsome whiskers," she confided. Taking her offered hand, Branscomb made a formal bow.

"May I inquire: How are your people? And dear Lucinda?"

"They are both well, ma'am. I thank you for asking."

"Lucinda has had the measles?"

"Yes, ma'am. It went through the family in March."

"I was so very sorry to hear of your brother's loss. The death of a child is—is a grievous trial."

"Yes."

Mrs. Powell made her voice bright, "She does such beautiful work, your sister. I am sure she stays busy *these* days."

"Yes, ma'am, that she does."

"Your uniform fits like a glove. I will write her today, to complement her skill and to say you have arrived safely."

Something like a harrumph was heard from inside the tent.

"Well," she said, lowering her voice, "There he is, my old bear. I mustn't keep you, Jimmy, but *do* let me know if I can be of any help to you while you are here. And *do,* won't you, remember me to your family?"

"I will certainly, ma'am. Thank you."

Miss Mary glided off on her rounds.

Beaumont entered the tent and motioned Branscomb to follow. Captain Powell sat at a small camp desk. He took the newcomer's crisp salute.

"Volunteer James Branscomb, Southern Rifles; reporting for duty, sir!"

It was a relief to finally encounter friends from home, and Branscomb visibly relaxed. Captain Powell did not. If anything, Branscomb received a more appraising stare than the one elicited from Roach. Like that corporal, Powell found no flaws.

"Sergeant: why is this man's jacket unbuttoned?"

Branscomb reacted with a downward glance, cut short by shouts, fore and aft.

"You presume *to contradict me*? How *dare* you." Rising from his chair, the captain's face was flush with insulted dignity.

"Eyes *front,* citizen," Beaumont shouted, and Branscomb, recognizing his error, focused on a point on the tent pole, opposite. Continuing his air of outrage, the captain resumed his seat only when his sergeant addressed the offending jacket. Choosing a random button to correct, Beau gave Jim a conspiratorial wink.

"That will be all, sergeant."

*"Oui, mon Capitaine!"* Chef responded cheerily, returning to his position near the entrance.

"Branscomb," said the captain, "for my money, the Southern Rifles are the best company in this regiment. And this regiment is the best regiment in Hampton Roads. I won't have you or any other man bring her disgrace. We keep high standards, here. From your previous time with us, you are familiar with those standards. You may, or may not, agree with them, but the question is not open to debate. Do I make myself clear?"

"Yes, sir."

"Then, whilst I have you, let me make certain you understand these other points: drunkenness will not be tolerated. Nor blasphemy. You will attend Divine Worship each and every Sabbath. I will not tolerate 'ladies of the village' inside your quarters. If you are in town and seen to enter a disreputable establishment, or, for that matter: should you appear on the streets consorting with strumpets, you will be dismissed. Do not think of darkening the door of '*The Lagniappe.*'

"I bear a responsibility to the parents and citizens of Union Springs, who have entrusted me with the welfare and morality of their sons, and I will not have those sons return home as heathens, nor allow anyone to disgrace this company. *Am I clear?"*

"Yes, sir!'

"Very well. Sergeant Beaumont: you will handle the details of this man's billeting."

"Sir!"

As the captain cast him a last critical eye, Jim Branscomb saw no trace of the friendly planter-politician-Sunday schoolteacher he knew from home. It was true: *the war sure changes people.*

"Dismissed."

\* \* \*

Chef passed Branscomb off to the escorting soldier, directing that man to handle his tent assignment. With a start, Jim realized the soldier was none other than his friend Neb, a boy from the same side of town as the Branscombs. In shaking hands, Jim noted the strength in Neb's grip, a hand newly callused and nearly as strong as his own. "Wondered when you would spot me," said his escort.

"Nesbit Battle, as I live and breathe. You're as brown as a Mexican! Last I saw you, you still had some baby-fat. You must have grown two inches, and lost weight in the process."

Pleased, Neb kept walking, checking the sergeant's roster to see with whom Jim would be tenting. "You're assigned to—let me see—yes: Mess Four," looking down the list. Passing the camp streets, Branscomb noticed each was devoid of soldiers. Though, through the smoky haze of mess-fires, he saw a legion of servants, mongers, cooks, and teamsters going about their business.

"Everyone's at Company Drill this time of day," said Neb, without looking up.

A large drum came thumping and bumping across their path, hindered in its course by the attachment of a small drummer. Neb greeted the later: "Little Joe," stretching out the name good-naturedly. Out of breath, Joe responded "*Bon jour,* Monsieur Neb. I am late." Neb explained: "Joe Baumer—Captain Woodruff's ward. Mobile Rifles. Everybody just calls him 'Little Joe.' Smallest man in the army, so they say, but a scrapper.

"Ahem. Now then, Mess Four should be a good fit: John Cameron, Mister Griswold, Rafe Herrin, Tom Johnson, McDevitt, McGowan, Cricket Underwood—yep, that's a good group." Jim knew most of them. They were nearly all the same age, excepting Griswold, who was pushing forty.

Branscomb's mind was still on Captain Powell, however, his resentment simmering over the captain's manner. Branscomb chose his words carefully: "I don't take kindly to undeserved abuse. The captain was—"

"The captain *is* your master here, boyyo," Neb shot back, completing the sentence. "Get used to it. Here, yer no better than a cotton-pickin' field hand. The sooner you get that through your head, the happier you'll be. Consider Chef your overseer. And when you lay eyes on Colonel Lomax, you'll know yer looking at the High Massa, himself."

Neb let Jim chew on this, and they walked the remaining distance in silence. Neb hated to rebuke a friend (for he was dying to ask for news from home), but the sooner Jim realized he was no longer in Union Springs, the better.

At Tent Four, Neb gave Jim a chit to draw his rifle, bayonet, and accoutrements from the quartermaster. Extending an olive branch, he said, "Head over to quartermaster now. Otherwise, when your messmates get back in, they will slow you up. And it is Corporal Fowler who has Awkward One. You will see him at one o'clock."

Ducking inside the tent, Jim was hit by the smells of perspiration, mildew, bacon grease, and gun oil. The tent was empty save for gear, all of it neatly-stacked. His own bags had been set down by the center pole.

Taking Neb's advice, he found the quartermaster tent, returning in due course with a greasy musket, rusty bayonet, battered cartridge box, and cap pouch. Rafe Herrin and Cricket Underwood were waiting for him, sitting outside on upturned Adams' crates. Rafe shouted a welcome when he spied his old chum. Cricket stumbled shyly through "Ha-Ha-Ha-Howdy."

"Wall, lookitchere, look-it-chere," said Rafe. "We saw yer traps, 'n wondered where you wuz." Spotting Branscomb's Springfield, he started laughing. "Sorry, Jim, but that is the most God-awful thing I have seen in many a day. Best not show up to drill with such. You got Awk'ard Squad, I bet. Get a bite to eat and I'll sic one of the boys on it." Rafe handed off the gun to Buck, the hire who worked for the mess. "Buck, rub this up for Marse Jim, won't you. *Hold yer dang hosses.* Don't run off so fast. Jim: you got a few cents? Take off yer boots 'n Buck'll run 'em down to Elsie; Elsie'll work his magic. Gotta make a good impression. Don't fret about the gun, they'll give you a new Enfield, soon's you sign the muster."

"When will that be?"

"Last Parade of the month."

Going inside, Rafe turned to Branscomb: "Well? You seen the Cap'n? What you think, huh? Ain't he sweet? He give you the ole 'We don't drink, we don't cuss; *Norfolk,*' talk?" Nodding, Branscomb smiled tightly. Rafe would never have uttered such a remark, two months ago. *More coarsening of war*, Jim supposed.

Rafe went on, "Marse Richard's 'bout all the cap'n we can take, ain't he boys? I tell you what—he lets you know right quick who de boss *is*, 'n it sure ain't us. Which is, I'm not sayin' they ain't wuss ones: Hunter and Swanson to name two. This camp is ass-deep in bosses."

Tom Johnson ducked through the flap. " 'Worse uns' 'n what?" he asked. Spying Jim, Tom greeted him with a single solemn handshake, as though his coming had been preordained.

"Wuss captains."

"You on that again? Cap'n Powell? I tell you, he's all right. He's got a big job, getting this sorry bunch to act like soldiers."

Jim had to smile. Army life hadn't changed ole Tom one whit. Still, Branscomb couldn't resist taking Rafe's side: "Acted like he didn't know me from Adam's house cat."

"Well, he must ha' been looking to see a soldier. Keep your hurt feelins' inside; all cats look alike to him. 'N don't look for sympathy from this crowd, neither. Who's next for ye?"

"Corporal Roach says I am to meet a Sergeant B-R-O-U-N, 'in full rig.' Full uniform and accoutrements, I take it. Neb told me to look for a Corporal Fowler."

"They will both be there. Fowler has Awk'erd One. He will

drill you till you drop, or, he delivers you to Awk'erd Two—whichever comes first—where ole Harley Broun will truly put you through your paces. 'Full rig' means: accoutrements, rifle, knapsack, bed roll. The works."

"Roach didn't say a thing about a knapsack."

"Exactly," Rafe snorted.

"Colonel don't want nobody thinking the awk'erds are an easy out from regular drill," Tom explained. "And not a light knapsack, neither."

"I don't have a knapsack. Just my bags."

"Here, t-take mine," said Cricket. "Ca-Ca-Cap'n Powell has to re-re-re—has to give you one."

As the rest of the boys came along, each greeted him in turn. Under the canvas, heat built up quickly and they were all soon outside again. Drill had soaked their uniforms through and they drank constantly from their canteens. Their faces were all alike: charred nut-brown from two months under the sun, their noses raw and peeling.

Sharing rations, he exchanged news from home for details of camp-life and politics. His bags held numerous letters from families and friends back home (and more than a few packages), but distribution was delayed by frequent interruptions, by the many howdies and thumps on the back. And a few jabs: "'Bout time you showed; What kept you—you walk here?"

Ten minutes to one, the drums began to beat. Branscomb's tentmates broke off in mid-sentence and, with remarkable efficiency, made ready for afternoon instruction: 'The School of the Soldier.' Buck returned Jim a beautiful gun that bore little resemblance to the one he had handed off, but the numbers matched. Polished boots, too. He thanked Buck most kindly, giving him a half-dime. Shortly before the hour, D Street was once again deserted.

Slipping on his cartridge box, haversack, and canteen, he secured all with his belt. Wrestling into Cricket's knapsack, he picked up his musket and set off in search of Awkward One.

## CHAPTER 13 — THE AWKWARD SQUAD
July 5, 1861


AWKWARD SQUAD ONE assembled by the Announcements and Postings Board at the center of camp. General Orders were posted there, alongside notices for the glee club, chess club, 'For Sale or Trade' offers, and so on. Egregious scribbling was promptly removed, but one bit of whimsy, a tattered survivor, had been allowed to linger:

*Lost:*
*Late on Thursday night, on leaving the steamer*
*St. Nicholas, between the wharf and the fair ground*
*– My Military Enthusiasm –*
*The finder is entreated to return same, without delay*
*to the appropriate Orderly Sergeant*

*"Fall in"* wiped the grin from Branscomb's face.

Squad One was for the most basic instruction: fall in line, proper intervals, stand straight, chest out, stomach in, shoulders back, eyes front, left face, right face, about face; how to come to attention, how to salute, when to salute, when *not* to salute, how to step off, how far to step, how *fast* to step. For Branscomb, nothing new, but all the fresh fish were put through it, usually for one, or two, or three weeks, depending. Occasionally, experienced volunteers were sent down to the squads to have their 'ears cleaned.' Branscomb suspected this was the case for Old Man Griswold. Griswold was no recalcitrant, he was simply deaf as a post and too proud to admit it, nodding 'yes' when asked the time of day. After two days, Branscomb and Griswold were promoted to Awk Two, where the small arms drill came under the exacting eye of Sergeant James Harleston Broun.

Broun's Awk'ards had their own corner of the parade ground. Corporal Donaldson formed the men into two ranks according to height: tallest on the right. He brought the men to attention and ordered: "Count off in ones and twos, by file." From there, the sergeant took over and conducted inspection. Rust spots found on their gun barrels got two men sent back to Awk One.

Broun now had Two's complete attention. He ordered the men to stack arms, a clumsy procedure unless each man (in every foursome), knew his role. Using Branscomb and three others, Broun went through each step until all could perform the order smoothly.

Next, he ordered them to unload their packs. Shanghai, taking note of each man's possessions, told them which items to exclude in future or (if missing), to obtain. He demonstrated how to roll a tight blanket, and how to pack a knapsack properly. Those arriving with light knapsacks (and, in Broun's eyes every knapsack was light), were allowed to make up the difference from a pile of bricks conveniently to hand. With packs bulging, the squad trotted lengths of the parade ground, with rifles at high port. Branscomb quickly got the hang of Awkward Squad Two.

Of all things, 'Load in Nine Times' proved his greatest challenge. Back in Union Springs, he could perform this drill in his sleep: load, handle cartridge (tear cartridge), charge cartridge, draw rammer, ram cartridge, return rammer, prime, ready (aim), fire. Executing the drill in under twenty seconds was the goal. In training, steps: seven, eight, and nine were performed in pantomime.

With "Order Arms," Sergeant Broun called out each step, in minute detail:

"One: 'Load.' You will grasp the rifle firmly, *with the left hand at the height of the right elbow*, bringing it vertical to the middle of the body. After shifting the *right* hand (he waggled his right hand) to the *upper* band, you will *then* place the butt of the rifle between the feet—your *own* feet—the barrel *toward the front*. Not *your* front, Mister Getty, *the front is out here*: thaaat's right, yes, where *I* am. Seize the barrel with the left hand—*near the muzzle*—which you will hold *three inches* from the body," pausing here to correct any misalignments.

"Two: 'Handle Cartridge.' Carry your *right* hand to the cartridge box, which-you-will-have-brought (for your personal convenience), to your front. Now, Mister Getty, *now*, *'your' front* and *'the' front,* are one and the same." Broun continued in this way, until every step was thoroughly italicized.

In their own demonstrations, each man called out the steps himself. *Any young boy can do this,* thought Branscomb. But never before had he been required to do it while a lunatic screamed in his ear; a role this sergeant seemed to relish. When Broun displayed this behavior to the first man in line, the victim stepped back, aghast. This man was returned 'unused,' to the end of the line. When the next man received the identical treatment, the squad understood the amusement had been devised expressly for them.

Old Griswold sailed through, Broun's yelling having no effect upon the deaf. When Branscomb's turn came, he was confident he would master this game.

He made it as far as 'Handle Cartridge.'

His error came in actually listening to his tormenter. Each rant was tailored to the individual, different from the one preceding; intentionally distracting and most amusing to hear, so long as it was not one's time 'under the gun.' The second time through, as Branscomb bit off the end of the paper cartridge, Broun got in his face, shouting, "Spit it out. Now *spit it out!"*

Broun's request meshed neatly with Branscomb's intent, but at this juncture (his thoughts being scattered) the wad became lodged in the back of his throat. Constriction of his windpipe aided the extraction, however, and with a cathartic hack, the soggy projectile landed squarely on Broun's breast buckle. Where it stayed. An obscenity hurled in church, could not have horrified its faithful, more. Services were temporarily suspended.

Third time up, Branscomb got as far as 'Charge Cartridge.' He succeeded in pouring most of the powder down the barrel—but dropped the minie ball. He was shamed by how rattled he had become. Next time through, the sergeant was perfectly silent, which proved more unnerving than the yelling.

He had managed to pour the powder and press the ball into the muzzle. He was pulling the rammer when the sergeant said, in a most reasonable tone—almost in a whisper—"All right, Branscomb, you know this. You can stop there. Go on back in line." The words stated so calmly that Broun's sincerity could not be questioned. Branscomb felt the fleeting glow of accomplishment before he realized he was, once more, at the end of the line. Five minutes with the ball-puller extracted the round.

Mr. Griswold remained at parade rest. In due course (Sergeant Broun's voice giving out), the others were allowed to join the older man.

The drill never failed to attract the attention of those off-duty and provided the camp wags ample fodder. For a time, Branscomb was celebrated as 'Spitwad,' or 'Ole Expectorant.' But from such small ways as this drill, the Awkwards would recall their lessons under trial, and in battle, remain steady.

For demonstrating proficiency at Load in Nine Times, the squad was marched to the range and allowed to fire their round. At one hundred yards Branscomb scored the lone bull's-eye. With an untried gun, he knew his result was pure luck.

\* \* \*

Branscomb was soon assisting Sergeant Broun, who, off duty, revealed himself to be a rational (even *sweet-tempered*) soul, though, as a member of Sands' Cadets, he remained all spit and polish. Broun received many offers of commissions outside the regiment, but his sole ambition was to go into battle as color-bearer for the Third, taking the position of greatest risk. There developed a mutual respect between he and Branscomb, the sergeant holding no grudge for being spat upon. "Comes with the salary," he said.

At night, the denizens of Tent Four would explain for Jim, what the rest of them were learning in battalion drills, using pebbles to demonstrate maneuvers and positions. They would rap out the different drumbeats used to signal orders, until he was familiar with them and could react properly. Rafe and Tom helped him identify the various Line Officers, the key sergeants and corporals, and to distinguish between each company's uniform facings. Soon, he knew who was ordering him about. Mostly.

Among his volunteers, Captain Powell remained a target of criticism. Rafe wasn't the only one to have gotten off on the wrong foot. In Union Springs, Powell was considered about the best man in town—an honest lawyer, a practicing Christian, a fair and humane planter.

Norfolk had brought out a different man: a petty tyrant, vindictive and narrow-minded.

"They's a time 'n a place to give orders, a time 'n place to take 'em," groused Rafe. "Ain't right for a 'Springs man to act so High 'n Mighty. Ain't right 'tall."

## CHAPTER 14 — THE ENGLISH OPENING
July 3, 1861

THE TWO were evenly matched. Each game—every move—requiring the utmost care, as anything less invited defeat. For the spectators, the tension was anticipatory, for otherwise it made for dull going. Armistead had been paired with Weedon too often, and each knew the others designs, several moves out, resulting in many a long, drawn-out battle. The two were second-tier players: Nott and Richey were better, having learned the game when Morphy was beating all comers. Sands and Lomax were said to be formidable, but they did not vie.

Chess was the one diversion that crossed all lines. Shinny enjoyed a large following, especially amongst those from Macon County, where their fathers had learned it from the Creeks, who told them the word meant: 'kill the ball-carrier.' For others it was cockfighting, or playing tip-catch—town ball—sometimes called base-ball. The drum corps preferred mumble-the-peg or the schoolyard combat of knucks. For the sedate there was whist, euchre, or seven up.

This evening the gathered had come for a match played for pride, *viz.* the pride of the Cadets and the Rifles—the cadres with the most to spare. The onlookers stood fanning themselves—and the players too, occasionally. Every small breeze was welcome, if only to give hard-landings to the 'no-see-ums.'

To the north, the great comet rose with even more splendor than the night before. Then, men had gathered outside their tents, watching for hours, that streak over half the sky. Tonight, the surprise and novelty were gone but its beauty shone undiminished. From the parade ground Zou's boys were hard at their lessons: *Mammy*-daddy, *Mammy*-daddy, *Mammy*-daddy, they drummed (endlessly); ragged efforts that carried all too clearly.

Armistead was a gentleman volunteer and, until the present disruption, arguably the best lawyer in Mobile. Dropped from the Cadets' muster at Lynchburg because of numbers, he continued on to Norfolk all the same, shouldering all the duties of a regular. Middle-aged and portly, he cut an amusing figure on the drill field. But he had *Hardee's* down cold, having come a long way since that night on the deck of *St. Nicholas.* Here, while his tent mates passed time talking moonshine, he applied himself to the study of tactics. He knew the evolutions for squad, company and battalion as well as any colonel.

He was also one of the 'Famous Fives'—Mess No. 5—Cadets possessed of servants, cots, inflatable mattresses, persian rugs. They would invite their superiors to dine, and be accepted. The Fives were mostly older men, each with some unique quality that placed them in the category of 'high private.'

To open a lane of attack, Armistead took a pawn with his knight.

Weedon saw the blunder and took Armistead's last bishop. A smug murmuring arose from half the onlookers, the others remaining silent, in hopes Armistead's play concealed some elegant design.

The rivalry between the Cadets and Rifles was unrelenting: the Rifles considered the Cadets swellheads—'ladies men' being the current dismissive; while, for their part, the Cadets did not consider the Rifles at all. Each was a militia of long-standing, their captains, veterans of the last war, brave and capable. The two companies often went head-to-head for honors and competed for the best prospects to fill their ranks. Armistead and Weedon, older than their comrades—and coming to it all rather late—found the rivalry a bore.

There was no grand stratagem; his defenses crumbling, Armistead conceded. Weedon took the opportunity to shake hands and take his leave. The onlookers dispersed almost as quickly, until only a single Cadet remained. This soldier waited politely for Armistead to relight his pipe, watching him bring up the coals with a few slow draws. Smoke kept the invisible pests at bay.

"Mister Robert? Sir? Have you time to give me a lesson?"

Through the cloud, Armistead peered up at the youth—one of the few elected to the militia last spring (one of only four under the age of twenty). Most Cadets were in their mid-twenties, with quite a few—like Armistead himself—past thirty. Nick was just eighteen, but a lean six-footer, and still growing; the son of the city treasurer. At Mobile, just before they were to board, the elder Weeks had approached Armistead, to ask he look out for his boy as much as was practicable. It was no great burden: young Nick was a fine lad, not childish or brash like some others he could name.

Armistead remembered that night—the night of their leaving—with many of the volunteers carousing their way to Montgomery—fumbling his way through the basic Manual of Arms while hoots and whistles rained down on his head. His 'standing' in Mobile counted for nothing in that crowd, with one exception: Nick Weeks. Nick, and the Ellison boy, had come down to offer their help.

As an unobtrusive way for Armistead to fulfill his pledge, Nick received the occasional lesson in chess; an opportunity to keep the youth from the baser temptations of camp life and, at the same time, draw him into conversation on a broad array of subjects. Armistead hated to think of Nick's fine, inquisitive mind going to seed beneath the boredom of an army camp.

With another draw and a puff, Armistead nodded his assent and, rising from his stool, said, "Let's go inside. We'll set the board up there on a cot, and be rid of these swarming devils."

\* \* \*

The tent was already occupied. Fast asleep was Armistead's younger brother, Bedstead (nee: 'Ed'). Robert and Nick made no effort to lower their voices. These past months the regiment had learned how to sleep through everything (excepting reveille, roast beef, and the long roll). The other man was Sergeant Broun, Mess No. 5's ranking member. From his long, custom-made cot Broun gave Nick a minute tilt of the head, before returning to his reading of Mackay's *Madness of*

*Crowds*. The rest of the mess had either run the lines or gone to the bonfire. Armistead turned up the lantern.

"The English Opening was all the rage some years ago. Comes up still, from time to time. Staunton used it to good effect over the Frenchman, Saint Something-or-other. So you should learn how it applies, offensively and defensively."

Armistead played white. "The English has little flash to begin with, but you recognize the opening by the initial move: pawn to D-four. It is a positional game, using flanking movements more than just head butting. But here," (tapping the white pawn in the middle of the board) "Here your little pawn can jump and shout, beat his chest and, gathering all his rosebuds, proclaim E-five, for his very own." His explaining stopped abruptly. He seemed to fixate on the pawn, and to select his next words with care. "There are several good responses from black," he continued, slowly, "including, a Queen's gambit (of which, you must be wary). The typical counter from Black, is: Pawn to. . . ."

His words faded away. The very spirit seeming to go out of him. Shoulders drooping, he leaned back from the board, his eyes darting from point to point, as they were wont to do, when he was assessing legal options. A final deep sigh signaled the resolution of some internal debate.

Alarmed, Nick leaned forward, but Armistead rebuffed the concern with an impatient waggle of his head. He renewed his study of the board, an examination which ended abruptly. With a flick of his finger, he rattled the board so hard, the pieces toppled over.

"Nick, let's explore a different game, what the British prefer to call 'the great game.' In our case: North versus South.

"You know, of course, I am here merely as a supernumerary to the Cadets? I have not signed the muster, and sadly, will not. Nor will I be in Norfolk much longer, as much as I might like to stay in this fetid swamp. So, I would have you know how *this* game may play out, for what good it may do you.

"Set up White on your side. I'll take Black, but you may array only your pawns, as bodyguard to your king and minister."

Bemused, Nick did as he was told. Armistead reached over and picked up Nick's unused pieces. Nick laughing, "I fear this: your 'game,' already."

"You should."

Holding up White's knights and bishops, Armistead dropped them over the side of the cot one by one, intoning as he did so: "Delaware, Maryland, western Virginia, Kentucky." Holding aloft two rooks, he dubbed them, "Fortress Monroe, and Fort Taylor, at Key West," before letting each go.

Nick remonstrated with the only argument that came to mind. "But this isn't chess."

"Overruled, my boy," the lawyer replied, "And, I believe, counsel for the defense means to say, 'I object.' Feel free, you *may* object, Nick. All you like." Pointing with his pipe to the unused pieces: "These could just as easily represent the machinery of State: military, bureaucracy, diplomacy, finance. So, object again if it pleases you. It pleases *me*. It pleases the court to hear you say it. But it will avail you nothing, for there is no judge to answer.

"Like our sister states up North, I am older than you, wiser, *meaner*. I have won many a hard-fought case, and used every trick in the book to do so, legal or otherwise, while you, dear Nick, were deciphering *McGuffy's Reader*. And I will tell you all the rules, as I—correction—*if,* I feel you need to know them. Look to your pawns there: You might as well face them each to a different direction, because ultimately (I assure you: *ultimately*) that is the absurdity of the States' Rights' argument. And, should we, by some divine intervention, win this war, what then? What will we have won? A dozen states all going their merry little ways? Beating their hairy little chests? Carving out their little fiefdoms? Dancing round, like our little English D-four, once did. May God have mercy on us, Nick.

"Here." Armistead picked up a black rook. Hopping its pawn, he slid it down the file until, knocking its opposite from the board, it held the redoubt on the back corner. He did the same on the other side with the remaining rook. White king and minister had two black rooks on their flanks.

"You have to let me make a move," Nick pleaded.

"Oh? Do I, indeed?" Armistead said with a whiff of sarcasm. "Well then, I *have* let you."

"What? When?" the youth spluttered.

"*Your* move was accepting the game. *Your* move was Fort Sumter. Whilst you were so proud of *that* empty square, I countered by simply holding onto Monroe, Key West, and Fort Pickens.

"Play 'what if' with me, Nick: If the governor of Virginia acts in concert with the governor of Alabama, and (purely as a 'precautionary' measure) takes Monroe on January four, (the day we took Fort Morgan) where does that leave the Yankees? What happens if (in concert with Maryland) we occupy old Fort McHenry. Even, should it later become our Alamo*?* What could have been *better* for the Cause, than that?

"Baltimore and Washington: we will never regain the one without we take the other.

"The mere keeping of St. Louis Arsenal locked Missouri to the union. Old Fuss and Feathers—fat, pompous, silly, vain, old Winfield Scott—did all that while seated at his desk. One of our brilliant Southern blowhards—Pillow, perhaps—should have *fussed* at Scott, insisting his hoary ole head was too old to remember how to win a war.

"Or perhaps it is Lincoln's hand which plays," he concluded with a curse.

Nick singled out a white pawn and, moving it down to the black king, knocked him from the board. Armistead smiled, pleased to see Nick was the quick study he took him to be. Still, the lawyer was dismissive, "Lincoln? Bah. I have more like him. It's the prime ministers you must watch, the Sewards and Stantons—"

"Then why fight, if that is how you see it?" Nick cut in, exasperated. "Have we lost already? Why are *you* here?"

"Good questions all, my boy. Let me answer the last, first. I am here because I believe the South has the right of it. Listen, all Americans hold sacred three documents: the Declaration of Independence, the Constitution, and the Bill of Rights. *However*, it is only the latter two have the weight *of law*. Mister Jefferson's opinion, 'All men are created equal,' is outside the law. As a lawyer, I can only see, in the Constitution, a badly drawn contract, entered into in bad faith by one, if not both, parties. Randolph and Macon saw it for what it was.

Be that as it may; I submit, the most egregious breaches have come from the North, long before Fort Sumter. Our problem is, we cannot see the forest for the trees; the trees being States' Rights. Or call them Yankees, and the woods, are us. *Ourselves*.

"We may not win, Nick, but we have not already lost. We can avoid losing, but only if we harness up and all pull together. Given the personalities on our side, this may prove unlikely. So, why fight? Well, why the hell, not? We are Southerners after all, it appears to be what we have been bred to do. The North isn't accustomed to war like we are. Since 1812 we have fought the British, the Red Clubs, the Creeks, the Seminoles, the War of Independence in Texas, the Mexicans. (If we could snatch away Nicaragua and Cuba, we would.)

"Am I making light of it? Yes. But in all candor, if we can make them howl long and loud in sixty-two, we will have a chance."

He continued in a more somber tone.

"Slavery is still (ipso facto) the eventual death of the South. It is immoral. It is suicidal. Had Mr. Jefferson written, 'All *white* men are created equal,' he would have become the laughing stock of Europe, and we would have become a footnote in someone's '*History of the Colonial Revolt.*' Later on, he called slavery 'a necessary evil,' and I agree: it is evil. Still would I argue, what makes it necessary? This is no quibble; Jefferson was a brilliant man, but could he see no further than this? The same man who found millions to purchase Louisiana, could not scrape together enough to set free one of his own slaves? Or his neighbor's ten, or one hundred by lot? Instead, like any other common, grasping, Yankee entrepreneur, he grabbed the chance to improve his holdings: to buy the farm next door. And *how* did he do this? I will tell you: *By taking a mortgage on his slaves.*

"*Damn* him; the *face of it*, Nick.

"I ask you: was it a necessary evil for England to keep her colonies permanently under her thumb? How could that have played out in any other way than as it did? Today, we repeat her mistake: three millions of slaves in the South; mulattos, quadroons, octoroons, abound. How can this necessary evil, turn out in any way but badly for us?"

This last hit Nick close to home. His childhood playmates, Susan and Vincent, were the decidedly fair-skinned children of Sarah, the Weeks' cook. At some point they had been hired out to another household and subsequently he saw them rarely. It was not a subject to broach to either of his parents. Or to Sarah.

"The courts groan under the burden of slave cases: 'Who can lash a slave?' 'On whose behalf?' 'If one borrows from a slave, has he stolen from a master?' 'Does a slave have a right to defend his life from murder?' 'Is it *his* right, or must he protect himself as his master's peculiar?' 'Can a wench maintain her virtue?' Does she *have* virtue? Hear me, Nick: it is *endless*. Goldthwaite's father adjudicates little else.

Long before this, we should have put our collective heads together to figure some way out of this mess—this 'bequest' of our forebears. Instead, we have allowed our pipers to call the tune, men like Buford and Yancey. And *have we danced.*

"In Boston, the Yankees pushed forth that serpent masquerading as a senator (I speak of Sumner, of course), to do the same thing. Caning him senseless on the Senate floor, only made of him a demi-martyr, just as hanging Brown merely sanctified *his* bloody hands. Every toddling step we have taken has been one of emotion over intellect. We have not played the long game. We are the errant child unwilling to wait for the pie to cool. So he steals it beforetime, and thereafter bemoans his burned mouth. Chess matches are not won with emotions. Children may play chess eye-for-an-eye; adults should not."

"May I approach the bench?" Nick interjected. Judge Armistead nodded.

"You say we have entered this 'game.' Is it a game of States' Rights, or of slavery?"

"Ah, there you have it."

"Have what, exactly?"

"The question our children's, children's, children, 'to the seventh generation,' will be debating through eternity. To us, it is States' Rights. Before 1789 each of the original thirteen states was a sovereign country. They made their own treaties (Massachusetts even had its own foreign policy); Virginia was half the size of Texas (and recall that Texas was an independent *nation* when it joined the Union); Georgia extended to the Mississippi. It was States' Rights first and forever, clearly enunciated and enumerated in the *proposed* constitution, of *uniting* states (heretofore referred to as 'the Contract.') *We–would–not–have–put–our–names–to–pa–per* otherwise. It is the trap Rutledge feared, and the conundrum John Calhoun exposed. As an aside, permit me to add that it is well known in legal circles the Constitutional Convention itself had little right to exist, and no *mandate* whatsoever. Old Alexander Hamilton convinced the States to send delegates to amend the Articles of Confederation. Once gathered, he changed the tune.

"To return to my point: To a Northerner, it is only about slavery. But hear the hypocrites, to wit: *they* (our Northern oligarchs) receive stolen goods (in the form of a man), taken against his will. In chains they secure him—*indemnify* him—his *life* is no longer *his own*, Nick; with others, spirited away across the seas, stacked like cord wood. They debase him, abuse him, break him by every outrage one human being can inflict upon another, *sell* him on our shores as a commodity (to the highest bidder), pocket the profit, build their mansions, educate their children at Harvard, Brown, and Yale, teach them there to 'tut, tut, tut' the poor black man *and,* the *present evil owners* (you and me). Then, have the temerity to demand of us (on behalf of said black man, of course), recompense for life, liberty, 'and the pursuit of happiness.' They would have us loose these millions of happy, carefree, *lash-scarred* blacks to roam free as they will; so long as they do their roaming in the South. Or pack them off to 'Liberia' to starve.

"'End human bondage, *Now,*' they demand. 'What monsters these Southrons be.'"

Ignoring the sarcasm, Nick countered, "Slavery is surely flawed—Agreed—but our servants are happy, secure, and better cared for than say, the hordes of Irish and—"

"*Pshaw*, don't throw your 'Professor' Dew on me. You embarrass yourself. After the Nat Turner massacre, Virginia came *very* close to abolishing slavery. *Very close*. Till that rascal tipped the scales with 'a merrier being does not exist on the face of the globe than the Negro slave of the United States.' Ole Dew played to their vanity. Nick, the same could be said of one's dog. He is fed well and secure. What of it? Would you contend the two are one and the same? Is the yard dog tied to his stake as happy as your house pet? Do either have any choice but to take your food and be happy? Either *may* bite you. Why do you suppose they do not? Real life is not the happy talk of minstrel shows."

"No, I ah. . . ."

"Listen, now: The Constitution counts them three-fifths of a human being, not as an indictment, but as a measure to weaken the South's representation in the old Congress, (or to strengthen the North's by two-fifths depending on your side of the equation). Subsequently, we made law to keep our entire five-fifths unschooled, so that we might pretend they are less intelligent." Armistead jabbing the air with his pipe stem: "They—are—not. They think, they feel, et cetera and so on; they laugh, cry, learn from their mistakes, grow angry, bleed, and curse, as any man might. You *know* this. Don't be fooled by those slack-jawed devils left to toil our fields. That is a circle of Hell all its own. No: teach them to read and write at a young age and they learn as quickly as any bright child would. And, I would add, they bear their lot with more grace than would we, should the Mussulmen of Africa one day turn the tables round, and permit us to serve them! No, the Negro has a resilience of spirit we would do well to emulate.

"Slavery is an abomination, foisted on the Americas by pious Puritans; upon ambitious, short-sighted fools: your great-grandfather and mine. Speaking rhetorically, of course."

Nick was too dazed to feel insulted, facing questions for which he had no argument. "So, what is the answer?"

"States' Rights, *and* the end to slavery. It is our right and (I daresay) our obligation, to right this wrong. The sooner the better. Slavery is the inherited wrong of both races. It is a greater serpent round our neck than Scott has ever dreamed of. But since we don't ask to interfere in the affairs of the North, they should not meddle in ours. Will our solutions be theirs? Will ours be perfect? Hardly. Each state must follow its own dictates. In chess, it is called the end-game."

"Then kill them all? Might not South Carolina's solution be to just kill all their 'hands' and be done with it? Is that part of the *game*?"

"Good Lord, boy, the rest of the South would drive the palmettos into the sea."

"Then States' Rights is a fraud! You cannot eat your cake and have it, too."

Checked, Armistead stopped, brought swiftly back to earth from the pleasure of legal dicta; his years before the bar enabling him to cover his reaction before opposing counsel.

*Nothing I cannot argue my way out of (of course), but the pup begins to bark.* He regarded Nick, anew: *A quick mind here.* He stalled by repacking his pipe, lighting it with a straw fired from the lantern. He took several slow draws.

A new voice broke the silence. "We should have conspired to let South Carolina secede alone." Harley Broun emerged from behind his book. "She has always wanted to, anyway," he said. "*There* is your true little pawn beating his chest. Maybe let Georgia run off with her too (throw in our own Barbour County for good measure), and hold the other states back. Our current perimeter is far too large to defend. We will be deflated like a balloon.

"We could have flooded those two with volunteers and

supplies, and made of them our cockpit, as Europe has used Belgium. Or, we could have waged another Peninsula War: guerillas at every crossroads—hit and run. The United States would have grown weary (as did France), of the drain on life and treasure. Once South Carolina is free, the precedent is set; the Union falls apart; to re-form later, perhaps, as smaller, but like-minded, nations."

"Hell," Bedstead chimed in, his voice muffled by his pillow. "We could have offered up an amendment freeing them in exchange for the population being counted at full value, increasing our power in Congress. Calling their bluff would see the bastards squirm."

"I would agree," Robert said, "especially about the perimeter. We can't prevent the comings and goings of our own people here in a twenty-acre camp."

"We could, if the men acted honorably, and reported violators."

"You make my point, Nick. If men reported violators, we would only need a token provost. We could do without armies, altogether. Instead, men will always look to their own interests. It does not serve them to report a messmate, any more than it pays to incur the enmity of your neighbor's messmate. If men acted honorably it would surely be a better world. I am afraid we are stuck with this one."

After a time, Robert reset the board, and motioned to Nick to make the first move. "We'll play a straight game, for pleasure."

The game was an interesting one. Nick ably countered Armistead's moves until his defenses collapsed under the older man's endgame.

"May I ask what your plans are, for after the war, Nick?"

"To be alive shall be enough, I think."

Armistead winced.

"I'm sorry, it was not my intent. . . Really, sir, I have not thought that far, beyond the war, I mean. Something in finance, I suppose. My father is—well, you know my father."

"I do, I do—I do, quite," he replied. "You must find me

after the war."

"I will, Mister Armistead."

"My friends call me Robert. 'Bob,' if you like."

They went on to speak of many things, the chessboard forgotten. Later, Nick wandered back to his tent, the comet so bright he needed no lantern. Taking a seat on a nearby stump, he gazed in wonder at the stars. The words of Edward Everett came to mind: *"The earth is but a foot-ball compared with its' starry hosts—stars like our own sun, numberless as the sands on the shore; worlds and systems shooting through the heavens."* [8] The universe was as vast as God's mercy, His ways beyond the ken of man.

A melody interrupted his thoughts: a jolly tune, from the direction of the old tree.

---

[8] Edward Everett (1794-1865) Governor of Massachusetts, U.S. Senator, Secretary of State; principle orator at Gettysburg, preceding Lincoln's address.

## CHAPTER 15 — THE OLD MULBERRY
July 1861

"DO YOU know this one?"

With a few flicks of his bow, the fiddler restated the question. The banjo player rolled the response. "Haven't heard that one for a while, Joe. *Vive la Compagnie*?"

*"Mais oui."*

'Cotton-eye' Joe Fort and Shanghai Donaldson sat under an ancient mulberry, by the ruins of a once-proud manor. All that remained of the house were its foundation stones, front steps and chimneys; charred memorials to some forgotten family. The site, uncovered in the process of clearing the woods for the parade ground, now served as the informal gathering place of the Third. Many nights a bonfire was set ablaze near it, where all things military could be set aside; a sort of sanctuary. On Sundays, the chaplain conducted divine services beneath the tree.

Sixty feet tall (seven in girth), the mulberry had weathered the events of nearly two centuries. Gnarled and fissured, its boughs were twisted in a manner familiar to hurricane coasts. Its trunk bore the mementos of assignations long past, while scars still fresh commemorated more recent visitors.

Under its leaves rank held no privilege; a matter of some concern around other, more distant, campfires; the opinion being such liberties would never work—s*hould* never work—a thing but one step short of mutiny. But the Alabamians regarded themselves as gentlemen, first and foremost and, outside official duties, the equal of any man. More importantly, Colonel Lomax believed this, that discipline could be maintained on the basis of mutual respect.

Weather permitting, the fire would be built up after dress parades. Those not posted, or sick—or running the lines—gathered to discuss (or mock) the latest rumors. Excepting vice, no activity was prohibited. One side of the fire might wish to hear a few chapters from Dickens, while another railed against Congress; (either one). The musicians claimed the side nearest the old manor. And often, they took center stage.

Joe rosined up his bow while Shanghai plunked his banjo—one of his two constant companions (Caroline being the other). Two more musicians came over: a civilian fiddler, and Gilbert Graves, the Tuskegees' drummer.

*Dixie* always drew a cheer, *Oh, Susannah,* too. But, after two months of this, Joe and Shanghai determined to expand their repertoire. For *La Compagnie* they consulted on the order of the verses; appealing for help from the Frenchmen. But neither Zou nor Chef Beaumont knew the song. Donaldson fah-lah-lah'd the melody for Gilbert: "*vive* la, *vive* la, *vive* l'amour. Not: vivala, vivala—"

"I know that one," chimed a female voice. "*J'adore La Compagnie*. Oh, you must play it for me. *Please* do."

Hearing her voice, the soldiers all rose to their feet, to see a woman in fashionable dress, enter the light, an escort on each arm, Colonel Battle on her right, beaming proudly, and on her left her brother, Vivian, a Cadet. Shanghai knew her only by her novels, but looking to his band, answered for them: "With pleasure, Miss Evans."

"If you will give me a fair start, might I sing a verse?"

"We would be honored, ma'am."

Divvying up the parts, Joe caught the eyes of the others and nodded out the tempo. Shanghai took the first verse.

> *Let Bacchus to Venus raise cheer to the past,*
> *Vive la compagnie*
> *And let us make use of our time while it lasts.*
> *Vive la compagnie!*
>
> *Vive la, vive la, vive l'amour*
> *Vive la, vive la, vive l'amour*
> *Vive l'amour, vive l'amour*
> *Vive la compagnie."*

Men from the circle's far side came round to hear the new song.

> *Let ev'ry old bachelor fill up his glass,*
> *Vive la compagnie*
> *And drink to the health of his favorite lass.*
> *Vive la compagnie!*
>
> *Vive la, vive la, vive l'amour*
> *Vive la, vive la, vive l'amour*
> *Vive l'amour, vive l'amour*
> *Vive la compagnie!*

Miss Evans joined in:

> *Let ev'ry married man drink to his wife,*
> *Vive la compagnie*
> *The friend of his bosom and comfort of life.*
> *Vive la compagnie!*

(Appreciative cheers drowned out the start of the chorus and the men began to emphasize *'l'amour'*)

> *Vive la, vive la, vive L'AMOUR!*
> *Vive la, vive la, vive L'AMOUR!*
> *Vive L'AMOUR, vive L'AMOUR,*
> *Vive la compagnie!*

Cotton-Eye Joe played the intermezzo. Shanghai, spying a tall man on the fringe of the circle, directed the next verse to him:

> *Come fill up your glasses I'll give you a toast,*
> *Vive la compagnie.*
> *Here's health to our friend our kind worthy host.*
> *Vive le compagnie!*

A great cheer was raised for the colonel, who, acknowledging the compliment with his famous smile, gave them an elaborate and courtly bow. Allowing the cheering to swell, Shanghai vamped a few measures, before leading them back:

> *Vive la, vive la, vive L'AMOUR!*
> *Vive la, vive la, vive L'AMOUR!*
> *Vive L'AMOUR, vive L'AMOUR,*
> *Vive la compagnie!*

There followed a spirited final verse that ended, nevertheless, on an odd note. Augusta Evans clapped delightedly, but only a smattering arose from the men, and fewer cheers. They seemed to have enjoyed the song well enough, but their mood had turned somber.

They pressed to be taken through the verses again. With each round more voices joined in, the harmonies improving as the chorus grew softer. Then, satisfied with the result, the throng (by now a small battalion) dispersed, as if by signal, drifting quietly back to their company streets.

Miss Evans whispered to Battle, "How queer how it moved them. They began as brigands, and ended as choir boys."

"They make use of their time 'while it lasts.' " Battle observed.

"Miss Evans?" Shanghai inquired, as the other players approached.

"Miss Augusta, may I present the orchestra?" asked Colonel Battle.

"I would be disappointed if you did not."

With a curtsey to all, she greeted them one by one: Donaldson and Fort, Zou, Gilbert, and others who had arrived in the middle of the second run-through. Shanghai saw Little Joe hanging back and pulled the boy forward. "May I present a fellow Mobilian, ma'am? This is Captain Woodruff's ward, Joseph Baumer, one of our best kettle drummers."

"I am delighted to meet you, good sir. But you surprise me, I did not realize the young ladies of Mobile were so foolish."

"Ma'am?"

"To let such a *handsome* man, depart for the army."

One would not have thought a face could turn so many shades of red. Taking Little Joe's hands in hers, Miss Augusta gave them a warm maternal squeeze, and another life-long reader was created.

"And this is Johnnie—Jonathan Wise—a local boy. His father commands a brigade nearby."

The author greeted them all and invited them to sit with her and tell her how they viewed Norfolk, army life, and of course, the war. She was an ardent and passionate rebel, having famously broken with her fiancé over politics. She asked each of them about their hometowns, and they found they shared many mutual friends. With Battle's permission, they talked long after the fire grew low.

It was a night long cherished. To the north, the great comet shone like quicksilver. Zou and Chef sat to one side, puffing on their pipes, sharing memories of old campaigns, and the companions of their youth. Caroline drowsed by Shanghai's feet. All eyes lulled by the repeating patterns in the flames.

"*Bonsoir, Monsieur: s'il vous plaît?* Where is your home, Monsieur Zou?" Miss Augusta asked.

"*Mobile,* Mademoiselle," said Zou.

Laughing, she begged, "No, please."

He relented: "Before I come to thez country, ah was in Algiers. An' before: Crimea—many places, Mademoiselle. My 'ome, long ago, is Prussia, then Alsace. You know Alsace?"

"I know of it. It is a beautiful province, I am told."

"Yes, yes. Little Joe, you meet, is too, from Alsace. I went a–way as a boy. Achoyne l'armée and zay teach me za droom." His fingers rolled a four-beat. "Ever since, ah haf been a soldier."

Zou wore his uniform proudly. The Turkish red trousers, sash, white gaiters, blue jacket and kepi (with red havelock) set him apart no matter how distinguished the crowd. He bridled at any association with the Louisiana Zouaves—Colonel Wheat's Tigers—who had cut such a public swath through the brothels and jails of Richmond. At their mention, Zou would spit, saying: "*Mon Dieu.* Zay are no Zouaves. Zay are Irishmen *in pillow casings.*"

Chef Beau came from a nameless village in the foothills of the Pyrenees, its precise location elusive. An associate of Eduard Kleber—nephew of one of Napoleon's field marshals—the two had come to Alabama following Harpers Ferry, enticed by a handsome stipend to drill the Tuskegee Light Infantry twice each week. On their advice, Battle and Swanson placed an order for one hundred Enfields, creating a militia as completely trained and equipped as any in the South.

Kleber moved on to greener pastures, but Beaumont stayed. He liked his new friends and settled near Union Springs. When that town formed a militia, Captain Powell called upon him, and together they organized and trained the local boys.

\* \* \*

It was long past lights out. The moon had set, leaving only the comet to cast shadows. On Bo–Lo Street all were sleeping soundly. Nearly all. Hugh Hardy nudged Joe Howard, next to him, whispering, "You awake?" The grunt offered in reply, was enough for Hardy. "That song will be in my head all night."

Howard did not answer, but his friend would not be ignored, and whispering more loudly: "I said, that song—"

"Could be worse," growled his neighbor.

"How so?"

"Could be, *Pop! Goes the Weasel.*"

For a long while silence enveloped the tent.

Conceding defeat at last, Hardy hissed: "You bastard."

## CHAPTER 16 — PRINCESS ANNE ROAD
July 18, 1861

HAVING PULLED sentry duty, Jim Branscomb and Tom Johnson had the following day free. Jim suggested they spend it in the city. A change of scenery would do them good and, if they kept to the shade, the stroll would be pleasant.

Henry Smith and Lon Stinson caught up with them, Henry his usual boisterous self. He relished every aspect of military life, especially Chef Beaumont's tales of Crimea and Africa; stories that had expanded Henry's command of colloquial French; vocabulary, not so much, but he could curse with the best.

Lon was the younger brother of Old Dick, the two, widely known for their good-natured bickering. Jim asked him how the Southern Rifles had come to be called the 'Bald Hornets.' Lon:

"We were the last train to reach Lynchburg. When we got to the fairgrounds, it was Hobbes' choice. Since we had no tents, we got quartered in the show stables.

"Anyways, 'The Great One' (Ole Dick) was busying himself hammering pins for the officers' tents, when this herd of wooly Tennesseans comes shufflin' by. Dick, now (he's ever so curious), puts down his mallet, and asks 'em: 'Where ya'll boys from?'

"They stop, and, this one big ole pachyderm says, 'We'uns the Ridgeville Hornets, Mister.'

'Where?'

'We'uns from Ridgeville,' says they, all together.

'Yes,' says Dick 'But, where is that?'

"These boys look't one t'other, then down at Old Dick, wonderin' if a display of pity might not be the politest way to go. First man says (slowww as molasses), says: 'Why, I *thunk* ever'body know'd *Ridgeville,* mister. S'over *thar*, south'ard.' Makin' this grand sweep of his arm in the general di-rection of, oh, say: Kentucky, Tennessee. *Ohio*. But he said: 'thunk' didn't he, Henry? *'Thunk,'* ya'll—hand to my heart."

"Gospel," Henry agreed.

"*Any*-ways, Dick's trying to think who might have a map handy, when this 'seed,' rememberin' his manners, asks: 'Who's you, mister?'

"Missin' not a beat, Dick says, 'Why, we are the *Bald* Hornets.'

'Huh,' says Wooly Number One. 'And whar ya'll Bald Eagles from?'

'We are from Bald Hill in Conecuh County.'

'I don't citely know whar them am,' sez he.'

"'Oh, thay's yonder,' says brother. Then he stands up—half-a-head taller'n any of 'em—and sweeps his arm in the general di–rection of Alabama, Georgia; thows in the Gulf of 'Meh-hee-coh,' fer good measure.

Them Ridgevillites: you almost see theys lil' wheels aturnin.' But you know Old Dick: can't he look 'bout as innerscent as a babe packin' a full load? So, cogitatin' on it, they figure maybe they got it right when they wuz talkin' to him *slow*. They give 'im a nod and mosey on. Dick sez he 'bout broke even in the matter."

"I can top that," says Henry. "Next morning, Lon and all us are out, busy, domesticating the quarters, when a party of citizens drop by.

"Word was abroad to the effect the Third's militias included a company of injuns."

To Jim's guffaw, Henry held up his hand. "'Injuns.' Cross my heart. 'Cause of our sunburned faces—all I can reckon.

"This delegation was one of several on reconnaissance, to confirm said rumor. By fair means or foul, they were directed to our digs, where we first seen them milling about. Lon here, steps forward and, with the polish of a courtier, puts his hands together just so (show 'em, Lon), rolls his palms over, as though to ask: 'How mayest I serve thee?'

"This teensy little lady steps forward, assumes command—throws her chest out, 'Where are the *Indians*?' she wants to know.

"Right then, comes a stir over by the stalls, and there, as if on cue, Mister Cargill rises up to greet the day: ole Mister Sunshine hisself—bare-chested."

A tall, raw-boned farmer, Boss Cargill was naturally dark; his long black hair, prodigious nose, and grave demeanor added to the picture.

"Boss sees our gawkers, assembled for his benefit, so it seems. Modesty demands he cover himself, so folding his arms, he stares right back at 'em."

"Pointing, Lon says: 'Why, there is one *now. How, Chief.*'"

"'*Aahhh*' say the townspeople."

"The little lady wants to speak to Boss. Lon says 'No. Best not approach any closer, madam. He ain't quite 'broke;' specially on a empty stomach. He is a *wild* man, don't you see; a chief among his people—the fierce *Comanche*—and he speaks our language poorly. His name is Bull Nose (you mustn't stare, madam) and, he has left his thirteen wives in charge of his scalps and papooses. At night, he howls for his life upon the prairie. We may have to put him down, for his own good.'

"Ole Boss, too distant to hear any of this, takes their stares. Then, having his fill, he gathers up his dignity, bows stiffly to his audience, and returns to his stall. The little woman, and all her friends return to town, happy as larks."

"Tell Jim what he said, Henry."

"Oh yeah. Once the ladies had gone, Boss says, 'Wal, I be damned if'n I 'listed fer somebody's show. Or 'spected to be stabled like *a hoss!*'"

Further down the road, Henry spoke again, to ask the others if they had heard anything about General Huger procuring a number of long ladders.

"You mean scaling ladders?"

"Well, 'long ladders' is how it was said. But fifty of 'em, yup."

"How you come by this, Henry?"

"I forget. Heard officers in Norfolk, I 'spose. I did not

think much on it at the time."

This was sobering news. Scaling ladders could only mean one thing: an assault on Fortress Monroe. Certain death.

Nearing the city, Princess Anne Road fed into Church Street, and they gawked at the fine old homes. Reaching Main, Jim and Tom turned towards Market Square to find a photographer, while Henry and Lon went in search of food.

Free of their companions, Jim turned to Tom, "Say now, what is this 'land nap' cap'n keeps tellin' me to steer clear of? Won't nobody tell me *what it is* or *where it is.* How am I supposed to stay away from somethin' I don't know what it looks like?"

Tom grinned. "Well now, hold up right there. I expect it's a bit embarrassing to some, and nothing I care to talk about, neither. But the 'land nap,' as you call it, is a blind tiger—"

"Stop. A what?"

"A bawdy house: whiskey and doo-dah gals, strumpets, *hookers.* You do know what *those* are, don't you?"

"Well yes, I'm sure I do."

"Thank you. Well, the land nap (now you have got me sayin' it), the *Lagniappe* is a nickname. It's actually a place known as 'The Forty Winks.' Somebody else (just as slow as you, no doubt), didn't know what forty winks meant. So, it got explained as 'a long nap.' Q.E.D. Do you see it now?"

Getting someone's initials thrown at him, Jim nodded uncertainly. "It's on one of these side streets going down to the docks. You'll never need anything more in this whole town, than what you can find right here on Main Street. But if you are foolish enough to run the lines, and stray to that part of town, you'll find all the trouble you want, and then some. Just look for the doors with the longest lines of men outside. Does that say it all for you?"

"Hold on now, Tom. Just this one: If the nickname is Long Nap, why ain't it called 'Long Nap.' What is this other thing, the 'land-knee-apt?'"

"Jim, I'll give you this and then I'm through: Somebody, in the Rifles—the *Mobile* Rifles—turned it into 'lagniappe.'

That comes from old New Orleans. Down there, it is the something extra a merchant gives out to a favorite customer—a baker's dozen, maybe. Now, I will say no more on it, or I'll be in no frame of mind to have my picture taken."

They joined the line at the gallery. When it came their turn, the assistant adjusted the blinds overhead and made sure the backdrop and props were just right. The professor promised them Norfolk's highest quality *cartes de visite* at an affordable price; special consideration for volunteers from Alabama.

"See here, Professor: you're welcome to full fare if you can make me look any better'n this," said Tom.

The professor did not see the humor. "I can assure the gentleman his loved ones will be proud to see their stalwart defender in uniform. You will have an heirloom to share and to treasure." Offered a choice of props, Tom and Jim each produced their own Navy Colts.

"Your *cartes* will be ready in three days' time, said the professor. "Payment in advance preferred, given the present *uncertainties*, shall we say. My assistant will handle the details."

On the street they ran into Neb Battle, himself heading to the professor's. The three agreed to meet later for the hike back. Jim and Tom were soon immersed in the bustle around Market Square, which was filled with uniforms of every style and color. Facings trimmed in red identified artillerymen, yellow meant cavalry—who often added black ostrich plumes to their hats. They stopped in at a saloon for a sandwich.

The Norfolk business district was much more compact than Montgomery (the only other big town either had spent time in). And its offerings more diverse. The blockade was having little effect, thus far: all the stores seemed well-stocked, if more costly. A cobbler's shop puzzled them, offering shoes made for each foot, 'left' and 'right.' Who would be so fussy? Ladies, they supposed. At a bookstall, the proprietor gently pressed a small tattered book into Tom's hands. Tom patted his pockets and spread his palms to plead poverty. The man insisted, explaining with a heavy accent, "No money. A *mitzvah*."

The bakers were doing a brisk business. The boys had a few coins, and made a purchase for the walk back. They found Neb Battle waiting with Chef Beaumont, and the four set off.

The talk of scaling ladders still weighing on his mind, Jim put the question to the sergeant, who immediately demanded to know the source of such intelligence. When Jim said Henry Smith had overheard some officers in Norfolk, Beau stopped in his tracks. Slowly rotating his neck, then flexing his shoulders, using the side of his hand to smooth his impressive moustaches, he turned to Jim. Assuming the drill sergeant's stance (feet planted squarely, fists on his hips), he leaned in.

"On-ree Schmeet! *Merde. I speet* on Schmeet! *Sheem*, you believe *zat? Ho ho!* Nibbet, leezen to theeze *wun!*

"You shall hear me vot zees boy make to me one time. He hear me say I want un mock bird, *oui? Mon Dieu.* Three days, zay pass. He bring me wun leetel bird, eh? He say, vor eem, I pay five dol-lar. I get cage *magnifique* vor dis bird. Ever' day zis bird, I listen for eez song." Extending a thumb, Chef counted: "Un week." His index finger: "*Deux* week. *Trois*. I keep ze tamm ting, and he grow. *He grow! But he no song!* Den, ez 'ead: eet turn red like, like . . . like *von* Zouave *Afrique*, eh? 'E eez no *mock* bird. NO! 'E nut but no-good, tamm *tree-peck bird!* Now you believe ze scale ladder, eh? *EH?* Henri yoost like make tamm fool of you to laugh. *Ma foi!"*

Before Jim could defend his friend, they heard a body of men approaching from behind, at the double quick: Colonel Battle and Captain Hunter, both officers mounted, leading forty men or so; a fair representation of the Third. Battle glared at the four as he passed. "Fall in at the rear!" he bellowed.

The column halted only after they had reached the camp gate, the summer heat leaving many near collapse. These men had come to blows with the Norfolk Juniors. It had started in town, right where Jim and Tom had been. Captain Hunter had taken offense at a pushy peddler, who, apparently insisted he purchase a book. Hunter had boxed the man's ears to teach him some manners, leading to words with a nearby corporal of the 12th, who took exception to such treatment of a Virginian.

*"A Virginian!"* Hunter had thundered. "You goddam insubordinate. I was not aware Disraeli's tribe reigned o'er the Old Dominion!"

One soldier explained: "We didn't care who started it; those Junior sons-a-bitches weren't gonna back-talk no captain of the Third."

With tempers flaring, the shoving began, drawing more soldiers into the fray. Battle had seen it starting and, riding into the melee with pistol drawn, he ordered, "Third Alabama Regiment: *Back* to camp. *Now!*"

The only Hornets to be caught up in the sweep, Jim, Beau, Neb, and Tom went before Captain Powell. He asked for no excuses and none were offered. Each man received an extra tour of sentry duty.

Battle restricted the regiment to camp, with orders to avoid all contact with the 12th. Not that that would put an end to it, but at least the immediate cause could be defused; rocky relations between rivals must be expected. He hoped the paperwork could be kept to a minimum. He would send a note to Colonel Weisiger.

Meanwhile, Jim wrote home to his sister:

> *"I am sorry to inform you that the much beloved Capt. Powell at home is the most unpopular officer in the company. . . . He is not the man I thought he was. He can never get ten men in the company to enlist under him again."*

## CHAPTER 17 — GRACIE AND HUNTER
July 1 – 15, 1861

AT MONTGOMERY, Lomax had briefly considered contesting Charlie Forsyth's petition. But personal wants aside, it was hard to buck the logic of putting Alabama's finest under an experienced West Pointer.

Withers 'wants' were all too obvious. After his election he was seldom seen, unless the sighting took place in Richmond. He was a brigadier by July, drafting orders for the War Department; Tennent Lomax was elected colonel, with only eight dissenting.

Hard work lay ahead. Lomax saw the Confederate Army for what it was: a gaggle of amateurs commanded by a smattering of professionals. Richmond hoped the crisis could be solved diplomatically, or with a quick victory. Lomax believed that nothing would come easy. The Davis administration needed time to address its shortcomings; more time than the Federals would likely allow. Missteps of the political, economic, and strategic, sort, were to be expected. Lomax's experience at Fort Pickens was a case in point: Alabama's allies had squandered that opportunity and, with the arrival of Federal reinforcements, the South had lost a vital port.

After Fort Sumter, the Third received every assurance of seeing action. Instead, they were packed off to Norfolk, where they were relegated to garrison duty; their chagrin only deepening when Fourth Alabama got the first taste of combat, winning laurels at Manassas. That many in the Fourth were literally younger brothers of men in the Third just added salt to the wound. The Fourth had lost their colonel at Manassas and more than two hundred casualties, besides—the most by any Southern regiment; facts not lost on Lomax. Neither did he ignore the reports of confusion and incompetence at the staff-officer level.

Still, praise for the 'Glorious' Third was seldom lacking— Lomax heard it often enough—while others were less generous, regarding the regiment as nothing more than a collection of over-privileged dandies. When General Huger first saw an assembly of the well-appointed Mobile Cadets, an aide informed him the 'M.C.' on their caps stood for 'Music Corps.' Overnight, the Third became the 'Band-Box Regiment.'

At the time of their posting, Norfolk had seemed a crucial assignment. To counter the threat to the naval yard, Jeff Davis had sent the best troops available. The Third was told: 'Every day you boys hold Norfolk, is a day won for the Confederacy.'

Perhaps. But soon enough it was clear, there would be no incursions at Norfolk; no need for the Federals to fight their way through fortified enemy positions, when they could be sidestepped. The post of 'honor' had become a backwater, and boredom their greatest enemy.

Lomax knew the lull would not last. He organized Schools of Instruction using Hardee's *Rifle and Light Infantry Tactics,* the favored manual of both armies.

The army's most glaring problem was the absence of experienced sergeants and corporals, critical cogs in any military organization. In the old army, its Southern officers *viz.* Lee, and Beauregard, and Longstreet, had been allowed to resign their commissions unmolested. But *only* the officers—not the non-coms and certainly not the rank and file. Desertion was a capital offence. The Confederate services were left to scramble.

Lomax insisted his officers identify and train talented subordinates. No regiment could be stronger than its weakest component. The schools would broaden the boundaries of command, allow his officers to share ideas, give them the experience of issuing and receiving orders, outside the normal chain of command. In battle, the chain would surely be broken, so every man received training two grades above his rank. Lomax's rigorous schooling would prove its worth over the course of the war: no candidate from the Third ever failed an examination before a board of review.

Sands, Woodruff, and Gracie were his most proficient captains. The former were Mexican War veterans, the latter, a graduate of West Point. All three were tasked with pulling their fellow captains through the finer points of *Hardee's Manual*. Once educated, these captains schooled the lieutenants, who trained the first sergeants, and so on. The schools revealed talents hidden within the regiment, and bolstered the confidence one officer could place in another. It also exposed those who lacked aggression, or were reckless, or who issued confusing orders—or did not follow orders.

Robert Sands was a devout Catholic. He was also a member of Mobile's upper crust. As an officer, he was demanding but just. From his time in Mexico, he was an assiduous student of military history. He knew *Hardee's* backwards and forwards. His reports were complete, precise, and timely, and he demanded the same from his subordinates; the Cadets maintained meticulous records. Lomax challenged Sands to impart the importance of this to the regiment's most-promising officers: Captains Bonham and Powell, and Lieutenants Mayes and Phelan. Sands' classes, were like his reports, and his students were apt.

Woodruff was a good judge of character, a hard-nosed officer, when that quality was called for. His captains were Ready and Swanson, and First Lieutenants Chester and Simpson. Of these, his toughest customer was Bill Swanson.

Authority suited Swanson. At home, he had a large and smooth-running plantation; fields that produced four bales of cotton an acre—year in, year out. His overseers were efficient, his hands (he held more than forty) unfailingly polite and never caught by the patrollers on night walks, *viz.* those clandestine visitations between plantations. Swanson was a formidable man. Though lately, he had developed a noticeable pot, evidence middle-age was gaining the upper hand.

One immune to Swanson's authority (or any other), was Simon—of Gracie's company. A lanky youth, Simon played the role of camp fool and was often seen marching through camp, banging a tin pot for attention, and looking for pranks to play. In short: he was easily bored, and favored anything that would upset routine.

The men looked forward to his mischiefs, as did many

of the (off-duty) officers. Their first night at Norfolk, Simon broke the decorum of lights out, with a loud and resonant "Good night, Captain Gracie," after a pause, adding a respectful, "Sir." Gracie, of course, was nowhere near, but a confederate replied, in a fair imitation of their captain's New Jersey accent. "Good night, my lad. Sleep tight." That set things off. Throughout the camp, men wished each other increasingly ludicrous 'goodnights.' It was the O.D.'s unenviable duty to maintain order at such times.

A few weeks after this Simon dressed up in an ancient swallowtail coat (oversized, and embroidered in a motif of green peacocks), with a pair of knee breeches covering his spindly legs; a tri-corner hat and long-beaked Mardi Gras mask completing his attire. He strutted through the company streets, just as the drums began to beat Dress Parade. Having wandered outside the camp, he was apprehended trying to re-enter. The Corporal of the Guard was summoned. Escorting his charge to the guardhouse, Corporal Roach had to cross a corner of the drill field, where the Parade was now in progress, a daily pageant witnessed by scores of civilian spectators. The contrast of Simon, goose-stepping his way to the guardhouse, followed by Roach, destroyed all sense of decorum. Roach prodded his charge into double quick time, and the increased pace only caused greater laughter, from the civilians and the ranks.

The Officer of the Day did not share this amusement. When the duo arrived at the guardhouse, Swanson was waiting. "Why, welcome, Puck," said the captain, in his most agreeable manner: "My house is your house." Simon received a shove through the doorway. Simon was delivered to the charity hospital that night. He never spoke of his experience in the guardhouse, but his antics stopped.

\* \* \*

The captains in Gracie's class, Andrews and Hunter, were a challenge of another sort.

The regiment's last West Pointer, Archibald Gracie, Jr.,

was a beefy six-foot-four, and a most imposing presence on the parade ground. this made little impression on Andrews and Hunter. To them, his crucial qualities were breeding, wealth, and bearing; they considered him their social equal. A notion Gracie would have found amusing.

Gracies were old money: Gracie Manor, on Manhattan's Lower East Side, had been a landmark for generations. After graduation Arch Gracie married Josie Mayo, of Richmond (her uncle was General Winfield Scott). Fulfilling his military commitment, he went to work for his family's interests in Mobile; a schism developing when he began to side, politically, with the South. (The breach becoming permanent once his militia stormed the gates of Mount Vernon Arsenal).

Andrews and Hunter were able to convince themselves instruction from Gracie was more in the way of an advisement, a courtesy, such as one gentleman might extend another.

Andrews was a successful clothing merchant catering to the gentry of central Alabama. When Lomax (then of the True Blues), was appointed colonel of the AVC's Second Regiment, Andrews was elected captain. He provided the Blues with new uniforms, impeccably matched and cut, from the finest lightweight wool. Andrews' strengths lay in artillery-drill and military etiquette, his weaknesses found in everything else.

His companion in all things was Winston Hunter, captain of the Metropolitan Guards. Hunter fulfilled his Metros every need: uniforms, shoes, haversacks, rifles, canteens, tenting— even flooring planks, to get his men off the ground. His largesse belied a fiery temper; he was quick to take offense, or to perceive a slight.

He loudly opposed the requirement that captains command their companies on foot. One of Alabama's oldest and wealthiest families, the Hunters held 500 slaves at their plantation below Selma. They ruled from horseback.

In a class on tactics, Hunter became famous for this exchange with Gracie:

"Captain Hunter: Define for us the difference between a withdrawal and a retreat."

"Certainly, Captain. In the former, one walks. In the latter, one runs."

"Expound, sir."

"A withdrawal implies a modicum of dignity."

Captain Gracie then asked how, under certain given circumstances, one would retreat. Hunter took umbrage at the question.

"Well, sir—I would not! I do not want my men to know how to retreat. I did not come to Virginia to learn how to retreat, and I'll be goddamned if I learn how to now, sir! I do not intend my men to learn that part of *Hardee's Tactics*."

Gracie's muttonchops betrayed a slight quiver, otherwise he kept his composure. The entire camp heard of the riposte. In the end, Lomax, Battle and Gracie were left to wonder whether 'Captain Goddamn' was crazy like a fox, or just crazy.

Neither Andrews nor Hunter relished the prospect of taking orders from younger officers, (Andrews was 35; Hunter, 42). But both realized they were too old to last long afoot, so election—or appointment—to field grade was critical. In a meeting with Colonel Lomax, the alternatives of transfer or of raising a regiment of their own, were explored, with Lomax adding: with volunteer regiments there would always be elections—*unpredictable* elections.

Through his business contacts in England, Andrews decided his best course was to purchase a battery of guns and transfer the Blues to artillery.

When Gracie accepted a promotion to the 11th Alabama, Hunter pinned his hopes on the forthcoming election. With Gracie out of the picture, it should be easy.

## CHAPTER 18 — DARK HORSE
July 31 – August 10, 1861

HUNTER HAD no intention of making his feelings known, not even to Andrews; but he was most put out with Lomax and the better class of officers; they had not talked him up properly. *After all I've done: this rigmarole. Damn their eyes.*

He thought his chances for major still were good. But falling short in the count the other night had taken him aback.

Gracie's grand exit was particularly irksome. *Has the gall to wave to me from his carriage like some grandee. Damn Yankee.* He closed his eyes to regain his composure. *Water over the bridge; under the dam—wherever the hell it goes.*

Collecting the most votes in the first round, Hunter's lead increased in the second—just short of a majority. Then, inexplicably, his support slipped: Ready led all candidates after the third round. Hunter felt like a groom left at the altar. *There can be no concern, whether I can afford the position, certainly.* He had met every need of the Metros from his own pocket. He could accommodate the whole regiment just as easily; a Hunter could buy anything worth the buying; pay off, or kill, anyone worth the trouble.

Recounting past successes: *I scattered those Knoxville Yankees, right enough.* His warning shot from the train, doing the job the local authorities would not. The constables (loath to question a train full of soldiers), let them go. Two weeks ago, when two from the regiment were arrested and jailed for cutting up those Juniors, he was the sole captain to support an assault on the place. *That impudent bookseller started it all, trying to sell me his used book. Those 12th Virginia boys should have steered clear, it was none of their affair. The damned little peddler deserved his thrashing.*

Then, last week, the murder of Lieutenant Adams. Though *that* could not possibly be laid at his door. *What manner of scum lurk under cover of night to fall on a defenseless man, to beat the life out of him?* He had seen the body.

With a shudder Hunter returned to the matter at hand: the election, and calculating his odds. He could not fathom this rally for Ready. *A goddamned democracy, this regiment— when it is a strong hand they need.* He decided to pay a call on Andrews, draw him out on this. *The mob: the 'Mobile vulgus;' Oh! Ha Hah: 'Mob-bile.' That's a good one (have to remember that one). They have had a night and a day to think it through, to see who would be the best man. Who is the best man. He felt certain the vote tonight would go better*

\* \* \*

As Scotty packed his knapsack, he was sure of two things. First, his vote would not be needed tonight and, second, the election would go to a Mobilian. He wasn't sure which man would emerge—he didn't much care—but he suspected the outcome would cause quite the howl.

Hunter and Ready had had their shot. His money was on the dark horse. If Hunter had a lick of sense he would have made an appeal to the Mobile bloc, or at least to their officers. *The bugger had offered to lead a jailbreak, for bloody sake. 'Steady Ready' was the better man, a fine officer—no politician, though. And a field officer needed that skill.*

Captain Woodruff had shown no interest, so Scotty guessed the old man must have a colonelcy in his back pocket. Then there was Captain Hartwell. but his health was bad; he would never be anyone's first choice. Ryder eliminated most of the second-tier officers: Chester had just been elected captain of Gracie's company. On the heels of that, it would be unseemly for him to stand for higher rank. Lieutenant Smith could fill the spot, but was still in jail for his part in the fight with the Juniors. Lieutenant Simpson would not want to jump over Hartwell, his friend and mentor. Marrast, would not have hesitated to step over Woodruff, but he had just accepted a captaincy in the Twenty-second.

He went down the list, ticking off each name: *Higley, Dickinson, Robbins, Weedon. Forsyth*—a pause there. *Hmm . . . Well, it hardly matters, at some point they are all alike.*

From where he stood, an officer's duties looked like nothing but headaches. *Glorified bookkeepers, they are.* He finished packing. He and Sergeant Goodwin had been ordered to map the roads between the camp and the ocean. Ryder thought it should be a pleasant outing; would do Goodwin good, too. Though the man was a Mainer, insisting every job be done quickly and well. *Why then had the fool ever come South?* Scotty grabbed more provisions. They would head out Princess Anne Road; with luck, reaching Kempsville by noon.

\* \* \*

While recognizing the telegraph would likely be the most important technical advancement in his lifetime, Cullen Battle regretted its invention. The consequences of near-instant communication were staggering. *This very war could not have begun before 1848! Speed is the new paragon: a torrent of electrified atoms sent racing through the wires. The world needs a little slowing down.* Messengers arriving at all hours, with orders from Montgomery, or from Mobile, or from Richmond. *It lets too many cooks into the kitchen.*

Battle was certain someone in Mobile was running up significant charges over the wire; meddling in the regiment's affairs, supporting one candidate over another. Nothing to be done about it. At least the voting tonight should settle the question; the regiment needed a decision.

Chain of command was the issue: colonels commanded from the center: First Battalion was under the lieutenant colonel and, Second, under whoever was elected major. Lomax and Battle could not perform proper drills with stand-ins, insofar as the whole point was communication and execution between the two wings.

Lomax had tried his best to draft Sands for the majority. No such luck. Then he appealed to Woodruff. Ditto. Gracie's resignation had truly upset the applecart. The big man would have been a steadying influence over the wilder elements in the regiment.

The Armistead brothers were leaving, too. And word had just come, the Rifles' two lieutenants were resigning. Woodruff would be left all alone to deal with his hellions. *Ah, me.*

\* \* \*

The companies formed near the mulberry, where a fly was pitched, with table and chairs set out for the paper work, and Captain Swanson to supervise. Junior officers and civilians, the non-voters and bemused observers, looked on. By tradition, the candidates were absent, as were Lomax and Battle.

The first sergeants tallied the ballots from their respective companies, and turned them over to the sergeant major. The sergeant major showed Swanson the result. Swanson nodded. He then showed the sergeants, asking each if they concurred. They did.

The sergeant major announced: "We have a major."

\* \* \*

"I'll be goddamned."

"What is it? Who do you say? *Charles Forsyth?* Little Charlie Forsyth *has been elected? Second–Looo*-tenant, Charlie–god-damn–Mo-bile–*Forsyth, is our new major? No sir. You are mistaken. They wouldn't. They couldn't. It can't be. It just can't be.*" Hunter was livid.

Andrews could only shake his head. Lieutenant Phelan had brought the news.

"He's not even in camp, is he?"

"No. Still on furlough, so far as I know," said Andrews.

"This is a—this is just—this is—" Hunter sputtered. "How *could* they? It does not follow. *That—Him?* I'm going to be saluting *him?* Oh, there is something rotten here, of that, there can be no doubt. Andrews, this is moonshine."

"The vote was square, Win. It is what our glorious volunteers want. Next week they will want a new man, you know how they are. But you also know, Lomax will never overturn it."

"He would be within—he—No, no, you are right, Andrews: you *are* right. That would require a set of bollocks. More than our Good Sir Tennent has got. He does not have the gumption to go up against the likes of Jones Withers and Old Forsyth. They struck a bargain back in Montgomery, sure as I'm standing here. They are behind this."

"Of course, they are," said Andrews.

"By telegraph; all done by telegraph, I'll wager. *Damn them. Goddam their goddam eyes!* Right there: right from the old man's *got-damn* office. Mobile, I swear it. Pulling his strings. Those stupid, *stupid,* men." He appealed to his audience, "*Charlie Forsyth?* A damn *child*. 'And a child shall lead them. . . . '" The phrase had a familiar ring, seeming apropos; he could not come up with the rest.

"Small but fierce. He does look good on horseback."

"What? Eh? What is that? How did Ready do? What was tonight's count?"

"Well, Charlie came in with three hundred twenty-one votes. You and Ready took most of the rest," said Andrews, referring to Phelan's notes.

"I came second?"

Knowing his friend was no longer listening: "Yes. Almost, Win. Almost."

\* \* \*

It was the result Lomax expected, and dreaded. He had not wanted Hunter, that *would* have been a disaster, but once again, the moon and stars had aligned to favor young Charles. All the recent decisions—starting with Captain Sands'—had pushed the door wider and wider for Charlie. Lomax wondered what Sands must be thinking at this moment. Forsyth: five years old when Sands received his commission. For that matter, what was Powell thinking, or Bonham? *I must not lose them*, he worried. *The regiment must not lose them.*

Cullen's misgivings notwithstanding, it was not a question of ability. Forsyth had performed all his duties, in commendable fashion. He had received good training at Georgia Military. No, Charlie could handle the immediate responsibilities of a major, and should pick up battalion tactics, readily enough. It was the man's lack of experience: he could handle men under him, what about those who once were his superiors? The boldness to seize opportunity might be an asset, but it is not enough. Lives will hang in the balance. Decisions must be made quickly, (instinctively sometimes), and, always the correct decision.

He did look the part, however, handsome on his little charger. Musing, Lomax's thoughts lingered upon Laura Forsyth—so like his Sophie. That the girl had spent time in the camp, charming every volunteer, had not hurt her husband's prospects any. *Yes, for some reason Dame Fortune has smiled on Charles Forsyth.*

*Enough.* Lomax requested Colonel Battle meet privately with the new major. He knew his brother-in-law had little patience for Charles, viewing him as an interloper, fulfilling the expectations of the father. The volunteers, however, had rendered their decision. Cullen and Charles would just have to work it out. For now, the silver lining: it should speed up some resignations, and thus, move the more promising officers, forward.

\* \* \*

Ryder and Goodwin completed their survey of coastal roads. Thirsty and tired, their twenty-mile circuit had brought them once more to Kempsville, where they had rested the first night, under the roof of James Garrison.

After supper, Garrison's daughter, Jenny, played piano for their guests. Wise beyond her years, when she caught the men fighting to stay awake, she abbreviated her performance. After playing a few chords of *Auld Lang Syne*, she switched to an older melody—one, Scotty knew instantly: *The Parting Glass*. He joined his voice to hers:

*"Then gently rise and softly call*
*'Goodnight,' may joy be to you all."*

After turning in, the song—and Jenny—continued to occupy his thoughts.

* * *

Cheers welcomed Charlie Forsyth's return to camp. The news of his election had come while he was in his father's office at *The Register*. For once, father seemed pleased. The rail connections had gone more smoothly than they had in April. More relaxing anyway, to travel with no one to answer to, no running errands for Captain Sands.

He was the best man for the job. He knew he was. And he was proud the volunteers had put their faith in him. *A field officer must have imagination, must take the initiative. A little political 'pull' doesn't hurt either. Not one bit.*

He thought of Laura. *She grows more beautiful by the day.* Mother had informed him Laura was with child. *The girl has a glow about her.* Whenever her gaze turned upon him, his heart would melt, lost in those siren's eyes. It pleased her to hear such things. Her coming to Norfolk had been a lovely mistake: so little time together. It made her absence, now, hard to bear—the furlough had passed in the blink of an eye.

*Major Forsyth. Charlie. Charles. I must insist on 'Charles' from here on.*

Charles wished Mobile wasn't so . . . social. He would have preferred to stay at home, preferred never to leave their bed. Instead, every morning was spent visiting; every evening, another invitation. When all was said and done, he knew he had little room for complaint; the envy of his friends, a hero in the eyes of his young wife, the scion of a distinguished family, heir apparent to his father's enterprise. A cloud passed over his face. Where his father was concerned, little was certain.

"Welcome back, *Major*," continued all along the road from town, right up to the camp's gate, where the halloos became handshakes, and he received thumps on the back (from his closest friends), and last: salutes from the officers he now outranked. *I will show them. I have the ideas: a dozen improve-*

*ments to operations. Tennent will hear me out, and see their worth, even if Battle does not.* He chuckled, as, from the corner of his eye he caught Captain Hunter making an about face.

The salute from Captain Sands was worth all the others put together: not a hint of rancor. Collegial, even cordial. *All in all: a most acceptable way to return to one's camp. Am I not the most fortunate of men?*

Presenting himself at Battle's desk, his jubilant mood withered and died. The lieutenant colonel did not rise, did not smile; did not extend his hand, or offer him a cigar. Nothing.

"Major Forsyth, you have, once again, placed self-interest above the good of your regiment."

## CHAPTER 19 — THE MINSTRELS
September 5 — October 9, 1861

A BEAD OF sweat dropped from Jack Goelet's nose. To wipe, or dab it away, was futile. And required effort. Norfolk required effort; more than Jack had in him. True: the idea of transfering out of the Cadets' reserve company had been his own. But trading garrison-duty in Mobile, for garrison-duty in Norfolk . . . was not representative of his best thinking.

*A fine mess you are in.*

*Yes, I am in Virginia, at last. But Virginia should mean Fredericksburg, Charlottesville, Leesburg; the Blue Ridge, the Valley—not this steaming, gnat-infested swamp. You have done it this time, Jack.*

*Gad.*

He scratched the welts on his cheek: 'No-see-ums' the locals called them—damnation in the flesh. The volunteers had dubbed them: 'D.F.F.'s' for 'Damned Firginny Flies.' From their run-in with the Norfolk Juniors, the regiment had re-branded them 'F.F.V.s'—First Flies of Virginia. Nowadays, a more-simple and vehement 'F.F.' was employed.

*How have the others borne this for four months? Four weeks here, and I have had my fill. In four measly weeks, my happiness is reduced to the annihilation of flies. Flies! Every Mobilian who steps off a train brings his family's heirloom mosquito net, yet even these prove inadequate. And the heat; this endless heat.*

Jack was weary of routine and weary of sweat and dust, and rust, and thirst; of cleaning guns, and smelly clothes, and—*Gad—I am even weary of me.* A recognition of his failings caused him to wonder whether his progeny, living in the far-off future, would ever suspect their ancestor fell, not in battle, but at the hands of mortal boredom? *Bah. What progeny? Doubtful,* he concluded. *Very doubtful.*

His messmates were still at parade. He was excused, per his sentry duty, yesterday. He might re-read old letters or, send new ones off: "Your favor of the 18th instant, has duly come to hand . . ." etcetera, etcetera—*Et in sæcula sæculorum. Humiliating, to be reduced to begging for correspondents. Perhaps I shall wander over to the old tree.* He enjoyed the entertainments around the bonfire: bombast always in good supply. Nothing ever resolved, of course. And should the colonels attend, the conversations took a higher tone. Their presence was increasingly rare, however; Lomax and Battle were often called away to this headquarters or that. Jack's thoughts turned towards home: *Oh, Mobile! Jack—you dull, dumb, dim, despicable dolt: why did you ever leave?* He longed for one more stroll along Government, one more supper at Battle House—*Don't think of food!*—the aroma of wild azalea; paying call at the villas along Shell Road, or, crossing the bay for a late-summer's jubilee; an evening spent in the company of some sweet young thing at the Tea Drinker's Ball. *Tant pis.*

As he burrowed deeper into self-pity, Hope appeared at his tent flap: a welcome face—a fellow Tea Drinker, in fact. Only one man could so butcher the French language:

"'*Dormez-vous, frère Jacques?*' Have you forgotten the Amateur Minstrels, mon?"

Jack sat up, laughing, "I had, frère Scotty, until this very moment. Is that tonight?"

"Yes. We shall have to shake a leg. I assure you they are worth the risk."

"No doubt. But I cannot join you."

"Why the devil, not?" said Scotty. "Is it plague? The trots? What?" Lowering his voice: "Is it 'The Pox?'"

Jack winced. "Spoken like a Rifle. It is my duty to inform you: I have mended my ways, sir—turned over the new leaf."

"I'm so sorry to hear that—em—mending your ways, means what, exactly?"

Jack laughed again. "I am being facetious, and beg your pardon. I have taken a vow of poverty and, to be honest, at present, I am enjoying a grand funk. I would prove a poor companion, Scotty. So, I shan't spoil your fun, and won't be running the lines with you. Have you a pretty girl picked out?"

"Pitiful. Ye are to be pitied, Jack, wasting away in this tent. A vow of chastity at your age."

"Of poverty." Jack corrected.

"There is a difference? And, our minstrels have worked so hard, just to please you. No, don't give me that look—I include myself. Rise to the occasion, Jack. '*Ah-rize-zah!*' (as the circuit riders declare). Or how will you ever again look us in the eye?"

"Lord, never, I know, I know." Jack hung his head, piteously. "I grovel before you. I am a drag upon humanity. What must I do, to make amends?"

"Oh! Well then, as to that—ahem—so kind of you to offer: I'll have the shirt off your back!"

"What?" Jack was at a loss.

"Nae, 'tis serious, I am. I'll trouble you for a suit o' clothes, so I can run the lines."

"Do you have a pass?"

"Don't be insulting. Whomever do you take me for?" Ryder held up his hands, fingers dancing. "Gloves?"

Jack pulled his trunk out from under his cot, searching for his gloves. "Why the haste?"

"I ran into old Goodwin, at headquarters—still on crutches from his fall. He can't attend, so has done me a good turn. Let's just say I have reason to make tonight's curtain."

"A-ha. And what is your reason's name, pray?"

Scotty simply smiled, as he changed into his friend's civvies. Blowing a kiss, he backed through the tent flaps, and made his way to town.

\* \* \*

Ryder was not one of the minstrels, but he enjoyed theatre, had contributed some bits to the show, excising some material, also—from the stump speech—only those, as might get Bill Averill lynched.

Arriving at the Opera House, Scotty greeted Goodwin's guests—the Garrisons, and their alluring daughter—and he explained their host's absence. As hoped, the family invited him to join them in the box. Given the two front seats, Jenny and he looked over a sea of undulating, hand-held fans. Occasionally these met, in pairs, to cover some private remark—or to flag some fashion faux pas.

The Amateur Minstrels—the regiment's glee club—had offered their talents to the Ladies' Aid Society. Almost overnight, the benefit had become the talk of half the town—the female half, to be sure—but the result was two sold out performances, before an enthusiastic audience that was mostly young, and pretty. The Opera House had had nothing on its stage since Fort Sumter, so the manager was ecstatic with the gate—nearly thirteen hundred. His expectations for the show were guarded, his hopes being these minstrels would not prove too amateurish. As the gas-lit chandelier dimmed, the audience grew still.

The clash of cymbals shattered the silence to announce the processional. The curtain rose to reveal twelve chairs arranged in semi-circle. Two troops burst from the wings, high-stepping in time to the lively music. The audience reacted with a roar: The Pride of Alabama parading onto stage in stylish chesterfields, top hats, and gleaming spats, set off by colorful vests and cravats. Stepping out, their dazzling white gloves shimmied in salute. Merging into a circle, they completed their cakewalk with the audience clapping time to *The Petersburg Grey's Quick Step*. At its conclusion each minstrel stood at attention in front of his chair. Then, bowing in sequence from one end to the other, they earned the night's first standing ovation. 'Mr. Interlocutor' returned the compliment with a respectful bow of his own. Then, drawing on his august dignity, he stared the audience into submission, before intoning the traditional opening:

"Gentlemens, be seated."

The First Part followed the form used both North and South: Jim Crow-badinage between Mr. Interlocutor and his troop, the routines anchored at either end by Mr. Tambo and his partner Mr. Bones. Following this opening, each minstrel performed a short turn, or, in combination with others, a 'crambo.'

Ryder knew everyone in the cast, but under the burnt cork they were hard to distinguish. Mr. Banjo was obviously Shanghai, and Cotton-eyed Joe was Mr. Fiddle. There was no mistaking John Hoyt or George Dunlap when they sang *Blue-Eyed Nell*—George had the best voice in the brigade. When Shanghai stepped forward for his solo, he was met by a parliament of hooting owls—his many friends and acquaintances returning in kind, his own greeting. The good-natured mimicry turned to laughter. Abashed, he took his seat and bowed over his banjo.

"We love you, Shanghai!" a sweet voice cooed from the balcony. Agreeable laughter. Applause. In response, the front rows heard a pleased little hoot.

The Second Part began with the traditional stump speech; Averill's use of dialect and malapropisms making, not only a subtle case for emancipation, but (with Ryder's twist on the end) delighting the ladies by his call for equal rights for them. Part of the audience sat on their hands while the females leapt up to shower him with bouquets and bravos.

Unavoidably, the finale was a lugubrious rendition of *God Save the South;* eight verses (found in the program), beyond salvation, and soon forgot. Delivering an encore, the troop took their final bows to thunderous applause.

After the curtain, Scotty steered his party backstage where they found a crush of friends and minstrels. Jenny wished to meet the one with the marvelous voice. Ryder spotted Dunlap (his partner was still in blackface) being interviewed by a Day Book reporter. Guiding his party through the throng, Scotty broke in to make introductions. While George was deflecting Jenny's compliments, Hoyt wiped his face clean, eliciting from the girl a nearly inaudible (and involuntary) squeak. Scotty urged his party along to meet Mr. Interlocutor. Over her shoulder, Jenny gave the two performers a smile, her fingers rippling a reluctant adieu.

After the ladies withdrew to the downtown home of relations, Garrison took Ryder round to several parties, where he met a wide spectrum of good fellows. Corks were popped, and many glasses raised to the Cause, to the Amateur Minstrels, the Rifles, the Juniors, Alabama, the fair sex, et al.

In the small hours, Garrison delivered his companion to Atlantic House, where Ryder had a room—both men now in their cups. His host's parting words sobered Ryder right enough. "If only you were a Virginian, my boy," said Garrison. "If only you were a Virginian."

\* \* \*

Captain Woodruff had no time for theatricals—a consequence of Adams' murder, and the transfers of Marrast and Weedon. For the past five weeks Woodruff had been sole officer of the Rifles. His senior sergeants having allowed discipline to slide, by September he had decided to confront the issue.

Still, his announcement demoting (Acting) First Sergeant Daily—in favor of Fourth Sergeant Hoyt—came as a shock. Daily was so incensed he stepped from the ranks and tore off his stripes. His friend, the third sergeant, followed suit.

Scotty had had his own differences with the captain, but in this case, he thought the demoted sergeants had rather proved the point. Despite his youth, Hoyt deserved the promotion. More selfishly, Ryder worried this shake-up might curtail his own ex-officio visits to town.

\* \* \*

The rest of September sailed by. Each day brought some new event, usually the departure of another volunteer. A number of Cadets received commissions in the 22d regiment, where they were under Robert Armistead, now Major Armistead. Both Marrast and Weedon were captains, there. Additional commissions had come from the 24th regiment.

From Chester's company, two men were dismissed by court martial; elsewhere, Bartee was deemed unfit; Willis Hall went down with typhoid; another was found to be addicted to morphine; some needed treatments for syphilis, and the 'Sunshine Patriots' purchased substitutes. New recruits were arriving all the time—Jack Goelet was one—so there was no appreciable loss in numbers.

Scotty resolved to stay on good terms with his new first sergeant. An excellent drill instructor when he applied himself, Scotty did so now—a reformed man. He even answered roll, and pitched in wherever he could help. Proving that no good deed goes unpunished, he was appointed fifth sergeant.

\* \* \*

Events in October buoyed everyone's spirits. In the first, the ladies of Norfolk presented the regiment with a flag.

The Third had come to Virginia with only their state banner and a seven-star national flag. This new flag was made of silk: blue on one side, white on the other. On the blue was painted the state seal of Alabama. On the white, a fine portrait of President Davis. Beneath his likeness: *'Lunctus ad Mare, Dividitur sicut Fluctus,*[9] an inscription which left the regiment's scholars scratching their heads.

In the second event, Scotty was given the task of laying out a new camp for winter quarters. The site chosen would be further out from town, in sight of the ocean.

---

[9] "United as the Sea and as Individual/Separate as the Waves." The regiment did not receive the first 'battle flag' until mid-June, 1862. In addition to the regimental colors, presumably each militia displayed its individual banner.

## CHAPTER 20 — MOSELEY'S CHURCH
October 15, 1861 – December 25, 1861

SCOTTY WALKED through his new camp, taking pride in his work. The men were just putting the finishing touches on the result: one hundred forty cabins, eighteen feet by sixteen, with brick fireplaces and shingled roofs; most with gun racks and tables, and many with mantelpieces and cupboards. They were diligently chinking the logs with mud, to make the cabins fit for winter.

The site was known by its church, at the crossroads near Lynnhaven Bay. It was the colonel's hope, the additional distance from Norfolk would stem the tide of those taking French leave—an irony not lost on Scotty (the regiment's most inveterate line-runner). For him, the work had provided a needed distraction.

In town, Scotty had run into Jenny and her mother. Jenny's letters had stopped soon after the concert, so, this chance meeting was awkward. Jenny kept her eyes down, while the mother rebuffed his attempts to converse with a stiff formality. Scotty was at a loss to explain the chill. A few days later Mr. Garrison came to call. The conversation was brief, one-sided, an unambiguous. Scotty's letters to Jenny were returned, unopened.

On a different plane, a court martial nearly brought the regiment to riot. One night, a couple of Hunter's men were caught running the lines—returning to camp—three sheets to the wind and looking for trouble. At the gate they were challenged by the sentry, a newly-mustered recruit. Snatching his unloaded rifle, they boxed his ears and knocked him down. The ruckus brought men from out of the cabins. When the Corporal of the Guard appeared, Hunter's men were placed under arrest, causing one to exclaim: "My only fault lies in behaving like an officer!" This earned him some derision, but there were those who agreed; who resented those privileges accorded their 'superiors.'

The affair would have blown over had the usual punishments been handed down, but with Captain Woodruff presiding, he felt it was time someone sent a message to the regiment's rowdies. He put the camp's carpenters to work erecting an odd structure—common enough in the old army—called 'the wooden horse.' An outsized version of an ordinary sawhorse, here, its legs were long enough to elevate a rider to such a height, a fall would be unpleasant. A 'ride' of two days was the norm—two hours on, and two hours off—morning to dusk.

Feelings were running high, when the same punishment was meted out to three additional men, one of them camp favorite, Zou Zou Hartman—for punching one of his musicians in the nose.

The wooden horse did not last long. A mob of Metros pulled it down. Emboldened by the act, they set off to rampage the camp. Descending on officers' row the mutineers were met by a line of Mobile Rifles—bayonets fixed—under command of Sergeant Hoyt. (Unbeknownst to the mutineers, Woodruff was in Norfolk).

The chief ringleader stepped forward: "We have a bone to pick with your captain."

"Volunteer, pick all the bones you want, with Caroline. Captain Woodruff is not available."

The man tried a softer tack: "We are come as gentlemen to lay our grievances before the president of the court martial."

Hoyt told him what he thought of gentlemen who ran the lines and came back to assault a comrade.

Lieutenant Phelan and Colonel Battle quietly appeared.

"At–ten–*HUT.*"

Battle stepped between the two sides. "As you were, boys, as you were." Staring down the mutineers, he addressed them all.

"Boys. Men. *Volunteers*: the horse will be rebuilt tomorrow. And it will be utilized. Its purpose is not to disgrace any volunteer. It is not even meant to punish; mere discomfort is not its goal. Its purpose is to stop behavior that is detrimental to the good order of this regiment.

"If you refuse discipline, you are no better than a mob. If you refuse to obey those who *you* have elected to lead you, the Third will be regarded as untrustworthy. There are those in Richmond (and even closer than that), who believe that of you already. They will send us home in disgrace.

"A mob will not stand fast before a resolute opponent. They will break and run—I have seen it—they do so, not from want of any man's courage, but because he harbors little faith in the courage of his fellows. Before Third Alabama becomes a mob, I assure you, *I* will resign."

No one spoke. At last, the would-be leader stepped forward and saluted the colonel. Battle was slow to return it. The horse was rebuilt and mounted next day, for its first and only use. Colonel Lomax accepted the resignation of Captain Hunter.

\* \* \*

Captain Swanson required a structure of his own. At parade the adjutant announced the new guardhouse would soon be accepting guests; indeed, the facility would open Christmas Eve. While the announcement was being read, all eyes were on Swanson, seen striking a defiant stance: chin up, arms folded across his chest—one leg thrust forward. Unfortunately, the pose also accentuated his potbelly. From the color company came a familiar voice:

"Don't he look jez like a goober with three *goodies* in it!"

For a breathless moment, the words dangled on the air like a noose. Then gathering momentum "looks like a goober" sped down the lines to the ends of the formation. When the volunteers were dismissed, a gangly young man was to be found in the middle of a great and admiring crowd, his back pounded by his many friends. Recently returned from hospital and awaiting a medical discharge, James Simon would to be known for rest of his days as 'Jester.'

'Ole Goober' stuck to Swanson like a starved tick.

\* \* \*

Private Ryder spent Christmas at *Chez Goober*—his loss of rank directly attributable to the holiday. Eleven others had preceded him—Rifles mostly. Hearing that Scotty was a guest, Jack Goelet allowed himself to be nabbed outside the lines.

As the sober gradually became the majority, they hatched a plan. Prizing the mortar from between the logs to get more air, they next dismantled the split-log ceiling. Gaining access to the underside of the roof, they worked through until they had an opening large enough to mount guard. In the spirit of the season, they hoisted a white flag and requested a parley; the Officer of the Day ignoring them, until his attention was drawn to the battering down of the door, from the inside.

The escape was short-lived. For the first time since May, the guards were allowed to load their rifles. The inmates were quickly rounded up.

To pass the time, they listened to one another's plans for when their enlistments were up. Most planned to transfer to cavalry or artillery units. Some desired only a furlough home. All planned to reenlist—but not with the Third; their desire was to volunteer with some *fighting* regiment.

\* \* \*

At Gosport, the call went out for volunteers to man the floating battery, *Virginia*. Jim Branscomb and a contingent of Hornets took advantage of Christmas Day to tour the ships and grounds. A polite lieutenant of Marines showed them through the ironclad after they all signed a document swearing allegiance to the Confederacy.

## CHAPTER 21 — A GOOD MAN
February 6, 1862

"YOU *DO* KNOW why you all are here, don't you?"

Packed into the small room, the twelve were confused by the question. They had been ordered to present themselves before the colonel.

Standing, at 'rest,' they would have been more at ease being barked at by a drill sergeant. Reading their names out at roll call Chef Beau had sent them to headquarters, no reason given. Flanked by Captain Powell and by the adjutant, Colonel Lomax addressed them from his desk.

"No? Well," he said, dragging out his words, "It appears the port commander is under the impression you boys now belong to him." He held up a sheet of paper by its corner, as though it were soiled. "This letter states you 'volunteers' are to report for duty at the Navy yard—this morning—by twelve, mid-day." His words were met by stunned silence.

"Et cetera, et cetera, et cetera."

Scanning the letter again Lomax pulled off his spectacles and, after searching his coat for a handkerchief, gave each lens a huff and a wipe. He held them up against the light for inspection. Satisfied, he looked towards the ceiling and asked the room, "Please tell me why I have received this letter."

A dozen explanations began at once. The colonel raised his hand, and the men fell silent.

"You," he said, pointing. "It's Branscomb, isn't it?"

"Ye—yes sir," answered Branscomb, caught off guard. "Ah, well, sir, speaking for myself and Private Cameron, here, colonel—I didn't know we *were* volunteering."

Ten heads bobbed as one.

"We talked to an officer on board *Merrimac,* at Christmastime—you know, sir, just asking—and he allowed as they weren't taking volunteers. Then, 'fore New Year's he comes round and says aren't we still comin' on board. I think we all said, *'Nooo, sir!'* I know me and Cameron did. We had only come to see the boat."

This account squared with the bobbing heads.

"What did you sign?"

"Well—nothing, colonel."

"How came he to know where to find you?"

The question produced another awkward silence.

"You all signed your names to *some* sheet of paper," said the colonel, pulling them along.

Jim began, "Just to get—" The room seemed to shrink some more. Jim tugged his collar.

"All right. You say you did not volunteer. Then we—"

"Beggin' yer pardon, colonel, but I did volunteer—for the *Merrimac*, er, *Virginia.* I have been a seaman—able body—under the Union Jack. Charles McDevett—Private McDevett, your honor, sir."

Lomax, peering over his spectacles, located the man directly behind Branscomb. "You are at peace then, with your decision, Mister—em, McDevett?" Glancing at the letter to locate the name.

"Aye sir. I am, sir."

"Very well. Return here with your kit and we will start the transfer—the *proper* sequence of events in these matters. The rest of you: you are up to your elbows in the 'ole tar baby.' You are excused drill, until such time as this evil is settled. Restricted to your street. I will have a word with Captain Powell. In the meantime, you are to have your rifles and equipage ready for return-inspection and your belongings packed."

Lomax arched his eyebrows, indicating the audience was over. "You may go," he said lightly, his eyes dropping back to the letter. "Dismissed."

The men scrambled out. The colonel turned to the adjutant and spoke crisply. "Mister Wilson: compliments to Colonel Battle. He is to forego his normal duties today. Ask him to step round, if he will. Next; alert Quartermaster Sanford he is to have personnel at the ready to effect any transfers."

Once they were alone, Lomax offered a seat to Powell.

"Well. Unhappy Hornets, Richard. I do believe you will

have the chance to dust off your debate skills. You had a gift for such, as I recall. We will need Cullen to insure the Navy accords the Army all due courtesies. But between you two old country lawyers, make no mistake: I expect you to extricate these men from their folly. My gentlemen shoveling coal for a floating battery? It simply will not do."

"I agree, colonel, but this is merely the tip of our larger problem: how many of our boys will go home once their twelve months are up?"

"That is one question. Here is another: what are your own plans?"

"Sir?"

"Hear me, Richard, six months from today—maybe less—there will be no forty-year old Captains of the Line."

"You mean Swanson, Woodruff, Hartwell . . . and me."

"This business is hard enough for men on foot. You know it. Woodruff will land a regiment, I have no fear, and, *entre nous,* Hartwell knows he cannot keep up. He will soon retire. You have seen Swanson's health suffer this past winter. He has lost weight. He is not the fearsome 'Goober' of old."

"It appears he has a rodent ulcer beneath that eye."

"Yes—too much sun for ole Black Bill. Doc Lee believes it is a carcinoma."

"That leaves, me—"

"That leaves you. Your health is good?"

"Fit as a fiddle. Though we know how swiftly that can change."

"As our senior captain, Sands is earmarked for major—and yes, I have spoken with him—he will take it this time. Should you be dropped, I will try to find something for you. But even if you *are* re-elected, heed my council, Richard: *you must get off the line.*"

\* \* \*

From D Street the Hornets watched Battle and Powell ride off, Sergeant Beaumont following. Once McDevett bid them farewell, the others passed the morning arguing over who first suggested talking to the *Virginia* recruiter. They exhausted the topic of whether Battle and Powell could get them off the hook.

Branscomb was not optimistic. His regard for Captain Powell had never recovered from that first day. The captain held himself apart, and inevitably, the volunteers thought the worse of him for it, his faults magnified in posts back to Union Springs. Most believed he should resign to avoid the disgrace of being voted out.

After drill, groups of Hornets dropped by to commiserate. They learned six others from the regiment, had volunteered for the *Merrimac*, Corporal Roach being the greatest surprise. 'Conscripted for ballast,' was the common judgment. Like men at the lying-in of an expectant mother, an uninformed dread hung over them. What could be taking so long? It was mid-afternoon before Neb Battle stuck his head in: "They're back."

Knowing they must wait for the summons proved to be the longest stretch of the day. Battle, Powell, and Lomax held a prolonged conference. Lomax finally emerged and returned to his quarters. Shortly after, a runner brought the order: "Step lively to Cap'n Powell."

\* \* \*

In the day-room, the eleven came to attention. Colonel Battle, and Chef, stood, in one corner, grim-faced.

"Boys," said Powell, "I'm afraid I have bad news."

The wind went out of their sails. The captain paused, lowering his voice.

"You Southern Rifles are to remain with us, here."

A moment was needed to grasp his meaning. Some were certain they had misheard. What? Truly?

"Boys, it was a near run thing, I assure you. Colonel Battle got you off by the skin of your teeth." (Battle, with an almost imperceptible shake of his head, indicated it was their captain they should thank). Overjoyed, the men nearly broke ranks, all they could do to resist hoisting the two and parading them through the camp.

That night Branscomb wrote:

> *You ought to have heard us thanking him. Sister, I know you have heard many a bad report about Capt. P but he is a good man.*

\* \* \*

The following week Johnnie Wise, the local boy, brought the news of Roanoke Island.

## CHAPTER 22 — HARD TIMES
February 8 — March 7, 1862

ROANOKE ISLAND lies behind the Cape Hatteras shore, a poor man's Manhattan, nine miles long. The first Englishmen set foot here a generation before Jamestown. It is where Virginia Dare was born, and from where her parents—and a hundred other souls—vanished; Raleigh's 'Lost Colony.'

Sand dunes, scraggly oak and pine; the island is unattractive in every way, save one: it is the gateway to Albemarle Sound and the waterways that cut deep into North Carolina. Roanoke commands the northeast corner of the state. An enemy controlling this corner threatens Hampton Roads, eighty miles north. By taking Suffolk, an enemy can cut off all practicable means of escape for the garrisons in Norfolk. Responsibility for the island belonged to General Huger.

Affable, charming—personally brave—Benjamin Huger's reputation rested on his ability to manage field artillery and supply. In the Mexican War, General Scott himself had awarded him Santa Anna's silver spurs. There was an orderliness to artillery that appealed to Huger, an attention to detail required of supply. If the army were a gigantic engine, his role was that of a vital cog.

He gave the defense of Roanoke to Brigadier Henry Wise. Third Alabama was familiar with the Wise plantation, being near Moseley's Church. Wise's youngest son, Johnnie, was a frequent visitor to the Alabama camp. It was his father who (as governor) had dealt so swiftly with John Brown.

Despite being a political appointee, Wise was capable, and understood the strategic underpinnings of his assignment. This did not alter the fact his new command was *not* capable: it was understrength, outgunned, ill-equipped, his requests for reinforcements repeatedly denied. Huger was convinced Hampton Roads bore the greater threat, and he would not spare Wise an extra man, horse, or cannon,

Roanoke's faint hopes rested on a breach of protocol. Going to Richmond, Wise appealed directly to Secretary of War Judah Benjamin, asking for one good battery of twelve pounders. While Benjamin was an astute lawyer—a one-time Senator from Louisiana—he was no military man. He did have enough of a grasp on the army's chain of command to send Wise packing: "Make the best use of what you have."

On February 1, Wise headed back to Roanoke, accompanied by his middle son, Richard. (Another son, Jennings, was under his command, as captain of Company A of the 46th Virginia).

Shaped like an hourglass, Roanoke's middle is marked by marshes and wetlands. There, on the only patch of dry ground, Confederate engineers constructed a chest-high rampart one hundred feet in length, the marshes to its front and sides deemed impassable. In the center, Wise improvised a battery of three guns: a 24-pounder, an 18-pounder, and a 6-pounder; all of them trained on the sandy trail coming from the landing beaches. The sole ammunition available was 6-pounder shot and shell.

Supporting these guns, was a battalion of infantry, with one company deployed into the marshes as skirmishers. The remainder of Wise's forces were stationed on the north end of the island ("Fort Huger"), in support of the battery guarding Croatan Sound.

Under the stress, Wise's health broke, and, on the eve of battle he was prostrate with pneumonia. Colonel Shaw, of the Eighth North Carolina, commanded.

He faced General Burnside's flotilla, which delivered more than 12,000 men. No time was wasted landing the three brigades (Foster, Reno, and Parke) on the south shore.

Next morning, under a lifting fog, the federals moved northward with six 'heavies'—Dahlgren naval guns—attacking the Confederate left and right through the impassable marshes; the Union brigadier, Reno (last seen surrendering Mount Vernon Arsenal), was pressing hard. In the center, Parke's 9th

New York made the final assault.

Jennings Wise, commanding the confederate skirmishers on the left, held his ground admirably until he received a mortal wound. His flank collapsing, Colonel Shaw saw no option but surrender; the entire command taken prisoner.

On the north end of the island, while the battle was still in doubt, aide-de-camp Richard Wise crossed to the mainland. After a ride of forty-eight hours, he delivered the island's final dispatches to Norfolk. General Huger sent no relief.

Dismissed, young Wise rode an additional seven miles to his family's homestead. Noise from the barn woke youngest brother, Johnnie, who, armed with a pistol, thought he would be confronting a thief. Only when he heard Richard's voice did he realize it was his brother, caring for his emaciated mount. The two had left from this barn just nine days before.

Word of Roanoke's fall spread quickly. Locally, its import was immediately understood: Norfolk was now indefensible. Rumors of incompetence soon were swirling through the cantonments. Third Alabama was ordered to abandon Moseley's Church and cross to the mainland, to secure the rail-juncture at Suffolk.

\* \* \*

February 13 was spent packing all critical supplies and equipment. Under a bright moon, the baggage train moved out, first; followed by the regiment a few hours later. Colonel Battle's orders: "Battalions: *Right, Face!* Countermarch by file left: *March!*" The column moved onto the plank road and headed towards Norfolk. Each company took a turn leading the others in song: *Bonnie Blue Flag, Dixie, Oh Susannah, Oh Lemuel, Rose of Alabamy.*

Norfolk turned out for her adopted sons, it's citizens lining their route. At the customs house, the color sergeants dipped the flags to General Huger. Brigadier Mahone took the column down to Market Square.

At the slave market, the regiment formed battalion squares. The sergeant major bellowed, *"OR-Der—Arms!"* Eight hundred rifles lowered.

"*PA'ah-Rade—Rest!*" The rifles rocked forward. The men eased their stance.

The absence of sound grew palpable, a transcendent pitch seeming to build, filling every ear, till broken by the notes of a lone fife. The regiment sang its adieu:

> *Of all the money tha' e'er I had,*
> *I spent it in good company.*
> *And all the harm tha' e'er I've done,*
> *Alas, it was to none but me.*
> *What I've done for want of wit,*
> *To mem'ry now I can't recall,*
> *So fill to me the parting glass*
> *Good night and joy be to you all.*
>
> *(So) fill to me the parting glass*
> *And drink a health whate'er befalls*
> *Then gently rise and softly call*
> *'Good night and joy be to you all'.*
>
> *Of all the comrades tha' e'er I had*
> *They're sorry for my going away,*
> *And all the sweethearts tha' e'er I had,*
> *They'd wish me one more day to stay . . .*
> *But since it falls unto my lot,*
> *Tha' I should rise and you should not,*
> *I'll gently rise and softly call,*
> *'Good night and joy be to you all'.*

\* \* \*

Ferried to Portsmouth, they marched to the outskirts, where they were halted at an abandoned camp known as Oak Grove (so named, apparently, for the absence of that tree).

It began to drizzle. The men had no more than the usual coats or gum blankets, to pull across their shoulders. Hardened to such low-scale miseries, it was the billeting that brought them low. Oak Grove had only thirty cabins for the eight hundred.

What happened to us going down to Suffolk? many asked.

Army bungling, was the short answer; the latest example magnified by the rain, cold, and filth, of their surroundings. Naturally, the baggage train was well on its way towards Suffolk. They received a ration of moldy pea biscuits and salt beef. The line officers protested; Lomax and Battle lodged their own complaints. Portsmouth's commandant—a transplanted Yankee brigadier named Blanchard—turned a deaf ear. These were Huger's pets, after all; they would need toughening.

In one of the cabins, Jim Branscomb watched leaks from the roof form a stream at their feet. He offered his take: "I don't think General Huger, nor this new one, knows his business."

*"No!"* exclaimed thirty Hornets. "You think so, do you? *Do* tell."

The knee-jerk reaction startled them all, and a raucous laughter ensued, Jim joining in.

They railed at the constant roadblocks set before them whenever it seemed combat was in the offing. Turning their attention to General Huger, they began to tally his faults.

"Before you get so wound up," said Tom Johnson, "Remember the fable of the frogs."

"What's that one?"

"The frawgs in de swamp: dems dat desire-red a king," he said, in the parlance of the field.

"So?"

"So, dey croaks *n' dey croaks* for a king. Dey croaks so long, dey wake ole Marse Zeus. He none too pleased, neither, hearing dis caterwaulin. "So dey think dey want a king, well Dey jus frogs, ain't dey?' 'n sends 'em—"

"A log!" chime several.

"You right as rain. Thohs 'em dis big ole log—wuch make a mighty splash. He tell 'em: 'They's you a king: King Log. Done and done.' Sceered to deaf by the splash, de frogs go hoppity off. But, bye 'n bye, dey works up dey Curge, 'n come a-creepin' back—sizin' up dis ole King Log. *'Dis ole boy got him no active campaign,'* sez one. 'Ain't gwine do but jez sit dere,' sez another. 'Ain't so big,' sez de terd. Soze dey gets real familler wid dis feller (as many a frog will), an' one by one dey mosey round 'n wind up sittin' on *top* dat ole log.

"Oncet dey comfy, deys commence to thinkin'. 'N deys thinkin' dey bin *skinned:* 'Why, dis heah log ain't no *proper* king,' sez one partik'lar big bull (name 'Ole Dick,' as I recall), sez, 'Zeus, he mus' jez bin *messin'* widdis.'

" 'When you right, you right,' dey alls agree.

"So, here dey comes agin a-croakin.' 'Send us a *real* king, Marse Zeus.,' 'Send us a *sho nuff* king.'

"Now, Marse Zeus, miffed (as you might 'magin, be woke now twice), he say, sez, 'Yassir, frogs, mose sorrowful 'bout dat. Wone 'tappen 'gin.' But here now, look he'ah, here you a king: here you a *good 'un*. Dis one keep you quiet, 'pon my honor."

"And he sends 'em Ole King—"

"Cotton!" says Henry Smith.

"No, no, now, don't be messin' with my story. He sends 'em Ole King Stork. And, wid dat, he brust his hands" (Tom demonstrating). "He walk da chalk. He say, 'Good night!'"

His hands on his knees, Tom hung his head.

"What did the stork signify?" asked one babe.

"Why, I got to say it?" Tom looked up, turning his head to encompass the cabin. "King Stoke, jez do like all stoke do."

"Well?"

*"Et 'em up, chile! What you think?* King Stoke et ever' last one o' dem dern frawgs."

\* \* \*

Newspapers began reporting the debacle of Fort Donelson: the key to Tennessee. Just as Roanoke was the key to North Carolina and Norfolk, Donelson was meant to secure the whole northwest of the Confederacy. At Oak Grove they asked: how could an army of fifteen thousand (many of them AVC militiamen) simply lay down their arms? The details of

General Pillow's conduct would not emerge for some time: after the defending forces had repelled the initial federal assault, Pillow relinquished his share of command, and, in the night, crossed the river to safety. General Simon Buckner was left to negotiate the terms of surrender.

From Fort Donelson a new phrase entered the public consciousness: Unconditional Surrender—the only terms offered by a third-string Union general named Grant.

\* \* \*

An escape of another sort was effected by Captain Andrews and transfer of his True Blues. The Blues' expertise was artillery. In Montgomery, patrons raised funds to purchase a battery, placing them with the Barbour County Light Artillery under Colonel Kolb, then forming in Eufaula.

While the Third would not mourn the loss of Andrews, the loss of a company *en masse,* was a blow, like losing a sound tooth. A number of Blues protested, and Lomax refused to approve their transfers out. (A new Company G would be formed in May, under Captain Bonham.) On the whole, the regiment wondered if Kolb and his officers knew quite what they were getting in Andrews.

Clearly, the regiment was dwindling. Nearly a third of the original volunteers had already transferred to cavalry or artillery units, or been promoted to officer new regiments. A surprising number had been medically discharged. The muster roll stood at seven hundred. Men talked openly of leaving, of their plans to return home and accept commissions elsewhere. The Hornets' Lieutenant Wilson began to cherry-pick men to come with him—into a new artillery battery—promising promotions to Neb Battle, Tom Johnson, and Jim Branscomb.

\* \* \*

The evacuation of the Roads gained momentum. Refugees, heading inland, streamed past Camp Oak Grove, their carts and wagons laden with possessions. The Confederate shore batteries were put on flat cars and spirited away. Martial law was declared.

Discipline was strictly enforced under General Blanchard. The Third was ordered to post all sentries. conduct all drills, and run all errands, under full packs. When one man was spotted without his pack, Blanchard ordered him bucked and gagged—the torture of trussing up a soldier like a hog, binding his hands to his shins, locked into place by a rod inserted over his elbows and beneath his knees; a gag to keep him quiet about it.

"Stand fast," said Colonel Lomax to the provost guards.

Not sure he had heard right, Blanchard ordered Lomax directly.

"Bucked and gagged, colonel."

"I call the general's attention: this man is a volunteer, not a conscript."

"I don't care if he's the goddam Prince of Wales—"

"Sir, I will resign the Army, before I see a gentleman under my command, subject to such treatment. The meanest conscript has the right to stand before a court martial."

Insubordination was itself a court martial offense, and Lomax was placing his career and his reputation on the line. Ultimately, higher-ups swept the matter under the rug, Lomax was too big a name—though the incident set off a fresh round of gossip. Those who did not know Lomax repeated what they had heard: he was lax, there was no discipline in his regiment, the 'Bandbox Regiment' existed only for show.

\* \* \*

After a week of rain, Second Battalion was relocated to a new camp behind the Naval Yard, last occupied by the Third Georgia Regiment and their body lice. Whatever name those boys may have given their camp, Second Battalion christened it 'Camp Hard Times.' Though a bit more spacious, the cabins leaked worse than at Oak Grove; storms left standing water, inside and out. The line for Surgeon's Call grew longer. Even Swanson wound up in hospital. A snowstorm blew in and turned all to ice.

Huddled for warmth, they read books and newspapers aloud to each other; smoking their pipes to pass the time and dreaming of home. It would not be long now: spring was just around the corner and their enlistments would be up in May. Every last man felt he had earned a long furlough home. They would reenlist, but they would not come back to Portsmouth; their next regiment, would be a *fighting* regiment.

## CHAPTER 23 — PIG POINT
March 8, 1862

THE WEATHER had moved on and the morning was beautiful. Snow was rapidly melting. Saturday, March 8th, would be a bright and temperate day.

So odd, then, for the streets of Portsmouth to be deserted.

Even more unusual, Gosport Yard was silent. The locals had become inured to the clamor coming from there, shifts working around the clock to get *Virginia* ready for launch. So, the absence of sound was immediately noticed. And interpreted: *Virginia* and her crew were steaming towards the Roads; a telegraph could not have spread the news faster.

Brogans clattering over Portsmouth's brick streets, Troup Randle and Neb Battle led a band of Hornets to the waterfront. At the crossings they found the ferries were away to Norfolk—where they would remain, abandoned by crew intent on following the tide of passengers streaming towards Sewell's Point.

An old woman called to them.

"If you boys're wonderin' where the town has gone to, you shall find them at the Navy Hospital, half a mile north." They could see smoke from the steaming squadron.

Down the street was a party of Thirds—Mobile boys—who had overnighted at Macon House, Harley Broun among them. He waved them over.

"That smoke is from *Virginia*," he said. "She chugged past here minutes ago, with all hands on deck."

The Hornets and Cadets weighed the pros and cons of making for Wise's Point, north of the hospital. They were disappointed to have missed the ferries. The thinking was Sewell's Point—nearest the sea-entrance to The Roads—would have an excellent view.

It was now almost noon. Neb interrupted the debate.

"Our Navy isn't going to let *Virginia* anywhere near Monroe's guns. Admiral Buchanan will head for the warships at anchor—*upriver*. Pig Point is where we want to be."

"It must be close to ten miles," said one.

"More like twelve," said Broun.

"So—?" challenged Troup Randle.

On the way, they encountered a courier galloping towards town. To Cricket Underwood's question "Wha–wha–wha . . ." The rider confirmed: "*Virginia* is steaming upriver."

Ripping! They had guessed right. *USS Cumberland* was there. And the *Congress*. Pig Point was five more miles, but the fresh intelligence spurred them on. Arriving at the point, they spotted the ironclad across the waters.

A battery of heavies defended Pig Point, but these proved no match against Portsmouth's civilians, who had overwhelmed the garrison and were now watching from the embrasures. Daring young women stood atop the wicker parapets with their beaux.

Their backs were buffeted by a stiff breeze. Other than the sounds from the gulls, slashing and kiting, and the pop and snap of the battery's flags, the spectacle before them unfolded in complete silence.

Somehow, Old Dick Stinson had beaten every other Hornet to the site and he had also thought to bring a glass. He pointed out one of *Virginia's* escorts—adrift in mid-channel—where it had been disabled, receiving a hit from the Union guns across the way. Run aground on the far shore, with smoke billowing, was a Yankee frigate. The artillerymen identified her as *Congress,* of fifty guns. She had loosed two broadsides into *Virginia,* to no effect. Without changing course, The ironclad had replied with her starboard guns and done damage.

A fresh report from Stinson: "*Virginia* comes on, bearing down on the *Cumberland*," still at anchor. Being a Saturday, her crew's wash hangs in the rigging, to dry. Firing broadsides of her own, *Cumberland's* salvos glanced off *Virginia's* iron plate like so many peas. Holding steady, *Virginia* closed on her prey, the deadly ram under her prow breaking the surface of the waves.

Swinging on her anchor, *Cumberland* attempted to get out of harm's way, but *Virginia* caught her beneath the main chains, plunging deep into her starboard. With a shudder, *Cumberland* began to sink.

Like two bulls locked in death, there was danger of *Virginia* being pulled under. In desperation, she fired into *Cumberland* with every gun that could be brought to bear, and the maneuver set her free.

The *Cumberland* sank rapidly—in under fifteen minutes—her gun crews manning their stations till one by one, each was silenced. Finding the bottom, *Cumberland's* topmasts remained above the waves, her flag still streaming. On both shores, the witnesses were stunned.

At Pig Point, the young ladies are no longer so brazen. Quietly, they fold their parasols and turn away. With nothing clever left to say, they are handed down from the parapets. The fight—so brief, so lopsided—is no cause for celebration. The sight of *Cumberland's* masts are a memory none will ever forget.

*Virginia* continues upriver, firing into the federal tenders and dueling with the shore batteries behind them. Making a long slow turn, the ironclad comes about and heads back down.

At four o'clock she is off the stern of the defenseless *Congress*. *Virginia* unleashes a broadside that rakes the length of her deck, a devastating blast that dismounts six guns, killing thirty sailors. Shell after shell is sent into the hapless ship, and at last *Congress* strikes her colors. A party off the *Virginia* ferries over to evacuate the wounded. Despite the surrender, fire continues from Yankee riflemen on shore and Admiral Buchanan and several others are hit. *Virginia* halts her aid (though the evacuation of survivors continues from the offside of *Congress*). Standing off, *Virginia* fires hotshot into her victim and she begins to burn anew.

*Virginia* turns her attention to a final opponent—*Minnesota*—run aground about a mile from *Congress*, where she has been exchanging fire with Confederate gunships.

Night is coming, however, and *Virginia* has many casualties aboard—from both sides. Retiring to the protection of Sewell's Point, she off-loads the wounded, while her officers assess battle damage. *Minnesota* will keep till morning.

Hoping to see the fight renewed, come morning, the Hornets and Cadets bivouac with the garrison. Keeping watch late into the night, they are mesmerized by the blaze across the water—the pyre that used to be *Congress*. Now and then flames ignite a gun, causing a loud explosion—heard clearly, now that the wind has shifted. The flames are visible in Portsmouth, where the outcome of the battle—even the fate of *Virginia*—remains a mystery. The sky over the Roads is blood red.

*Congress* is the ammunition ship for the Union fleet. At midnight the fires reach her magazines. All anticipate a mighty explosion, but when it comes the degree of violence is staggering: the blast rocks them where they sit. Windows shatter for miles; men are jolted from their bunks. Heard up to forty miles away, the reverberations echo for minutes.

Next morning the Alabamians got their encore. Over a sea as smooth as glass, *Virginia* steamed out to finish *Minnesota*.

With her tormentor approaching, *Minnesota* commenced to fire, but her shots either glanced off *Virginia's* iron plates, to bound across the water, or plunging, sent spectacular geysers into the air. Once again, *Virginia* maneuvers to advantage. Standing off, she makes every shot count, and methodically begins to dismantle the bigger ship.

Just as *Minnesota's* fate seems fixed, Stinson reports fire coming from her away side. When the smoke clears, glasses confirm salvos coming from a new combatant: a tiny vessel with an iron turret like a cheese box. The much-touted *Ericson* battery has been rumored near completion at Brooklyn. If true, she has arrived in the night and, if their eyes are not deceived, she appears to carry but one gun.

This should not take long. *Virginia* dwarfs the newcomer. But the fight goes round and round. Smoke and distance hinder any meaningful narration, but after three hours neither ship has gained the advantage.

Eventually, the Yankee captain breaks off and seeks refuge in the shallows, refusing to return to the main channel and battle the deeper draft *Virginia*. The latter returns to Sewell's Point. The show is over for now, and the exuberant volunteers head back to camp.

At Portsmouth, the streets were now jammed with citizens, all in a carnival mood. All hail *Virginia's* heroes: the blockade is breached—if not broken completely. At Camp Hard Times, the Mobilians stage an impromptu Mardi Gras, creating rump societies overnight, each competing for attention with louche parades.

More good news arrives the following week: the regiment will be reunited, and return to Moseley's Church. The resulting march through Norfolk is a triumph.

## CHAPTER 24 — LOMAX
March 14 – 27, 1862

THE SIGHT of Moseley's Church was sobering. The camp had been looted of everything of value: furniture, furnishings, books, clothing. Cabin doors were missing and even floor planking. The cabins along True Blue Street stood empty and abandoned, simply underscoring that loss.

The end of their own service was in sight, as well—six weeks more. Officers and staff were nervous, and counting heads. A sufficient number of reenlistments would be needed, from every company, to preserve the organization of the regiment. Many volunteers had signaled their intent to serve elsewhere. Will Grist of the Rifles used his furlough to raise a company for the 32nd Alabama. William Smith went one step too far: hand-picking his company (for the 22nd Regiment) from among the ranks of the Third. He was ordered to desist.

To replenish the ranks, exemplary soldiers were sent home to recruit, but all across the South, the volunteers and the patriots—the 'easy pickings'—were already in. Only the exempt, the infirm, and the shirkers remained.

Bounties and incentives were offered the old volunteers. When the government rescinded these, morale plummeted further. The non-coms reported a growing number of disorderly conducts and insubordinations.

In this state of affairs, Lomax ordered every man to be present at Parade on March 27. No exceptions. Moseley's Church would be closed to outsiders.

\* \* \*

The regiment was drawn up, E Company (the color company) front and center. George Ellison and Milton Boullemet formed part of the color guard. When the adjutant ordered: "*PA*-rade: Rest," the colonel was standing between two raised lanterns. Removing his hat, he began:

"Comrades. First, a confession: I owe each of you a heartfelt apology, and I stand before you, in all humility, to beg your pardon.

"I have spoken with many of you in recent days. And I have made promises, promises of furlough for re-enlistments; promises that I can no longer honor, despite my honest intentions." He paused to let this sink in.

"My promises, and my orders—and my intentions—have been countermanded. Not (I should add) by our own General Huger, but by no less than the President of the Confederate States—Jefferson Davis." This news caused a stir.

Lomax read the president's order. It applied, not only to those *desirous* of furloughs, but recalled all those *currently* on furlough. The implications were obvious.

Many of those present, had been with Lomax at Pensacola, and some (he observed) before that. And such men, who had been faithful then, would not waver now. "I am humbled to command such men, a regiment that is universally acknowledged to be the finest in the service; men of education, talent—of everything which a proud country or state can boast—as attested to by every visitor to your camps." But he had also heard it said, that "'Third Alabama is nothing but a set of damned rascals.'" The smattering of laughter caused Lomax to smile.

"But I know better," he said. "We all have our failings—I have my share—*but by the Gods, boys, I am a patriot!"*

He recounted how those—longing for rank—had transferred out of the regiment. "Still others have charged that I desire to rule—to play the great man. I hurl the slander back in their face. *It is our country, our cause, our homes; our mothers, wives, sisters, and sweethearts that are in jeopardy, here.* Faced with that, it makes no difference to me, whether I command a regiment or serve in the ranks."

He turned to the position Virginia was in, of needing the aid of her sister states: "Outrages are daily committed upon Virginia, wherever the accursed have gained a foothold. And yet, some of you grumble, complain of fighting 'Virginia's battles.' *Virginia? God Almighty.* Don't you realize that by fighting the enemy here, *in Virginia*, you prevent such scenes from occurring in our own beloved state?

"Here, you are an impassable barrier to the advance of the enemy; back home, your loved ones are safe. The soil of Mobile, and of Montgomery, and all the rest of Alabama, will never be polluted. . . They intend to confiscate our property, to liberate our slaves, so *they themselves* may hire them out to replenish the government purse.

"You see all this, and yet . . . and yet, you must 'go home.' You say: 'Only for thirty or forty days, Colonel Lomax.'" Looking across the assembled ranks, he exclaimed: "The Yankees *can be done with us*, in thirty or forty days! All their damnable schemes may be accomplished!"

He announced he had already re-enlisted—as a private. "In the ranks—I mean to carry a rifle. And I will use it, too.

"And, should you men choose another to lead you into battle: no one will show greater obedience to our new commander, than myself."

There was nothing left to say. Battle dismissed the formation and the men marched quietly away, back to their darkened streets. One company after another, from scattered points around the camp, raised three cheers for the colonel.

\* \* \*

The hard times had begun. April brought news of victory at Shiloh Church, a place in Tennessee. Many former comrades were now with the Army of Tennessee, including most of the officers for 22d Alabama; Robert and Ed Armistead, Weedon, Nott, and others.

Jubilation was soon tempered by the report of Albert Sidney Johnston's death, the Confederate commander, which foreshadowed a long toll of casualties, defeats, and withdrawals. The number of casualties was nearly incomprehensible. Nick Weeks saw Bob Armistead's name among the fallen. Arriving letters would later report him relinquishing command of his regiment, and leading his horse to the rear, where he wrote brief letters of farewell. Shot in the belly, he died in agony a few hours later. John Marrast now commanded the 22nd Regiment.

In the middle of the month, details of the Conscript Act were released. No law passed by the First Congress so demoralized its patriot volunteers. The act locked them all into place by banning transfers to the other service branches, while granting choice to those who had, thus far, avoided service altogether.

The new law also required the discharge of all volunteers above the age of thirty-five, or under age eighteen. This affected about one in ten of the Third volunteers. The younger ones could simply sit out their time before reenlisting, but requests for assignment to their original units were rarely approved. The over-age volunteers were relegated to home guard units or partisan bands.

More salt into the wound: the law condoned the purchase of substitutes, codified exemptions, and authorized bonuses to entice new recruits. The *one* inducement extended to the volunteers (namely furloughs for those reenlisting early), was the first one rescinded by Jeff Davis, once McClellan started to move.

## CHAPTER 25 — ON THE WING
May 2 – 15, 1862


FEELING AS wet and disagreeable as the night, the sentinel slogged towards his cabin. Mud from off his shoes mingled with the slurry covering the boardwalk, making the planks all the more treacherous. His rifle was slung barrel-down to keep the muzzle dry, but more importantly, to give him better balance. Keeping his eyes cast down, too, he took short, careful, steps. Still he slipped, and he cursed each betrayal; a fall now would make his miserable day complete. Rain fell in sheets but it could not cleanse the boards as fast as traffic added to it. And by the looks of it there had been a lot of traffic. The soldier cinched his raincoat tighter. Ahead, his cabin was aglow, an inviting light pouring through the chinks. Other huts were lit up, too. The entire company was up past taps. Come to think of it, he hadn't actually heard taps, and he noticed the lanterns still burning along officers' row. Nearing his cabin, he heard riotous laughter: Rafe Herrin—the magpie—mimicking Major Forsyth:

"Make haste, you men. You, thayah. Yas—you with the fine mess boy—Colonel Battle insists you tote your own gun. That's right, knapsack, too, m'afraid. Can't be helped—the war, you know."

More glee. The sentinel made use of the boot-scrape and, ducking through the door was met by a gratifying warmth. Rafe was also there, smiling broadly. Rafe was not usually so welcoming, and the soldier was immediately on his guard. "Herrin, this is no night for foolery." But now the others all were standing, and one, towards the back, by the little fireplace, moved in a particular, familiar way—though bundled beneath several blankets. The sentry saw nothing but grins all around. Rafe said, "And may I introduce—"

*"Lewis!"*

The cabin erupted in cheers as Jim grasped his brother's hand—quickly exchanging it for a long and earnest bear-hug.

Even draped in blankets Lewis shivered uncontrollably. Jim pushed his brother out to arms-length, "You've grown—and filled yourself in. Lewis, what has happened to my 'little' brother?"

Eyes glistening, he hugged Lewis a second time. Lewis was all grins and embarrassment. "W-W-William and J-John are h-h-here, too," he said. "W-W-With Cap'n Jelk's company. They are setting up."

"You are excused duty?"

"N-No. I mean: I am here. *I am a Rifle, too.*"

Which earned another cheer, though several shouted the correction: "Hain't no *Rifle*, boy—you a *Hawnet*." Jim shouted to be heard, "I am glad, of course, but how is this, now?"

"Cap'n Jelks tells me him and Mister Powell shook hands over it his last trip back. So I am yours, I suppose."

"A more welcome 'suppose' I never heard. Heigh Nelly, what a day. Look everybody, *it's Lulu!*" Jim put his hands onto Lewis's chest, and playfully shoved him away.

Lewis was of a more solid build than his brother, a little shorter; his broad face topped by a mop of dark hair and a shadow of beard. He had a pleasant and easy way about him. His upper body would sway, as he talked, shifting his weight, restlessly. Swaying to-and-fro now, he reached into his haversack for letters—for Jim, and for others—calling out their names. The fortunate ones snatched the letters greedily and flopped down onto their bunks to read. He delivered 'howdies' from uncles, aunties, friends, and loved ones back home. The blankets warming him, he dispensed news from home: the spring planting, a fire in town, families in mourning—which required repeating, for every new arrival. Finally, Jim had to push him outside and, locked arm in arm, they went in search of their older brothers.

The new recruits included an entire new company—The Dixie Eagles. From the Norfolk depot they had marched seven miles through the downpour, arriving drenched and chilled to the bone; grateful to find a hot supper and ready bunks on True Blue Street. They would become the regiment's eleventh company: Company L.

The lamps stayed lit in the 'hives,' for some time. The Branscombs weren't the only ones to discover old friends, relations, and neighbors among the newcomers.

Fresh orders soon put a stop to the reunions—the brigade was to abandon Norfolk. Adding to the scramble, company elections must be held—part of the reorganization mandated by the Conscript Act. The volunteers had only a few days left, to cling to their democratic pretensions.

\* \* \*

In their election the Tuskegee Light Infantry felt they had improved their lot. In poor health, and hoping to salvage a portion of his dignity, Goober Swanson resigned just before the balloting. Robert Mayes was elected captain, by acclamation; Charles Bryan, his first lieutenant. Tom Bilbro was elected second lieutenant and Sam Johnston was elevated from the ranks, to 'third' lieutenant.

The only other captain to be dropped was Bonham, his ouster expected, but for different reasons. Bonham was the original recruiting officer for the Beauregard-Lowndes, and popular enough—but as a practicing dentist he bore the stigma attached to men in trade. Lowndes County was the jewel of central Alabama; that a 'tooth-puller' commanded the sons of some of Alabama's most influential families, had been an issue.

He had been at odds with his senior lieutenants from the start. The two were first cousins—both named Cornelius Byron Robinson (the first lieutenant went by Neil, the second by Byron). Many of *their* cousins were in the ranks. The Robinsons were early pioneers of the state, with large holdings and wide influence. Lieutenant Neil felt the majority of the 'Bo-Los' had volunteered expecting to be under the command of a gentleman. But a September election went against him and both cousins tendered their resignations.

As Lomax expected, this did not end the matter—too many in Company H owed fealty to the Robinson clan. But he didn't want to lose a good line officer, either. So, he and Battle prepared a contingency plan for Bonham: creating the position of *ad hoc* major. When this failed to get approval, they made use of the departure of the Blues, to appoint Bonham captain of a new Company G. Known as the Lomax Sharpshooters, it was comprised of thirty former Blues (those who had not wished to follow Andrews) and twenty-five Beauregards (who had no wish to find a new tooth-puller).

Neil and Byron Robinson returned in April, bringing with them thirty new recruits; enough to secure Neil's election as captain.

The remaining companies all stuck with their original captains. Even Powell was confirmed. Five new first lieutenants were elected, including drillmaster James Broun of the Cadets and Troup Randle of the Hornets. There were some resignations, some bruised feelings, but nothing of lasting moment. The May elections would be the last shakeup to the officer lists; promotion via ballot box was over, and seniority, a settled matter. Seniority was of grave importance, for each captain was literally an 'officer of the line.' In line of battle, the position each company held, was determined by their captain's seniority. As attrition erased field officers, seniority determined in what order, captain(s) succeeded to higher rank.

A final vote was taken for command of the regiment. Lomax and Battle were both returned with near unanimity; Forsyth with a solid majority. Preparations began for the evacuation of Moseley's Church. Contracts with local hires were severed. Going forward, hands would be the responsibility of their owners.

\* \* \*

The evacuation brought an ignominious end to their time in Norfolk. There was no fanfare, this time—no nostalgic serenades. On their march through the city, the Third was relieved to have so few witnesses. At six a.m. the column halted at the depot. A few men from each mess were permitted to secure food. Corporal Boullemet used the time to pay a last visit to his benefactress, the widow Walke.

Anticipating his coming she had put out a hearty breakfast for him, and prepared sacks of sausage and biscuit to carry back to his comrades. The widow, having no children of her own doted upon Milton. Her niece, Mary, plainly adored him. If before, Mary had been a reluctant churchgoer, it was Milton who improved her enthusiasm. Mary was a planner, and Milton had come to figure in her plans. She made him swear to write her every Sunday, even if a battle were going on—*especially if a battle was going on*—because then, he wouldn't go running around getting shot. Milton pledged his word and crossed his heart.

Leaving his trunk and belongings with the widow, he asked they be burned before letting the Yankees have them.

In the doorway, his arms laden with food, the widow kissed him on the cheek and said a blessing. Setting down his bounty, Milton knelt to give Mary a hug. With her clinging to him, he asked: "Will you keep something for me?" Reaching into his haversack he brought out his silver cup.

"Mary, you best take care of this, till I can come back for it—it will only get lost where I am going."

Needing to blow her nose, Milton handed Mary his handkerchief.

"Best keep that, too."

The Norfolk & Petersburg Line provided the cars to Suffolk, where the Third's captains requisitioned much-needed tents. They were then transported to Weldon, North Carolina. Their baggage train—under Lieutenant Greene—moved much more slowly and arrived in Suffolk just as the Third pulled out.

Troops entering a town fell under the orders of the local Post Commander. At Suffolk this was Brigadier Lewis Armistead. Lieutenant Greene was directed to report to Armistead's headquarters. The lieutenant found the general seated at his camp table scanning a report while he heard a lengthy, and defensive explanation from its author, a quartermaster. Dusty and parched, Greene hoped to find a pitcher of cool water in the tent. When he did not, he sat on a campstool, to wait his turn.

Armistead was 'Old Army'—a West Pointer—though not a graduate; expelled for breaking a plate over the head of his roommate, Jubal Early.

"Very well. Dismissed." Armistead ended the interview with the quartermaster. That officer gave Greene a worried look as he made his escape. Greene rose from his campstool.

"I know of only one regiment, with officers so presumptuous, as to sit in the presence of their superiors—well? Speak up. Report, if you know how—or do you expect me to guess?"

"Startled by the rebuke, he stumbled a reply: "L-Lieutenant Greene: Third Alabama Volunteers, sir."

"A *gentleman* of the Third, you say? Do tell. Take your hat off, mister! Were you raised in a barn? Present yourself: Stand at attention! Do you know how to salute? Are you the best your regiment has to offer, or are they all like you? This is how you represent the State of Alabama? God have mercy—*By God, I have seen illiterate bumpkins do better;* seen Mexican peasants show more respect. Next time you appear before a superior officer, you *will* have a better grasp of military etiquette. There will be no slovenly militia habits here, sir. Why *are* you here, boy?"

"To—Sir, to report—Sir, Lieutenant Greene—"

*"Jesus Christian Christ. Get* out of my sight. You are a disgrace to the uniform. Come back when you can deliver a proper report. Be gone, mister—get out of here."

The regiment arrived at Weldon; fatigue, sporadic rations—and new strains of common diseases—meant the sick list grew longer each day. Lulu Branscomb and those others were sent ahead to Petersburg. The rest of the brigade followed a few days later, as the pace of events began to quicken.

## CHAPTER 26 — DREWRY'S BLUFF
May 13 – 29, 1862

EACH ORDER brought them closer to Richmond; each stage of the journey erasing the taint associated with 'garrison troops.'

At Petersburg depot, they were met by a squad of bright-eyed recruits—lined up at attention, on the platform with Sergeant Ledyard—their spotless uniforms trimmed with Cadet satin. Next to them was the stationmaster, who was himself attended by an ancient dog—the mortal remains of a bull terrier. As the regiment de-trained, the dog began a soliloquy of mindless barking.

The old Cadets eyed the new, with a mixture of envy and disdain.

"Look at 'em. Have you ever? Mint-condition, brand-spanking new, baby Cadets—right there—right out o' the box. Lookit 'em. Lookit 'ose uniforms, them shiny cuffs, 'n shiny brass. Don't they know no better?"

"We weren't never that pretty," said Chighizola.

"What a difference a year makes," said Jack Goelet.

"Speak for yourself, Chigger—I was a beautiful baby," said Averill.

"What a difference a bath makes, you mean," said Krebs.

"Think they don't still have goodies from home? Lookit them full haversacks."

"I bet theys fingernails iz even clean."

"And in one piece."

"You bring us newspapers from home? You best have; admission to this car is one Mobile Advertiser."

"Lookit that dawg. How ole you figger dat ole boy be?"

"By the look o' him, *bound* to be an F.D.V."

"Bet he's barked at ever' train thas ever come through here."

"Hey, mister! Do Miles Standish know you got his dawg?"

"I know Standish would be surprised to hear ya'll talking

like field hands," snapped Lieutenant Broun.

The dog, having said his piece, ceased barking, to begin a regimen of personal hygiene; the process eliciting more comments from the bored young men.

Sergeant Ledyard introduced the newcomers:

"This one is Lincoln, Livingston here, Mulden, Newburg and Seawell, all recruited by Captain Sands on his last trip. Give 'em a cheer, boys!" And the older boys obliged.

"Lincoln? I hear that right? We got us a baby Lincoln?" asked Chighizola. "O, I hope 'tis little Tadpole."

"Thas some powerful recruitin' raht'chare—getting' us a Republican this late in the game. Cap'n Sands' got him that silver-tongue."

"Hey, fish!" Chighizola yelled to the recruits.

The fish—knowing they were fish—turned their heads in unison.

"You on the end: Yeah, you. You get your ration of coffee?"

"No, sir," said the fish called Livingston. "We didn't know to ask. But I have a pound bag in my kit—shall I get it?"

Amid the laughter, Sergeant Ledyard pleaded, "Let 'em be, boys. Let 'em be, now. (Corporal, show 'em where to fall in)."

"Didja hear Cap'n signed up little Johnnie Forsyth?"

"Go on! 'Johnnie Forsooth'? Ole Trip don't know whether to sit or stand."

"Wait. That ain't all, word is he overslept and . . . *missed the train.*"

Hoots and howls of incredulity.

"*Haw!* Don't ye know *that* must have pleased Cap no end, scraping the bottom of the barrel, just to have it oversleep on you."

"All right, all right—you boys have had your fun—"

"Dollar a dime these cherubs are sweet little altar boys, too; Cap'n's done cleaned out Spring Hill."

* * *

Next morning, General Lee wired General Huger: 'SEND IMMEDIATELY GENERAL MAHONE WITH HIS BRIGADE OR PART

OF IT'; meaning to Drewry's Bluff, site of a fortified battery overlooking the James. Reports had the ironclad *Monitor* and *Galena* steaming upriver to test Richmond's defenses.

Receiving no response, Lee repeated his order the following day.

During this layover, the Rifles learned Captain Woodruff would depart, having received his commission as lieutenant colonel in the 36th Alabama. John Hoyt, not yet twenty-two years of age, was elected captain-in-waiting; John Lake, his first lieutenant.

Lee fumed over Huger's slowness.

In a downpour, the brigade was ferried across the Appomattox the night of May 15, halting on the other side, at the Petersburg-Richmond terminus.[10]

They waited for cars to be switched. Then, as no one knew their exact destination, they waited for Huger to be found. The agent in charge had been ordered to provide cars for a regiment, but failed to accommodate for the field and staff's horses—shorting the cars needed, by two. They waited on these. At four in the morning, the men finally boarded, but the train was at capacity before the Rifles could board. They were to remain at the station, to wait on a second train.

The first troops arrived at Halfway Station (Drewry's Bluff) before dawn, the short distance covered at a crawl. The rain was clearing as they de-trained and the men received a ration of crackers for the march to the bluff, where they were deployed along the riverbank as skirmishers. Within minutes, *Monitor* and her support rounded the bend, a mile downriver. Obstructions in the river would stop them short of the bluff.

On the following train, Hoyt and his Rifles could clearly hear the bombardment begin. Just short of the Halfway Station they encountered another delay. An hour passed, in which

---
[10] There being no railroad bridge across the Appomattox River.

the firing increased. Finally, the train chuffed ahead—*past their stop*—continuing on a few miles, to the next, where they were met by Major Forsyth. At the double quick, the battalion commander led them back through the woods.

The Union ships concentrated their fire on the heights. *Monitor* approached under a hail of shot and shell—too close, in fact, for her guns to bear on target. While drifting back downriver, her armored escort, *Galena*—at the proper distance—was able to dismount one of the Confederate guns. Shells screeching and whistling up to their targets, the bolts resembled 'lampposts.' Occasionally a shell burst over the skirmishers, but most of the action was between the big guns. *Galena* was subject to galling fire from the Alabama riflemen along the banks. Her marines did what they could to protect the gun crews but eventually *Galena* had to limp away as well, with substantial casualties.

Hoyt's men contended with obstacles. Enemy shells had downed trees across their path and they crossed a field furrowed by shell. In a pine thicket on the far side they discovered two ammunition wagons. A mule had been eviscerated moments before, and the drivers could not move the munitions away from the danger. A man, his arm blown off, was borne past them on a litter, and Hoyt realized his Rifles had been halted just to the rear of the battery. Charlie had led them to the most lethal area of shelling.

Fortunately, the incoming fire quit almost immediately. Filing in to the cantonment, the Rifles spotted the Cadets manning one of the guns; gunners from CSS *Virginia*, working the other two.

The Union ships drifted downriver to safer waters. The last explosions came from Colonel Battle, dressing down Major Forsyth for exposing his men to naval fire.

\* \* \*

Generals Lee and Johnston rode down from Richmond to

assess the damage and gauge the battery's future needs—and to have a word with General Huger. Standing on the bluff with Mahone and Lomax, Lee watched the operation to recover the dismounted cannon and the regiment got its first look at the man called the 'King of Spades.' Lee was pleased with their efforts. Drewry's Bluff must never be taken, for Richmond would surely follow. The bluff controlled access to the capitol by river. It also kept the rail link open to Petersburg, the vital corridor for men and materiel.

As night approached, the men's thoughts turned to matters of food and shelter—details overlooked, in the army's haste to get troops to the front. There were few facilities at the bluff: no barracks, no supplies. Though less than ten miles from Richmond's warehouses they might as well have been on the Moon. Till the roads dried out, the regiment's commissaryand baggage train'(with its newly-made tents) could not move.

Being dropped into an unfamiliar and sparsely populated area would try the skills of any forager. Competing for necessities with a brigade of like-minded men raised the stakes considerably. Lacking even the tools to erect shelter, the men were at the mercy of the elements, with little more than the clothes on their backs.

They made bivouac in the woods near Drewry's home. Lomax and his officers accepted the captain's offer of his house and occupied every inch of floor space. The sergeants shared the barn with his livestock. The men erected 'shebangs'—lean-tos—built of whatever materials came to hand. Another storm came over the Blue Ridge, bringing rain as cold as ice. The volunteers learned the value of partnering—especially the art of spooning. Men who initially scorned the practice, soon changed their tune.

Those who had sickened in route to Petersburg, were deemed fortunate to be recovering there in the comfort of hospital beds. For their comrades in the field, the wet, cold nights were only the start. Three were dead by the end of the week and more than two hundred would eventually be sent back to Petersburg with pneumonia, or 'debilitas,' i.e. intermittent fever coupled with exhaustion.

Powell's young servant, Amos, demonstrated his resourcefulness. He and Elzie Randle were given a pass and sent south on the Post Road, returning the following morning with a bag of flour, molasses, fat middling, and three hens. The flour was stretched to provide the Hornets a breakfast of ashcakes.

Zou Zou Hartman was another who took his circumstances in stride. The cats of Norfolk had hated to see him go, for he had always fed them well. Indeed, he loved cats and kept the best mousers in his quarters. It was no surprise then, that he adopted one of the Weldon town-cats and brought her north.

Foraging came in many guises. Colonel Battle had a knack for locating those campfires with resourceful chefs. An enticing aroma drew him round to his old friend Zou, whom he found relaxing with his pipe before a fire; a spider of stew, bubbling over the coals. Zou and his mess (the musicians), got to their feet.

"As you were, boys, as you were. I see you are about to serve, I shouldn't intrude—"

"Not at all, *Mon Colonel. 'Aide-toi et Dieu t'aidera.'* God helps those who help themselves. Sir, would you care for a plate of my Alsatian burgoo? We should be honored to share."

"Well, I would not want to . . . do you have enough to go around, sure enough?"

"More than enough, Commandant."

"Well dern, then, aren't you kind? I would hate to see any go to waste."

He produced a plate and a silver spoon, and soon the mess had made short work of the 'special;' conversation suspended long enough to empty the pan.

"An interesting flavor your stew, *mon ami. C'est magnifique*. You exceed all! My compliments, monsieur."

*"Merci, beau coup."*

"You must save a dab for your cat. You know my fondness for cats. Where is she?"

"Absent with leave, sir. Rest assured, she is nearby."

"If I had a scrap I would give it to her."

"You are most kind, sir."

The rest of the mess bowed over their plates, sopping up the last bits of gravy.

"Has she a name, your cat?"

"All my cats have names, sir. Thez one I call *'Nuef.'*"

"Hah! *That's rich*. They say a cat has nine lives." Battle used his thumb to pick his teeth.

"Exactly so, sir. *Ni plus, ni moins*. No more, no less."

T. Jeff Cloud had a coughing fit as a morsel went down the wrong way.

Full stomachs putting a drag on conversation, the colonel knew not to overstay his welcome. He stood, signaling the drummers to remain seated. Battle sucked his spoon clean, gave his stomach a pat, nodded his thanks to one and all.

"Duty calls—carry on," he said, as he wandered off.

\* \* \*

Each morning, the lines for Surgeon's Call grew longer. Doc Lee sent the most serious cases down to Petersburg: fevers, sore throats. Some exhibited a general malaise and loss of weight. If a rash developed on their palms or on the soles of their feet, he recognized them as symptomatic of syphilis; a disease that befell city boys more than not. When a man said he could not march—and had no obvious excuse—well.

" 'A night with Venus, a lifetime with Mercury' " said Tom Johnson to Jim Branscomb. "And *now*, Jim, you know why 'tis called 'The Lagniappe.' "

\* \* \*

Lulu returned to the regiment: the Branscombs boys all together once more. The roads began to dry and the much-maligned teamsters arrived with the baggage wagons, bringing eighty new Enfields for the Lomax Sharpshooters, courtesy of their namesake. The commissary soon was providing full rations again, and the men were able to regain weight.

\* \* \*

Captain Woodruff's commission came and, a few days later, he and Little Joe departed for Montgomery. As he had pledged the widow Baumer: "Where *I* go. *He* goes." 36th Alabama would form up at Mount Vernon Arsenal.

\* \* \*

Battalion and company drill recommenced. When the Eagles' Captain Jelks fell ill, Scotty supervised the drill for his company. Will, the eldest Branscomb brother, came down with measles on May 25, and was packed off to Richmond. He died June 19.

Except for sounds of coughing, Drewy's Bluff was quiet.

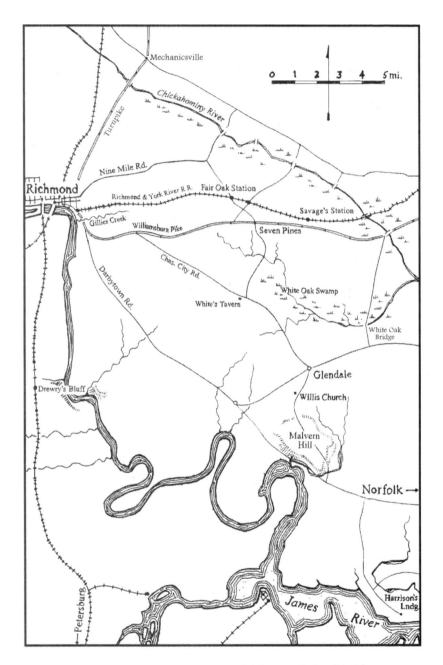

THEATRE - SOUTH AND EAST OF RICHMOND 1862

# King Log

*"Ahem, I say, General . . ."*

Maj. Gen. Benjamin Huger
(in the uniform of a brigadier)

## CHAPTER 27 — GILLIES CREEK
May 30 — 31, 1862

JOSEPH JOHNSTON read the skies over Richmond. The portents appeared favorable; May in the Tidewater had brought her gifts: torrents of rain, creeks over-topping their banks, bridges carried away, roads impassable—perfect conditions for defense. So long as the Chickahominy was up, his opponent's forces remained divided—not by the usual meandering creek but by a raging river, fifty yards wide. The thought of 'Little Mac' losing sleep, produced a twitch at the corner of his mouth, suggestive of a smile.

The general had waited for just this opportunity, ignoring the many demands for action. By concentrating his divisions, the Army of Northern Virginia could destroy two Federal Corps isolated south of the creek: Keyes' IV Corps (holding a wide front east of Fair Oaks station), and Heintzelman's III Corps, in reserve behind Keyes. A decisive thrust forward should do it, and Johnston knew just the place.

Over a map, he had laid it all out for Longstreet: "Nine Mile road meets Williamsburg Pike southeast of Fair Oaks—*here*, at this juncture they call Seven Pines. Keyes holds that crossroads in force. He's put Couch's Division up here in the woods, and Casey's, entrenched in the fields to the west. We will hit Fourth Corps simultaneously, from three directions: you, on Nine Mile; Hill, striking eastward from the pike; Huger's Division converging from the south, off the Charles City Road. Easy as pie." Longstreet hadn't said much, but then he never did.

\* \* \*

The following morning before daybreak, an officer riding west over Williamsburg Pike came to a swollen creek, and its makeshift bridge. On the opposite side, Chimborazo Hill was aglow with campfires: the army of his nation. Providing the countersign, he dismounted.

Normally, Gillies Creek was an obstacle of little consequence, but the rains had carried away its regular crossing and the replacement did not inspire confidence: two rough-hewn planks atop a half-submerged wagon. Between duty and risk, he had no choice. "Is this Huger's Division?"

"Yes, sir. Sure is."

"I carry a message for the Officer Commanding."

The sentry pointed to a group of tents. "General's yonder, lieutenant, on that rise. Best lead yer mount. Fer a bridge it ain't much, but ain't nobody falt in yet."

Crossing without mishap, he picked his way through the encampment, past rows of ragged color lines and sodden shebangs. There was little stir: a few hands going about morning chores, a few soldiers stumbling about to relieve themselves in the minimum number of steps. Others stood wrapped in mud-caked blankets, round balky fires, a Stonehenge of flesh and blood, shifting this way or that, according to the dictates of the smoke. From every side he heard men coughing—the interminable hacking of the 'just shoot the man' sort. On his ride he had passed many such bivouacs. Besides these sights and sounds, the camp was virtually asleep. Such a camp did not exist under the ken of his commander, Major General Daniel Harvey Hill.

At division headquarters he roused a servant to wake someone in authority. A captain and a sergeant major soon appeared, the former buttoning up his fly.

The captain informed him: "Father has received no fresh orders since late last night and, that last one, more in the form of advisory, to move down Charles City Road, today, 'as early as deemed possible,' to 'increase our force' before the enemy." Pointing to the swollen stream the captain shrugged. "Yon footbridge might do for infantry, but never for ordnance."

He waggled two fingers: "Two alternatives present, lieutenant. Wait to rebuild the bridge or, leave the guns behind. As my father is an old artillery man, the latter is a no go."

"My orders are to ascertain General Huger's intentions and serve as guide—"

"At the Point do they not still teach: 'The march must

never be so hurried as to arrive unfit for service?' To be fit, a division needs its guns, would you not say? Regardless of the artillery, the infantry would spoil their ammunition, were we to send them across.

"In point of fact, a second message followed the first, to the effect, he (our esteemed commander, General Johnston) hopes to have cavalry determine the enemy's forces *before* our start. I copied the messages into the division ledger myself."

The lieutenant went in search of more intelligent signs of life. He approached a soldier who offered assistance. At the soldier's side stood a filthy cur—a bitch—the regimental mascot, one would presume. She inspected the lieutenant, lifting her muzzle to fix his scent. The soldier spoke to her softly and she relaxed.

The two escorted the lieutenant to brigade HQ where he was introduced to Brigadier 'Billy' Mahone and Colonel Lomax, the division's odd couple. The lieutenant restated his mission: Hill was holding the Confederate center, in the woods this side of Seven Pines, opposite Casey's batteries. Storming the position would be bloody work. "The general has word to expect Huger's Division to advance this morning, to cover his right flank. I am to guide you to Charles City Road and report back."

As Huger's vanguard, Mahone was exhilarated by the prospect of action. He had his column assemble and make ready to cross the creek. Huger's staff thought otherwise: "As materials arrive, the pioneers will build a proper bridge." Mahone was ordered to stand down. The division would cross as one.

A new (and lengthy) column of troops appeared, from the direction of Chimborazo and, without ceremony, began to file across the plank bridge. The boards were muddy, and wide enough only for one horse or one soldier. These men were Wilcox's Brigade, vanguard of Longstreet's Division. Mahone apprised Huger's ADC of the development.

Longstreet himself, rode up.

Johnston's first message to Huger had advised him to cross Gillies Creek, then advance down Charles City Road to White's Tavern, where he would meet and relieve Rodes' Brigade (freeing them up to rejoin Hill's Division). The tavern was only five miles, a relatively easy march, regardless of conditions. Johnston's messages, however, gave no hint Huger's advance was the critical first step to his entire battle plan. Indeed, the messages made no mention whatsoever of offensive operations. Huger was in the dark. By contrast, Longstreet's Division appeared to be moving with a purpose.

Huger and Longstreet were as different as two men could be. Huger descended from an old Charleston family, graduating West Point near the top of his class; polished, sophisticated, competent. Expendable. As Winfield Scott's chief of ordnance, he served in Mexico with distinction, commanding the siege guns from Vera Cruz to the capitol. In recognition of his service, Scott presented him with Santa Anna's silver spurs. Some years later, he was the obvious choice to send to Crimea, as observer. When Huger resigned his commission in '61, he was a full colonel.

No one ever accused Old Pete of being polished. Raised by his uncle (the famous author and publisher) in Augusta, Georgia, he gained appointment to the Academy through a relation in Alabama, where his widowed mother resided. Though good with numbers, Pete was no scholar and graduated near the bottom of his class (seventeen years behind Huger), a class that included many future stars. Rosecrans, Thomas, Pope, and Doubleday, would stay with the Union, while D.H. Hill, McLaws, and Gus Smith would fight for the South. (Smith was one of the most decorated heroes of the Mexican War and, at Seven Pines, General Johnston's second in command). Longstreet was particularly close with a man in the class just behind his own; they were, in fact, in-laws. Sam Grant was married to Pete's first cousin. In Mexico, Longstreet served in the infantry, receiving two brevets to the rank of major.

Wounded at Chapultepec, he had handed the colors off to yet another classmate, his lieutenant, George Pickett.

In June 1861, Major Longstreet sought opportunities with the State of Alabama before tendering his resignation from the U. S. Army. Since then, his postings had been most fortunate: near to (and under) the eyes of Jeff Davis, Robert E. Lee, and Joe Johnston.

Huger and Longstreet did share a remarkable convergence: both had received their commissions as brigadiers (in the Confederate Army), on the same day: June 17, 1861. On October 7, the War Department elevated both, to the rank of major general.

Huger watched Longstreet's Division cross Gillies Creek, at the rate of a dripping spigot. A word with his colleague would straighten out this little *contretemps*. His division, being the smaller of the two, could cross in half the time and be on its way. *Besides*, he reasoned, fluffing out his whiskers: *Age before Beauty, and all that.*

Certain he also held precedence of rank, Huger rode up to Longstreet and made the blunder of his career.

"*Bonjour*, General Longstreet," he said, without salute. *"Le monde appartient à ceux qui se lèvent tôt."* Longstreet, chewing the nub of a cigar, responded with a curt nod, his eyes never leaving the crossing.

With a sigh, Huger lowered his sights: "I see you are the early bird. I did not expect you to require this route over my creek." When this also produced no answer, Huger pressed the issue. He did not know these younger fellows as well as he should, and wished Longstreet no embarrassment—especially in front of staff.

*There is no call to be rude. However:*

"Ahem. I say, General, do you know which of us two is senior officer here? I profess I do not."

As though wakened, Longstreet twisted slowly in his saddle, to take stock of this man. He was at once reminded of those foreign popinjays common to West Point: swells, from one duchy or another (brandishing titles a mile long), with their gaudy uniforms and boots gleaming like glass. Now comes this old fool with his white hair and formal courtesies. Longstreet half-expected a whiff of perfume, and, ah, yes—there it is.

Cigar clenched between his teeth, he said:
"*I* am."

Huger was struck, not only by the tone, but by the blatant lie; his face reddening, as he realized Longstreet's reply was a *coup de main*. If he had said (as any gentleman should), 'I *believe* I am,' Huger's response would have been prompt: 'I believe you are mistaken'—proper dates and facts, to follow.

But among the brass, were many of the opinion General 'Ooo-zer' was too old for this game; the debacle of Roanoke Island cited as a case in point, his tardiness at Drewry's Bluff as another. Whatever validity these opinions might have, of one thing, all could be certain: Benjamin Huger knew *exactly* where he was on the army's seniority list. The list was a short one with simple rules: rank conferred on identical dates was resolved by last rank held—in the *old* army. Huger had been a full colonel, Longstreet a major.

The stark answer; "*I* am," left Huger only two options: to contradict the general in front of staff, would (in essence) call the man out for a liar. Officers were presumed to be gentlemen, not liars. The older man's upbringing embraced the *Code Duello*: no insult shall be suffered without formal apology, or the letting of blood. Huger did not shy from *affaires d'honneur* but, such a course would require his recognition of Longstreet as an equal.

The remaining option, was temporary acquiescence; placing his trust in army bureaucracy for future redress. And retribution. Looking forward to this prospect, he found his voice: "If you know it, sir, that is sufficient."

It was nearly ten o'clock, the sun was clear of the trees. Benjamin Huger (and his division) were now under command of James Longstreet. Flipping the cowl of his cape over his shoulder, Huger sat his horse, stiffly correct—an obedient subordinate, awaiting the pleasure of his commander. Neither man thought the situation merited putting a second wagon into Gillies Creek.

Turning his horse, Longstreet looked back with a cold smile. "There's your creek," he said, pointing with his chin. "If your boys are not afraid of a little water—be my guest."

## CHAPTER 28 — FROGS
### 4 AM: June 1, 1862

*2d Battalion*

*Hal Martin (C)*

THE SLAP jarred Hal Martin awake, scattering his dream. The one of home, stalking game on a wintry morn with his father. In silence, they weaved through woodland; the game is there, ahead, somewhere—when he hears the faint call of his mother.

"Hen-*ree*," she cries, the last syllable searching him out; *'reeee'* flies over fields and streams, curls through the bottoms, sometimes taking a form only he can hear.

In the dream, Pappy nods to him and they turn for home, which becomes an endless meandering. Stopping to rest, Hal realizes his hands are free. Bafflement is followed by shame, then alarm, as he begins to search for his gun.

"Hen-reeee?"

"Where is it?" his father demands.

"I must. . . ." But here, things always fall apart. Even in a dream, he would never forget his gun. Nor offer an excuse. But the dream is not about that.

"Hen-*reeeeeeee—eee—EEE—eee,*" warbling closer; the whine persists, becoming tangible. The mosquito is dispatched and Hal opens his eyes—to total darkness.

Blinking—he knows they are open. *They must be*. Eyelids wide, then shut; now open again. He squints.

Nothing.

He gulps, *I am too young for*—when the calming burble of water all about, mocks him: *Fool: use your head, not your eyes. Dern swamp. All eyes are blind if there is nothing to see.* He searches the pine tops for the evidence he knows must be there. But the moon is down. With a hunter's patience he spies a flicker of light. S*tar light, star bright.*

Though his legs were nearly numb, his clammy trousers confirmed his sense of touch. Lowering his kerchief, he took a deep breath, inhaling the musty rot of the place. The taint of death stops him: *Wish you might—this ain't no dream.*

Aware of a variety of sounds: whispers, coughing, someone blowing their nose. *Here we are, hundreds of us in the same fix. Surrounded by an army of mosquitos, too; legions of them (less one).* He pulls his kerchief back up. On the edge of his hearing he makes out a call, like in his dream, but nothing like his mother. The Buglers' Signal tells him the armies are stirring.

Whether he had been totally asleep, he did not know, his mind too weary to judge. *The last night we slept, actually slept on dry ground, must have been at Drewry's. How many days back? So very tired.* A second night spent standing. *If I might just lay down, someplace.* Flexing his knees, he plucked at his trousers to free the slime trapped inside.

Last night, the colonel had ordered the regiment off the road, into a V: battalions to left and right, the color guard centered on the road. E and L were sent out to form the picket line, while one company from each battalion, remained on the road. The road was plenty churned, but at least it wasn't under water. The road let one sit or lay down, if one had a mind. Hal couldn't remember which company got the road. No matter, wasn't them.

Hal had fixed bayonet, and aping his comrades, plunged his rifle into the muck, as a support. The rifle's weight was off his shoulder and safe from slipping out of his hands. A quick swab-out, would be all that was needed to restore it from chin-rest to weapon.

More noises. A hawk and a spit preceded a stream of . . . Well, Hal himself had no urge; his bladder as empty as his canteen. Amos and the hands had collected those last night—as many as they could carry—hiking back to the tavern for potable water. *They should be back soon.*

Nose wrinkling at the scent of smoke. *Nothing burning that I can see. No, there it is: a little fire in the road, where the officers are. Officers, drummers and horses.* He wished he were one of Zou's drummer-boys again. *Hell, I'd settle for being a hoss. Any of those over there, would do. No, actually.*

*I wouldn't, neither—I take that back.* The smoke from the fire could not be the source of the smell. This had an oily smell, like barbecue. Not as pleasant. *Don't think of food.*

By ones, then twos and threes, the Tuskegees cursed themselves back to life. *That is Eddie Varner's laugh—cutting up with the Alexanders.* Eddie, one of the fresh fish Captain Mayes pulled in. Marse Varner had insisted Eddie finish his year at Athens. *Nobody at Athens now.*

Through trees, he noticed another light, the broken glow of a torch held aloft. The glow became two, each going its separate way.

*We will head towards that oily smoke, I wager. Where the fight has been.* The smoke smelled very odd—nothing like the brush burns they set back home.

A shower fell from the trees shaking off last night's rain. Though still quite dark, he began to detect edges in the overcast. He looked across the line in the direction of the Rifles. *Must be the dickens on city boys.* At least he knew what it was to sit and wait for dawn; for game. Many a day spent hunkered with Pappy in the Calabee, a swamp much like this one. *Course, we have blinds—and a solid stump to sit on, and cracklin' to nibble.* This sent his hand crawling into his haversack once more—like a bloodhound, it found his extra pair of socks, his tin fork, spoon, and plate. It continued its exploring, his fingernails raking the seams for crumbs previously jilted. Hal whispered:

*"Psst*—Hey, Toby, you awake?"

A non-committal grunt from the darkness.

"Got ennythin'?"

"Nary a cracker. Hollowed out myself, since yesterday."

Hal knew this, of course. Toby, his messmate and friend, sharing everything. "Just makin' talk."

"Yup, yup, yup. Hear ye. *'Hey, fish:* You get your ration of coffee?'"

"No, sir!" Hal answered the cue. "But I have this one-pound poke right here in my kit. *Shall I get it?"*

"Shall I get it?" always got him and he laughed out loud. It remained a popular trope across the regiment.

The sound of a horse pawing water caught his attention. He could just make out the colonel, talking with someone beyond the color guard; the adjutant, Lieutenant Sam, he guessed. Hal heard a new bugle, blowing a ragged reveille. Another, better, and nearer, followed quickly. *Must be the Twelfth back at White's.* Close by, the Third's bugler sounded, crisp and loud.

The drummers beat 'First Call.' Followed soon after by 'Assembly,' signaling all to slosh back to the road, where they formed up by the glow of torchwood. Last in were the pickets. Some of them had spoken with a courier, who told them the enemy had been swept yesterday, and the road ahead was clear. (General Johnston was rumored to be gravely wounded, however, and General Smith in command.) No, the courier could not tell them which General Smith.

The corporals went down their companies, distributing canteens—the hands had made it back. The corporals also passed out strips of white cloth: "To tell friend from foe. It's Orders. Shut up and put 'em on. May save your life."

They received the password: 'Our Hearths' (and the countersign, 'Our Families'). File mates helped one another tie the strips to their arms. Others tucked them into chinstraps or onto their cartridge boxes, one making of it a pretty bow for the front of his kepi. Another Jonah, caused his to hang from his fly. Preacher Tate stared him down: "You know where they'll be aiming, don't you?"

"Boys," said Tate, raising his voice, "This is the day which the Lord hath made. Rejoice and be glad in it." 'Amens' were returned. "We all gonna have smoked *Yankee* for breakfast. Lord willin' and the *Creek* don't rise."

Hal chuckled along with the others. For a sergeant, Preacher was a good fellow. "All right," Tate ordered, "Tuskegee Light Infantry: *Fall* in."

Tate allowed them a few extra seconds. "Arise ye frogs, rejoice, and be glad. C Company: Attention! *SUE*-port, *H'arms.*" He took out his book and pencil.

"Acrey," he began. Silence. "Hey, Acrey: Get the wax out

your ears, 'n listen up."

"Here, Sergeant," came the yawn.

"Don't vex me, Acrey; Alexander, *James*."

"Here, Sergeant."

"Alexander, *John*."

*Corbet Ryder (K)*

The Rifles' routine was identical. When each man's name was called, he brought his rifle to shoulder arms and responded, before lowering it to ground: Order Arms.

"Campbell."

"Here, Sergeant."

"Cherry."

"Sick Call, Sergeant," his file mate answered for him. Shanghai made the note.

"Cherry," he said aloud, "Surgeon's List. Okay. Then, um, lessee: Childress. . . ."

"'*Creek* don't rise?'" Ryder muttered to Charley Keeler. "How does that merit laughter? It ain't even proper English."

"Thas' ole East Alabamy talk, Scotty. 'Creek' meanin' Creek *Injuns*—that the *Injuns* don't rise. Get it?"

"Creek Indians?"

"Fort Mims, Horseshoe Bend. Chief Maubila, 'n all. Way 'fore your time."

*Charley's in no mood for gab*, thought Ryder. *Ol' Woodcock, now* (his usual file mate) *would talk my ears off.* Woodcock had fallen out yesterday. *Probably has his feet up, in a soft hospital bed; a down pillow—lassies to coo over him.*

"What's eating you, Charley?"

"We shoulda been up there yesterday."

"You mean the fight? What's yer hurry?"

"Brother Henry is with Rodes. In the Twelfth."

"Sorry, I'd forgot—"

"Knock it off, there," warned a corporal. The roll continued.

"Crowder."

"Here, Sergeant."

"DeBell."

"Fecal detail, Sergeant."

"Huh? Oh, yes—right. Demerit."

Ryder had not reckoned on the flooded landscape, or the mud—his imagination failing to concoct a circumstance whereby he would be ordered to stand for hours—*under arms, mind*—in a swamp. He smiled ruefully. *What I would not now give for a good night's sleep in my auld corner at Goober's.*

Shanghai continued. "Diamond."

"Here, Sergeant."

"Donaldson."

"You're here, Sergeant."

Shanghai ignored the remark. He was as tired as everyone else.

Ryder looked around. The Rifles had not been hit too hard with sickness. *We should be seventy or so to answer roll.* Roll: the usual game of bait-the-sergeant. As Shanghai called each name, the responses varied greatly. A simple: "Here, Sergeant," was all that was required, but *Hardee's Manual* failed to anticipate the creativity a volunteer army could put into those two words. So, in a head-down monotone against a background of croaks and ribbits, Donaldson persevered, through Ellis, W. pretending hiccups; Garrow (*"Ici, Chef"*), pretending French. Some conspirators worked in concert: farts syncopating Gazzam, Geaudreau, and Getty; efforts wasted on their jaded audience.

Big Bill McDonald earned the morning's *cum laude* with a sultry, "Aye, Thar-gent." Donaldson's pencil paused over the ledger, but he did not look up. *Summa cum laude* must be earned.

"McGuire."

*Dick Stinson (D)*

"Steen-sone, Alonzo."

"Here, Sergeant."

"Steen-sone, Mee-cah-ya."

"Yup."

Muttering a curse, Beaumont let the response stand. 'The great One' was the only volunteer he allowed such license. It had nothing to do with size—Chef was not himself a big man, but he could handle the likes of Old Dick. Still, Chef had never gotten more than 'yup,' no matter how many times. . . . What *galled* was the knowledge Stinson was no bumpkin. "*Qu'est-ce que c'est 'yup'?*" Chef demanded of his fellow sergeants. They assured him the answer did not connote disrespect. It was just Old Dick being Old Dick.

"Steen-sone, *To-mas*."

"Here, Sergeant."

Old Dick had slept poorly. Mosquitos partly; worries mostly. Standing in rank, weariness enfolded him, making him feel dull, though he listened out for his brothers' responses. Lon and Tom both sounded hale. Good.

It was Alonzo had gotten him to volunteer at the get-up. As a husband and a father, it was neither required, nor expected.

The fitting by the tailor was memorable. Recording Dick's length and breadth, the little man turned giddy, took his measure twice. Through a mouthful of pins, "I should be using cubits." To get his brother's goat, Dick turned to Lon, "Hear that, Shorty?"

Not the thing to say. Barely six foot, Lon was sensitive about his height. He was a tough knot, however, and despite the occasional spat seldom gave Dick cause for concern. No, it was Tom, he worried over. *So thin*. And at six foot three, clearly, he had some growth left in him. Dick wished Tom were anywhere but here. Joining them right before the evacuation, the Hornets had immediately named him 'Babe.' Dick tried not to hover. Sickness could hit a man hard the first weeks. But Tom remained healthy as a jake.

Dick was always on the right—always a 'one'—'the great One,' owing to his height. Company Ones were always first to form line, establishing the proper spacing and alignment. His wife's youngest brother (her favorite) was all the way over on the other end, one of the 'shorties.' But even at five-foot-four, Frank Bickley was more than a match for most. (Much like 'Chef Beau,' come to think of it.) Dick knew better than to come back home without Frank.

"Yarring-tone, Ro-bare," and "Yarring-tone, To-mas," completed the roll call.

"Prepare for Inspection."

Setting the rifles before them, the men pulled the ramrods and, giving them a flip, let them slide through their fingers down the barrels, each sounding a gentle ping as it hit bottom. Together, the pings sounded like wind chimes, a sound that always reminded Dick of home. He had made a wind-chime for Emily when they were courting; others for the children, as they came along.

Lieutenant Randle stepped in front of him. With eyes locked on each other, Dick presented for Inspection. Randle snatched the rifle away. Giving the weapon a practiced jerk, he nabbed the rod. Releasing it, the additional ping verified the barrel was clean. Eyes dropping to the weapon, Randle cocked the hammer to safety, working the trigger, looking for any sign of dirt or rust in the lock or in the nipple. Easing the hammer down, again their eyes met. Without a word, Randle shoved the Enfield back at Dick, who recovered. Sidestepping to the next man, the procedure repeated.

Dick removed the rod and grooved it back into its slot, returning the rifle to his side. He resumed breathing. No one ever twice-failed a rifle inspection to Troup Randle. Dick felt unnerved by only two men: Troup Randle when he was angry, and Troup Randle the rest of the time. Troup barely came up to Old Dick's chin. But in a peculiar way, that was what bothered him. At these times, Troup, looking up, would cock his head—like a cottonmouth—fascinated by the throbbing pulse under the jaw. The night of the reorganization, then-sergeant Randle lit into the faction still carping on Captain Powell, shoving the truth down their throats, till they were ashamed to vote for anyone else. For good measure, they elected Randle first lieutenant.

When the mood suited him, Randle could also be funny as hell. It was a mystery to Dick, why Randle allowed him to get away with 'yup.' Three files down, Randle stopped before a new boy.

"Double-knot those shoes, *re*-croot! Think we're off on some *got*-damn picnic? The war supposed to wait on you, while you look for your shoes?

"Anyone here think we're going on a picnic today? Speak now if you do. Speak up! Hand that man your rifle and tie those shoes. Who is your squad sergeant, boy? Sergeant Baker? Sergeant Baker: why does this *re*-croot think he is going on a picnic today?"

"I cannot say, sir."

"Have you scheduled a picnic, Sergeant Baker?"

"No, sir."

"This *re*-croot seems to think you have."

"The recruit is mistaken, sir."

"Not even a small one? Some sublime affair you have forgotten to tell me about?"

"No, sir! No picnic is scheduled."

"The picnic you-would-have-*invited-me-to*—had you scheduled one."

*"Yes, sir!"*

"Good, Sergeant. I am *always* to be invited to company picnics."

Leaving the sergeant to deal with his recruit, he moved on. A few files down, a ramrod landed with a muffled thud. No one breathed.

*Major Forsyth*

Forsyth moved his horse a few paces off the road, awaiting the colonel's orders; keeping one eye on Second Battalion inspection, the other on Lomax, who was in talks with Battle and Sands. A courier arrived, reporting to Lomax. The colonel, nodding, sent the adjutant off to convey his orders.

Lomax had been in an odd mood earlier, so Forsyth was reluctant to insert himself here, *persona non grata*. Lomax had made Sands brevet-Major without any consultation. Battle rarely spoke to him—then, only for the minimum required by military necessity.

He leaned over for his servant to tie the white cloth on his arm. The teams that had brought up the six-pounder last night were re-hitched, to move the piece back to the rear. Huger must want it back.

Captain Powell approached.

"Captain Powell."

"Major Forsyth. Sir: I raise a question regarding seniority on the line."

*Hal Martin (C)*

Hal counted forward from the last day that he could remember being dry: *The twenty-ninth, maybe? Boarding the cars at Drewry's Bluff?* When the colonel had addressed the regiment: "Third Alabama has long wished to get into this fight. We are now going where I can promise you: we will soon be engaged." Interrupting their cheers, he continued: "Keep your wits about you. Maintain discipline. Keep cool—be *silent,* that you may hear your orders. In line, touch elbows—close ranks—guide to the colors.

"And may God bless you, and bless our cause."

From there to Richmond had been all about polishing and cleaning. Their trousers grown shabby from two weeks in the woods, many kept Parade clothes for just these occasions, the Third having its reputation to maintain.

From the train Hal caught his first glimpse of the city; a citadel bristling with weapons and fortifications, unassailable, unconquerable. The state house perched on its hill made a worthy Parthenon. The capitol at Montgomery was large, yes, but—well, it was just large. It could not compare to the grandeur of Richmond.

Left of the state house was Washington's column, George

and his horse rearing o'er the trees, at the ready, as though the nearby steeple was their starting post. More church steeples punctuated the horizon. Nearer them, by the river, Tredegar's smokestacks belched smoke, testament to the guns being forged there every hour of every day.

Easily, the most beautiful city he had ever seen, Richmond was worth the fight.

Peering through the slats of his car it was cheering to see shops and buildings again. *Look at all the brickwork. Granite! That one must be the Spotswood Hotel—six stories high,* he counted. The city was surrounded by trenches and redoubts, and by clear fields of fire. *Must be miles n' miles of 'em. If this be the work of Granny Lee, he is rightly named 'King of Spades.'* Lee's star, once so bright, had been dimmed by the loss of western Virginia. *I hope he is better at ditches.* From the trestle over the James they saw Belle Isle set up to receive Yankee prisoners.

They had not exactly arrived in style. While yet over the river, during the last slow crawl into the station, the men took the opportunity to relieve themselves, the cars temporarily transformed into an ill-made fire hose. Accustomed to this spectacle, ladies, waiting in the terminus turned their heads or engaged in animated conversation.

As the men clambered down, they brushed straw from their uniforms and helped one another don packs, making themselves presentable. Hal watched the Mobile boys pulling out their gloves, white gloves (and black cravats) being a required part of their dress uniform, the proper dress of a gentleman. Invariably, the practice invited their provincial comrades to hold their pinkies aloft in mock salute. Macon County's boys didn't use gloves. *Though that sure would have been a good day to have 'em. Mobile did look grand.*

*So that was the twenty-ninth—No, the thirtieth. Where does that extra day come from?*

The brigade assembled outside the terminus, commands bouncing off the huge brick warehouses, hobnailed boots clattering and slipping over the pavers. Amos and the other grooms led staff officers' horses through the bustle, the horses laden with the officers' needs, and spare mounts with staffs' tents, poles, and cots (commissary and baggage, once more, miles to the rear). The men had all they could carry, haversacks bulging—the hard lesson learned at Drewry's.

At the head of the street, Lomax and Battle and Forsyth waited for the sergeants to bellow the men into ranks. When all was ready, the adjutant commanded: *"Third Alabama!"* The alert was repeated forcefully by the captains of battalion. "Ah–ten—*Hut!*" The men snapping together like a steel trap, the surrounding brick walls echoing its own syncopated applause: sardonic, mocking, fading.

They wait.

The colonels confer with city officials. Runners come and go. The adjutant remembers to order Parade Rest. The grateful troops shift their rifles, only to wait some more.

In the swamp, Hal's reverie is interrupted by Mr. McGinty's coughing up phlegm. A process. *They should send him home. We can't be so hard up. Swamps and marches no place for bad lungs.*

All of Richmond turning out to cheer her heroes, the brigade heard the roars billowing from Capitol Square, five blocks away; earlier-arriving regiments are there, parading beneath Washington's statue—answering the citizens' cheers with hoo-rahs of their own.

Though the day grew warm, the shadowed streets near the station remained cool, ventilated by the breeze from off the river. Orders arrived. Lomax straightened in his saddle, tugging his coat. At the signal, they moved off in route-step, up the hill at Eighth Street. At Cary, a provost, seeing their banners, offered: "The Alabama warehouse is down this street. 'Cross from the Spotswood Hotel." Repeating this loudly for each passing company. Richmond warehouses had been contracted to support the states' hospitals, and to provide storage for her regiments. "All right, boys, you heard the man," said one comic, "It not jes yo' momma 'n sweethearts we afightin' fer—all yall's socks 'n drawhs is countin' on you, too!"

At the top of the hill they made column right, coming to right-shoulder shift, falling smoothly into step for the final march to the square. Rifles gleaming, few regiments could match the turnout of the Third, a picture of pride, polish, and precision. The cheers became a roar once the crowd spotted Alabama's flag. Many in the crowd knew boys in the Third. Many more had heard of their handsome colonel and his famous 'kid glove regiment.' They were not disappointed. In perfect cadence front to back, not a head bobbing out of step, those white gloves rising and falling like a metronome, they entered the square. "Eyes—"

*"Left."* Every head snapping round to the dignitaries, their left arms crossed their chests in the classic salute.

Halted before the capitol, they went through an arms drill, eliciting applause and whistles. *To have been part of that.* The memory brought a lump to his throat.

Restricted to the confines of the square, the regiment stacked arms and rested in the shade near a small statue of Henry Clay.

Tricked-out like a state fair, Capitol Square displayed banners of every size and hue. Tables were dressed in linen and laden with platters of food. Ladies' societies vied to see which would provide the best or the most—or prove most popular with 'the boys.' Tables with the prettiest servers had the longest lines. Food was on Hal's mind. He had never seen such spreads. In line for seconds, an elderly matron spoke to him. "Now, Sonny, where might you be from? Alabama? Oh my! Oh, my gracious me, that *is* a long way, isn't it? You must be homesick. Well, you just help yourself to what–so–ever–you–want, dearie—there's plenty. Oh, you are *so* like my grandson, so tall and so handsome. Billy Taylor; do you know my Billy? You might know him as Master William Taylor—of the Powhatan Taylors? But he's still just our sweet little Billy. Anderson's Brigade? No? Well, they are *quite famous,* I assure you. You *really* don't know them? No, I don't know his *regiment*, but he is in Captain Harris' company. Or is it—land sakes, well. . . . Pardon? Yes, there are so many of you boys. Now, you go on, take another biscuit for your side-bag. Chile, I swan, you are nothing but skin and bones. What would your mother say? Go on now, take another. Don't make me fuss at you."

Later, when the windstorm came, it seemed conjured just to sweep them out of town, a great cleansing, in the wake of the army. The army bivouacked east of town, on Chimborazo Hill, and, for a time, all enjoyed the thunder and rain: nature showing off. When a bolt of lightning hit a cluster of men, not a hundred yards from them, the aesthetics lost all its allure. When the gas works flooded, the lights of the city blinked out. When the tents blew down, the pies and biscuits were ruined. Not a man in the army had been dry, or well-fed, since that night.

The following morning, Huger's Division marched a short distance to camp beside flooded Gillies Creek. Hal thought: *more like Gillies Marsh*.

*The Thirtieth!* He was certain. *It was next morning General Huger and Longstreet had their set-to. That would have been yesterday. So, today is the first of June—the Sabbath—the day of rest.* Hal was satisfied they had been drowned only two full days. It seemed like two months.

*1st Battalion*

*Brevet Major Sands*

"All present and accounted for, sir."

"Thank you, sergeant. Carry on." Broun returned Ledyard's salute.

Standing to one side Sands watched the exchange, his frustration mounting with every hour, towards those higher-ups responsible for this mess. He was (in the new parlance), 'pissed.' *Yes. Somehow that does convey the right spirit, however vulgar.*

The new major did not display his pique, maintaining an air of imperturbability before the men. But he was not happy.

Lomax had informed him of his brevet rank in route from Drewry's. "I want you on a mount for the coming fight," Lomax had told him. "Your place in the chain of command, evident." Lomax confided he had been assured a brigadier's commission; he would soon be leaving the Third. Given that eventuality, he said, Sands' promotion would be permanent. Departing from his beloved Cadets would be difficult, but Sands had every confidence in Harley Broun. Casey Witherspoon was just as able.

He did wonder at the callousness required for one to order a regiment into a swamp, and, to keep them there, unfed, un-watered—*unable to rest*—on the eve of battle. He should have been able to point to Huger as the obvious incompetent. But the general's authority had been publicly usurped. Longstreet's Division had taken three hours to cross Gillies Creek.

At White's Tavern, couriers had come with details of the long, drawn-out fiasco: Longstreet's Division completed their crossing by early afternoon. General Wilcox, left in command, remained in place on the far side, awaiting Huger's Division. Once that was accomplished Third Alabama (and Mahone's Brigade) was detached to double-quick down Charles City Road (with the remainder of Huger's Division following at a normal pace), in front of Wilcox.[11]

There was more: Further orders came from Longstreet: Huger's two brigades were to halt, so that Wilcox's five could pass them to take the lead. Fine. All marched in this arrangement for a short distance, when fresh orders arrived *to countermarch.* Longstreet meant them to be on Williamsburg Pike. All now reversed (Huger's brigades leading once more), back to the starting point. They had retraced their steps one mile, when yet another order was received: they were to reverse

---

[11] By proceeding down Charles City Road, Huger was merely executing the last orders he had received from Johnston (having received nothing counter from Longstreet at Gillies Creek). Should Wilcox follow the same route, it was a matter of no concern to Huger.

course *again* and parallel the furious fighting that could be plainly heard from D.H. Hill's position on the pike. Guides finally arrived, who took them through the flooded woods, cross-country, towards the fighting; the troops wading in some places, through water waist deep. With nightfall, they halted in the swamp, still short of the pike.

*A Maypole dance would have been better managed,* thought Sands; *Longstreet seeming more at sea as to his instructions than was Huger—no easy thing. Something very odd was afoot. And how can Longstreet be senior to Huger? But that is their business.*

Avoiding most of this comedy of errors, the Third made good time. By the time they arrived at White's Tavern, however, the impatient Rodes was gone, released by Hill to march to the sound of the guns. In doing so, Rodes saved the day.

Mahone's trailing regiments arrived in due course. The brigadier ordered Lomax a half-mile north, and once there, to deploy his men across the road. Half of Turner's Virginia Battery went with them. 12th Virginia, 41st Virginia, and the remaining section bivouacked at the tavern.[12]

There was no lack of comment regarding Longstreet. For all the marching to-and-fro, it was offered: a two-mile trench must be the result, where the legs (and arms) of eight brigades had gone for naught.

Darkness coming on, Chester's Infantry went into the swamp where the outposts formed a curved line. One of Turner's guns remained on the road to back them up. Behind the regiment, the Cadets, and the second gun, served as rear guard. Broun picketed Witherspoon's squad 100 yards out.

Some hours later, Witherspoon, hearing a column advancing, discerned a dim light, low to the ground, bouncing to-

---

[12] At this stage of army organization, each Confederate division had an artillery battery attached. Turner's guns presumably made it across Gillies Creek late on May 31. They did not advance to Seven Pines due to the flooded conditions.

wards them at the cadence of a walk. With a whisper, the sergeant is sent back to alert the artillery officer. With thumping heart, he stepped forward and issued the challenge:

"Halt!"

The bouncing light stops. Behind it, the squish of a marching column also slows to a halt; the sound of a horse blowing. The light, quivering in place, pivots abruptly to the left and goes out. Curses follow. Witherspoon realizes the light is merely a lantern extended on a boom—a road lamp.

"Who comes there?"

The horse walking slowly forward.

"Who comes, I say? Another step and I fire!"

The horseman halts.

Witherspoon hears a hurried back and forth. Finally, an exasperated voice: "*You* say it."

The second voice clears his throat, and offers: "Friends?"

"Stand, friend. Advance one, on foot, with the password."

The invisible stranger comes forward and stops. His senses on edge, Witherspoon hears something resembling a croak.

"Speak up or die," he states.

The stranger replies: "Our Hearths."

## CHAPTER 29 — CASEY'S REDOUBT
Morning: June 1, 1862

"IT IS FORTY-FIRST Virginia, general, leading Mahone's Brigade. Third Alabama follows, then Twelfth Virginia. No artillery." The aide de camp had spotted 'Little Billy' straight away and, lowering his glass, began to rattle off the names of the brigade's field officers. The general was in no mood. "I know who their officers are, lieutenant."

*Who else would it be: a day late, and a dollar short?*

Harvey Hill's relentless soliloquies were a way of coping with the fools (believed) to be surrounding him; a blunt and caustic man to all but family. *Little-Less Billy and Colonel Lummox. Aren't they the pair? The tavern boy and Mister Silk-Stocking himself, both under the wing of that doddering buffoon, Huger. Heaven help us.*

Hill and his aide stood atop Casey's Redoubt—west of two large frame houses known as 'the Twins,' the center of yesterday's fighting. The battery was taken only after the most desperate struggle. Firing from up in the trees, sharpshooters had cut down the Yankees' artillery teams, preventing the guns withdrawal. The fallen still lay in heaps, horrible in death. The Southern portion, having been removed, were arrayed in rows—where they had begun to bloat. Moans and cries emanated from the Twins, where the surgeons presumed to work.

Longstreet had paid his visit, and, while leaving Hill no meaningful instructions ("You have taken the bull by the horns, and must fight him out"), did leave him fresh brigades from his own division. From Wilcox's column: Wilcox, Pickett, Colston, Kemper, and Pryor. Behind them, two from Huger: Armistead and Blanchard. And now, literally the last: Mahone's Brigade.

In the absence of their own division commanders, Hill ordered Armistead and Pickett and Pryor into the woods north and east of the redoubt. *Let them get their feet wet. They're fresh—and true-blue Virginians. Mostly. Pryor has a mixed bag.* Hill expected a report from Armistead at any moment.

He focused on his ugly ducklings, knowing all he needed to know about the Third. He had heard the talk and his expectations were correspondingly low.

*Just look at them: 'Make way for fortune's favorites.' Covered in mud, head to toe. 'Oh? Sleeping in the swamp last night, were we?' Bless their hearts. And, this morning, Mahone deigns to let them tour our battlefield. Will miracles never cease?*

"Compliments, Mahone, and get him over here," Hill instructed the aide, sending him off while he continued to monitor their progress. *I'll be . . . the devils are peeling off to plunder the supply barn. Men died yesterday so these 'gentlemen' can loot Yankee coffee; Mahone can't be bothered to report to me first.*

Through his glasses Hill saw the aide pull up to Mahone, faces turning and arms pointing in his own direction. Hill resumed his muttering: "Thaaat's right, Billy, run along over here. Headmaster is here." *Damned Chihuahua.* He could not look upon Billy Mahone without recalling those nasty little ratters down Mexico way.

Mahone's entourage cantered towards him. He did not see General Huger. *Just as well. Would muddle the chain of command. Probably still at his breakfast.* Standing outside Casey's former headquarters, he identified Chambliss of 41st Virginia, and Weisiger of the 12th. *And now Lomax, the man who can't bear the thought of his regiment being disciplined. No buck and gag for the 'Bandbox Regiment,' no sirree. Who else is with the Third? Battle? Yes, the great lawyer. We know all about him. Got his boys off the Virginia. Must have been afraid they might actually have to fight. That one prancing his little charger must be the Forsyth boy–'the boy Major.' How old can he be? No doubt Daddy bought that promotion for him too. Well, well, well . . . And what was that amusing tale Armistead was telling, of his encounter with the wagon master from the Third?*

Colonel Gordon, Sixth Alabama, approached. Hill awarded him a wan smile; the Sixth had fought like heroes yesterday. Before Gordon could speak, a rattle of musket fire from the north woods.

\* \* \*

Emerging from the swamp, Rafe Herrin felt he had thrown off the lid of his own coffin. His rapture was brief. Picking up their pace, from file, the brigade formed columns in cadence. As the sun broke through, they got their first look at a battlefield.

"*Shee-eee-it*. Ain't this inviting as all," said Rafe. The landscape, such as it was, was unlike anything the volunteers had ever seen: devastation in every direction. The fields lay flattened beneath sheets of standing water, broken here and there by mounds of mud and by rows of felled pine dragged into place for defense. A dozen columns of dense, yellowish smoke rose skyward. All the convenient fuel—branches and fence railing—had been consumed by the Yankees; planks from the turnpike had been re-purposed for breastworks. Like ants on a mission, men trudged back and forth to the woods, seeking firewood.

At Seven Pines crossroads was a cluster of houses and sheds. About half a mile west, the two identical houses. They fronted a line of shade trees, under which numerous horses and vehicles were drawn up.

They marched towards the redoubt, past a cantonment of mildewed tents occupying the area south of the Twins. Nearing the redoubt, Rafe realized the mounds of mud were not earth at all, but mules, still in their traces. More than one had been carved up for rations. Smaller mounds had not been touched, but they were not mules. Idle soldiers lined their route, inspecting the new regiment.

Smoke and pine resin added a heavy tang to the air, but did little to cover the odor of excrement, until a fourth stench overpowered all. Rafe and his comrades recoiled in disgust. The officers were indignant: "Uncover those mouths, you men."

Passing a barn, filled with captured supplies, they caught a whiff of coffee—real coffee. A squad from each battalion was permitted to enter and scoop up provisions, and distribute the first rations any had received since Richmond. The foul air had no effect on Rafe's appetite. Studying one torso, its ribs splayed like lamb cutlets, he pondered whether he was viewing someone's front, or back.

Hill's ADC arrived at the barn; Mahone and his colonels sped away to report. Rafe heard the musketry to the north.

At Hill's headquarters, preliminaries were brief—everyone had met one another over the past months. A crude map of the area was on the table. Barely a word was uttered before a staff officer rode up and reported. Pointing north, the rider declared, "Yankees are advancing in yonder woods, general."

With a cold eye upon Mahone, Hill swept his arm in the same direction: "General, take your men in there. Be advised, Pryor's Brigade is in column to the north." Mahone protested the poor condition of the terrain. His men would become mired, and make easy targets. The observation was not worth his breath. Hill dismissed Mahone and his colonels, to return to their commands, who now were at the redoubt.

Hill estimated the Third's lengthy ranks—six hundred, or more—twice the number of any other regiment present. But he had expected more, having been told the Third numbered nearly half again as many. They wore the white cloth bands he had ordered, a few tied playfully into cravats or bows. He indicted them with a sour look. *High time these dandies learn war is no game.* Hill looked towards the survivors of Fourth North Carolina—staggering losses yesterday, eighty-percent or more; 12th Alabama: fifty percent. He surveyed the rows of dead, where the bodies remained obscene, their trousers and jackets tight as sausage casings. Many were barefoot, but not all: some shoes could not be pried off. Those men with abdominal wounds—gut shot—had died in groping anguish, trousers unbuttoned.

And the flies. Of course, the flies: feasting on the wounds, foraging over eyes; inspecting nostrils, and mouths, and ears. *God, how they ate us up in Mexico.* Hill turned to face the mud-encased Third Alabama. Some were employing bayonets, to scrape down their trousers. *Bandbox indeed.* So that his contempt could not be mistaken, he leaned forward elaborately, and spat upon the ground.

Standing at ordered rest, the eyes of the entire regiment had followed Hill, a fresh actor upon their stage. Hill had a reputation, was said to be a hard man—as hard a man as his brother-in-law, the great Stonewall.

At Hill's insult, they stiffened, each reacting as though he had been personally slapped.

"Well, *lar–dee–dar,*" growled someone from down the line. "Peckerhead," muttered Old Dick. Someone in the back rank let go a loud fart.

"*SILENCE* in the ranks!" Chef Beaumont bellowed.

"'Couter up, boys, I believe we got us a King Stork," said Rafe.

"I know zat voice, *volontaire,*" warned Beaumont.

To reassert control, the companies were ordered to attention, to count by files. Duets of "One. *Two!* One. *Two!* One. *Two!*" sped down the ranks. Useful, if for nothing else, to remind the new boys their correct positions under maneuver. Old Dick, reaching in his pocket, pulled out a small pack of cotton. Tearing off two wads, he rolled them and punched them into his ears, passing along enough for Tom, who did the same.

Orders rang out. "Brigade: *Atten-HUT. Column.*" 41st was near the road, Third, by the redoubt, then 12th Virginia.

Charley and Oliver Keeler, having a brother in 12th Alabama, had been granted a moment to search for him. Along a row of bodies, Charley stopped, and signaled Oliver over. Wasting no time, he knelt to cut a lock of hair, then searched inside Henry's jacket. Standing quickly, he stopped the arriving Oliver, handing him what he found. The two trotted back to their places in column. Charley fell in next to Scotty.

"Found him."

Following the 41st, the Third marched west along the pike, skirting the defenses around the redoubt.

Lomax spied Colonel Gordon standing with his staff in the shade of the Twins. Reining his horse over, Lomax greeted his young friend.

"You are a long way from the Raccoon Roughs, Colonel Gordon."

Gordon grinned. "A few are still with me, Brother Lomax. Their tails a mite worse for wear, I do allow."

Time was short.

"I was hoping I would see you. Give me your hand, Gordon, and let me bid you good-by." He leaned over to grip the younger man's hand. His next remark wiped the smile from Gordon's face. Noting the reaction Lomax sought to put him at ease. "It is all right, my friend, it is all right." With an easy smile and salute, he spurred the horse and was away. The exchange staggered Gordon. Turning to his staff officers, *"Did I hear him right?"*

General Hill to his aide: "Complements, Colonel Weisiger, Twelfth Virginia; he is to take his regiment due north—short of the woods—where he will establish a defensive perimeter parallel to the Pike, to protect the redoubt." The aide echoed the order, geed his horse and sped away, catching up with Weisiger at the rear of Mahone's column.

Hill looked about him, at the wounded and the dead of his division: Rodes', Jenkins', and Garland's Brigades, and at the ambulance men tending them. He looked to the west, where survivors of yesterday's battle sheltered in the woods.

*We pay a high price.*

Hill winced. His back. The pain was killing him. *God's will—why should today be any different?*

\* \* \*

Mahone, and his regiments, in columns by company, neared the western border of the field. He directed them at the north woods. One hundred yards from the trees he ordered: "Right, and forward into line." Swiftly, each company formed two seamless ranks. Mahone looked round for Weisiger— wanting 12th Virginia in reserve—and was astounded to see them marching away at the oblique. His remaining regiments continuing their line of march: 41st Virginia on the left, Third Alabama on the right. The latter seeing where Armistead's brigade had preceded them, a causeway of fresh-trampled mud leading to the woods.

Weaving through fresh-cut pine stumps, both regiments' lines repeatedly broke up and reformed. Lush with undergrowth, the woods ahead were dark and foreboding.

## CHAPTER 30 — NINE MILE
8AM: June 1, 1862

### *2d Battalion*[13]

JOHN HOYT, feeling the burden of a hundred details, tried to anticipate the next sequence of orders. Dropping their knapsacks and pulling down chinstraps, the men executed 'Right, and forward into line.' On the right, Battle ordered: "Load and prime," pulling the Dixie Eagles out of line to create the First Battalion reserve. The Cadets—Company A—dressed to the colors, rejoining I, B, G and F. Forsyth mirrored Battle's order, holding back Chester's Infantry. Lomax, arriving at the canter, ordered: "Forward, Third!"

Stepping off, the battalions skirted the rows of felled pine and were soon entering the woods, the drummers following, just ahead of the field officers and couriers. A line of servants, themselves armed with muskets, came last.

Immediately, the Rifles encountered elements of Ninth Virginia—men of Armistead's Brigade. They had been ambushed and were leaderless and disorganized, many without rifles. They were reluctant to exit the woods in the face of Mahone's advance. The Rifles pushed through them, only to be halted shortly after by a similar band, still wearing their white armlets. Bolder than those previous, these men had had enough and wanted to get to the safety of the open fields. For once, the Rifles said nothing, and simply watched them go.

From here the undergrowth was formidable, and they began to appreciate the Ninth's behavior. Hoyt lost contact with Forsyth and the other companies of the Left, though the Tuskegees—left flank of First Battalion—were in sight on his right, and, occasionally, the colonel and his staff, hacking through the tangle. Sporadic fire came from their front, the bullets zipping through the foliage.

---

[13] Presumably, 2d Battalion's line is arranged per *Hardee's* dispersal of seniority, i.e. from left to right: **D**, **H**, **K**, E, **C** (E in reserve); 1st Battalion LOB is: **I**, **B**, **G**, **F**, L, **A** (L in reserve). See chapter notes.

Arriving at a section of beaten-down vegetation, the Rifles found the Ninth's abandoned color line and evidence of the recent attack. Some rifles were still in stacks, others toppled over, underscoring just how unaware the Virginians had been to the proximity of their enemy. Contempt vanishes when a volley blows through their own ranks—the source invisible, but straight ahead. Fortunately, the fire was wild. With a cheer, the Rifles plunged headlong into the brush. The shiver of foliage indicating the enemy was falling back—just beyond their reach through the hanging smoke. Hoyt signaled his sergeants to spread the line; Jimmy Howard to re-establish contact with the Tuskegees, or with anyone else he might find that way. Forty more yards brought them to a boggy little hollow.

Ahead, they spied a Federal encampment, with its troops not yet formed. From their concealed position Hoyt brought his men into a tight line and, with a single volley, sent the Yanks reeling. Crossing the road they entered the camp, just as their enemy melted away. Dashing ahead, Caroline gamboled through the tents, returning to Shanghai's side, with a rasher of bacon in her jaws.

Down the road, the Wetumpkas, and elements of First Battalion, emerged from the woods, followed by the Tuskegees From the other side, the rest of Second appeared and shifted down the road towards them. The Yankees, meantime, were taking pot shots from cover. Lying prone, the Rifles returned fire, and for a minute or two the Yankees were game. But the marksmanship of the Rifles—sighting their targets beneath the rolled-up canvas of the tents—took its toll and the enemy fell back.

The Rifles have three casualties—one shot dead. Hoyt directs the body to a nearby tent.

The Tuskegees had worked their way through the difficult woods too, before finding the road. Mayes was disoriented until he saw Hoyt and the Rifles. The Wetumpkas (left flank of First Battalion) were already on the road. Ready directs them towards the camp where the regiment is reforming, Robinson

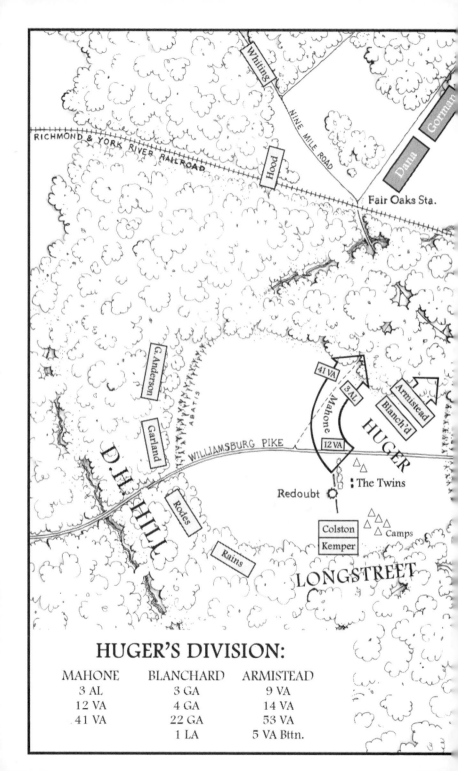

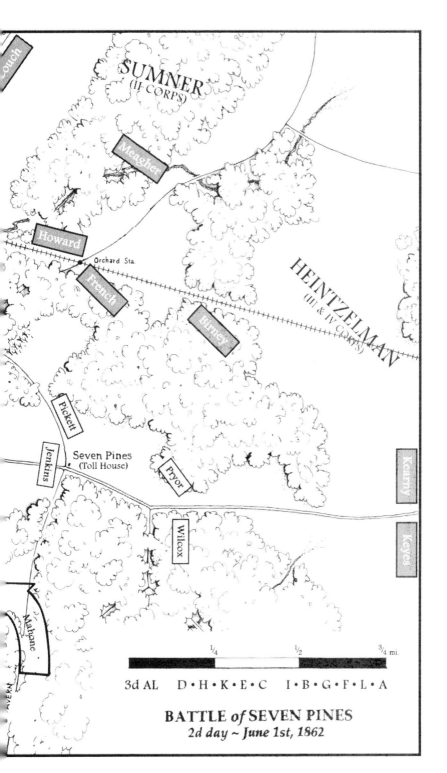

sends a runner to bring in Powell's Hornets. Major Forsyth, with his aide and couriers, also emerges.

Ravenous, the men snatched rations straight from the pans, or went pillaging through the tents. Hal Martin found a canteen full of coffee and several tins of sardines. Stuffing one into his jacket he flipped the extras to Toby and to Toby's elder brother, John. Johnny-come-latelies have to accept Preacher's prophesy of 'Yankee' for breakfast—the chance for anything more quickly vanishes.

The sergeants and corporals began to work in concert. As the men assembled, the noncoms made sure everyone was loaded and capped. A soft-spoken 'Attention,' brought each company to Order Arms. Lomax issued instructions to Battle, to Forsyth, and to Adjutant Johnston: Find the enemy and press him.

Before the battalion commanders broke off to return to their posts, Lomax directed a horse be brought up for Sands. Staff aides (and servants, often) were ponying remounts for this purpose. These remounts, and the surgeons and other staff personnel, entered the clearing. Last in, was Zou, looking about as happy as a wet cat. He received a sardonic cheer. A minie ball had ruined his drumhead, briers had shredded his trousers, and his gaiters were black with mud.

Once Doc Lee had set up under a fly, the ambulance men paired off to bring in the wounded.

Lomax surveys the scene. His charger champs impatiently; sixteen-three and clipped for brush, the bay seems to say: *Let me go*. But the colonel has him well in hand. With a word to his aides he wheels the horse, and sidestepping, centers on the regiment. The colors are uncased: the white and blue regimental and the Stars and Bars, the men cheering loudest for their state's blue banner. 'The Time Has Come,' emblazoned above the star, dances, and seems to taunt. Lomax flashes his smile, vanishing the moment he stands in his stirrups. Brandishing his sword overhead he thunders his orders, his voice ringing through the clearing, syllables rising and falling like a chant:

*"THIRD A-la-BAM."*

Six hundred men: shoulders square, eyes front.

*"FIX!"*

Six hundred rifles swivel forward, left hands poised.

*"BAYONETS!"*

Six hundred blades sweep from their scabbards. The saber-like 'Yankee ticklers,' catch the morning light. They flash in arcs, leaping like powder fuses that dazzle the eye. There follows the distinctive, clapping, clattering rhythm of steel on steel as the men place them, turn them, and lock them down.

Returned to Order Arms, the men stand still as stone. Smoke, lingering from the musketry and overturned campfires, spreads the morning's glare. For a moment the colonel is enveloped in this aura: the regimental behind him, billowing, and set aglow by the sun. The weariness and hunger of days past, the frustrations of fourteen months, the scorn of rivals, forgotten under his gaze: *their* colonel. The charger, contemptuous of delay, snorts once again. *Let me go.*

Senses heightened, every man feels cleansed beneath the warming sun; in the moment, hearing the smallest sounds: the creak of leather on leather, the soft jangle of bits, the sound of canvas as it billows and pops.

*"SHOUL–DUH,"* the order echoes down the line.

*"ARMS!"*

The rifles are hoisted as one.

*"BAH–TALIONS—"* (the captains relay: *"COMPANY—"*)

*"CHARGE . . . BAYONETS!"* Lowering their rifles with a heavy step forward, the men present *en garde.* Lomax, reining his horse towards the new woods, swings his sabre forward.

*"THIRD ALABAMA!"*

Hoyt, inside the tent where the men have lain Tom Bell's body, hears the colonel's command as clearly as though he were just feet away:

*"THIRD ALABAMA: DO YOU HEAR ME?"*

The men roar their response.

"I say: DO. YOU. HEAR ME?"
The roar comes back even louder.

*"DRIVE THE BASTARDS!"*

In the time it took Hoyt to pull the blanket over Bell's face and dash outside, Third Alabama was gone.

## CHAPTER 31 — SEVEN PINES
8:30 AM: June 1, 1862

*2d Battalion*

*Hal Martin (C)*

"DON'T JUST stand there, boy—*Hark to him.*"

Hal Martin needed the push from John Pride to realize 'Drive the Bastards' was an order. And not one executed at the double-quick step, neither—men ran. A clumsy, clanking, flapping sort of run, but run, they did: clear of tents and campfires, skillets and coffee, an enormous pack of eager youngsters, steadied by their elders, yelling and yipping, shouting, stumbling, kicking—laughing—as they tore through tents and ropes and gear; a shrill sound: inarticulate, primal, and joyous—the sound of Hunt, old as time. Taken altogether, it was a melody familiar to Hal. He had heard such music before in the woods back home, ole Marse Hardaway hunting his 'dawgs' over Martin land. Now a part of it, it sounded times ten. *Times men, I swan. Now, it is me—now, it is times me.*

Battle and Forsyth raised their swords as they passed Lomax. He, by similar salute, restored them to command of their battalions. Then, following his men into the trees—Sam Johnston right behind him—Lomax vanished.

The new woods were second growth, full of vines and brambles thicker than those which they had just come through. And wetter: a sump of trapped drainage off the roadbed of the Richmond & York River Line. Their charge slowed to one of lurching strides through the tunnels left by the retreating Yankees. Growing mindful of their footing, the rebel yell petered out, too; the lines, ragged once more. Hal was still nearest John Pride, an excellent marksman, but here, even now, a shameless punster. "Hal, old son: *Pride* goeth before the *tall.* Don't move into my fire, boy. Hang back." To his brother: "*Et tu,* Tobias."

*Lewis Branscomb (D)*

On the left of the line, the woods grew thick, but remained peaceful, the sounds of battle muffled—nothing to distract a regiment surging forward snapping saplings, slogging through muck. The stronger saplings fought back, exacting a toll in wales and curses. Lewis Branscomb heard one of Zou's boys banging away—somewhere—presumably the command locator for the regiment. In this wilderness they needed all the help they could get. Some captains used tin whistles to direct commands.

Sergeants and corporals kept up their usual: "Dress that line—Close ranks—Mind the guidon," to little avail: beyond twenty feet visibility flickered once or twice, then disappeared altogether. The men close by, were all that one could see. The sergeant major, conspicuous in his red sash, was having a hard time connecting his superiors to their subordinates. Never before had the regiment experienced wilderness like this. Cedar grew amongst the pines, and their broken branches were as lethal as arrows. After a hundred yards, the growth began to thin.

'Awn-ree' Smith gave Lewis a nudge to draw his attention. "Look there, to the left—eye level." Lewis glimpsed a palisade or embankment, the Hornets' line of march converging on it at the oblique. Now and then he saw black hats bobbing on the far side, but the trees were too dense to furnish a clear view. The Hornets closest to this puzzlement slowed their pace, a caution that caused the rest of the line to bow. The situation could not be ignored and the Hornets' corporals, themselves unsure, looked around for orders. Captain Powell sent a messenger to Forsyth. "D company encountering troops unknown, on our flank." A gap in the line was created as the rest of the battalion plowed steadily onward.

Their comrades on the left yelling alerts, Hornets in the middle files felt something like an electric charge run down to them, hearing oaths, and shouts for orders to fire. "Yankees," "Countersigns." "See them *plain*, goddammit." All of it drifting back to Lewis as bedlam. He wished Jimmie were with him and not assigned to the ambulance squad. A man near him cried out, *"Lord Jesus."* He strained to see around him. Beaumont, at a dead run behind the line to see for himself, stopped near him, gasping: *"Oh, la vache,"* Lewis needed no translation.

At the top of his voice, Troup Randle shouted: *"DROP, goddamn—"*

The last words Lulu heard before the world exploded.

*Major Forsyth*

*Worse than useless. Tells me nothing. Powell knows better than to . . .* "Complements to Captain Powell. He is to withhold his fire. We have Virginia troops to our front, the Forty-fourth—Pryor's Brigade. We mustn't draw first blood from amongst our own. Captain is reminded of the signs and countersigns." The major looked down at the runner. *The lad looks like something the cat dragged in. A Cadet would never present himself in such a way.*

He sent the runner back.

It was the second report to come from the left, of unidentified troops. But this was to be expected. The men were tired, anxious at going into their first real action, and overreacting to every sight and sound. *Has not Mahone received assurance the enemy is in retreat? Hill surely knows the whereabouts of the enemy. The camp on Nine Mile confirms they have broken, probably abandoned yesterday and used overnight by pickets—or stragglers, most likely.* He also had to consider it was units of Armistead's brigade. He was confident Powell would keep D in order. Robinson and his Lo-Bos were over there, too, and they knew how to handle themselves.

The Rifles, to his immediate front, were the only men he could see. Mayes was in the brush somewhere ahead and to the right. *Never have I seen woods so dense.* A runner approached from the right—one of the Tuskegees.

"Captain Mayes establishing contact, requests orders," the man relayed, gasping.

"Reply: There is nothing to be done until we emerge from this wilderness and regroup. Stay calm and press ahead. Dress to the colors whenever possible. Wait for instructions from Colonel Lomax."

Dazed and exhausted, the man just stared.

*Patience.* He spoke deliberately: "Tell Captain Mayes to press ahead. We will regroup in the next clearing."

Nodding, the man confirmed Forsyth's instructions and departed.

A rattle of small arms fire was heard from the far left.

*Damn it, Powell.*

Before he could form a second curse, a large volley blew across the front from left to right, followed by one straight ahead, just as heavy. Buck and ball. The zip and fly of shot was on every side. A third broadside came from the right oblique, loud and close. *How close? Fifty yards? Less?* Deadly range. The Tuskegees answered with a sharp volley of their own.

## *1st Battalion*

*Brevet Major Sands (A)*

On the other side of the regiment, the Cadets held the right flank of First Battalion. They had come through the first woods unscathed. Enemy resistance had been light, though they had sometimes heard, sometimes seen, the fight that was growing on the left.

The second woods were tightly packed, menacing, and almost as marshy as the first; the pace of Lomax's 'charge' dictated by the thick underbrush. Lieutenant Witherspoon sent word his platoon was finding enemy casualties; details were escorting the walking wounded to the rear. Acting-Captain Broun had just relayed this information to Sands, and was returning to his position when Yankee skirmishers, crouching behind cover, stood up and fired. Sands saw Broun stagger and fall. Rushing over, he found Broun already sitting upright. Looking at Sands like a sheepish schoolboy, he said, "Captain, they got me."

"Where are you hit, James?"

He placed his left hand lightly over his left breast.

Fifty feet away, Sands heard Lieutenant Yniestra's commands: "Cadets—Fire by file. READY, AIM, *F*—" the final word obliterated. The Cadets kept up a steady defensive fire by twos: down the line, right to left—in rapid but disciplined succession. Spearing his sword, Sands supported Broun's elbow, got him to his feet. James, raising his right hand in apology, turned his head to spit out a mouthful of blood, the bright red in marked contrast to his face.

"Do you think you can make it back to that camp?"

Broun took a careful breath. With an effort, he swallowed. "Yes. I think—"

"Doc Lee will take care of you there."

"Yes."

*"CADETS!* Fire by *RANKS,*" shouted Yniestra. *"FRONT rank—"*

The strapping young man Sands had watch grow from a boy, already looked like a ghost. Broun stepped gingerly back through the flattened underbrush towards the camp. Colonel Battle was to one side waving on Captain Phelan. Retrieving his sword, Sands found Sergeant Ledyard waiting to guide him back to the Cadets. He shouted into the sergeant's ear: "Mister Ledyard. Find Lieutenant Witherspoon—he commands A."

*Nick Weeks (A)*

Corporal Weeks hurried past the destruction wrought by the Federals. Squishing through the bog, his shoes in ruins, he tried to leap through brush, got entangled, tripped and went sprawling over a downed man. It was young Foy, hit in the arm and in the hand, looking ready to faint. Nick inspected the wounds and motioned him to the rear. Going a little further, he found more Cadets, either prone or, sitting behind trees firing Indian-style. Crouching low, he hurried up to them, bullets whirring past. Kneeling by Redwood, that sergeant asked,

"What do you hear? Have you seen the captain?"

"Mister Broun is hit."

"No! Bad?"

"I was told it is. Witherspoon has the company. Captain Sands is okay and should be up presently. I passed Sergeant Ledyard, and saw Foy. I sent him back. He's hit in the hand, but can walk."

"Ledyard?"

"No. Foy."

"Alright. Go down the line—that way. Find your squad."

Nick crabbed off but did not go far before diving behind a log, where he found Andy Woodcock and Charley Sands. There was not much to see except smoke and the occasional flash of fire. The underbrush here was as impenetrable as elsewhere, but fusillades were rapidly thinning it. Their log receiving a few thumps, Nick noted the enemy rounds were high. A double-loaded rifle—fired too close—rang his head and muffled his hearing. In the obscuring smoke, things turned dreamlike and slow. Cecil Carter's words came to him: 'Where *are* you?' He wasn't sure. The drill-ingrained steps of Fire and Reload, seemed to take him forever. Nick hoped to catch a glimpse of Cecil. Instead, over Woodcock's shoulder, he saw two of the new recruits—Babe Lincoln and Doc Livingston—both in trouble. Lincoln was cradling his jaw, blood seeping through his fingers. A picture of pain, jutting his head out so the blood would not ruin his uniform. Lincoln and Livingston were inseparable. Livingston was not firing, but doubled over, cradling his rifle. His head clearing, Nick felt a momentary shame: Babe and Doc were in his squad; they should be in school at Spring Hill instead of on a firing line. With a start, he recalled both were older than he was. He crawled over. "What's the problem, Doc?"

"My gun won't fire."

"Is it loaded?"

"Yes."

"'Yes, *Corporal*.' But just with one round? You haven't loaded it twice?"

"Yes, Corporal—I mean, no, Corporal."

"Give it here. Use mine—it *is* loaded—needs a prime. You got a cap?" They exchanged rifles, and Nick fingered his pouch for one of the tiny mercury caps. He felt no sense of urgency. His thinking was clear now, as though he had been trying to kill human beings—and they, him—all his life. He got hold of a cap. He felt a heavy blow, as though someone had brought a club down on his shoulder, the force of it bowling him over and planting his face in mud. Raising his head, he looked at Livingston. The boy had a gaping wound, high on his ankle, the foot beneath it, off at a sickening angle. This puzzled him: *Was that there before?*

"*SECOND rank,*" shouted Yniestra. *"READY. AIM—"*

## Lt. Col. Battle

*"Push on, Push! Forward, Alabamas! Good man! Good— Get after 'em*, Mister Bonham." Battle had his Firsters advancing nicely, and he was close behind them. He had seen Captain Sands go to Harley Broun's aid. Making his way to the rear, Broun had spotted the lieutenant colonel and, changing course, had made directly for him. At Battle's side, he came to attention and drawing himself up, saluted as smartly as though he was on parade. "Colonel, they have got me this time—Sir, may I retire?"

Horrified, Battle could only focus on the dark stain seeping through Broun's frockcoat, spreading about the waist where it was held temporarily in check by his sword belt. A dribble of blood came from Broun's mouth as he held his hand against his chest. Battle returned the salute. "Permission granted, lieutenant—pardon me: *Captain,*" was all he managed to say. His battalion advancing, Battle spurred his horse. The image of Broun's salute followed him.

Each step forward infused First Battalion with confidence and momentum. The enemy's first volley was the only disciplined fire they had received, and, subsequently they paid no heed to individual fire. In contrast, the Cadets were snapping off crisp volleys like a stamp mill—a punishing toll exacted every ten seconds: front rank, second rank, front rank, second rank. The enemy vanished under the hammering. One moment there was a mass of soldiers in their front, the next, they were gone, leaving only writhing bodies to be stepped over. Battle recognized the enemy had withdrawn, or their line had broken, one or the other. Remembering Lomax's instructions, Battle had a rider bring up Sands' pony.

"Major Sands! Major—you boy, get him over here—*call him*. Get him that little horse."

The rider didn't make it all the way to Sands, but the pony did, and Sands mounted. Advancing, the battalion began to see more enemy casualties, finding kepis and knapsacks marked: '81st Penn.' Battle knew the Eighty-first to be in Sumner's II Corps. Edwin 'Bull' Sumner. Looking constantly to his left, Cullen hoped to see Lomax there. His horse shuddered and stumbled, throwing him forward over its neck. Getting to his feet, the horse remained down, killed instantly by something. Somewhere. He saw no wound. One of the couriers came up, dismounted, handing Battle his reins.

"Save my saddlebags and pistols. Then the saddle," he ordered, before riding off to catch the lines.

The area was lightly wooded in pine saplings, but a scrim-like curtain of smoke obscured the landscape and kept visibility poor. Unable to fix on targets, Battle's battalion dressed to the center and cautiously resumed its advance.

A courier: "General Mahone's complements. You are to withdraw immediately. You are a quarter mile in front of our line."

Battle relayed the order to his captains.

To withdraw in the presence of the enemy, second rank grabbed the belts of front rank, who, still continuing to face forward were guided backwards. The smoke clearing unevenly, they soon discovered they were operating in a gap between two Federal battalions. Battle's men occupied ground won from the left wing of the 81st Pennsylvania—withdrawn or broken—their colonel left upon the field, shot through the heart. But the 81st *right wing* was still in place. On Battle's other side was the 52nd New York, entire.[14] The smoke clearing further, they saw a third regiment to their front—Sumner's reserves. (All three units a hive of activity, their officers repositioning to address this breach without firing into their own). Speaking over their shoulders, Battle's front rank offered encouragement to the second rank. "Step it up there, fellows. Lively, if you please—*Merci beaucoup.*" After a suitable distance, Battle ordered:

"Face to the rear. *BAT*-talion: *AH*-bout—*FACE*."
"Battalion: *Forward*."

### *Reserves*

*Lt. Kennon (L)*

The reserves were left to wonder how the fighting went. The close proximity put them even more on-edge. As the violence in the woods grew louder, they willed their eyes to peer through the curtain of trees; their friends were there—their brothers.

Witnessing the flight of the Virginia regiment only buttressed faith in their own. They were veterans of Drewry's Bluff after all. Had they not 'seen the elephant,' too?

When Lomax and his line were first absorbed by the woods, they were followed by Zou and his drummers, and next, by a thin line of body servants, twenty-five or so Negroes in an assortment of hand-me-down uniforms and muskets. The servants' line was the last the reserves had seen of the regiment.

Eventually, came the explosions and massed volleys that made the onlookers flinch. After an eternity, Zou reappeared with his battered drum, trousers, and gaiters. "A *merécage* is no place for a Zouave." Indignant at the savagery practiced by amateurs, he passed to the rear.

On the edge of the woods, the Hornets' Buck was also

---

[14] The 81st Pennsylvania was in Richardson's First Division, First Brigade (Howard); the 52nd New York, the same division, Third Brigade (French).

returning, with two more hands, Amos Powell, and Elsie Randall—Amos being supported by Elsie. Lieutenant Kennon sent out a detail to bring them in. Nearing the trio, these men heard a loud commotion from the woods and brought their rifles up, as a wild-eyed young man broke from covert at a dead run. He did not slow in passing the Negros, nor did a dozen rifles leveled at his breast divert him from his goal.

Recognizing the uniform of the Hornets, Kennon shouted, "Hold your fire!"

Reaching 'home,' it was all the boy could do to form words; aid for the blacks evaporating whilst the volunteers gathered round the breathless comrade.

"Gone—All gone. They're gone," the youth gasped. To all appearance he was unscathed. Bent over, catching his breath, he raised one palm against Kennon's rapid-fire questions. "Who's gone? And where?" Kennon wanted information, and wanted it now. Was the regiment advancing? Falling back? Was this soldier sent back with orders? "Spit it out, boy."

"Dead—Mowed down. Never seen the like," he said. "They're all dead!" The horror of it all, etched on his face. He remembered to add: "Sir."

Buck, Elsie, and Amos hobbled past.

"One moment they were all there. The next, they *gone*, I tell you. *A single volley.* We never knew what hit us."

"'Sir,'" came the prompt.

"Sir."

Those near enough to hear, reacted with disbelief; the notion the Third could be annihilated. "Rubbish." "Can't be so," they muttered. Others further back, shushing them to hear more.

Kennon's mind reeled. *How can this be? Can this be? Wait. Who commands now? Chester, of course—Must tell him.* "Sergeant—"

"Sir, there's plenty of fire coming out those woods, yet," said the sergeant, recognizing his lieutenant was rattled, needing a moment to gather himself.

"Those 'dead' men are still putting up a fight and, by the

sounds of it, a good one. The Third is still kickin' hard in there, sir."

Kennon stared at the sergeant, the words sinking in. "Yes. Yes, of course, sergeant. What are you men doing out of line? Sergeant Martin, reform your men."

Two more soldiers staggered from the woods.

## *2d Battalion:*

*John Hoyt (K)*

Hoyt spit out another mouthful of dirt. Seemed every time he opened his mouth, a minié ball came along to shovel up a clod. He blew his nose on his sleeve. The Rifles were taking heavy fire, the enemy so close they could be hit by rocks.

He had needed only a minute or so to reach the fighting, on his way he had stepped through a line of fallen New Hampshire men. Catching up to the Rifles, they were thrashing forward, though unable to gain on the retreating enemy. As he resumed his position behind the line, a platoon of Federals rose in ambush. If not for the trees and skittish marksmanship, the Rifles would have been finished.

But the storm of missiles kept coming, exceeding all Hoyt had ever imagined. Going to ground behind a sapling, it seemed every bush and twig would be cut down. Near him, Bart Jordan was firing from a prone position. It being difficult to reload while on the ground, Jordan rolled onto his back. Pushing off to right himself, he was struck in the thigh; Hoyt heard the bone crack. Turning to his right, he came face to face with Ben Roper. As he began to speak, he realized his friend would never answer.

Shanghai, was behind a tree, loading and firing, cool as ever. Looking over, Shanghai saw John, then Ben; his 'owl' emitting a single mournful hoot.

Caroline needed no orders. Dashing among the trees, splashing between the lines, she was all set to retrieve those thousands of birds that, at any moment, must surely fall from the sky.

For the Rifles the situation was grim, but there was no panic. Picking their targets, the men maintained a disciplined fire. Hoyt's senses were acute: trees receiving hits from the left, he surmised the battalion had Yankees on that flank. Then the trees began taking bullets on the near side—friendly fire— source unknown. He wondered where Mayes and the Tuskegees might have gone. *Mayes should be on my right. Where is Colonel Lomax in all this?* A Yankee lieutenant came too close to Shanghai's tree. While that officer was looking in one direction, Donaldson reached around from the other, jerking the officer off his feet, and dragging him into the lines.

Orders from Forsyth to pull back.

Hoyt ordered: "Fire at will." Under this cover the wounded were moved to safety. The Rifles fired and fell back by rank, fired by second rank, and fell back, fired again and again, until they had separation between the lines, the Federals more than willing to see them go. 12th Virginia was the source of the friendly fire; Major Forsyth negotiating that ceasefire.

All the tramping and musketry having cut swaths through the wood, the battalion had no difficulty withdrawing to the abandoned camp on Nine Mile. At least this was true for the Rifles and the Tuskegees. The Hornets and Bo-Los could still be heard blazing away from that side. Forsyth was anxious to locate Colonel Lomax; he had received no orders since the opening salvo.

The Tuskegees' Captain Mayes had been killed at the outset. His men now gathered around his body, as Preacher Tate spoke over him.

Shanghai's prisoner proved to be a talkative New Yorker, who said the Third had been facing the better part of a division—brigades made up from New Hampshire, New York and Pennsylvania. He feared their losses were heavy, he had seen his own colonel fall.

Forsyth continued to inquire after Lomax. A wounded Wetumpka man said he had seen the colonel cut down in the first volley. Many more had received wounds in the attempt to recover his body. They *had* managed to retrieve Sam Johnston.

The Rifles had been mauled. Besides Tom Bell, Hoyt knew that Roper, Bill Robeson, and Will Garrow were dead; McNulty, Swain, Crowder, and Sitchwell had disabling, if not mortal, wounds; Joe Skinner and Savvy Thompson not much better.

Hoyt looked around—a third of his company missing. Consulting his pocket watch he stared at it in disbelief. they had started from this camp just forty-five minutes ago? Giving it a shake, he held it to his ear. Lieutenant Gardner limped over to him, a bloody flesh wound soaking one leg of his trousers. He had been helped back by Neville who himself had a broken arm, and was waiting his turn at the surgeon's tent. Hoyt sent Gardner there too.

Shanghai assembled the company. This time, roll was not slowed by banter; the responses were straightforward, each man doing his best to recall those he had last seen, and where. Shanghai reported forty-nine present—twenty missing or otherwise unaccounted for. Hoyt directed him to return to the field with a picked squad, to search for the absent.

Battle and Sands came in: First Battalion was still intact. On the right, the Wetumpka Light Guards and the Cadets had taken casualties. Forsyth reported to Battle, whose first demand was for news of Lomax. Forsyth repeated what the Wetumpka man had told him. Battle greeted this with silence, then asked after his friend, Robert Mayes. He was shown the body. Lastly, he asked if Lieutenant—rather, *Captain* Broun's—whereabouts were known. No one had seen him.

Shaken, Battle sat on a stump. *Not today, Lord. Please,* he prayed. *Not this day.* Realizing every eye was on him, he regained his composure, and standing, reasserted command. "Major Forsyth: I do not see Captain Powell's company. And where is Captain Phelan and his Metros?"

"Sir, Powell was last seen on the flank of Second, when Colonel Lomax was—when he was fired upon. I presume he is on the left, taking fire. I have no information on the Metropolitans, as they are not under—"

"I see," Battle interrupted, his face turning dark. "You

'presume.' Powell is *there*. *Phelan* is God-*knows*-where—and yet, here you be, sir. Here *you* be."

*Lewis Branscomb (D)*

Lewis felt the heat from the volley rake his back. And the sun was in his eyes. Attempting to pull his cap lower, he came up empty: the bill had been shot away.

He heard Captain Powell: "HORNETS! RISE. *Quickly,* men." Lewis and his comrades got to their feet.

"Front rank. Steady, now. On my command: Ready. Aim . . . *FIRE!"*

The rifles discharged as one. Powell's commands kept the men focused on their duty, just as they had been schooled.

Lewis was aware of nothing more than those immediately to his left and right. His world narrowed to feeling for cartridges, biting off the end, pouring the powder down the muzzle, then: pull ramrod, tamp; percussion cap, fit it on the nipple. Await the orders to fire. If the enemy were still out there, they had become invisible.

Powell: *"FIRE AT WILL."* On Louis's left, Henry Smith loaded, aimed, fired, reloaded. On his right, Fisher McGowan fell; Lewis glanced down at him and was sorry for it. Bullets coming so thick and so fast, it reminded him of scattering feed to chickens.

Powell ordered a withdrawal back to the road. Lewis was pulled to the rear and, stepping over a body, noticed 'Alfo. Bagby • So. Rifles' painted across the canteen, realizing how widespread the carnage must be. Gil Vaughn, using his rifle for a staff, hopped along to keep up. Wounded men pleading, "Don't leave me behind. Take me, boys. Come on now— *please*," the plea so much worse when the man called you by name. Old Dick had taken Chef under one arm, the sergeant's trouser leg split to the crotch, the material tied in a knot to slow his bleeding. Lewis looked for his friend, Babe Stinson.

Making for Nine Mile, Powell remembered passing a small hollow during their initial run. He ordered the company to rally there, to make a stand. Several Tuskegees were already there, still game. Together making a force of fifty or sixty able bodies. The wounded kept coming in and passing through their line.

The Federals continued pressing, hoping to catch the rebels on their heels. Focused on the camp, they came through the woods, passing in front of the Hornets, their right flank 'in the air.' A volley taught them the error of their ways. Powell's hollow made an excellent redoubt and they repelled the subsequent counterattacks with ease. General Mahone coming up, dismounted to observe. Though the general made for a tiny target, his mare did not, and she fell to enemy fire. The general's aides pulled him back and, by keeping the road on their left, escorted him through the trees towards Nine Mile. With the Federals' attacks petering out, Powell and his men followed Mahone's path through the brush to safety.

They arrived just as Shanghai and his squad were returning with more of the battalion's wounded. The ambulance men had found Bart Jordan and Joe Jackson, and Squeegee Sullivan—all three in a bad way. Hoyt took a quick headcount of his effectives. Thirty-three.

On a remount, General Mahone asked the whereabouts of Colonel Lomax. Informed the colonel was missing in action, Mahone sent orders to Battle to withdraw the Third from the north woods.

## CHAPTER 32 — COWARDS
11 A.M. June 1, 1862

BY ELEVEN O'CLOCK Mahone was once more on Williamsburg Pike, watching his regiments (two of them, at any rate) exit the woods and establish defensive positions. They were badly cut up, the officers of Third Alabama and 41st Virginia adjusting their lines, their reserve companies moving up and assisting the wounded, moving prisoners to the rear, battalion officers ordering their companies to rest under arms.

Battle rode over to report. He found Colonel Gordon standing with Mahone, both men anxious for word of Lomax.

\* \* \*

Harvey Hill lowered his glasses. He had seen enough, seen about all he could stomach, seen what he expected to see: The Third had broken soon after they entered the woods. *This is what comes of packing all those fops into one regiment.* He had seen many flee to safety without their weapons. *Silk-stocking trash: that one fool broke from the trees like a fox on fire, then, instead of shooting the coward on the spot, everybody stands 'round, consoling—making certain 'Somebody's Darling' is all right. Yes, here they come now—the rest of Madame Mahone's boys streaming out—those that haven't already run for home.*

*Damned Yellowhammers.*

\* \* \*

'Somebody's Darling' was mortified: his behavior displayed for all the world to see. *How could I have been so foolish?* 'Shame' did not scratch the surface—he prayed the earth to open up and swallow him whole. Yet soon his eyes were brimming with tears of joy, to find so many of his friends—friends he thought he would never again see this side of the grave—emerging from the woods. Having fled for his life; having reported his entire company wiped out—by a fiendish new weapon, no less—he felt every eye was upon him.

No judgment could be harsher than his own: *I am an ass. There is no hiding from it; nothing left but to face the music.* The first Hornet to come in he embraced in a bear hug so fraught, the man was left a little puzzled. He hugged a second man. "I am so sorry—I am so very sorry. I thought you all were dead."

They came in disheveled and filthy, with torn, mud-covered uniforms, their shoes encased in it. But there was also an exhilaration that soon encompassed the reserves. Hugs, handshakes, reunions, spread from man to man; an urgent need to talk, to explain and compare. The Eagles were close with those from Tuskegee and Union Springs; Chester's men felt the same towards the Mobilians. Craning their necks, they searched for friends in sister companies. The morbidly curious gathered around the wounded. The reserves handed over the knapsacks, or looked for their missing owners. A mound grew from those left unclaimed.

Old Dick was relieved Frank Bickle was still in one piece. He began to search for Lonz and Tom. The knot in his stomach slowly growing.

"Anybody seen Sid?"

"Took a ball in the leg. Had to leave him. Mister Keiser is back there too, staying with his boy."

"Ollie Keeler? Anyone in First Battalion seen my brother?" asked Charlie.

"Lou Branscomb, that you under all that mud? Is that all the hat you brung back?"

"Where are Phelan's boys? Anybody see the Mutts? Anybody seen the Abbetts? What about Jeems, and Big Jim?"

"Here comes Carter and young Weeks. I'll take those rifles, Cecil—Nick, you're almost there, lad. You're gonna make it. Keep 'a going."

There were none from Phelan's Company to banter with.

Officers restoring the lines, the ambulance men took the

injured to the Twins, already filled to capacity; the freshly wounded were allotted space in the yards.

"*GET out of those ditches,* you filthy cowards!"

The challenge was so loud, it made every head turn. All activity stopped. The Alabamians looked behind them, curious to see who was being called out.

It appeared General Hill—his face red with rage—was addressing them.

"Cowering, spineless cowards. Yellow—the lot of you. Who made you run—*a few Yankee skirmishers?* Stand up, you dogs, and learn what it means to fight like men."

The volunteers were struck dumb. Obediently, those on the ground (the wounded) struggled to their feet. Forsyth riding up, saluted.

"Major Forsyth, General. The men—"

"What *men*?" Hill sneered, looking down at Forsyth. "I *SEE* no men, '*Major.*'"

Forsyth's brown face darkened further, and he stammered a reply. "General, if, if you, or, or any other man says this regiment acted. . . ." Mahone arrived with his entourage and Colonel Taylor of the Twelfth. Mahone launched.

"Anyone who says my brigade has run, is a goddam liar, and I will hold that man to account hereafter. Personally responsible. I ordered those men out of the woods, General. The Third and Forty-first were following my direct orders."

"Soooo? You leave a gap for the enemy to break our line? I do *deeply* beg their pardon. I stand corrected: it is their *commander* who is the incompetent."

"Colonel Lomax has fallen, sir," said Mahone, shocked by such a remark.

"*Indeed! I mean you, YOU DAMNED TOM THUMB!*"

Battle and Gordon pushed between the two, Battle using his horse to turn Mahone, who was searching for his brace of pistols—*Where are they?* Confused, until he realized they were still in the woods, beneath his dead mare.

Speaking calmly but rapidly, Hill's ADC convinced the

general to let him handle this. In a fury, Hill rode away to inspect the next brigade.

Mahone was hustled away, also, the latter cursing so bitterly that spittle flew.

Leaving the regiment with a hundred mouths agape.

"Cowards? "*What in Hell?* What did *we do* but fight all morning?" they asked one another. "Does he take us for the Ninth?"

"Did he say Lomax has fallen?"

"What? The colonel? 'Fallen'? You mean, as in *dead?* Can't be true—*fallen off his horse*, maybe. Knocked *out*, maybe."

All had heard the insults. But once said, the words took on a life of their own, began to twist. One man would ask his neighbor, who told his cousin, and so on, until only one phrase stood out: Hill had said, "Then Lomax is a coward." By noon, it could not be argued he had said anything less.

Left to wither by neglect was the humiliation of one lone Hornet. There was but one topic: Daniel Harvey Hill.

\* \* \*

One o'clock found Major Sands and Sergeant Ledyard standing to one side, waiting for casualty figures to be tallied—normally the duty of the adjutant. Sam's absence being already felt. Sands' old company had fourteen casualties, one killed. Only two Cadets were still unaccounted for: Captain Broun and Corporal Keeler.

Captain Simpson had twenty-six casualties: four dead. Lieutenant Bilbro reported the death of Captain Mayes and estimated at least twenty wounded or missing, in addition to the known dead. Melton feared Ready was near death, with thirteen others wounded or killed—the Wetumpkas had been in the thick of it with Lomax. Melton had not seen the colonel fall, but Ready had been wounded in the attempt to recover the body. The Tuskegees were still coming in. With each scan of a company's report Sands saw not only the toll to the regiment, but to the families back home.

A lieutenant—'14 NC' on his cap—approached.

"Captain Sands?"

"Major Sands."

"I stand corrected, major. I was directed where to find you. I have the personal effects of Lieutenant James Harleston Broun, sir."

"I beg pardon, my hearing is shot. Broun—*Broun* you say?"

The lieutenant spoke louder: "Yes, sir. Of your Cadets. I found him on the field."

"He is alive?"

"I regret to report, sir, he is not. He had been dead for some time, when I found him, about an hour ago, by the side of Nine Mile road. I—I took the liberty, sir, to recover from him such items, as might be a comfort to his family. I have his purse, here. And his watch. His name engraved inside."

"Then you knew him?"

"No, sir. Seeing 'Mobile Cadets' on his buttons, I knew where to come."

"Of course."

Sergeant Ledyard stepped forward. "I will take care of this, major. I'll make sure these get back to his family."

Sands nodded absently. "Keep an eye out for Keeler too, if you will." To the officer he said, "I thank you, lieutenant. This will mean a great deal to the father—as it does to me. I am in your debt. If I can be of any service. . . ." losing the thought. "My regards to, em, Colonel Tew."

\* \* \*

Shanghai handed Hoyt K's casualty list. Seeing the many names, Hoyt's eyes filled with tears and, in shame, he turned away. Pulling out his handkerchief he pretended to mop his brow.

"How many, sergeant?"

"Sir: twelve dead, twenty-four wounded."

Shoulders slumping, he scanned the list to find those he had not yet been aware of. Crowder, McNulty, Sitchwell, and Swain were dead; Coco Colburn, Jackson, Moore, and Savvy Thompson would be lucky to make it through the night. Neither Jordan or Will McKerrell would ever march again, nor Loper, Neville, or Skinner shoulder a musket. Big Bill McDonald (whose lisping had given Shanghai pause) was missing, as was William Ellis, one of Hoyt's former messmates, a great friend from the old days. *Twenty minutes under fire—Was that all it was?*

"Will you make a separate list of casualties for me, Sergeant—"

"Yes, sir."

"And another, to tell me who is still al—, still present for duty."

Three more soldiers stepped out of the woods. Two of them—the two in blue—held their rifles aloft, by the barrel, in token of surrender. They were on the bayonet point of the third man, Awn-ree Smith.

Smith had been cut off at the railroad embankment when the Hornets fell back. Submerged in the water and obscured by brush, the enemy brigade had passed him by. Laying low while the fight raged at the hollow, he waited for the Yankees to fall back, then got the drop on these two stragglers. Mahone, hearing of the exploit, shook his hand, feeling the honor of the brigade reestablished by such bravery. Next, Smith—overhearing Mahone's grumble over the loss of his saddle and his pistols—walked back into the woods. He returned thirty minutes later, with the items in hand. Mahone recommended Smith's promotion on the spot.

"Young man, I must tell you if I had had these pistols one hour ago, I would now be under arrest for murder."

\* \* \*

Old Dick also returned to the woods, to search for his brothers. He figured wherever he found one, he would find the other. In this, he was wrong.

At the point where the Yankees opened on them, he discovered Fisher McGowan. He found L.B. Day's canteen, and Lonz's rifle—but no Lonz. About to head back, he heard moaning and, following the sound, walked past the Hornet's original line to the railroad embankment. There, six bodies lay side by side: four Federals and two Hornets. Some Samaritan had dragged them out of the water. But two had slid down and lay submerged to their chests. One of these was Tom—cotton still packed in his ears. He took them out. Reaching into Tom's jacket he removed the pocket Bible and letters he found there.

Alf Bagby was the source of the moaning. Dick couldn't say how long he would last; he didn't look good. Taking a last look at Tommy, Dick tried to memorize his face, his freckles. He glanced at the eyes, but not for long. He pulled a button off Tommy's jacket. He picked up Bagby.

\* \* \*

At two o'clock, a bad day turned less so. The Metropolitans, cut off since morning—missing and presumed lost—came in; Captain Phelan with a ball in his thigh.

The Mutts began the day with forty-eight. For them, Hell was found in the swamp after leaving the Yankee camp. Following the direction taken by Lomax, they had gotten caught up in the firefight over the colonel's body. With the numbers against them Phelan ordered his men back. Advancing a second time, he thought he was on the line the battalion had taken, but he never reestablished contact. In the dense smoke and underbrush the Metros soon were isolated, with Yankees in every direction. More than once they were called upon to surrender. Phelan ordered his men to remove General Hill's white arm bands. "Take those bloody rags off. We're giving them targets. We'll have to fight our way home, boys."

Concentrating their fire in one direction, he gauged the response. Wherever the return-fire appeared weakest, they moved, losing five killed and seventeen wounded in the process. Of the wounded, seven had to be left behind. When finally, they made contact with Mahone, the Metros numbered thirty-six (twenty-six fit for duty). Before passing out, Phelan relinquished command to Lieutenant McAnerney, until May, the Metros' first sergeant.

\* \* \*

'The Hornet who ran' not only escaped censure, he escaped all notice. Immersed in the day's other events, his leg bail was recalled by few and, among those, filed away as merely a humorous footnote. Still, the recruit felt the shame of having let his comrades down. He sought out Captain Powell. "Sir? I need to report myself."

For Powell it was like one of his Sunday schoolers confessing to lustful dreams. Troup Randle was within earshot, Mr. McGowan too, but the young man made no effort to exclude them. When the story was told, the captain sat a moment, thinking it through. How strange battle must seem to an eighteen-year-old. He looked the youth in the eye, expecting to see a boy, but finding a man. Responding to the soldier's candor, Powell said there had been so many mistakes made (by so many), the man's sins could only be those of pride, greed, and avarice.

"Should you persist in claiming the biggest share of blame for yourself," said Powell, "I shall think the less of you for it."

Clasping the young man's hand. "We are all new to this, son. You will do better next time. And, so will I."

The youth had to pass by the fearsome Randle, who had given no indication he had heard a word. But in leaving, the youth had the distinct impression of receiving the officer's quick, approving, wink.

The sergeants took command of the men.

"RIFLE INSPECTION! By platoons—thirty minutes! Corporals: half your squads to clean rifles, the remainder on the line. Old-timers: make sure the new fish do a proper job. You have thirty minutes, gentlemen—that means fifteen."

## CHAPTER 33 — FOOLSCAP
Afternoon—Midnight

PICKETT'S BRIGADE anchored the defensive perimeter; Mahone's on the right. Gustavius Smith—who had been directing the fight since Joe Johnston was wounded—was relieved of command by Chief of Staff Lee, who ordered an immediate halt to all offensive operations. Together, the two rode over to Williamsburg Pike to assess the situation there. They found Longstreet in casual conversation with President Davis and members of his cabinet.

Longstreet was in a talkative mood and began to outline for Smith, the current status of his divisions. Smith (wondering how likely could it be, Davis had failed to inform Pete of the change in command), directed him to make his report to Lee. Other than to observe Huger had gotten a late start crossing Gillies Creek ("Must've been afraid his boys would get wet"), Longstreet said little of the mismanaged battle. Staff began to generate the orders to pull the divisions back to their starting points. By six o'clock, Lee and Smith were back at Army headquarters on Nine Mile Road.

Hill set his division to recovering abandoned equipment, salvaging more than 6700 muskets and rifles in the process. Still smarting from Hill's insults, Mahone had to be dissuaded from demanding satisfaction; his aides pointing out the unseemliness of challenging a man who had publicly denounced dueling; Hill's personal bravery was beyond dispute. While conceding the point, Mahone would neither forget nor forgive.

In reserve, the Third bivouacked near Casey's Redoubt. Three days exposure to the elements (a fourth, spent in battle) rendered their camp quiet as a grave. The officers admonished the pickets to stay awake and remain vigilant. The Rifles and Cadets were exempted of this duty.

There was an awkwardness to be found around the Rifles' fire: that one blaze should accommodate the whole. Despite its warmth, Scotty could not stop shivering. Jack Goulet appeared, and, dropping down beside him, the two gazed into the coals.

After a while Scotty pulled a small, worn, notebook from his jacket and began to write, jotting down the names of those Rifles who had answered Morning Roll. After a series of starts and stops, and lengthy pauses, he put down his pencil. "We went in with seventy-three," he said, eyes fixed upon the pyre. "I tally thirty-six dead, wounded or missing. Half."

Jack was silent. His own Cadets had suffered losses, but nothing to compare with this. They shared news of this fellow or that. Scotty had heard of Harley Broun's death, while Jack had just come from Tom Scott's side. Doc Lee had been unable to stop the bleeding.

"Those new boys got shot all to hell: Babe Lincoln in the face, Livingston in the ankle. I saw the ankle—he's done. Nicky Weeks got hit in the shoulder. Casey, too. Flesh wounds is all, I think." Jack rambling on, to avoid his own thoughts.

"The Wetumpkees who saw it, say there is no way the colonel could have survived. But until we have the body. . . . We'll get up a party tomorrow and go look for him. If we find his horse, we'll know what happened. The great horse will mark the spot. I think they have recovered Sam Johnston." Changing the subject: "Colonel Battle did all right today, I think. How about Forsyth? Say, why weren't all you Rifles on the flank of Second, when we were in that camp?"

As if newly aware of Jack's presence, Scotty tore his eyes from the fire. "Woodruff is gone, so, Powell is the senior. We got moved—Forsyth was there—I don't know. I didn't see him till we came out." Fatigue getting the better of him, his words began to slur.

When next Jack looked, Scotty was out. Teasing out the notebook and pencil, he slipped both inside his friend's jacket. "Gad, Corbét," he said, softly, "Haven't we had a day?"

\* \* \*

No one took the day harder than Battle. When he could

get away from the eyes of his men, he reviewed the orders and decisions. *We are undone. By a word, a sentence, or an ill-considered gesture. Today, of all days!*

He stopped, horrified by the shallowness. *Shameful, Cullen. Vade retro Satana!*

The men had fought bravely; no one would deny—hard as Harvey Hill might try. No, they had done all that could have been asked of them. More. The poor showing rested squarely on the commanders. Huger and Hill certainly, Mahone, somewhat. Battle condemned himself. They had all made mistakes; even Tennent. *Poor Tennent.*

What more could we have done? *Waded* across Gillies Creek? *Risk the ruin of our ammunition? Put skirmishers out? Insist that rations be issued at Richmond?* In the event, it was hard to fathom how *'these things work out for the best.'*

Reviewing each moment, searching for different outcomes: *We should have deployed skirmishers, that is certain. But how could we have anticipated enemy fire, so near Hill's Headquarters! Where were his pickets? We could have been more cautious, but Hill waved us—WAVED us on, without a. . . . as though an enemy sighting were nothing more than a flock of pigeons! The bivouac we stumbled upon, so established, their coffee was hot! Tennent ordering "Charge" as one might "Tally-Ho." And his smile—that smile: that sweet, beaming, so at-peace-with-the-world-smile. Ahh, Tennent, Tennent. . . .* He wished he weren't too old to cry.

*What the devil was Forsyth thinking? He had Powell's men—good men, too—reacting correctly to the Yankees they sight. So, who is it, mistakes them for Virginians? Why are Powell's men ordered to hold fire? First Battalion saw nothing—I hear the volley—shouts; Lomax and his horse disappear into the smoke, and the woods vanish, too.*

His attention was drawn to the sight of John Pride and Hal Martin assisting Toby to the field hospital. Next came a squad of Tuskegees, carrying the body of Robert Mayes; ambulance men rushed to them with a litter. Preacher had been standing next to Mayes when he fell, and reported his last words were of his wife. William was distraught. The two were extremely close, hunting and fishing together since childhood. Now, there was not enough water for the servant to wash his master's body. *Poor Clara,* thought Battle. *And the boys: What ever will I say to them? What will I say to Clara? What can I say?*

*Sam Johnston's mother: what does one write to a widow who has lost her only son? Her only means of support? Who will provide?*

Sam possessed no sword when he was elected lieutenant. Battle had presented him his own; as he did, teasing Sam about his frock coat, for its dark patches, where the chevrons had been.

He would talk tomorrow with William, about sending Robert's body home. Purchase another steel casket, for Sam; use the one he already had, for Robert; Preacher would help with arrangements.

But first things first. He need to appoint as adjutant and fill other vacancies. The younger Swanson—Beau Swanson—should do: a good soldier, mature, and well-educated.

Another twinge of pain. Reaching back, Battle found the hole in his britches, began to work on the minié ball lodged in his buttock.

\* \* \*

For the present, Sands and Powell shared Sam Johnston's duties, designating details: one to secure rations, another to locate their baggage train (if their wagons had even made it through Richmond) and, if so, to expedite their arrival. A third detail was sent to scavenge, borrow, or steal anything useful to a bivouac; a fourth to locate potable water, another to fetch firewood. The officers continued to receive reports and to tally casualties. With night approaching (another without shelter), the details stumbled and shuffled through these duties. Subdued by the day's experience, it was easy to distinguish combat veterans from those who were not.

The missing continued to come in, each with a tale to tell. Casualty reports adding up: perhaps a third of the regiment, companies in Second Battalion faring worst: Powell and Robinson each losing twenty or more; the Tuskegees more than thirty, the Rifles, thirty-six. Roll call proceeded at a crawl. The numbing response: "Left on the field," repeated with regularity.

Companies E and L took picket duty, allowing the others to establish shelters. Powell and Chester, and most of the sergeants and corporals, worked through the night. It was not a quiet night, but one that grew quieter over time.

Lewis Branscomb had nothing but his rifle and accoutrements. And a Yankee blanket. He had tossed his cap away, and had no idea where his knapsack may have gone. As muddy as he already was, he had no qualms about lying down in it to sleep. Willie Waugh was standing near, propped against a pine. Having sustained several broken ribs, his body had begun to stiffen. He waved Lewis over.

"What's a broke-rib like?" asked Lewis.

"Ducky. The pain is novel. You can't—imagine it. Can't breathe deep. So long—as I'm standing—or sitting—it's tolerable. But going—one to the other—is the devil. Steals all joy—from a cough—or a sneeze, I declare."

"How can I help?"

"Would like it, if I could get off—my feet. Stand there—in front. Grab my elbows. Okay, now, ease me down—slowww."

As Lewis began, Willie let out a gasp and went rigid. Lewis stopped immediately, tightening his grip, so as not to drop him. Willie's face went white. Through teeth, Willie struggled to regain his voice—his mouth working, but in silence.

Holding him up, Lewis said, "I cain't make out what yer saying. Tell me what to do."

Indecipherable syllables followed. Lewis finally made out one breathless word:

"Please."

Willie repeated it, gasping out clearly: *"Please."*

"'Please.' Okay," said Lewis, "Please what, Willie? Please

*what?*"

Trapped in this ludicrous embrace and against all reason, Willie began to laugh. His mirth quickly choked off.

"Tell me *what to do*." Lewis pleaded, the distress on his own face nearly a match for Willie's. He leaned in to hear.

"Please—" The word had been established.

"Got it. Yes. 'Please.' Go *on*, Willie."

With a last-ditch effort, Willie exclaimed, "God's sakes—won't you? Just—let—me—*da—*"

*"I cain't just let you die."*

"Let me—*down,* Goddam it! Just let me down!"

Given this epiphany, Lewis complied. Then, hard as he tried to suppress it, he too began to chortle; Willie trying desperately to ignore him.

Heads turned, at sounds so out of place, the first heard on that field that day, though one's sounded more like hiccups of pain.

"I thought the Yanks done sent you to finish me, Lulu! Lord have mercy—Oww—you liked to killed me—'Just let me die'—*Jesus.* Who *raised* you? *Please*; no more help—Ahh—*Oh!*"

\* \* \*

Powell found Amos and Elsie around a separate campfire. Doctoring Amos, the captain put a fresh dressing on the wound asking, as he did, after Buck, and others not present. Elsie spoke up:

"Cap'n Richard? How' do, suh."

"Elsie."

"Bad day, suh."

"Yes, it was."

"Cap'n, I larn't sumpin' 'bout white folk t'day, suh. Sho did."

"Oh? What is that, Elsie?"

"Well, suh: Ya'll's a heap mite faster'n I would 'spect, fo' dis."

"Are we? How so?"

"This mornin,' Amos, Buck 'n mysefs in line behind yo Hawnets. An' jes' fo' we get to'em dern woods, we starts to hear dem bees."

"*Bees?*"

"Yessuh. Bees singin' 'round our ears, Cap'n. We starts aswattin' 'em. Den ole Amos heah, alla sudden, he drop lock a rock. An' Buck, he say: 'Fool—dese heah *hain't no bees!*' Jes den, heah come dem ole Virginny boys, outta de wood, lock lightin'."

Elsie's dramatic pause would have made an orator proud.

"Nah, Cap'n, back home, I been chase by manys de pattyroller, nights when I'ze takin' my walks. Tain't one cotch me yet. Always found it easy to distant any white man. But suh— wid 'spect—in a race twix a minnie ball an' a white man, ah puts my money on de white man. Dem Virginny boys run pass us *like we standin' still!*

"Cap'n Powell, ah say: Ain't no fasta critta dis here wide green urt' thanna white man runnin' fo' his life. Den, he could whup a railroad car."

\* \* \*

Midnight found Sands addressing his final duties as commander of the Cadets. *Who knows what tomorrow may bring? I must put this right.* Walking to the redoubt, where lights still burned in the officers' tents, he was provided a field table, camp stool, paper and ink.

Opening his journal to June 1, 1862, he found this entry:

*June 1 – L$^t$ Col. B —— b'day 33*

The penciled line was a cypher, meaning nothing, though the hand was his own. Slowly, his tired mind filled in the blanks: *It is Battle's birthday, today. His thirty-third.* Making the Sign of the Cross he began to jot down words and phrases, times, places, and names—orders received and given—that he would later expand, to record today's events. Then it would be up to others to make sense of this senseless day. Finishing, he cut a fresh point. On a fresh sheet of foolscap:

*Camp near Richmond V$^a$ June 2, 1862*

*My Dear Sir*

*You have no doubt ere this, learned by Telegraph, that your son, James H. Broun, my First Lieut. has nobly fallen on the field of battle. Yet, I feel that a line from me, his Captain, and friend, would not be unacceptable or out of place. . . .*

\* \* \*

# King Stork

*"Drag out the drones and cowards."*

Maj. Gen. Daniel Harvey Hill
Army of Northern Virginia

## CHAPTER 34 — BRASS
June 2 – 16, 1862

IN THE STRUGGLE to get his letter right, the writer made several false starts. It was not the sort of thing he could seek advice for, much less hand off. *Harder than it looks: recruiting words to follow orders—*

Wadding up his latest effort, he leaned back in his camp chair, his hand tapping impatiently against his knee.

*How to play this out?*

Though reputed to play a mean hand of draw poker—a master of the bluff hand—in truth, he seldom gambled, preferring to size up his opponents, lying in wait for favorable odds. A fight was a different matter: there, he was a brawler—aggressive and tenacious—a soldier's soldier. Not much of a talker. At six foot-two, and solid as wood, he didn't need to be.

*Even a fool, when he holdeth his peace, is counted wise.*

He had heard that one often enough.

Surprising, nonetheless—to have come so far in the army. He had not sought exalted rank; it had come to him. At the beginning of the war, his expectations were modest: to be assigned to senior staff. A paymaster through much of the 1850s, he had earned a reputation for irascibility, but (more importantly) one for competence. His accounts were always in order. Lesser men might lie, but his balance sheets did not.

And, as any fool could see, the South's balance sheet did not look good: a large country, thinly populated, poor roads, minimal rail, problematic rivers and coasts; no navy to speak of, yet an economy largely dependent on a single export; harvested by a large population of . . . 'servants.'

It didn't add up; not in any good way—but his own options were also limited. Putting the decision off as long as he could, he resigned his commission and offered his services to Alabama—where his streak of luck began.

Informed he was the highest-ranking active officer attached

to the state, Governor Moore promoted him brigadier of the AVC (over Lomax and Withers). President Davis secured him a lieutenant colonel's commission in the Confederate States Army, followed by the Secretary of War promoting him brigadier (CSA). A mid-level officer, of limited means and expectations, suddenly playing for high-stakes. With house-money, no less.

Joe Johnston had taken a shine to him, and Davis and Lee obviously thought highly of him, too. Yet, on the eve of Seven Pines, it was his old classmate and rival, Gustavius Smith, who was Johnston's left-wing commander, the second in command.

For reasons known only to God and Johnston, the Old Man had not taken Smith into his confidence, not shared with him the plan of battle. In fact (so far as he knew), Johnston had not shared the plan with anyone. But secrets never die of loneliness, and the night before the battle Johnston summoned him, bursting at the seams to blab the whole thing to *somebody*. To him.

Now, here he was—one week later—sitting at this desk, his career in the balance.

*In the jakes.*

He had gotten something terribly wrong. *It was late: Johnston's hand was darting all over the map; the man so keyed-up he couldn't string two sentences together.* There had been the usual interruptions. *The Old Man simply assumed I could see it all as well as he.* "An early start," Johnston kept repeating, "We must have an early start." That, he remembered clearly—he could not be accused of missing that. Though his start was a tad off-line: ninety degrees, give or take.

His first inkling things had gone awry was at the creek. *Where that sorry prig, "Ooze-air," tried to pull rank.*

But it was too late, even then. *I would have looked the fool turning them around. Wilcox knew something was queer, but was smart enough to keep his mouth shut. Anyone else lurking out there, willing to speak up? What might Huger know?*

Under his own command was Harvey Hill, who had gone

forth that day armed only with such detail as he needed to know; another friend from the old days—but Stonewall Jackson's brother in-law had to be kept in the dark.

The final risk was Brigadier Whiting, who, on May 31, had waited in vain on Nine Mile road. (Where, the writer now knew, he should have been, himself). He would need to tread lightly with Whiting, careful what he committed to paper.

The upshot of it all: Headquarters did not know his whereabouts until mid-afternoon. Missing. Lost—with a third of Johnston's forces with him—the center of the army. When a courier eventually found them on Williamsburg Pike, he rode back to report what he was told: the forces were engaging the enemy while awaiting the sound of Whiting's main assault on Nine Mile road.

Johnston was stunned by the reply; his plan was hours behind and in shambles. Disgusted, he said, "I wish the troops were all back in their camps."

Yet something might still be gained. Johnston rode forward with Smith to launch Whiting's Division at the Federals. No sooner done, than Johnston was knocked off his horse by shrapnel. It fell to Smith to corral the missing division. At this juncture President Davis and General Lee came riding up. Appalled by the disarray, Davis relieved Smith of command, turning the army over to Lee. So went the thirty-first of May.

*And yet, one good bluff might salvage the hand.* Knowing the odds favor the dealer, he led.

> *Headquarters*
> *June 7, 1862, 11 A.M.*
> *General Johnston, C.S.A.:*
>
> *General—Your kind favor and present are received. I hope you won't think that I could visit the city without doing myself the pleasure to see you the first thing. I have desired to go in every day, and for no other purpose, but I have been afraid to leave my command for a single moment. It has so turned*

> *out that I might have done so, but I did not know it. Not knowing what moment I may be called upon, I am afraid to move. I shall not fail you the first moment that I consider safe.*

This was where he always stumbled. The opening was satisfactory, striking a balance between concern and adulation, and, it presented a good reason not to be at Johnston's bedside. An actual face-to-face must be avoided at all costs. It might go badly for one (or both) of them. Johnston must have some worry his orders had not been clear.
*The shortest distance between two points . . .*
Before him on his desk was Johnston's present (a *carte-de-visite*.) Taking a deep breath, the writer plunged ahead:

> *The failure of complete success on Saturday, I attribute to the slow movements of General Huger's command.*

He exhaled. Good. Leaves the baby at the door, but not across the threshold. *No need to detail why Huger was so slow. And I have left him a backdoor: his subordinates let him down.* The general wrote carefully, as carefully as anyone would, who might next be reading this before a court martial:

> *This threw, perhaps, the hardest part of the battle upon my own poor division. It is greatly cut up, but as true and ready as ever. Our ammunition was nearly exhausted when Whiting moved, and I could not therefore move on with the rush that we could, had his movement been earlier. We did advance, however, through three encampments and only stopped at nightfall.*

'Is' works much better here than 'was.' 'Our' and 'we' also may serve: safe, inclusive words, embracing whomever the reader may choose.

> *The enemy ran in great confusion, but their troops were arranged en echelon, and we encountered fresh troops every few hundred yards. These readily fell back, however, as the fleeing ones came to them closely pursued.*

Hill did great work there, *but under my command*—so needs no mention. Now, close with a passing opinion, a whiff of regret—something the Old Man can hang his hat on:

> *I can't but help think that a display of his forces on the left flank of the enemy by General Huger would have completed the affair and given Whiting as easy and pretty a game as was ever had upon a battlefield. Slow men are a little out of place upon the field. Altogether it was very well, but I can't help but regret that it is not complete.*
> 
> *With kindest expressions for Mrs. Johnston and the members of your staff, I remain,*
> 
> *truly and sincerely yours,*

He read it through. Read it once more, slowly—word by word. He dared go no further, but could say no less. Burning the earlier drafts, he wrote out an exact copy for himself, blowing lightly across the page to fix the ink. He signed his name:

*James Longstreet*

## CHAPTER 35 — RED TAPE
June 10 – 26, 1862

*"Brigade and Regimental Commanders will institute
a rigid inspection at once of the sick camps and
hospitals and drag out the drones and cowards."*
– Maj. Gen. D.H. Hill

HILL TIMED his order perfectly—eight days before the launch of Lee's counter-offensive. His intent: to confound the shirkers and to stiffen the spines of his surgeons. Hospital beds must be preserved for the brave.

So far as the Third was concerned, his timing could not have been worse. The regiment's hardiest souls, those who had warded off Norfolk's brew of measles, mumps, and whooping cough; who had survived freezing rain and short rations ever since Drewry's Bluff, were finally succumbing to the army's neglect.

At Seven Pines, human and animal waste lay alongside blood, vomit, and viscera, creating a reek that curtailed speech and curdled thought; flies beyond number. A scarcity of potable water and wholesome rations reduced conditions further. Ordinary prostration—*debilitas*—was the first symptom. Camp fever, diarrhea, and typhoid, came next, decimating the ranks. Life in the Richmond cantonments was somewhat better, but even there, the traditions of the Army outranked common sense; illness was dismissed as malingering, medical negligence as 'toughening' the men.

By Hill's lights Third Alabama was a prime example of the problem. *Before the first whiff of gunpowder, Lomax allows two hundred of his 'finest' to waltz into Petersburg's hospitals. Seven Pines drove the remaining cowards into similar havens around Richmond.* Hill had only contempt for the Third's volunteers—accustomed to servants, warm beds, and full stomachs.

Regimental surgeons, he accused of 'trifling'—sending on any man with a hangnail. Under his new orders they could make all the medical recommendations they wished, but each malingerer would be reexamined by the respective *brigade* surgeon; their maladies certified, before being forwarded. Ultimate approval would rest with the Division Surgeon, with whom Hill had had a most constructive talk. This surgeon was responsible for five brigades, plus eight batteries. Simply finding the man was a challenge. The runaround this created earned the sobriquet: Red Tape and Bows.

\* \* \*

John Hoyt punched a new hole in his sword belt, the third in seven days. To forestall a fourth, he dragged Jimmie Howard along for a foraging expedition.

The past week had not been pleasant, much of it spent visiting his men in hospital, making enquiries, writing letters of condolence. One letter he kept putting off concerned Jonathan Moore, last seen being loaded into an ambulance at Seven Pines. The captain had visited every hospital and parsonage on Church Hill, had placed notices in the newspapers, and enlisted the aid of Mr. Lancaster—his father's business partner—to ascertain Moore's whereabouts. All to no avail. He had 'lost' one of his Rifles.

The hunt for food was another challenge. As an officer, Hoyt was allowed to search further afield than his men. His best chance for success would be outside the usual ranging. He and Jimmie headed west, towards the city.

Coming to a well-kept farm they spied chickens near the big house—goslings and ducks in the back pond. Their mouths began to water. Executing a two-pronged attack, they hopped the fence and were nearing their objective when they encountered a breastwork in the form of a large black woman. Her withering glare reducing his age by half, Hoyt inquired if the master of the house was to home.

"All de white folk been done gone, chile; better'n three week."

He asked if the house could spare any food.

"Hmmph. Ah notice you was 'bout to spare us some chickens, wasn't you? Well, *wasn't* you?"

The boys bobbed their heads ruefully.

"Mm-hmm, thas what I thought. That pou'try ain't for sale. Other folks got to eat too." She looked them over. "You git on up the house. You find two ole dinahs dar in the kitchen. Dey do sumpin' fer you young gen'mens."

Grateful for the reprieve, the two quick-stepped to the back of the house, where they found the cooks and struck a bargain for cornbread. While the bread baked, they set off to explore further, to see what else might be obtained.

Blocked by wetlands, they were of a mind to turn back, when they heard a cock's crow. Following it, they crossed the bog, coming to another large home. An older gentleman was chopping his garden alongside three tow-headed boys. The man straightened at their approach, taking out a kerchief to mop his brow. In unison, the youths also stopped, to stare. Tipping his hat, Hoyt introduced himself and made his appeal.

The old man considered. "I don't know, son. Provisions are mighty scarce hereabouts. Don't know as I can spare you any. Tell you what, I will call my daughter and ask her what she thinks we can do for you."

Bobbing amongst the strawberry bushes at the other end of the garden was an enormous sunbonnet. The old gentleman called to it:

"Margaret."

The bonnet continued its bob.

"Mar–gar–ret," he said, louder.

Nothing.

"My daughter," he called, sweetly. The bonnet ignored him.

"Daugh–ter–er."

No change.

"Oh Mag-g-g . . ."

Ditto.

"You Mag!" he said, sharply. Silence. " 'Pon my soul, I believe the chile has gone deef," the old man becoming most agitated, while his boys remained expressionless.

The bonnet, having completed its task, turned its attention to the gaggle of men. Under its shadow, Hoyt beheld a lovely girl of sixteen, if she was that. Pulling off her gloves, she strolled towards them, graceful and unhurried. Whatever coquette may once have batted eyes with gentlemen soldiers, had vanished long before. With a glance to her father and brothers, she took command.

Sweeping off his hat, Hoyt made his best bow and, encouraged by her small smile, introduced his confederate. The father entered their plea.

"We can make you some bread, and let you have some buttermilk," she said. "I'm afraid we have no ham, or chickens, nor even any eggs to spare."

She noticed the holes in their belts and, as if on cue, Jimmie's stomach rumbled. The corners of Mar–gar–et's mouth turned up. Removing her bonnet, she revealed hair as light as her brothers.

"Let me see what we can find." To one of the brothers, she said, "Willie, pull some milk for these gentlemen, won't you? And a pitcher of water." Willie obeyed.

To the soldiers: "Come up to the house in a bit. Rest a spell." Then, keeping to the shade, she walked towards the cookhouse. The soldiers observed a moment of silence.

Making themselves agreeable to the old man, they complimented him on his garden.

"Damn me if it is worth the trouble."

"Would grapevines grow here?" Hoyt inquired.

The man looked at him as though he were daft. "You mean for wine? Nothing you would want for your cellar."

"We have a small vineyard back home. Your strawberries look well enough."

"Pshaw. Strawberries will grow anywhere, young man. Plainly, you are no farmer. Best you stick to soldiering."

As though he had thrown a switch, the remaining sons returned to their labor. The gentleman beckoned the soldiers to follow him up to the house. There, while waiting upon the bread, Jimmie went out onto the front portico. Hoyt and the old man sat in the parlor.

"How goes it, sir? First, I take it you are not from here."

"No sir. We are Alabama men: Third Regiment of Volunteers. I am from North Carolina myself—late, of Mobile."

"A captain, I see. Line, judging by the condition of your uniform, if you will pardon the observation. Your hat . . . 'M.R.C.'?"

"I am captain of the Mobile Rifles, yes, sir."

"The Rifles, you say? I have heard of the Mobile *Cadets*."

"They are allowed a supporting role in our regiment, yes sir."

"Who are your people?"

"My people come from Beaufort County; the upper reach of Pamlico Sound. My father is Mister James Hoyt of little Washington. Jimmie—outside—is from there too. My mother is a Brickell."

"They are safe, I trust."

"Thank you. I believe they are. At least for now. Burnside has made no show towards that place."

"That is well. What can you tell me of Seven Pines? The accounts have been full of 'glory.' Facts, on the other hand, remain in short supply."

"I understand you. Yes sir, it should have gone better. Most of our division—we are under General Huger—marched up and down Charles City Road, all day, that first day."

"I understand he is a great nincompoop, your General Huger."

"The marching up and down was not his idea."

"I see. That is discouraging. And the rest of it?"

"A wasted chance, I think. General Hill did good work the day before we joined the fray, though at frightful cost. If he had been properly supported—had we been used (if I may be so bold)—he might well have destroyed two enemy corps. At minimum, he would have chased them back to Williamsburg. Politically, such a calamity would have been devastating to Lincoln and his henchmen. To McClellan, too. As it was, the effort was so piecemeal, by the time we got in the fight the

Yankees were in large force."

"'Man proposes, but God disposes.' Saw the elephant, did you?"

"Saw the elephant, yessir. Sufficiently close."

"And the elephant saw you?"

"Eye to eye, toe to toe, tusk to tusk."

"Yes. And since?"

"Too soon to tell about old Lee. He is called 'Granny' by the men. His expertise seems to be entrenchments. Of a defensive mind, I gather. He came down to Drewry's Bluff while we were there. Joe Johnston and President Davis came, too."

The description of Lee elicited a "Hah!" from the old man; the exclamation both ambiguous and unexplained.

"I am well acquainted with old Drewry." *There* is a farmer."

Mar–gar–ret entered the room with a pitcher of water. Hoyt stood.

Looking past him, she brought a hand up to cover her smile. Following her eyes, Hoyt saw Jimmie outside, enjoying the vista, the seat of his trousers so worn his drawers were in plain view. Hoyt was relieved: *At least he has drawers*. A rap on the sash got Jimmie's attention. His friend did not spare him.

With haversacks bulging and toting a jar of buttermilk, the two waved goodbye to Miss Margaret (Jimmie backing away). Swinging by the first house, they picked up their cornbread. At camp, they were in time to hear the latest good news-bad news. The good: the regimental baggage train (absent since May 29), had been sighted and was due to arrive. The bad: Hoyt and company were to head out for a week of picket duty. Immediately.

On the hike to the front, it began to rain. Due to the proximity of the enemy, they could not have fires. John, Jimmie, and the Rifles bivouacked in damp clothes for the next two days.

The third day, Forsyth (as Major Commanding) brought forward the remainder of Second Battalion for a reconnaissance in strength. The Rifles were ordered to deploy in skirmish line through the woods, to 'feel' the enemy. Another mile brought them within hearing of a Federal camp. Here, the woods were so dense they could see nothing farther than ten yards. Hearing an enemy patrol passing to one side, they left it alone. Hoyt was running a high fever by this time, and, worried they would get flanked, recalled his men to safer ground. Eventually, they went forward again, skirting to the right of the enemy camp. The lead scouts crawled back to report Yankee pickets straight ahead. A man was sent to report this to Forsyth, who ordered them to withdraw: mission accomplished.

Hoyt collapsed on the return, and was carried back to camp.

Red Tape did not apply to officers. Nevertheless, Hoyt was very ill. His brother James telegraphed their father, who solicited his business partner, Robert Lancaster.

* * *

Among the Hornets, it started with Nan Germany's chills, which progressed to joint pain, fever, and confusion. But he was a new boy; they were always getting sick. When Billy Farrior and Willie Waugh—messmates of Nan's—woke the next day with muscle-soreness and queasy stomachs, the others took notice. Billy was always fighting off some cold or fever, but (other than his ribs) Willie had never been sick a day in his life. Captain Powell had Lieutenant Greene look in.

Rutherford and another messmate fell ill on the third day; the lieutenant on the fourth. The assistant surgeon quarantined them all. By then, the first victims had blinding headaches and high fever. Worse, Farrior and Waugh had a telltale rash of tiny pink spots. The assistant informed Doc Lee and Major Forsyth.

The men knew typhus when they saw it. Several had contracted it while the regiment was at Portsmouth. More had succumbed at Drewry's Bluff and were still in hospital at Petersburg. How it spread was a mystery. Unclean conditions certainly—but whether it was borne by vermin or by other means, no one could say. The Petersburg hospitals were clean, well maintained, and equipped, and those who landed there stood a good chance for recovery.

Neb Battle took care of Billy Farrior—they were neighbors back home, and friends from childhood—tending also to the others, as each took sick. On the fifth day, Neb felt lousy.

\* \* \*

For Forsyth, typhus in Company D came at an inconvenient time. After Seven Pines, General Lee had ordered all regiments to be brigaded by states. Under protest, the Third was transferred out of Mahone's Brigade, to Rodes' Alabama Brigade. Rodes himself was acceptable, but Rodes' Brigade was in Hill's Division (newly under Jackson's command). On June 17, after serenading their beloved brigadier, General Mahone, the Third marched to their new home among the Fifth, Sixth and Twelfth Alabama Volunteers. (The 26th Regiment also came in under the new alignment.)

Lee issued orders mandating the number of wagons allowed each regiment, and the Third was obliged to pare its complement to seven. While the reduction was a challenge to many, no regiment hauled as many wagons as the Third. This did nothing to improve Hill's opinion of the Alabamians. Her officers could only watch, as their cots and air mattresses got forwarded to Richmond's hospitals.

A new brigade and division meant forging new relationships. With Battle recuperating at home, Forsyth found it difficult to navigate the new channels of authority; his youth (and his father's reputation) worked against him. Before he could focus on the regiment's health issues, he lost a couple of days to the paperwork of inventory and transfer; another two, to locate the brigade surgeon.

Captain Powell did what he could—as did the regimental surgeons—but Hill's edict carried weight. Any push to get men into hospital needed to come from a field officer. Concern was easy enough to find; someone to buck the system—

to buck Harvey Hill—was not. The run-around was into its second week before the brigade surgeon made his call on the sick Hornets. His recommendations were overruled by the division surgeon.

Troup Randle took a different approach.

The top surgeon was alone, writing reports by lamplight when Randle took a seat across from him at the small camp table. Without preamble, he said, "Doc: here is what you are going to do—"

The surgeon barely gave him a glance. "Lieutenant, do you have any idea to whom you are speaking?"

Troup, raising one hand to signal caution, used his right to rest a Navy Colt on the table, barrel to the surgeon, finger on the trigger. The doctor's face grew red.

"Doc, just hear me out. One question: does this look like I give a good goddam?"

The surgeon had not risen to his present rank being buffaloed by lieutenants. "Mister, you will have to do better than that. Discharge that firearm, and you won't make it ten yards from this tent. And you don't look the type to stand in front of a firing squad. Get the hell out of here before I call the guard."

Troup's head canted over. "Guard? You think there's a guard? Ain't nobody gonna be passing this tent anytime soon. Not till we finish here—"

"How *dare* you!"

"Now Doc, now—now listen, you're not *hearing* me. I'm not the one you have to worry about. This Colt here, is just to get your attention—"

The surgeon had had enough, his voice rising: "Why you *impudent*—" he started to sputter. "Lieutenant, I'll give you exactly—"

"—it is that fellow behind you. It is *he* you want to worry about."

"What kind of damn fool do you take me for?"

"If I were dealing with a fool this would be tricky. But I don't take you for a fool, Doc. No, not one bit. I take you for someone who wants to live a long and peaceful life. Someone who wants to sit in front of his fireplace, someday—once this shit is over—bouncin' grandbabies on his knee; tellin' 'em stories of the great war.

"But if you raise your voice one more time: you will die. And I will have to go through this again, with your successor. Simple as that, Doc." He leaned forward: "So, I would stay very, *very*, still, and be very, *very*, quiet, and *listen*, were I you."

"You son of a bitch, I could—"

"Ah, ah, ah, now—I hear you. I do." Randle leaned back, taking a soothing tone. "If the shoe were on the other foot, why, I don't rightly know how I would play this myself."

"You say an assassin stands behind me—To what? Slit my throat?"

"Oh, no, no, no, no, no! *No* sir. I've seen too many rascals survive that procedure. No sir, he's holding a common, every-day, bayonet. The sort we call a 'pig-sticker.' Should come out right about where you're flapping your gums. The man there behind you watched his brother die. Just yesterday. Of Red Tape."

The surgeon's forehead was glistening.

"You ever hear of such a thing, Doc? A misery called Red Tape? I never heard of it neither 'fore last week, but I'm just a country boy, you know. They tell me you fix it with the dip of a quill, a little ink, a little scribblin'."

"There is no. . . . "

Randle's eyes shifted from the surgeon's face.

A man cleared his throat.

The surgeon made to swallow, but his mouth was dry. His face, once so red, drained of all color. He was very still.

\* \* \*

The brigade surgeon was surprised to see the approvals come in so late. Knowing General Hill would have larger fish to fry, he forwarded the order without delay; Lee's mobilization had begun.

Rodes' Brigade marched on June 26. Powell left the sick men in the care of their remaining messmates.

Nan Germany died first, on the day spent securing transport for the others. Everything with wheels and hooves was engaged in moving the army. By the time the others got to Second Alabama Hospital, [15] their care was competing against the wounded arriving from Mechanicsville. They were placed in a back corridor. When they got moved outside, they had no strength to protest. The ward superintendent did not know where they had gone. Billy Farrior died June 29. His friend, Neb Battle—the corporal who had guided Jim Branscomb through camp—died the next day. Willie Waugh and Frank Rutherford were cousins. They died together, on July 1. The lone survivor was Lieutenant Greene, his health so shattered, he would never again have to face General Armistead.

Captain Jelks, who had fallen ill at Drewry's Bluff, was also in the city, in a private home. It did not save him. Captain Powell did not learn the fate of Jelks and the others till days later, on Malvern Hill. Where his focus was on rebuilding a regiment out of the shattered remnants of the Third.

---

[15] In addition to the Confederate government, the states also supplied doctors and facilities for their contingents. Alabama's Richmond Hospitals were under the able supervision of Julia Ward Hopkins, of Mobile.

## CHAPTER 36 — Cold Harbor
June 27, 1862

T.B. FOWLER never did learn whether it was *that* Poe's farm. Probably wasn't, but there wasn't anyone to ask after the families got cleared out. *Might be some relation though.* The farm was their section of 'the works' (as the entrenchments around Richmond, were called). The past weeks had been an idyll of normalcy; the most time he had spent in one place since leaving Tuskegee, providing some idea what garrison duty in Norfolk must have been like.

His school of fish hadn't been at Moseley's long enough to gather an impression, let alone a pass into town. Those were days of packing, weighing, discarding, re-packing, loading, forwarding. Once, he had sat on stoops, watching sunsets, with some of these same boys, a glass of lemonade, or ice water, to hand. To see them grown into soldiers was a revelation.

*Good ole days.* The phrase popped into his head; one he had heard all his life, from the old folks, both black and white. Until this moment never giving the words much thought—

A whoosh, then a whump: the ground shuddering as something big landed near them, smashing his reverie. Came another, and another. Mildly concerned, his mind returned to its present: he was still prone, still sweltering. He wondered how long he had been out. Not asleep, exactly—just somewhere else. *'While I nodded, nearly napping, suddenly there came a tapping, as of someone.'. . . Someone, what? Rapping? Gently rapping*—no gentle rapping here.

A twenty-pounder screeched overhead. *Quoth the Parrott?* The fire was steady, but having little effect. Its face in a ditch, the past hour, the regiment was pinned by a second foe. If they did not soon move, sunstroke would begin to take its toll. The cut by the road protected them from bursting shells, but the noonday sun made it hot as a broiling pan. Caissons and limbers racing to the front raised great clouds of dust; the ambulance wagons and couriers making smaller donations.

Another cloud rolled over, daring them to breathe. T.B. closed his eyes tight, holding his breath through the worst of it. The coughing started. His head resting on his forearms, he swiveled his face away from the road. Next to him, Henry's face was caked with dust, white as an egg. Opening his eyes, the effect was startling. The two mouthed their stock greeting to one another: 'Why, what are *you* doing here?'

Back when Captain Mayes was home, recruiting, T.B. had joined the line outside the courthouse, minding his own business, when old Mrs. Drakeford found him. Fixing his arm in her claw, she demanded: "Why, Edmund Fowler, what on earth are *you* doing here?" Edmund (he was Edmund back then) was at a loss. It was Henry Foster who spoke up: "He's here for his colonels' stars, Mrs. D. Same as me!" It gained him a sharp look from the matron, but amused the line of recruits. She stalked off, "*Well, I never!* Young people today— just as impudent as the day is long." That the *Fowler* boy had enlisted became the talk of the town.

Before this, he and Henry were barely acquainted. Henry was older by a year, and a good deal bigger, ran with the fast set. Most of that set (like Henry's brother, Wilbur), had gone off with the Third the year before.

Afterwards, when it came their time to take the cars, Henry took the seat beside him—no one else would have. By Columbus, the two were fast friends.

T.B. was small for his age; would always be so, and was resigned to seeing the world from five-foot-four and three-quarters. While he was not the youngest of the fresh fish arriving in Norfolk, his fair complexion, freckles, and beardless face supported that assumption, even among the drummer boys.

Clarence Tate was first to spot the fish, and singled him out as "Minnow." Tate's wit was of the cutting sort and he quickly honed his creation: "You too small to keep, boy. We just gonna call you 'Thoh-back.'" And Thoh-back, he became.

He had been called worse.

Everybody had a nickname; most bestowed in the natural way: Bubba, or Trey, or Torch. Tate's older brother was the one they all called 'Preacher.' These were volunteers, however. In the army's caste system, Edmund was a "recruit," meaning he barely had the decency to join up 'fore somebody "come got him." Nicknames were assigned whether you wanted one or not—some appellation was needed, if only to distinguish one "hey you" from another. The names were not meant to be spiteful, necessarily. Hiawatha Taylor earned his name on the firing range, forgetting to remove his ramrod.

In his own case, Edmund knew better. Tate (and some others) had a low opinion—not just of him, but of his parents. "Thoh-back" was a challenge to see if he dared be one of the boys, to see if he was easily offended. He wasn't (easily offended). All the same, he was relieved when Thoh-back got shortened to "T.B." (not that that was a vast improvement).

Henry remained Henry; a strapping lad, he was not one to take guff from the likes of Clarence Tate. Was Henry who tagged him: "Tater"

The shelling stopped.

Awaiting orders, the men stayed put, but immediately took up the wry commentary first begun in Montgomery. Colonel Forsyth and his wings—Sands and Powell—were on their feet, conferring. T.B. thought Forsyth looked unwell.

When the officers' mounts were brought up, the regiment got to their feet, a cloud rising with them as the new boys began dusting off, bringing down curses from the volunteers. Dust cakes wherever sweat collects: chests, armpits, collars, crotches. Like manure—best to let it dry. T.B.'s face was as chalky as Henry's, and he wiped at it with his sleeve. At commands, all talk ceased. At 'Shoulder Arms:' they were once again on the move and, T.B.'s mind, back to its wandering.

When the fish were first getting broke, the old boys gave them this advice: "First thing: Don't offer yer opinion. If we want it, we know where to find it. Second thing: a recruit is to be seen—not heard. Third thing: *remember the second thing.* Fourth thing, and most important: you are most definitely a *'re-croot.'* All us *volunteers* jined up in Sixty-One—so put that in yer dern pipe." The point was brought home one day when a recruit greeted Boss Cargill with *"Why, hullo, Chief Bull Nose."* The jonah could not have come off his feet any faster.

Sound advice never offended T.B. One word was all he needed. He held the old militia in high esteem anyways, regarding them always as "The Company," Macon County's best men (least ways, the best men still single) cutting the figure with their shiny buttons, frock coats, and patent leather shakoes. Squire Battle, Mister Swanson, and some others, had chipped in for the outfits. Had bought the Enfields, too.

In Virginia, the company was, if anything, more impressive. Their coats might be gone—swapped for grey jackets, the shakoes for kepis—but a year of work, drill, and maneuver had brought out their better qualities. Lean and fit, they fell to their duties (and to their pranks) with a spirit, missing from old Tuskegee.

Moseley's Church had been a chaotic time, what with company elections and all. At T.B.'s first roll call, Swanson announced his resignation, displaying a weeping sore on his cheek. And he had lost weight; a far cry from the man who once had ruled Macon. He departed for home next day, accepting a promotion, to school conscripts at Notasulga. It might be, he left without ever hearing the name Goober said out loud—only a fool would have said it to his face. Regardless, the result was a good one for the company: Mister Mayes was elected captain.

A shame about Mayes.

Then it was Drewry's Bluff, those dispiriting days of rain and cold, fever and hunger. And this ugly incident: a parcel, arriving from his father, deliberately crushed. He heard sniggering behind his back, when the corporal handed it over. It had not been the usual thing soldiers received, containing biscuits and jams. Being a pharmacist, Mr. Fowler had filled this box with scarce and valuable drugs, patent medicines and ointments, intended for the benefit of the entire company.

The Fowlers were Tuskegee's own "Damn Yankees." Not that they were the only pro-Union family in the county—not by a long shot—but his folks were the only ones from the detestable commonwealth of Massachusetts and, the only ones who lived right on the square. Mrs. Fowler saw no reason to adapt to local mores, other than to hire wenches to do the cleaning and cooking—there being no Irish girls. It became difficult to find black women willing to work under her heavy hand. "Southerners are backward, willful, *and ill-mannered*," she declared; pronouncements which were not helpful.

Once Edmund had enlisted, and gone off, Mrs. Fowler had gone to a ladies' sewing bee, uninvited—to help make uniforms. Entering the silent room, a woman of "good family" greeted her with a sweet smile—and spit in her face.

T.B. lodged no complaint with the corporal.

At Seven Pines he stood his ground as well as any. The better men began to pass round the word: "Ole Thoh-back, now, is better'n he looks—he's all right." T.B.'s first sergeant made sure the information circulated amongst those who mattered.

Marching gave Edmund time to notice many things. The man marching in front of him, for instance: the seat of his trousers was worn through and he was in discomfort, twitching and reaching behind. Edmund suspected piles. Woody Salve or Oil of Canada Balm would help that, and he would have offered it, but it was things like that, that were in the destroyed parcel. The man's shoes were in good shape, but many of the others, tramping along nearby, were not. Entrepreneurs would pick up spares from the abandoned camps, tying a single shoe to their cross belts, a tacit offer to sell or trade.

T.B. heard the footfalls of someone coming up at the double quick, and Sergeant Tate hove into view, trotting slowly past. Preacher spotted the recruit. "He hath filled the hungry with good things, and the rich He hath sent empty away."

"But they that seeketh the Lord shall not want any good thing," Edmund responded.

"Psalm Thirty-four. You good to go there, Thoh-back?"

"Yes, sergeant."

"Very well." To the column Tate announced: "Thoh-back say he all right, ever'body. Knows the Good Book. Close it up, there—here now, Otis. Close it up, boy! Don't disgrace yourself."

"Too late," said Otis.

"Amen. Just keep up—keep it tight, *'Serrer les rangs'* as ole Beau might say. Close enough to pick up their scent, lads." From the column came a well-timed fart. Preacher laughed along with the rest, the men rattling and clanking ahead, to close up on the Guards.

Looking back on it, T.B. knew he was fortunate to have missed the regiment's first year. He was as patriotic as the next fellow, but service under Captain Swanson would have been onerous.

Now that Captain Mayes was gone; Mr. Bryan was their captain. Bryan was "quality." So was Lieutenant Bilbro. Wherever they led, Edmund would gladly follow.

Presently, this meant marching through one continuous encampment. Mile on mile of abandoned tents, equipment, overcoats, knapsacks, shoes (singles); "bullet-proof" vests, stray dogs, crippled mules. A euphonium. Obviously, the North was sparing no expense to bring the South back into line. At first the pursuers picked up whatever treasure struck their fancy. But even cornucopias grow heavy before they are worthless, or traded for smaller mementos. Servants were now relegated to the baggage train, so, every soldier carried his own kit and every man learned the value of travelling light.

At two o'clock the division came to Burnett's Tavern (also known as Old Cold Harbor), a way station for army couriers and provost men. Across from the tavern, beneath the boughs of a large chestnut, a crowd of thirsty men waited their turn at the well. The vanguard of the division came to a halt. The Third, at the opposite end of this concertina, came to a shuffling stop by the tavern itself.

The occasional pop of musketry from the front, now

roared to life and greeted them properly, the smoke clouding a neighboring hill. Punching through the rattle, was the steady boom of field pieces. The guns, calling to Edmund's mind, a prizefighter he once had seen at the fairgrounds. A big bruiser, he was—paid to pound the lights out of feisty little fellows— them as had more spunk than brains.

At the halt they were silent, waiting for the next development. A boy-Paul Revere came tearing down the column: "Stonewall is come—and driving all before him!" eliciting a lusty cheering. "By land or sea?" asked Henry. Rodes' lead element moved off the road and through a scrim of young pines. Dismantling a fence, they quickly reformed and dressed to the colors, marching into a large field, the Federal guns on their left.

Waiting their turn, the regiments pulled their cartridge boxes forward, unbuttoning the flaps. Edmund pressed down the cork on his canteen and made sure his haversack was fastened. Henry Foster did the same. Fussing over details helped. Edmund heaved a deep sigh; Henry yawned—starting a like response from others, that finished in self-conscious laughter. Some flexed their shoulders or rotated their wrists, cracked their knuckles—whatever thing might ease the stress without earning a bark from their corporal. They expected this fight would be over entrenched positions and much different from the free-for-all that was Seven Pines. Musicians from the various regiments flowed past them to the rear, where they would be assigned to ambulances. The drummers and buglers stayed put.

Shambling the last few rods down to their position, the regiment made right face, slipping between the pines and over the collapsed rails, into the field of trampled grass. Southward, behind a low line of trees, were two Yankee batteries entrenched near the crest of the hill—ten or twelve guns, with a clear field of fire—likely the same ones they had heard all day. The rest of the brigade were already marching away to a skirt of woods running along a bottom, a thousand yards southwest. Hill's other brigades were massing there.

The color guard strode to its place and uncased the banners; *"No Lo Me Tangere,"* on the regimental, looking rather ironic. On the other hand, their large new battle flag was bright, and unsullied: a starry St Andrews cross on a field of red, the whole bordered in orange; '3d' and 'Ala.' flanking the center star. That these simple abbreviations should be the flag's sole embellishment was a source of anger. The other flags in Rodes' Brigade all proclaimed: 'SEVEN PINES!' in large, neat, letters across the top—only the Third was lacking; Longstreet and Hill decreeing regiments accused of plundering had no right to the accolade.

The Tuskegees formed on the left of Chester's men. The sergeants were all business, dressing the lines as though on parade. Behind Edmund, the drummers took up *Jefferson and Liberty*. Across the way, the Federal batteries continued their slow, methodical fire. He followed the shells arching over, to where they landed on the north edge of their field. With deafening booms, the small Confederate batteries answered.

*LT McAnerney (F)*

The Metros acting captain did not relish the thought of crossing this ground. But the boys stepped off like they were the kings of Capitol Square. Second Battalion (under Captain Powell) marched in the lee of the wooded marsh. Risk depended on a number of factors, but Mac thought they must look like sitting ducks to the gunners on the hill.

He had not slept well. Last evening's artillery duel at Beaver Dam Creek had been beautiful—from their safe distance—but hardly conducive to sleep. The bright fuses of competing shells, rolling gracefully back and forth through the night sky, bursting in silence like ripe cotton bolls; mesmerizing, until the gut-thumping explosions arrived. The opposing batteries, lit up by each salvo. Whatever was moving in the creek bottom became illuminated, captured for that instant, a spectacle in its own peculiar way. Occasionally the groans of the dying were heard through the din, and dispelled the illusion. The display eventually stopped and, at midnight, Lee's orders came down: Rodes' Brigade would renew the attack at dawn.

The regiments accepted their sentence. It was their turn. Such missions were 'forlorn hopes.' It was madness to charge guns so strongly placed. McAnerney knew these next few hours, would most certainly be his last.

At one o'clock, they moved forward into a shallow vale. The men lay down. To set an example, Mac closed his eyes and pretended to sleep. For a brief time, the charade was no pretense.

When he awoke, the air felt dense; a puny breeze trying its best. Against the glow of camp fire he read his pocket watch: three o'clock. Jones, who had not slept, came over. The sergeant knew his job, no need to issue him orders. The sergeant set off in search of his squad leaders and a pot of coffee. Rodes' Brigade was under orders of silent reveille, for whatever good *that* might do. The Federals would not be napping. Besides, there was always some peckerhead in the neighborhood feeling the need to rattle his drums.

The company executed a quiet count-off, roll call and inspection: thirty-two present—ten fewer than yesterday. Jones handed him a cup of coffee. He winced at the taste, but did not complain. It was wet and, like the breeze, trying it's best. The regiment was brought into column.

It is a mystery how a cheer can be raised without sound. That it is possible, cannot be denied. When Forsyth passed the word, that the Yankees had pulled out, the men experienced a joy known only to those who have cheated fate.

The rest of that day was the usual stops, starts, halts, and shelling, to which they were accustomed. Reprieves being impermanent things, McAnerney took the Metros into the field at Old Cold Harbor. But this was not the certain death they had been facing twelve hours before and, as they marched, each man believed the odds would favor him.

To maintain Line of March, McAnerney kept his eyes on Colonel Gordon and his staff, remaining alert for orders from Forsyth. It seemed to him the Federals were directing fire at the brigade's leading regiments: the Fifth, Twelfth, and 26th. Gordon and the Sixth kept to the original line. Their goal appeared to be a small space between Anderson and Ripley's brigades. Breaking into double quick the Sixth sped away. The Third kept its pace: ninety steps per minute, twenty-eight inches to the step.

*Corbet Ryder (K)*

The Rifles stepped over the rails at shoulder arms. The old A.V.C. militias still cared about appearance: their lines remained ordered by height—tallest men on the right. Scotty's place was in the middle. Singleterry had been on his left for a year, but the clap had got him. Now, Lecesne was there. On his right, Yeates was where Skinner use to be. Skinner. He shook off the morbid thoughts.

Ryder's outlook was skewed by the habits of his profession. A bookkeeper before the war, his days spent recording profit and loss, assets and liabilities, margins, percentages, accounts receivable and payable; costs fixed, and variable. Da had often told him: "Every enterprise of man can be reduced to numbers, lad." Sometimes, he longed to be free of them. Joining the militia had been an escape—socially, at least. And until Seven Pines he would have entered his experiences with the Rifles under Assets. But battle had changed the calculus: the First of June represented a gross loss of two hundred. Line ditto: those rain-soaked weeks at Drewry's Bluff. Since then, one hundred more, fallen sick. The regiment left Norfolk with nine hundred, ergo: the loss of five, leaves a net of four hundred this morning. Of these, exactly thirty are Rifles, and the Rifles are not the smallest company.

He inventoried the brigade in like-manner: fifteen hundred perhaps, no more. In the last sixty days Rodes' strength had been more than halved. He shook his head. Pessimism did not come easily to Scotty: such profligacy he likened to embezzlement.

During Hoyt's illness, Lake was in command of the company. Scotty liked the lieutenant, but wished he could order a faster pace. Scotty's Enfield was nestled in the hollow of his shoulder, his hand tightened about the trigger guard.

*Edmund "T.B." Fowler (C)*

Crossing the field was not so bad as Edmund had feared. Watching the color guard out front, marching so confidently, was an inspiration for all. Nearly all. He heard someone reciting the twenty-third psalm.

The line encountered a few craters, a few casualties, but he had not been forced to step over any. The Yankee gunners were directing fire ahead of their march, over the lines of the first regiments. Arriving at the boggy bottom, the trees provided little actual protection, but the men jammed in under their shade, clinging to a notion of safety in numbers.

So many, in fact, unit cohesion was impossible; impossible for commanders to order their battalions, or for companies to hear their captains. In lieu of commands the men pressed forward. Edmund was soon thigh deep in the bog, struggling to keep his footing. Pushing through the mire brought them against the side of a ravine. Here, the ooze only covered his shoes. Well, his left shoe—the muck had pulled off his right. Henry Foster grabbed his sleeve and pulled him toward a cluster of Tuskegees. Henry's eyes were bright and Edmund realized: *He's enjoying this.*

Iron and lead whistled all around, the sound interspersed by frequent thumps, occasionally a crack, as the missiles slammed into tree trunks. They were soon beneath a cascade of leaves, looking out for branches and limbs. The shade was welcome, but its coolness was more than offset by the body heat of hundreds. The afternoon light was diffused to a golden hue by the smoke of battle. Orders came down, were shouted and relayed: "Hold your fire."

Shadows appearing across their position, T.B. looked up to see silhouettes charging them, his heart pounding, as several hundred men rushed downhill to their embankment, plowing and clanking and scrambling down into the huddled masses in the ravine. He waited for an explosion of gunfire and slaughter. Instead, those nearest the melee stood up to make room and, with hearty slaps on the back, made the newcomers welcome. The silhouettes were Colonel Gordon's men—all that remained of the mighty Sixth. They had sloshed through the swamp and kept going, till they found themselves unsupported and under heavy fire. They were ordered to fall back. Last into the ravine was Gordon himself, skidding his mount down the bank, the horse nimble and alert—ears twitching to follow the singing lead. Below Gordon's saddle blanket, the grey horse was stained black.

Gordon was about the thinnest man T.B. had ever seen. Once, back home, a man had brought a half-starved dog into Pa's store. He called it a greyhound—was meant to look like that, so the man said. Gordon looked like that. The same sharp features and dark, luminous eyes. More weapon than man.

Captain Bryan pulled Edmund from behind and motioned him to regroup with the rest of the Tuskegees. Lieutenant Bilbro, Cotton-Eyed Joe, and others were there. Henry Foster crouched behind Hal Martin.

*Corbet Ryder (K)*

Lieutenant Lake searched to locate Colonel Forsyth, missing since they first went in to the field. First Battalion was apparently leaderless. Lake had volunteered Ryder to go search for him when Captain Bonham and Major Sands rode up.

Sands huddled with the captains: Colonel Forsyth was ill and had been removed to an aid station. Sands had command of the regiment—Powell would take First Battalion, and Bonham Second. Orders were to keep their heads down, to not return fire. There soon would be a push.

Scotty was encouraged. Sands should have been in command all along. *Best officer in the regiment, even if he is one of the high and mighty Cadets.* Twisting around he looked to catch a glimpse of any of his friends down that way—

couldn't—too many bodies between. He hoped Frère Jack was all right. Word was passed that Cherry was killed crossing the field, and that Yeates (somehow), had put a minié ball through his own hand. These two appeared to be the only casualties. *Knock wood*, he rapped on his stock. As if in answer, a double whack came from the tree trunk behind.

The sun was melting into the horizon. If a push was to come it better come soon. The soldiers near the front edge described the landscape: an uphill slope of four hundred yards covered in rows of young corn, an orchard of some sort on the crest where the Yankee batteries were at work with their usual effectiveness.

Fighting on the right increased. They had been pounding away over there for hours, but now the rattle appeared to be reaching a critical phase. Looking behind him, Scotty saw another brigade arriving at the marsh, begin to slog across— Georgians. When he looked back around, his comrades were up and shouting—something inarticulate, but suitably warlike. The horde went up and over the bank, rushing away up the hill towards the last of the light. With a grunt he too rose up and, leaving the safety of the bog, joined his shouts to theirs.

*LT McAnerney (F)*

Having used the flat of his sabre to swat a straggler, McAnerney took a moment to assess the situation. In the orchard up top, the Federal's were paying little attention to those advancing through the corn. Rather, the batteries appeared to be concentrating fire upon their left flank. They wore white straw hats, those gun crews, and the lieutenant thought it an odd choice. Following the direction of their fire, he saw a tide of Confederates break from the gloom of the far woods and spill across the hillside. At this distance, they seemed mixed-in with glowing sticks, jittering reds that stood out against the darkening landscape. He was transfixed, until a muzzle flash revealed them to be overheated rifle barrels.

The Federals began to waver. Mac crossed more cornrows, encouraging the men onwards. Nearing the crest, he saw that the battery had been taken. Across the hill, he saw the Yankee Bucktails massed in an ordered withdrawal. Others—panicked units and individuals, both—ran in front of and through the Bucktails, disrupting their field of fire. Confusion became contagious, the panic manifesting when the Texas flags topped the slope. Hood's Brigade had made their charge over the creek and up the hill, evidently without firing a shot, because upon reaching the crest they knelt and sent a storm of lead into the Yankee defenders. The Bucktails' 'modicum of dignity' fell apart.

Taking this in at a glance, Mac did not pause to celebrate. The light was nearly gone. They must continue to push, to knock these Yankees off their hill. He was nearly through the corn when the ball blew through his right forearm. He had been moving forward. Now, forward lost all meaning. *What has happened?* Gaping at his coat sleeve as it turned black below the elbow, more black dripping off his cuff. On his knees, all seemed out of kilter, the horizon spinning. Where had the sun gone? Dazed and nauseous, pain broke over him like a wave. He could see his hand. It was still there. Why couldn't he feel it? *Why can I not make it move?*

\* \* \*

T.B. ran up to the captured guns. With comrades egging them on, several men assumed heroic stances atop the limbers and guns. Bathed in the last of the light, one suddenly clutched at his throat and pitched backwards. *There are old soldiers, and there are bold soldiers,* T.B. had often heard it said. *But there are no old . . .* His hand reached into his cartridge box. Pulling a round, he brought it to his mouth, biting off the end. His eyes scanned the hilltop, alert for both friends and foes. Confident danger was not imminent, he continued to load, pouring the powder, by habit tamping the rod gently to seat the ball. He turned to look behind him—to see how far they had come, and how high. He was disappointed. The hill seemed so much longer and higher when he was running over it. Cocking the hammer back to safety, he flicked the spent mercury cap off the nipple, and fished for a fresh one from out of his pouch. Below, many were still advancing, swarming like ants. To his eyes it was strangely festive. It was the mangled and the groaning who seemed out of place. With the rifle balanced in his left hand, he seated the new cap and pressed it down. In the twilight, he witnessed an officer struck by a ball spin to his knees. The officer stayed there, holding his elbow, rocking back and forth.

On top of the hill, soldiers were whooping, congratulating one another, exulting. "Did you see those Buckteeth run!" cried one. Another—likely one of the Texans—let loose a bloodcurdling war cry. In the growing darkness T.B. heard a bellow coming from the far slope: "Third Alabama!" Two horsemen rode past him, one of them (with enough braid to be a general), swaying in his saddle. Edmund heard "Third Alabama" again, followed by: "Macon County—Mobile—Montgomery men!" Sounding like Captain Powell. "Wetumpkas—Third Alabama—form on me. You Bo-Los . . ." Closer, and, in similar manner, sergeants and officers from other regiments competed for the ears of their own men. He recognized Preacher Tate taking up the call. T.B. headed towards him, keeping an eye out for Henry Foster—and for a good right shoe.

## CHAPTER 37 — SAVAGE'S
June 30, 1862

TWO RAIL-STOPS east of Fair Oaks, Savage's Station was the primary supply dump for the Union army and the site of several field hospitals. Bull Sumner, commanding the Union rear guard, could have held this ground till Christmas. And would have. But McClellan (always fearful he was outnumbered), ordered his generals to fall back to the James, destroying all supplies that couldn't be saved. Sumner withdrew—only after McClellan threatened his arrest.

From the Chickahominy, Rodes' Brigade watched the supplies go up in smoke.

Next morning, the Tuskegees were deployed as skirmishers, and were first to enter the area, emerging from a wide ravine north and east of the depot. Standing outside of the field hospitals, nurses and stewards flapped towels and sheets, in token of surrender. Another white sheet flew from the flagpole, beneath the usual red banner. On the other side of a community of blankets and shebangs (used for the overflow of wounded), the skirmishers spotted a line of wagons. Each, stenciled with a large green shamrock and '$2^d$ Corps Medical.' In army parlance these were Authenrieth wagons. In the haste of retreat, Christmas had come early.

Waving the nurses and walking-wounded out of their way, a band of Tuskegees sped towards the wagons. Captain Bryan held the rest in check, to verify the camp was filled only with non-combatants. He ordered Bilbro to get the names of those who had broken ranks.

Commanding Second Battalion, Powell rode up and reported to Major Sands. Confederate surgeons and ambulance men came next, to assist the wounded. Assured a one-hour's halt, the captains ordered their men to keep their rifles handy, and to stay within sight of the flagpole.

Savvier volunteers knew an opportunity to rifle medical wagons was well worth the punishment. Each Federal brigade had a complement of eight ambulances and four Authenrieths. Ambulances had litters, bandages, and splints—and not much else. The medical wagons, on the other hand were practically small dry-goods stores, with: coffee, tea, sugar, honey, cans of condensed milk. Of particular note: each contained a case of medicinal liquor, *viz.* whiskey. Desirable for consumption or trade, these items went to the sharpest eyes, or the strongest arms—more disciplined soldiers were 'a little out of place.'

Wading through a crowd of gun-holders and optimists, Thohback reached the last wagon. John Pride was clambering down from the front bench with two army blankets across his shoulders and a roll of gutta-percha under his arm.

"Cleaned out?" T.B. inquired.

"Not quite, but there ain't much left 'ats of any use. This is the last of the rubber cloth. What I can't use I can sell. You want a couple of yards, best speak up now. You ever seen such a sight? Must be three thousand head o' Yankee 'round this place, 'n that's jess the ones can't walk." John trotted off to find his gun-holder.

Parting the canvas, T.B. made a quick survey. The whiskey had flown: its crate displaying twelve empty nests. A surgeon's pannier lay open: clamps and syringes—all manner of medieval devices strewn about. Plaster of Paris had been spilled, the powder all over the medical instruments. Walking around to the rear, he expected more of the same. Lifting the backflap, he found bottles of alteratives. His father didn't put much stock in elixirs but, insofar as alcohol made up a good percentage of their contents, they were empty. He smelled ammonia and other spilled chemicals. The wagon's sliding casements had been rifled—but *look out*: the bottles inside were intact! Unable to decipher the labels, the boys had left them alone.

T.B. turned a small bottle in his hand: *'Antimonii et potassium tartratis.'* Over a second bottle he mouthed the words: *'Ceræ albæ.'* Edmund smiled. *No: 'Nothing here of any use.'*

Making himself comfortable, he began to inventory.

\* \* \*

The hour having passed, Gordon ordered the regiments to fall in. Showing off their more legitimate trophies, the Tuskegees were the envy of all. Down the road, they passed Savage's battered home, and then the station itself, hallooing the other divisions assembled there, and falling into step; the tramp, tramp, tramp, always a boost to morale. General Jackson was to one side, questioning Yankee prisoners, his eyes wide and animated. "Eyes Right," was ordered. While the officers and N.C.O.s dutifully lifted their swords, Jackson focused on the interrogation, oblivious to all else.

On the south side of the rail line they re-crossed the ravine, following the road to White Oak Bridge. The Tuskegees returned to the skirmish line. It was not till much later, they discovered Morris was missing.

Several remembered trading shots with a Yankee bushwhacker that afternoon—the one Bilbro had dropped. All agreed, the lieutenant had made a fine shot, but Morris was now missing and, *only now*, did the last skirmisher on the left speak up to say Morris had been over there, too. They had become separated; a common-enough thing, given the rough terrain and the distance between skirmishers. All agreed it was not in Morris's character to desert—or to get lost. T.B. and some others, volunteered to go back and look for him. At minimum, they should be able to confirm the dead Yankee.

Morris was a late recruit; Charlie Moore's man. Moore was sent home for bad eyes, and though it was not required of a medical discharge, he hired Morris for his substitute. Being a hired substitute was not a pleasant way to start with a company (any more than it was to have Yankees for parents), but at Drewry's Bluff, Morris proved such a willing soldier and successful forager, he won over his new comrades. At Seven Pines and Gaines Mill he continued to show his mettle.

He was first to spy the wagons at Savage's and, by so doing, claimed a first-rate oilskin raincoat—just like the one General Jackson was wearing.

It was T.B. who found him—right where Bilbro had put him—still in the black talma he had possessed for less than a day. At a distance, black looked like the dark-blue federal coat. Mistakes like this were made every day. When Bilbro learned some of his skirmishers were taking fire, he came over to take stock of the situation. They pointed out the solitary rifleman.

Veasey was the best shot in the regiment, but he was sick, so Bilbro, looking around, asked Hal Martin for his Enfield—knowing his gun would be properly sighted. Two hundred yards away, the stranger peeked out from behind his tree, and the lieutenant drilled him. Nobody thought twice about it. "Man needed a bigger tree."

Now, Thoh-back stood over poor Morris. The ball, hitting the bridge of the nose like that, had made a mess—but that was Morris's chin whiskers, right enough. His uniform was 'commutation'—homemade. Rifling the pockets of the raincoat (the nicest thing he owned), he found some letters to send back home. T.B. waved in the rest of the search party. T.B. had not had much experience viewing dead men. And *there* (he couldn't help it, the search had become second nature), right there, on Morris's feet: a perfectly good pair of shoes. Union issue. Hobnails. Morris must have traded for them back at the station. He felt bad for Morris, (even worse for Lieutenant Bilbro), but good fresh shoes. The right size. Right there.

His mother would have pointed out such callousness was a reflection of the company he kept, but shoes were critically important and frightfully scarce. Last night John Pride had gone on about it: "Why, when I was a lad, brogans covered the plains—far as the eye could see (or a man could walk). Now the herds is in decline, I say, *brought to heel*, they have become shy, *cowed* little critters—nocturnal—'specially in this, the *mating* season. Just the other night I saw one go to ground, its *tongue* hanging out, the *last* of its kind, forty thousand smelly feet *on the heels* of this one frightened little *sole*—just too painful to witness." Pride the Incorrigible.

T.B. couldn't take these shoes, he just couldn't, not even to trade. The one he found two nights ago was about as wore down as the one he lost. He had expected more from the Yankees, but he supposed they had been doing the same marching as them—just backwards. Morris's shoes were practically new.

The others harbored similar thoughts. Taking Morris's shoes meant bringing him back barefoot and everybody back there looking to see who come in with extras. Human nature. Morris could keep his shoes—so long as no one was looking, anyways. Pride lifted the body under the shoulders and, with the others grabbing the corners of the raincoat they started back; T.B. carrying everybody's guns. Morris's rifle was about the same as his own.

\* \* \*

They had no trouble at White Oak Swamp. The crossing was the usual strong position for the Yanks (the Federals were seldom without artillery support), but at this point in the skedaddle, they were putting a premium on government property. The Third was halted, and the Twelfth allowed to pass through, to establish the night's picket line. Next morning, the Twelfth was ordered back to Savage's, where they collected the wounded prisoners and escorted them to Richmond.

## CHAPTER 38 — WILLIS CHURCH
Morning: July 1, 1862

ROLL CALL WENT quickly. No smart remarks from Garrow, or from Gazzam or Gueadreau. The sergeant skipped over Colburn and Campbell. Ditto: Crowder and McDonald; ditto, ditto, ditto . . .

"Here, Sergeant," Scotty answered, tallying the numbers. *Jim Young, the last man. Twenty-six, I make it.* Same as he had arrived at last night. Twenty-five on the sick list, a dozen more recovering from wounds. The bookkeeper fidgeted over which column to put Yeates in. *Bloody stupid, using his rifle for a hand rest. Nae better than a conscript.*

Sergeant Traylor executed the about face and reported to the sergeant major, who turned to Lake. *Twenty-eight, then, counting them.* Scotty mouthed a curse. *We had seventy-three, one month back; one bloody month—almost to the minute,* he realized. Looking down the line: *Bonham has only thirteen down there, the Cadets and Wetumpkees, forty or fifty apiece.* In Second Battalion he counted twenty-six Mutts. *About forty Guards; Tuskegees, the same, give or take. The 'Glorious Third:' two wee battalions—make it three hundred-fifty.*

Sergeant Major Dunlap accepted the report from the lieutenant and delivered it to the new adjutant.

Attune to detail, Scotty liked the way the Lieutenant Lake was handling his duties. *Efficiently, without the nonsense. Absent Captain Hoyt (and Shanghai), he is doing all right; has the confidence of the boys. And why shouldn't he? It's there for anyone who can keep us alive an extra hour, an extra day.*

*We'll be in good hands so long as we are under Major Sands and Captain Powell. And the regiment will follow Colonel Battle. But the first two are outranked, and the latter is still recovering at Tuskegee. Charlie Forsyth has a ways to go; Colonel Gordon, now . . .*

Gordon was operating coal mines south of Chattanooga, when war came. His miners—burly mountain men—promptly elected him to head their local cavalry troop. They next demanded to be called the 'Raccoon Roughs' and, arriving in Milledgeville, wished him to offer their services to the State of Georgia. That governor took one look and replied his state required no more cavalry at present.

Rather than miss the war altogether, the Roughs gave up their mounts and, as a company of infantry, headed for Montgomery—raccoon caps, and all. There, they got a warmer welcome, and were tacked onto the rolls of the newly formed Sixth Regiment. Backed by his miners, Gordon was elected major. In the reorganization of April, Colonel Siebels tendered his resignation and Gordon was elected, becoming the youngest colonel in Rodes' Brigade.

His ability was obvious. When Rodes was wounded at Seven Pines, there was no objection to Gordon assuming command. He was a tall man, with striking good looks; straight as a ramrod and razor thin, a natural leader. His fighting spirit was contagious.

When the Third was transferred to Rodes' all-Alabama Brigade, it was no love-match. Rodes was in D.H. Hill's Division. Fortunately, Gordon (acting commander in Rodes' absence) was not Hill. He was uniquely Gordon, and he took a personal interest in Lomax's orphans, supervising the Third as it toiled over his parade ground, each sizing up the other, executing every maneuver in the manual (and many more besides). The Third came to believe in this commander, and their trust was reciprocated.

* * *

Gordon had Third Alabama on point. From Glendale, Second Battalion went down Willis Church Road and Powell put the Rifles out as scouts. Scotty reflected sourly on the sequence of orders that put him in front of the entire Confederate Army: *'Mousie,'* he grumbled, *'thou art alone.'*

The landscape was one of abandoned camps, pillaged vegetable gardens and trampled pastures; the same as they had found marching down to Cold Harbor. The only new feature: no livestock. No *live* stock. Investigating a terrible smell, the scouts found the slaughter of two hundred or more horses and mules: the lame and the worn out. The entire Union Army had come through here, so tracking them through manure and rancid pools of blood was as unpleasant as it was unavoidable. Viewed across a trampled field, where earth met sky, was a distinct haze of greyish-green: flies. Ryder appreciated their professional courtesy: *They prefer blood and shit to soldiers, thank the saints.*

The scouts moved into skirmish line, spreading out to a distance of seventy-five yards to either side of the point. They tip-toed through a ripe latrine-line. Knowing they were closing with a camp, they moved slowly and methodically, their senses keen. Coming to a road, they found red-flagged stakes, reading 'III Corps Hosp,' on lacquered cardboard—with helpful directional arrows.

The hospital was a four-columned framed stucture: Willis Methodist Church. Today it had the reek of an abattoir. Its pews had been pulled outside, some broken up for planks, cushions placed under the wounded. Shallow graves already filled the nearside yard, with the far side reserved for the wounded too injured to move. At the side entry to the sanctuary, they discovered a four-foot-high stack of flesh: arms, legs, hands, feet—all beneath a glaze of flies. A foot flew from the nearest window. Its landing causing a cloud to rise with an audible buzz. The sight prompted more than one scout to heave. Inside, the Union surgeons were still at it, their rubber aprons dripping. They took little notice of the interlopers. If ever there was a time the riflemen wanted to push on, this was it. Lieutenant Lake ordered a halt.

While Lake spoke with the medicos, the Rifles walked among the wounded—two or three hundred here—offering water; hardtack, if they had it. Exhaustion and fevers appeared to be as common as wounds. Some men had tags tied to their clothes, labels reading: 'V.S.—shoulder;' or 'V.S.—left hand.' Some read: 'Debilitas.'

Scotty stopped to offer his canteen to a sergeant whose hands were wrapped in bloodied bandages—the left, disturbingly short.

"Whit's your outfit, Sarge?"

"Eighty-Seven New York. Third Corps," answered the man, as casually as if greeting a friend on Broadway. "Who are you boyos?"

"Mobile Rifles, Third Alabama Volunteers, D.H. Hill's Division, Jackson."

"Shit. 'At's a mouthful. What's the 'D.H.' stand for?"

"Dun— " For once, Scotty held up. "Em, Daniel Harvey. So, his mama say." A diamond-shaped scrap of flannel, sewn on the man's tunic, caught his attention.

"Whid's tha' smart red patch ye ha' there?"

"Means: 'Third Corps' is all. Our General Heintzelman came up with that. Puts it on everything. We are in Kearny's Brigade."

"Oh, We 'ave heard of him. Kearny, *le Magnifique*?"

"The same."

"So, thae bonny blue wagons with the red wheels. . . ."

"Yep, 'at's us too. We busted up all the ones we couldn't move. Did we miss any?"

Scotty laughed. "Nae. Ye dun weel. Here Sarge, Corbet Ryder's my name," touching the man's right forearm lightly with his free hand.

"Burdett. Brooklyn. I bet they all call you 'Scotty,' am I right?"

"Aye. Ye always hae this gift?" He inspected the tag pinned to Burdett's collar. "Whit does 'V.S.' signify?"

"'You-all' a 'special correspondent' down 'thar' in 'Mo-bee-yul'?"

Scotty didn't rise to the bait.

His silence earned a shrug: "Just means I'm gunshot." The man took another pull from the canteen. "Latin's my guess. Who knows?"

Scotty held the canteen so Burdett could not empty it. "How did the bloody Romans come up with 'gunshot?' Ne'er saw such in my Latin Reader."

"Burdett pondered the question. "Huh. Never thought—but I take yer meanin'.

"Ye ken the letters: 'V.S.'?"

"A smart Alec has told me, it stands for 'Very Shot up.' I've seen it spelled out 'vulnus something,' I can't remember the S word."

"Vulnus is the latin for 'wound,' I remember." said Scotty.

"'Sclopeticus.' That second word is sclopeticus," declared a man nearby. "I had the same question. Never did get an answer. Don't mean 'gun,' that's fer sure. Got any more water there, pard?"

Scotty shook his canteen, gave the second man the last swallow; Lieutenant Lake emerged from the church. "Whit then is this 'smart Alec'?"

"It is someone who is one sass away from a punch on the nose," said the second man.

"Then, we have plenty of smart Alecs, too. Listen Sarge, been fine gabbin' with ye— Looks like we are set to move. Good luck with your paws. Dinnae fesh, they'll take good care of you in Richmond."

"That's what I'm afraid of. Obliged for the water. Say, is this Monday, do you know?"

"Tuesday. The first of July." Scotty stood to leave, feeling a bit shameful. "Weel—I'm sorry for yer hands."

"Yeah, you and me both. I think this one will be O.K. The other one'll have to grow back."

"See you Johnnies down the road," said the second man.

"Johnnies?"

" 'At's what you are."

\* \* \*

Crossing the churchyard, the Rifles entered the woods behind, land sloping gently towards a creek. The woods here were not thick—the land used to shelter cattle. Men had also been here in number, their detritus all around: rifles, cartridge rolls, gear, clothing, bandages, soiled drawers, pools of congealed blood, flies. They found evidence of a large herd, but no beeves.

Hopping the stream, they climbed through woods on the opposite slope. Lake ordered a halt and threw out Ryder and the Mosby brothers, to scout and report back. Others he sent back to the stream to fill canteens.

The scouts, keeping each other in sight, moved cautiously, their arms at port. E.C. Mosby came to the wood's edge. Kneeling, he signaled the others to halt. A road crossed his front. He looked to the right and spotted a Confederate line resting among trees about a quarter mile away. Finally, he looked south, and motioned Scotty and his brother, Mac, forward.

At the top of a long open rise, three-quarters of a mile off, they saw the guns. Dozens of them being positioned in a continuous line across the ridge, practically hub-to-hub; more cannon in one place than any of them had ever seen. Behind the guns was a cloud of dust kicked up by the artillery teams. There was not enough separation to count the pieces individually, so each man made an estimation and they compared the result: fifty, easy—just those they could see. Scotty went back to report, and soon returned with the lieutenant and the Rifles. The rest of the battalion came up, and halted by the creek. First Battalion joined them. Powell and Sands dismounted, to study the scene through their glasses.

"Major, I see Parrotts: tens and twenties; Napoleons and Howitzers. There is a line of skirmishers digging in fifty yards down from the cannon."

While they watched, half of this line rose up to reposition.

"Green coats. Like Colonel Gordon's."

"Sharpshooters," answered Sands. "Berdan's men, presumably."

The green coats established a second line, a short distance downhill from the first.

All right," Sands said, lowering his glass, "I suspect we are here awhile. Mister Lake, you will keep your eyes on them.

Report any fresh deployment or positioning. Until you are informed otherwise, I am in command of the regiment."

" 'Valley of Death,' Tom—even if it *is* on a hill. Cannons *'above'* for heaven's sake. Only thing missing are the Russians. I don't like the looks of this. Don't like it at all."

Lieutenant Bilbro could see Captain Bryan was uneasy. Though he was more optimistic, both men spoke *sotto voce*.

"We won't have a Balaclava here, Cap'n," said Bilbro. "Both sides know their Tennyson. Think of it as just 'Cannon to the front of them.' We'll make a show—they'll throw some shells; we'll all settle down for the night. They'll skedaddle, and we'll be right on their heels."

"I hope you're right. I *sure* do hope you're right. But if we cut them off from the river, they'll stand; *then* there will be hell to pay."

"McClellan has perfected the art of 'changing base.' You'll see." Tom sounded confident; Bryan was not.

Others arriving reached similar conclusions: The Federals held too strong a position to attack, at least not in a frontal assault. Maybe Jackson could get behind them.

The Hornets had their own opinions.

"Lookit all 'em guns up 'air," said Rafe Herrin. "And that's after we borried half they batteries from Casey's Redoubt and Gaines Farm. Where're we hiding ours?"

"Gen'l Hill handed Casey's guns off to Ordnance for refit and re-supply," said Jim Branscomb. "They went though all their shells at White Oak Swamp."

"Sheeee-eee-ee-it," said Rafe. "*Ree-fit!* Dung Hill's gone done it a'gin, you mean.  Wern't nothin' wrong with them guns that turnin'm round hunnert-n-eighty de-gree wouldna' fixed. Easy enough to bring up shot and shell."

"Above brigade, they do things by the book."

"Then best they write *a new book*. Anybody gets past them sharpshooters, will get a mouthful o' cannonball."

"Canister," said Tom Johnson. "They'll use canister if we make it that far. Makes those cannons big ole shotguns: fifty iron balls the size of grapes."

Rafe looked queasy. The new sergeant knelt by the men.

"First Battalion's going out there about a hundred yards: skirmish line. Nothing's going to happen for a while—other divisions are coming down. So, for now, stack arms, but stay in arm's reach."

"Sergeant Tom? You really think we gonna' take on those guns?" asked Lulu Branscomb.

"Nah." Tom scoffed. "But what do I know? If they want that hill, not for us 'to reason why.' You boys all right? Got caps? Cartridges? Water?"

"I could use a solid crap," Rafe said.

"You manage one today, Rafey old son, tell us your secret."

"I wish we knew something of Neb and Frank and Will and them," Lulu said, not quite asking.

Tom shrugged. "No more'n me. They're in the hands of the Lord, now."

"Amen," they all muttered.

"They'll be fat and sassy by 'n by, you watch," said Rafe.

"They'll pull through," agreed Lulu.

Knowing it wouldn't last, they savored the shade of the woods, opening their jackets and fanning away the bugs. Troup Randle passing by, they all fell silent, their eyes following him, ready for any order. "As you were," he said, lightly. "Put your feet up."

"Yes, boys, get some rest," said Tom, standing. Before his first step, the guns on the ridge spoke in earnest. The thought of stacking arms evaporated. With a groan the men rose to their knees to better see the play of the guns.

The sergeant major received his orders from Major Sands. He faced about:

"Third Alabam—FIRST 'n SECOND: *FALL* in."

## CHAPTER 39 — THE HIGH GROUND
July 1, 1862

VIEWED FROM the north, Malvern Hill appears to be one of Virginia's lesser efforts, terrain hardly worthy of a name. Where one road meets another, fields of grain and corn rise in gentle stages to a level crown, half-a-mile wide. A modest farm belonging to the West family, is there surrounded by a parched picket fence and a few shade trees. From the yard, the road coming down from Willis Church can be seen crossing a small creek by the church parsonage, before joining the road from Carter's Farm.

The parsonage was substantial. A two-story structure made of brick, that enjoyed a fine view of the hill and its fields. The sheaving of wheat has begun, though the scythes still have many acres yet to reap. Shortcuts, made by men in a hurry, have marred the crop.

One shortcut goes directly to a third home, known locally as 'the old Crew place.' Behind it, the hill drops some eighty feet, through reedy woods down to a creek that flows to the James. Along this precipice a footpath connects a row of slave cabins with the main house.

All three homes: parsonage, West, and Crew, lie in sight of one another.

Altogether a handsome neighborhood, but the true beauty of the hill is not evident to civilians. Artillerymen see it at once. Pouring over maps from the safety of a gunboat on the James, George McClellan has seen it: high ground, protected on three sides—a perfect killing field.

He orders the Army of the Potomac to continue its 'change of base,' to Harrison's Landing, a march of nine miles. There, by the river, the navy's guns can protect his army. All will be well. Artillery will hold and defend Malvern Hill.

\* \* \*

A few miles north, at Glendale, another old artilleryman, reading his own maps, draws similar conclusions. Consulting a local farmer, D.H. Hill confirms the massing of Union ordnance up ahead. *If the artillery is there, Henry Hunt is there––a man who knows his business.* At Willis Church, he comes across Lee and Longstreet, and offers his take: "If McClellan is there in force, we had better let him alone."

Longstreet, nestled between his commander and a former subordinate, sees the free play, and taunts Hill in terms he would never dare use on Lee. "Don't be scared, now that we have him whipped." Facing an enemy at bay, and knowing his lines of communication were poor, Lee remains cautious.

Hill, ordering Rodes' Brigade to his right, sends them into the woods near an exposed knoll. Gordon, wearing his singular green coat, throws a portion of Third Alabama out as skirmishers, to cover *his* right flank. First Battalion got the assignment. For two hours, they waited for further developments.

On the hill, the Federal artillery was also waiting. Colonel Hunt, without space enough for his batteries to operate efficiently, sends half of them to Malvern House, on the southern end of the plateau.

Completing his personal reconnoiter, Hill could see but little chance for success and sent to Jackson for instructions. Jackson shares his own orders, and the reply finds Hill near the parsonage where he shows the message to his brigade commanders:

> *"Batteries have been established to rake the enemy's lines. If it is broken, as is probable, Armistead, who can witness the effect of the fire, has been ordered to charge with a yell. Do the same."*

The message leaves Hill uncomfortable. It is signed by Chilton, Lee's Chief of Staff. *Maybe Lee knows something he's not telling.* As the others rejoin their units, Hill asks Gordon to remain. They dismount, and walk towards the front of the home, where they can better judge the effects of the promised cannonading. It does not take long.

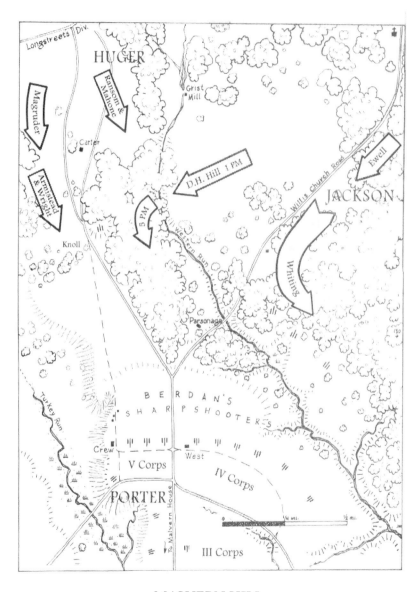

MALVERN HILL
July 1, 1862, Afternoon

Seeing the threat on their right, the Union guns open with devastating force before the Confederate batteries are even set. Having no batteries of his own to add (those acquired at Seven Pines, ordered to Richmond), Hill reacts: *A farcical effort—has there ever been such a waste of iron? Pendleton should have sent my replacements ere now.* His eyes linger over the Federal line, envious, admiring their discipline: deliberate, methodical fire; choosing their targets. Henry Hunt must be there; remembers Hunt's reputation—every shell must be accounted for. The story goes: "Young man, are you aware that every round you fire costs two dollars and sixty-seven cents?" Hunt would pull a gun whose crew fired too fast—indicating a poorly trained crew, one lacking nerve.

Frustrated, Hill moved to a large oak and, to rest his back, sat beneath it facing the enemy. As he began to make notes and scribble orders, Gordon expressed concern:

"General, hadn't we best move—at least to the other side of the tree? Their spotters can see you."

"Don't worry about me, Gordon. Look after the men. I am not going to be killed before my time is come."

"Spoken like a rock-ribbed Presby—"

A shell exploded directly overhead, showering both men with shrapnel, ripping Gordon's coat and rolling them both in the dirt. The general, first to his feet, was bruised and shaken—but miraculously, neither man had sustained more than minor injuries. Knocking the clods and grass from his coat Hill sat back down under the tree, this time on the side away from the guns, and resumed his writing. Gordon shakes his head. Returning to his brigade, he deploys Sixth Alabama on the left, Third Alabama on the right—a wide gap between. The Fifth and 26th behind the Third.

Beneath his tree, Hill awaits the expected shout from Armistead's Brigade.

## CHAPTER 40 — PRIVATE QUARTERS
July 1, 1862

"MARSE JOHN? Folks's come t'see you. Shall I show 'em in, suh?"

"Thank you, Joseph—yes," said Hoyt, opening his eyes. "A moment, please."

Accustomed to an afternoon's siesta, the captain was loath to cut this one short. A corner of the Lancaster's front parlor had been screened off for his privacy (Mr. Lancaster, being a friend and partner of Hoyt Sr.). He and Mrs. L. have treated the Hoyt sons as their own. Every home in Richmond, it seems, has adopted sons.

A nap always followed Hoyt's tramps around the city. Like many of his fellow convalescents, he was hoping to rejoin the army as quickly as possible. It was a common sight to see them marching to-and-fro, uphill and down; stopped, on occasion, by General Winder's plug-uglies demanding to see their papers. These 'detectives' had had to learn the hard way, not to accost a certain class of soldier. The medical board had taken note of his progress and anticipated his return to full duty by the ninth of the month.

At first, he was exhausted after a twenty-minute walk. But each day he went just a little further, and today he had kept a steady pace for more than two hours. This progress came at a price: one restorative siesta. Hearing Joseph bring the visitors to the parlor threshold, he swung his legs from off the cot.

"Captain Hoyt?"

Unexpectedly, the voice was female—familiar—but he could not place it. He had expected to hear one of his Rifles, Corporal Treat perhaps, bringing Lake's report, or a visit from one of the other men; Shanghai and Caroline usually stuck their heads in around suppertime.

He knew Mrs. Lancaster's voice. She was at the hospital; in any case, she would not need to be announced. Peering from around the screen he saw a beautiful young woman. Her attire more practical than fashionable, but showing her to advantage. Removing her bonnet, the face grew more familiar. "There you are, sir—come out, come out, now—I see you. Don't be shy." It was her escort, a solemn, tow-headed youth, that sharpened his memory.

"Mar-gar-et!"

"Why, as I live and breathe, Captain Hoyt, you remember my name, almost. I am so flattered."

Abashed, he stammered, "My apologies, I beg your pardon, Miss Guest. I grasped for the first thought that came to mind."

"No, no—quite 'O-Kay'—time of war, these things. I must say I hardly know you—you must have put on fifteen pounds since last we saw you. It suits you. Brother, don't you agree? Don't you think he looks splendid?

"Captain, you may call me 'Maggie.' If you promise never again to call me 'Mar-gar-et.'"

"Thy will be done—I am 'John.'"

"Oh, no. Thou art 'Captain Hoyt,' and shalt remain so."

"Even if I am promoted?"

"One must not presume. We will cross that bridge when we come to it."

Hoyt extended his hand, the gesture a puzzle, till she realized he was offering his word. Eyes dancing, she took his hand, lightly—sealing the bargain—pleased with him.

Witness to this, her brother stood by, immutable as a cigar store Indian.

"Of course, you remember my younger brother—"

"Yes, of course—Willie."

"No. This is John. Take off your hat, indoors, Johnnie."

"John. Yes. Good day to you, John."

"Say hello to the captain." Johnnie nodded his head.

Hoyt invited them to sit.

"Just for a moment. Private Howard told us you were here. I hope this is not an intrusion—Papa thought you might like some fresh strawberries, and so, sends these 'round," handing him a basket—enough to delight a family for a week.

"That is most kind of, er, your father. Please tell Mister G. I am much obliged."

"Papa took a shine to you, Captain Hoyt, he certainly did, and to poor Mister Howard too. Said: 'Those boys are too thin to cast a shadow.' Papa told me to say that, should you resist the strawberries at all. You haven't, but I'll say this to you anyway: I don't think you have cast a shadow since last we spoke—certainly not upon our front door. Have you allowed Mister Howard a new pair of trousers? No? Then for shame. One would think you both terribly embarrassed—to say nothing of the Army. Such things cause talk, Captain Hoyt, and will encourage our enemies."

"The last time I saw Mister Howard, he was. In uniform, that is, I mean."

"We are so relieved."

"You have older brothers in the service, I recall. I hope they are well."

"Yes—so kind of you to inquire. At last report both are quite well—touch wood—though we have heard nothing for days. James and Joseph, their names."

"The Fifteenth, I believe your father said."

"Yes! The Henrico Guards: Captain England. There has been a terrible fight near the old tavern—Cold Harbor—some place it at Gaines Mill—I am sure you would know—at any rate, the papers say we have won a great victory, for the Yankees are reported 'skedaddling' for the river. If we are chasing them, we must be careful not to catch the tiger by its tail.

"I hope when you write—to your loved ones, I mean—you write a better letter than do my brothers. 'Nothing new' they say—every letter. They could be at Waterloo, or the Sandwich Islands, and still they would write: 'All routine—nothing new—nothing to see.' Most vexing."

"There is something to be said for dull letters in time of war."

She looked at him boldly. "Have you sisters, Captain Hoyt?"

"An older sister and a younger. Most vexing, the pair of them."

She ignored the sally. "You can write what you see, can't you? What you hear? You soldiers have conversations, don't you? Besides orders and commands, I mean: 'yes sir,' and 'no sir,' 'right away, sir.' You actually speak to one another, I do think. The army can't be so much gazing out to space. Then tell us what you talk about! It is the waiting for word that is so terrible. After a while, most any word will do. 'I read a book today.' Fine; then, tell us about it."

"My sister Clara tells me much the same. Lately, I have had to depend on my brother to keep me informed of all political goings-on, and how these changes affect our regiment. The Third has been transferred to General Rodes' Brigade during my absence."

"My point precisely: a perfect topic to share with your sister—without delay. She has probably never before heard of this General Rodes.

"Well. I shall keep all of you in my prayers, Captain—" She wished to say more—started to, twice—but, upon reflection, resolved to remain indecisive. Rising from her chair: "Well. Well, now—Captain, Johnnie and I must complete our rounds, or Papa will have something to say on the subject." Deepening her voice, she confided, "He will express an opinion, you may recall."

"Your father is most well-informed."

"Information is not a prerequisite for his opinions."

Hoyt saw the two out to her buggy, and there, he handed Margaret up. In the back, under cover, were several plants from her father's garden.

"Errands," she explained.

"Thank you for the strawberries. You have no idea how delighted the Lancasters will be. Treats are rare enough these days, Miss Maggie."

"Do be careful, won't you, Captain? We should miss your shadow on our door, however insubstantial it may be."

A distant roll of thunder ruffled the quiet of their shady street. An older gentleman, taking his stroll, stopped, turned, and then cupped an ear. All turned to the southeast.

"That is not thunder. Not from that direction." Hoyt pulled out his pocket watch.

Goddamn them their war, thought Maggie. "Oh dear," she said.

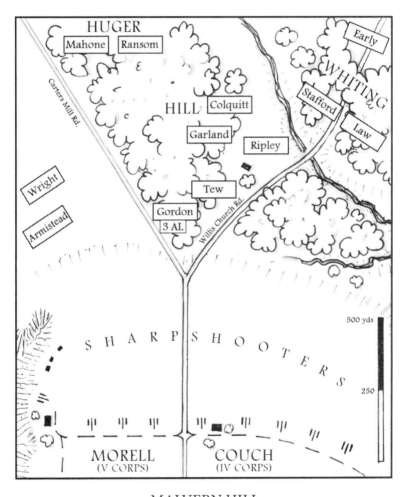

MALVERN HILL
July 1, 1862, Evening

## CHAPTER 41 — MALVERN HILL
4 PM: July 1, 1862

THIRD'S BATTALIONS (Bonham commanding the left, Powell the right) formed behind the smoldering ruins of Grimes' batteries deployed on the knoll, 1000 yards from the enemy's guns. The guns had been dealt with swiftly: a horrible thing to witness at close hand; more nightmare than reality. To close this gap, Gordon had Sands bring his skirmishers back by a left-oblique march, the execution of which sent them marching off towards the enemy. Reordering his line-of-march with "By the left flank," Sands delivered his men back to relative safety, under a dip of land. The discipline of his men during the initial blunder, so impressed the enemy gunners they saluted the feat with huzzahs.

All kept an eye out for the occasional shell lobbed from the river. A hundred-pounder landed twenty feet from their line. Mercifully, it proved a dud, and the battalion offered up a sickly cheer. Mid-afternoon, Sands received orders to push his skirmishers forward, to 'annoy' the enemy guns; the Cadets confirm the guns are easily provoked. Ambulance men speed in to carry away the wounded, while the rest wait their turn.

*Cecil Carter (A)*

Waiting it out, was Cecil Carter with his usual mates: Dunn, Herpin, Matthews, Prichard, Price, and Sprague; the smaller men on the left, dubbed the 'Mouse-kateers.' A term never successfully uttered twice.

They faced Berdan's company of sharpshooters. The Greencoats had had plenty of time to dig in and were keeping up an enviable rate of fire. Cecil certainly envied them their rifle pits. Fortunately, firing downhill, even good shots tend to shoot high.

Reloading a rifle from prone position is an awkward procedure. Cecil worked the powder and ball from out of his cartridge then tamped them down with the rod. Rolling onto his belly, he looked for a target. Hitting a Berdan man was luck as much as anything—having your sites on just the right part of their line, at just the right moment. He saw a hat bob up and he fired. Confirmation of a hit would come via an increase in return fire. His shot must have missed. One of his comrades down the line cried out: "I'm hit." The boys stepped up their firing, to cover aid to the man.

Looking beyond Prichard, Cecil noticed Soto's guidon stuck in the ground. The little pennant had a couple of fresh holes. If he wished to see the corporal himself, he would have to rise up—an effort he thought should wait. During a lull, he wondered as to the time. His pocket watch had been worthless since Seven Pines, but he still carried it. Maybe Lieutenant Yniestra would give it a look. Off his right shoulder he found the sun: a dull orange through the smoke—and gauged the time to be nearing six o'clock. They had been out here since noon.

*Time, fellows. Time. Fish or cut bait.*

Before he could voice his preference, he heard the sergeants yelling again. This time: to load, prime, and hold. The rest of the regiment was moving up in loose order. Soto and the other non-coms were scrambling to their feet, Soto looking decidedly green. Orders came for the rest of them.

"MOBILE CADETS, form ranks. On battalion! Move boys: *Move, move, move!*"

They withdrew to the woods where Rodes' Brigade was crouched in a dip of land. Colonel Gordon appeared at their front. He was in his shirtsleeves, now. Sergeant Ledyard, of the color guard, took off his jacket, and offered it. Gordon put it on as he mounted a stump, shouting above the din.

"Alabamians!"

The entire brigade stood. Behind Carter, a sergeant instructed, in flat, urgent tones. "Dress left: touch to the center! Move on down."

"Alabamians!" Gordon repeated. "There is a battery over on that hill. And Alabamians have got to take it." Looking up and down the ranks, he let the import of his words sink in.

Cecil looked left, shuffled left, didn't have to adjust again, standing so close to Soto. His left elbow was on Prichard when a shell exploded, launching that recruit backwards. Cecil shuffled down to Soto. Eyes front.

"All that will follow me— " Gordon turned to his left, repeating his words: "I say: all that will follow me, say 'aye!'"

"AYE!" the ranks responded.

"Then follow me!"

They obliged with a yell. Cecil focused his ears to the rear, listening for orders. A bullet zipped between his head and that of Price. He felt another pluck through his haversack, another thump into the blanket roll across his chest, stopping him momentarily—like walking into a wall.

"Carter!" his corporal shouted, shoving him back into line; he tugged his cartridge box forward.

Captain Powell was shouting to be heard:

"FIRST BATTALION!"

Yniestra, the officer closest to Cecil, echoed the order:

"CADETS!"

Powell: "FOR-WARD—"

"FORWARD," Yniestra repeated.

*"—MARCH!"*

A shell burst over them as they emerged from the woods. Cecil kept his eyes straight ahead. A second shell burst behind. Cecil's instincts took over, replacing the commands he could no longer hear. The men nearest him stepped forward, so he did, too. Price stumbled, but recovered, stumbled again and was left behind. Dunn came up from the rear rank to fill the gap.

"BA-TAL-LI-ON.*"*

"CADETS!" roared Yniestra.

*"CHARGE!"*

They responded with the Rebel yell, and some Yankee sharpshooters, unnerved, broke from their rifle pits, becoming targets soon as they did. This 'leg bail' blocked the line of fire of the enemy batteries, momentarily silencing them. Crews began hauling their guns up the hill, keeping out of reach. Cecil could not have imagined the volume of sound enveloping him. Clouds of smoke rolled over them and blanketed the charging ranks.

The smoke clearing with neither rhyme nor reason, he saw the Greencoats breaking to the rear. Cecil was thirty yards from their lines when the last one turned tail. Firing from the hip, he hit the man mid-torso (*latissimus dorsi* his father would have said), dirt flying off the man's back. The man kept running. If anything, moving faster than before—which made an impression on Cecil.

Leaping over the line he saw the rifle pits littered with equipment and spent cartridges; the wounded and the dead the only occupants. He knelt to pilfer a cartridge box, but the cartridges were Sharps—not compatible with his Enfield. He had seen a Sharps before, but never seen one demonstrated. One lay nearby, but this was neither the time nor place to get schooled. He found another cartridge box with rolled cartridges, and began scooping its contents into his own, finally just tearing out the tins themselves, his hands fumbling with fatigue. The dash uphill had exhausted him. Others, having gone further, were now fighting hand to hand. But their momentum checked, they began to fall back. He reloaded. A fresh brigade—Georgians—came up and passed through the Thirds' line, establishing a new firing line fifteen yards on. Colonel Gordon and Major Sands used the pause to re-organize the Third's reduced ranks.

Cecil felt engulfed in a flash. More witness than participant, his mind formed a singular thought: *So, that is what they mean.* A great pitchfork had found him and, like chaff lofted into the sky, with exquisite slowness—*Yniestra will never be able to fix this*—he floated headlong down the hill.

## Milton Boullemet (E)

Milton Boullemet was feeling wobbly. Again. And again, he had a raging thirst. He told himself: *Soon it will not matter.*

*This is borrowed time anyway.*

He had fainted back at Drewry's Bluff, before they ever boarded the cars for Richmond. At Dress Parade no less. Men dropped in the ranks during Parade all the time: the effects of hunger, thirst, fever—sunstroke, on occasion—carted off or cooled off, or sent to the surgeon. They recovered and came back. Usually.

Doc Lee felt his case was different and sent him down to Petersburg. Petersburg: where the linens were so white and the food so plentiful, the matrons and the old gentlemen-doctors so solicitous. He could not wait to leave there.

While he was under clean sheets, his company—so he learned—was slogging through the swamps at Seven Pines. Just before battle, E Company ('The Infantry' as they still called themselves), was pulled out of line and told to guard a battery, while the rest of Second Battalion plunged into the woods. A consequence of that minute change: Hoyt's Rifles had been destroyed instead of them.

The surgeon told him it was diabetes. No need to spell out consequences of that. The medical board concurring in the opinion, he was offered a discharge, or a transfer to the home guard. He refused. The board concurred with that, too, and granted his request to rejoin his company.

*Just a little further now.* In Milton's position, behind the ranks, (an acting-sergeant), he relayed orders and enforced discipline. His old messmate, Coot Turner, gave him a reassuring nod. Lieutenant Bagby repeated Chester's command, and off they stepped. The past month had seen The Infantry's numbers whittled down to forty-one. Milton saw Captain Chester fall. No one halted.

Milton had tried to write home about this—his illness. But Father had enough burdens to deal with. Times were hard. Especially for auction merchants: 'Tables, Clothing, Farm Equipment, Negroes,' their handbills proclaimed (Too many sellers–not enough buyers, was practically their family motto).

Instead of a letter home, Milton used the last of his Yankee stationery to write the widow Walke and Mary. By some arrangement, mail was still getting through to Norfolk.

Shell bursts—front and side—brought him back to the present, but only for a moment. He said a prayer for his closest friend, wounded at Shiloh. He had not heard from Miss Nimms since April. His thoughts grew fuzzy. A shout from George Ellison: "Let's go, boys."

The men responded with a yell and advanced at the 'weak shuffle.' Fast or slow, the pace no longer mattered; the Federals would make them pay, regardless.

*Corbet Ryder (K)*

First Battalion passed the front line of the sharpshooters, the area littered with the quick, and the 'not-quick-enough.' Scotty witnessed several Rifles fall together, enveloped in a bouquet of pink mist. Canister. He went to ground, too, while he had the option, sheltering behind the inert body of a Greencoat. To cement the arrangement, he used his bayonet.

Clods of dirt and other things began flying up from the left, his position too low for him to see what, exactly, was happening there, but he guessed the Hornets were catching it. Everyone was spread-out in a ragged line about halfway up the hill. No chance of spotting Jack through the smoke—under the grime everyone looked alike. He fired several rounds before looking back to gauge the progress of the rest of the division. He saw no division. There was not even much evidence of the brigade. None but their own officers and sergeants—though they were moving about purposefully. *There is Lake; there Dunlap . . . Surely, they don't—*

"LOAD AND PRIME, you Rifles. Load and prime."

*They don't mean—*

"BAT-TAL-YAWNN—" ordered Captain Powell.

"RIFLES—" commanded Lake.

*Jesus in a manger.* Scotty began the only prayer he could recall: *Our Father—"*

"FORM RANKS."

*Oh God.*

He, and about twenty others scrambled to their feet. Lieutenant Dunlap and Corporal Treat came down the line, moving quickly never pausing, bullets zipping past.

"Touch to the colors. Quickly now, boys, quickly—Single line, single line."

Scotty located the color guard about one hundred feet to his left and followed the dress of the man next to him. He didn't know who this man was—he was not a Rifle. Ryder inched about until he was properly aligned. He felt a breeze on his right thigh and, glancing down, found a hole rending the inseam of his trousers. He gulped.

"EYES *FRONT,* RYDER!"

His eyes snapped around just in time to see the Mosbys blown out of the line.

"BAT-*TAL*-YAWNN . . ."

"RIFLES—"

*Our Father, who art in heaven—*

"BATTALION, AT THE QUICK STEP: *FORWARD!*"

*Our Father who—who . . . hallowed name . . . heaven—*

Scotty stepped off. Like so many others, he remembered no subsequent orders. The Rifles went forward, leaning as into a gale. Thirty yards. Forty.

*"Kingdom come . . . power, glory—Amen."*

"DRESS TO THE COLORS."

He tried a more familiar verse. One ma taught him: *'Wee, sleekit, cowrin, tim'rous beastie—'*

Each time he glanced left, the colors were nearer, with new men holding them.

The stranger who had been next to him no longer was. A Yank popped up from the ground, putting a ball through some poor bastard before he himself got sliced in half. The banner in tatters now. Debbel Innerarity doubled over—to his knees. Stayed there. Over the distance of a few intense yards, men went to ground, wounded or not.

—*'Ye need na start awa sae hasty.'*

"Keep moving, boys," Corporal Treat, pleading.

When there was not a man still standing within ten paces, Scotty dove for the safety of a smoking crater. He wondered when the reinforcements would arrive; a reasonable question, he thought. To the rear, two hundred yards, he saw brigades forming into line—or possibly they were reforming. As they moved forward, he saw wide gaps appear inexplicably, gaps where (one blink before) he was sure men had marched. *What has become of all that wheat?*

No orders. Even the color guards were reconsidering. If only Treat would cooperate. Treat was a cool one: much too pious for Scotty's blood, but the boy had grit, he would give him that—getting to his feet to relay communications between lieutenants. He did not see the first sergeant. Looking about he recognized some men of the Third—Macon County boys, he guessed—*Yes, there is that big fellow: the one they call Old Dick.* The big man looking his way. Scotty nodded to him, giving him a wry face. The man made a rigid grin of his own, his teeth and eyes gleaming from the midst of a blackened face. Looking further, he saw the remains of his regiment scattered across the area of their 'charge.' Here and there, units appeared to be coagulating to make another rush; Colonel Gordon he located within one of these, scuttling this way and that, still wearing Ledyard's jacket.

Using his bayonet, Scotty pushed together a flimsy palisade on the leading edge of his crater. Peering over the rim, he made the distance remaining to the Union batteries at near one hundred-fifty yards—a line of Union riflemen lay much closer. He had forgotten the cannons, so focused had he been on his immediate front. *Cannons there are. Scores of 'em. There is no way: what are we doing here?* He rolled over to get at his canteen. Burst by a splinter, he cast it away. The dead would have canteens—though none appeared to be within reach of his lifespan.

An informal roll was hollered, to see who would answer. Sisemore said James Young had been hit, was complaining of being cold (of all things), had given him his ground cloth—

Should be all right if they could get him back to the field hospital.

Treat stood up and, like the target at a turkey shoot, ran down the lines, "Up, you Rifles. Up!" he cried. "One good push and we have got them!"

*'Weds the bloody coof thinking of? 'One good push' for the love of—* 'Scotty ignored him, looking for proper orders to come any moment, sensible orders, orders to withdraw.

Treat grabbed the Third's new battle flag—a tattered ruin—began to wave it dramatically. "Forward! Third Alabama," he shouted. "Follow your flag. Up, you men." The corporal started up the hill, a trickle of men following, dropping off quickly one by one. Soon, Treat was entirely alone.

Shot and shell along his path, bullets sought his head. Treat kept moving through it all, his flag—fixed to one of John Brown's pikes—growing smaller and smaller. The flag remained upright while, inexplicably, the firing slackened. Feeling sick to his stomach, Scotty peaked over his parapet. *They are letting him come . . .*

## CHAPTER 42 — RAVENS
Night: July 1, 1862

*Milton Boullemet (E)*

MILTON OPENED HIS EYES. It was dark; a light rain falling. No idea of the time. He felt neither cold, nor even especially wet, though the spattering rain hit his face. He could not move a muscle. His arms felt numb, pinned to his sides. Whatever lay atop him, held him completely immobile. In the darkness he could not suppose what it could be. He fought down his panic. Obviously, someone, or some thing, had landed square on him during the battle. He did not remember being knocked down.

The roar of battle had ceased, replaced by sounds of suffering: entreaties and groans; a few yelling their heads off. The light rain muffled the sounds, as beneath a quilt.

A most irritating noise was a few feet away, a labored rasp—followed by a shrill wheeze, made all the more tedious by its regularity; conjuring memories of lying awake through the penance of childhood naptimes—interminable hours spent entombed in his Nana's bedroom, enduring her rhythmic and inescapable snoring. Admonished not to make a sound of his own, all his desire centered on the wish to be set free: to get up, to race outside barefoot through the new-plowed fields. It is a slow death to endure another's snoring—"'tis where Time goes to die," his grandfather once remarked.

This rasping and wheezing was just like that. Whoever this was—and Milton felt sorry for him, he truly did—he prayed he would die. *And soon, Lord.* (Adding the hope it would not be anyone of his mess.) Contrite, he prayed it not be anyone he knew. He tried adding his own cries to the night: for help with whatever this was that held him down. But his throat was parched, and he could not draw breath enough to shout. After a while he gave up and, growing drowsy, he drifted out of consciousness.

*John Gilmore (E)*

The wheezing was John Gilmore, strangling on his own blood. Choking had woken him from a horrible dream, only to drop him into a greater nightmare. His last memory was Foley's teeth exploding from out his mouth.

A ball had broken J.G.'s leg; something else had struck him on the foot. It was useless. Foley had been nearby, pressed against a plank of wood, shot through both arms and slowly bleeding to death. Gilmore crawled over and bound his wounds with handkerchiefs. As darkness gathered, Foley felt more clear-headed and able; enough to move off the hill. But in the attempt they were met with a hail of bullets, and they fell back behind their meager protection.

"Hang on a little longer," Gilmore encouraged. "I'll stay with you till it's good and dark, and then we'll get out of here together." Huddled for warmth, they settled in to wait, faces only inches apart. That was when the bullet blew Foley's head apart. An instant later Gilmore was struck, the ball crashing through his right shoulder, shattering his right arm before lodging in his chest. He lost consciousness.

He awoke in the night, head down, gasping for breath, from the wound to his lung. The battlefield was quiet, the rain falling steadily. Repositioning his head so it would be above his wounds, he used his good arm to free his canteen. The water cleared his throat and relieved his suffocation, but not his wheezing; his remaining lung doing all it could do. Those parts of his body he could still feel, hurt like hell. In the dark, knowing he was next to the pulp that once had been Foley, Gilmore thought he would never see another day.

*Dick Stinson (D)*

Old Dick lay in one of the rifle pits below the Yankee batteries, glad his brother had missed this dance—by virtue of being under lock and key at some place called Fort Delaware. Lon's name had been read off a Prisoners' List at the last Parade Dress.

There was no way to reckon the time, but Dick estimated

the chill hours before dawn were yet to come. The Yanks had fought hard as long as there was light, and (to prove the point) for a good while after. The ordnance at the top of the hill had turned the night red. The boys had answered as best they could—returning fire till each man came to the last rounds in his last tin. If a squad of Yanks had rushed them, they would have scooped up the entire division.

Instead, the Federals had gone about on tippy-toe, hitching up the field pieces one by one, pulling them out of the line. *Who do they think they're foolin' being quiet?* In this dark, who was going to stop them? *Who would want to?* Old Dick had not heard any orders to withdraw. Till he did, he would stay put.

Horsemen were approaching from further down, the mounts picking their way, each hoof making a distinct sucking sound, as it pulled free of the mud. From time to time, the riders paused, exchanging words, but Dick couldn't make out what was being said. As they drew closer he recognized the voice of General Hill.

"What command is this?" Hill asked a soldier.

"Rodes' Alabama Brigade, general," came the answer. "Are we relieved, general?"

Stopping two rods closer to the guns, Hill asked another: "What command is this?"

"Major Sands,' Sir. Second Battalion, Third Alabam, general: How did the battle go, sir?"

Hill replied, "I will inquire," and rode on.

A third man spoke:

"I'm pretty done in, general—permission to be taken off the field?"

"Stand fast until relieved."

Dick heard a new voice. "That you, general?"

Hill replied, "What command do you belong to?"

The riders were stopped a dozen paces from Dick, faint outlines against the glow of a Yankee bonfire burning supplies back of Malvern. Hill, gathering intelligence, repeated:

"What command do you belong to, soldier?"

The voice said, "Just us Third Alabama cowards up here, Gen'l."

"Who said that?" demanded one of the riders. *"What man said that!"* gigging his horse a few steps forward. Silence. The horse took another step. Dick recognized the voice of the 'coward'—*George Ellison, sure as I'm dyin.' There, a few feet away, as good a soldier as they get. And about to get stepped on—in more ways 'n one.*

"T'were this old boy next me, Cap'n," a new voice broke the silence. "His last dying words, more's the pity. That boy, he has breathed his last."

*Well roared, Lion.* Dick discerned a figure rise to his feet, the barrel of a Sharps catching the gleam from the firelight. Lowering his voice, the silhouette spoke directly to the aide: "Come closer, sir—I'll show him you."

*Oh Fathers—Here we go.*

The rider pulled up, the horse fooling its bit. A gust of rain rattled across the hill.

"That will do, captain," ordered the general, who was out of earshot. "We move on."

Peering at the figure, the aide directed a curse and reined his horse over.

*Jesse Carter, M.D.*

The doctor made good his escape from the hospital with the assistance of an ambulance driver named Hardy. Small world: the young man was from Lowndes County, was one of the Third Alabamas. The young man did not know Cecil, personally, but knew who he was.

"He kin, sir?"

"My son."

"Don't you fret, then, sir—we'll find him. I know where they were last at—last night."

Hardy kept up a chatter: a medical student before the war—wanted to go to Jefferson. *Hell,* thought the doctor, *Doesn't everyone, these days? Before the war, of course.*

That was all right, he supposed. Jefferson was where he

would go, if he were just starting out. But he had trained at Pennsylvania, and his skills were miles ahead of those grey-bearded blood-letters back in Richmond: *'Laudable pus' for the love of God*; old men, unable, *or unwilling,* to learn. From what he had observed, most hadn't cracked a medical book in years; willing to patch and stitch, so long as the soldiers came to them, and the morphine held out. And they could go home to their wives each night. Judging from the evidence, many of them—sage and prominent men in the field—had performed their first amputations this past week. *Not one in five would have passed muster at Penn.*

Hardy had found the doctor on the steps of the Second Alabama Hospital.

"Want to do some good?" he asked.

"If you are heading to the front, I do."

"Hop on, then."

Carter grabbed his coat and bag.

Countless 'thank you ma'ams' later they arrived at the staging area at Savage's. The doctor was promptly sent down the line to Willis Church. On they drove, the sound of battle increasing steadily. Nearing the church, they were caught up in a jam of disorganized wagons and teamsters. At the sanctuary, Carter was soon standing in pools of blood. When one exhausted surgeon collapsed, he stepped in. Next to him was a surgeon named Bowie. A passing good operator too, from what he could see. Yet another Lowndes County man who had kin in Third Alabama. A kindred spirit: over the course of his trip to the front, Carter had heard Hardy sing the praises of Doc Bowie.

Napoleons and parrotts sent waves of concussions crashing against the little church, shattering its windows, rattling its walls. Eyes followed the dust coming from the rafters, and prayers were lifted that the roof would hold. The evening's stream of wounded became a torrent by nightfall. Carter worked without break. There were bandages enough, but the more humane supplies were soon gone—and the most desperate injuries, just arriving.

*Corbet Ryder (K)*

*What a bloody mess*. Staggering about, Scotty was not referring to the mud. He could not keep his candle lit and, in scouring the battlefield for friends and comrades, found he was reduced to searching for them by borrowed light. It made him jumpy, sidling up to lanterns belonging to God-knows-who. More than once he was startled to hear an Irish accent, or that of a Dutchman. Prudence dictated he use his native accent, to broadcast the neutrality of his birth. He had no desire to be carted off at this late hour by Yankee trash. He soon realized his fellow searchers were more intent on cooperation than conflict, and was reassured to hear an increasing number of southern accents. On the hill above, the Union field pieces were being pulled out of line. They would be gone by morning. He called out to his friends, and, growing bolder, for Third Alabama. He had not seen Jack Goelet, or Stuart McGillivary since early afternoon, nor Deb Innerarity, nor Davy Taylor since before Treat's Charge. It was a long and miserable slog back to the parsonage, even more tedious to trudge up the hill, to Willis Church. He had helped all those whom he could, friends and strangers alike, but he could not help everyone. About midnight he found two Rifles huddled together: Hurter and Jones. He took Hurter to the hospital, returning for Jones by recounting his steps from the road (ignoring the entreaties of others he passed). But he did not find Jack. *I will look again as soon as it is light*. Dropping to the ground he pulled an oil-cloth over his head, and was asleep.

*Jesse Carter, M.D.*

Carter had been on his feet since early afternoon, but kept at it, hoping to hear word of Cecil. A Lieutenant Kennon, from Macon County, came in. How he was still standing, was beyond the doctor's experience: the fellow's mandible blown open, hanging together by a thread. Some Good Samaritan had wrapped his head together. The shrapnel, having come out beneath the chin, had broken his clavicle on its way to the shoulder. Forceps plucked teeth from the wound, and, a gummy mass, that was was the better part of Kennon's tongue.

It was past midnight and the rain still coming down, when one of the Mobile Rifles brought in Will Jones—Judge Jones' boy. Shortly after that, Carter recognized one of Cecil's friends, Marshall Redwood. Redwood's left arm had a deep gash, but it was not broken. If he could keep it clean till it could be sewn, he should be all right. When the doctor asked after his son, Marshall said he had seen neither hide nor hair of Cecil.

Doc Bowie had also gone non-stop. Now, in the early hours of July 2, Willis Church was out of everything but whiskey, and almost out of that. His last man had died on the table beneath a blade so dull the nurse had allowed the leg to wobble through the cutting. Bowie cursed the man: "Great balls—you can't hold a leg steady for thirty seconds, find me someone who can!"

*"NEXT MAN*—Where's that bucket?"

The bucket-man rinsed off the planks. A small, grimy, soldier was brought in, soaked to the skin, clutching a knapsack to his chest. On the makeshift table, Bowie ripped open the boy's trouser, glanced at the mangled foot. He examined the leg above the knee: no obvious wounds. Manipulating the tibia and fibula, he found no fractures. The limb was intact down to the sub-talar.

"Son, you will soon have nothing but dead meat below that ankle. So, that foot is coming off. We have no anesthetics, and—no dancing around it—you are in for a rough time. Gather yourself. I'll give you a fresh blade—we'll go as fast as we can." To the nurse, he growled: "Take that knapsack and get him a strap."

"I think this is one of our boys, professor," said Hardy. "Third Alabama."

The youth nodded he was—he was Third Alabam—but no one was looking at his face. "Co . . ." Coughing, he tried to clear his throat. "Company C. Tuskegee," he croaked. But no one was listening.

Bowie turned to the man next to him:

"Your hands are clean: reach into my vest, fish me out that cigar. Now: tell Doctor Carter—that short one, there—we have a boy from his son's regiment. If he is at a point where he can stop, I would appreciate his opinion, here. But this boy won't be up to answering any questions if he doesn't come now. And if it helps the lad to hang on to his knapsack, let him."

Ashen, but with eyes fever-bright, the patient noticed everything: the grim surgeon—disheveled, oily black hair, black beard, clad in a black rubber apron from collar to ankle. He saw the sweat-drenched ambulance men, the filthy instruments and dirty towels. Not reassured by these sights, he raised his head, tried to speak, but nothing came out. Hardy handed the surgeon a towel and Bowie wiped his hands on a corner. The boy cleared his throat again, rasping:

"Na—knap—sack—"

The nurse, stationed behind his head, pinned his shoulders. Another took the knapsack and placed it on the floor.

"My knapsack!"

The boy felt a man lean heavily upon his hips, felt the tourniquet tightening over his femoral, above the knee.

"We'll take care of your knapsack, sonny, don't you worry your head about it."

"Don't rile yourself, partner; 's over 'fore ye know it," from the faceless nurse, behind. His lie, grown careless with repetition, had the opposite effect: the boy attempted to rise. In response, the hands gripping his shoulders turned to iron, pinning him flat. Others began to move about him like mechanics. He could still lift his head; when he did, by chance, the operator was looking his way, giving a silent nod to the hip-man, who began to force a thick leather strap between the boy's teeth.

Thoh-back thrashed his head left and right. Seizing him the nurse cajoled, "Come on now, pard, come on, you don't want to lose your tongue, too, do you?" More threatening than soothing, he added, "It's gonna be all right. Courage."

With all his strength, Thoh-back roared: *"Look in my damn*

*knapsack, you ass!"* The shout cut through the local carnage. At his feet, the operator was staring at him, eyes red with strain and fatigue. *Is he mad?* T.B. wondered. *He is a raven: nothing more.* Preacher Tate was by his side. "I'm here. The Lord watcheth over thee. It will be all right, son." Making his voice a facsimile of reasonableness, Thoh-back repeated: "Look—won't you look in my knapsack? You will find what you need: *chloroformi, argenti nitratis, quinine, morphine*. You are welcome to it. Take all you want."

## CHAPTER 43 — BALACLAVA
July 2–4, 1862

THE RAIN moved off before dawn, leaving a ground fog and an overcast sky. Cecil woke to excruciating pain. As the day grew brighter, he steeled himself to take a fresh look at his mangled leg. His father had taught him enough anatomy to assess injuries. With great effort he worked himself upright, and uncovered the wounds.

The round shot had torn his thigh open, and a slab of flesh dangled from his right calf. The entire leg was swollen, the wounds red and ugly, but saw no signs of festering. His knee was intact, and he felt no broken bones. Maybe he would be lucky. The good news was the limb had good color—discounting the purple bruises—his leg was getting blood.

He had resisted the temptation to hobble off the hill. In the dark, a fall would mean his death, and the rain only increased that risk. He knew the benefit of prompt care, but also the importance of keeping his wound clean. So, he kept the limb elevated and used a gun sling for a tourniquet, loosening it as necessary. When the rain was falling hardest, he cut open his trouser legs to expose the injuries. The wounds cleansed, he applied the compresses his father had supplied him for just this circumstance.

Eventually, a couple of boys from the 26th came along, and settled him under a fly behind the parsonage. An ambulance man found him there and asked if he had been treated already—asking, because he did not have an identity tag on his jacket. When Cecil replied he had not seen any doctors, he explained the bandaging. The man inspected the work and expressed his approval: "Better'n I could've done." Writing Cecil's name and regiment on a card, the man scribbled 'V.S.' on the opposite side and strung it through the buttonhole of his jacket. He promised to take Cecil up to Willis Church as soon as a litter was free.

"'V.S.'?" Cecil had to ask.

"Doctor talk, for: 'You been shot.'" The man moved on.

Cecil recognized some Third Alabama men. Most he knew by name, but not all. He saw Goelet's friend, the dotty Scotsman, bringing a man off the hill. Finally, an officer, recognizing his uniform, limped over, using his bent scabbard for a cane.

Lieutenant Yniestra saw clinched teeth shining white through a begrimed face. The Cadet was in obvious pain; kneading his fist into his upper thigh.

"Cadet, who are you? Can't tell one of you from another. What have you done to yourself?"

"I'm Carter, lieutenant. Messed up my leg pretty bad, sir."

"Does your father know you are here?"

"Sir?"

"Your father. I saw Doctor Carter last night at the church."

A welcome surprise. "I was not aware. If you see him, sir, I would be much—" Words were an effort.

"I know. The next Cadet I find—one standing and walking, that is—will go fetch him."

Carter nodded his thanks, his body passing through a spasm of pain.

"You have water? What can I do to help you?"

"Thank you, sir. They have given me a full canteen and they are doing their best for me—May I ask the lieutenant if he has seen anyone else?"

"We are all over the place. Able Cadets are to assemble for morning Roll Call at eight o'clock. Most are still on the hill searching for wounded." The lieutenant gave him the names of survivors he was certain of. Taking out a small notebook, he asked: "What can you tell me?"

Cecil named those Cadets he had seen fall. The lieutenant recorded the information.

"Sir? What came of our boy with the flag? Our color guard—I think it was Corporal Treat, of the Rifles. I saw him take off up the hill."

Yniestra's face grew darker. "Everyone saw that. For a time, it stopped the whole fight. Treat got to maybe thirty yards of 'em before he stopped. Saw that he was all alone.

Must have known it was over—had him dead to rights. We all knew it. They sure weren't going to let him come back down. The Yankees were jeering him: 'Come a little closer, sonny.' 'Where's yer army?' Laughing at him, the fiends. The bravest man on that field—*jeering* him.

"If he had kept on, I think they would have simply taken him prisoner—but that was a fate too humiliating to bear, I suppose, so he just—he had to—well, fact is—he just stopped. He was up there what seemed like forever—looking back at us. Someone must have said *something,* cause his head whipped back around and that's when he pulled his revolver. That was all it took. He was the bravest of us all."

"Yes, sir. Lieutenant? Can I ask you?"

"Go ahead."

"What is *our* 'Reason Why,' sir?"

Dangerous ground for a junior lieutenant. Promoted from the ranks, Yniestra knew the proper response to such a question, was silence. Instead, his mind discarded the obvious answers: 'lack of support,' 'outgunned,' 'uncoordinated attacks.' He settled on the truth.

"The 'Reason Why' is the same 'why' it has always been, Carter. What it always will be: Stupidity. 'Balaclava.' Balaclava is just a fancy word for stupid."

\* \* \*

At eight o'clock Gordon assembled the brigade in a pasture down from the church. Sergeant (David) Dunlap conducted roll for the Rifles: Aubert, Atkinson, Bryant, Maybin, Ryder and Sizemore. Collier, Mabry, Taylor and Williams were still detached to the ambulance corps. Eleven. In addition to Corporal Treat being killed outright, fourteen Rifles had been wounded. Prayers were asked for Clark, Inerrarity, Jones, and Charlie Keeler. Mac Mosby's leg had been taken off last night; Doc Lee thought he had a chance. Mac's older brother, "Easy," had caught one through the lungs. They did not expect him to last the day.

Lieutenant (George) Dunlap appointed an acting second sergeant and a first corporal. Across the army, surviving officers were filling similar vacancies. The adjutant announced Rodes' Brigade would remain in the area the next several days (barring unforeseen events), for Rest and Recovery; pretty talk for burial detail.

By dint of constant inquiry, Scotty located Jack; he was with other Cadets in a mechanic's shop off Willis Church Road. Plain to see Jack would not recover, case shot had exacted a terrible toll. His face was swathed in blood-soaked bandages, an opening for his mouth, a tiny, dried-up little tongue in there—like a parrot might have. Scotty was told he would not take water, it causing him to convulse. Kneeling, Scotty laid his hand atop Jack's good hand. After a long while, he felt a response. Or imagined one. Scotty spoke to the area of Jack's right ear. "This is Scotty, old fellow. I will be with you as much as I am able. I have to leave now, but I will be back."

The Cadets had a good fix on their numbers: thirty casualties out of the forty-two taken into battle. Among the dead: young Will Caulfield and Paul Lockwood. Ryder had known Paul well; he had been one of those advancing the flag. The detail to identify the fallen, worked slowly in the heat.

While searching the crown of the hill, Scotty came upon Corporal Treat. Of the flag and the John Brown pike there was nothing. Pulling the stiffened remains onto a gum blanket, a detail of Negros brought Treat off the hill.

A runner camp up. Lieutenant Lake required eight men for a mission of mercy.

## CHAPTER 44 — **LES MOUTONS**
July 9—12, 1862

AT THE INSPECTOR General's office, Hoyt got the clerk's best guess where to find Rodes' Brigade. Retracing the steps of their march from Capitol Square, he went past the sprawling new hospital grounds called Chimborazo. A mile past that, his papers were examined by the provost guards at 'the works.' He was glad to be away from Richmond. There was a pall upon the city: her streets rutted with use and foul with manure; windows cracked or boarded-over, shops closed. Civilians in black, *while the speculators, the pimps and the strumpets grow bolder*. Richmond was no place for a child.

Outside the entrenchments, he found wagons belonging to Fifth Alabama. An acquaintance among them said the Third was up on the railroad, opposite his present line. The wagons were heading to the division's sick camp if he cared for a lift. Taking the offer, he arrived with them, late in the day, a mere three miles east of his starting point. Finding some of his Rifles there, he threw in with them, and heard accounts of Malvern Hill.

Next day, he had covered fourteen miles by one o'clock, allaying the fear he could not keep pace with the marches to come. He came upon one of the Third's wagons, and those men suggested he stay right where he was, as the brigade would be passing this point later that afternoon. Walking over to a house, its owner invited him in to rest a spell. The man's home had been used as Federal headquarters, and this gave Hoyt the opportunity to read month-old New York newspapers and what they had to say of Seven Pines. *Harper's Weekly* had their fight at Drewry's Bluff on the cover—calling it the "Battle of Fort Darling." The engraving was first rate. With amusement, he read the accompanying article:

> "We publish in this week's paper views of three rebel cities [Richmond, Memphis and Mobile], all of which we hope to be able to report have fallen into the hands of our brave troops by the time our next paper is published."

As promised, the brigade appeared down the road. Hoyt examined the column through his glasses, before he was satisfied it was, indeed, Rodes' Brigade; it's length was so short. Bringing up the rear, Third Alabama was choked in dust. Expecting to spot the regiment's distinctive pikestaff, he nearly missed them, for there was no pike, nor even a flag. The regiment tramped past him without a word. He fell in beside Lieutenant Lake—his nose and mouth covered by a kerchief. Lake looked twice at Hoyt to be certain, then offered his salute. The lieutenant was much thinner.

"Right happy to see you, captain."

"Right happy to see you, Jemmy." Lowering his voice, he asked, "Is this all of us?"

"Every able body."

"How many Rifles?"

"Should be nineteen, in all—counting me and Georgie. Twenty, with you."

"And the regiment?"

"About two hundred."

Hoyt could not afford to display his shock. He re-tied his bandana across his face.

"It's not so bad as that: every few days, three or four show back up. We don't expect any of the wounded—those furloughed home—to be back before September."

"New recruits?"

"Few and far between. To hear the staffers tell it, we will be accepting conscripts by summer's end."

"Lord. What of General Rodes?"

"He resumed command only two days back, so we still don't know much about him; a good man by most accounts. A tough disciplinarian—no nonsense—but Colonel Gordon is our man. He will march us to an early grave, but he is brilliant—the Fifth and Sixth swear by both men. Would follow them to Hell."

Hoyt raised his eyebrows.

"Sunday last, he preached over us."

"Gordon, you mean? Where?"

"There was this little country church we used for a hospital down there at Malvern Hill—anyways, that's where we were—and the wounded who had not yet been moved. McDonald, and Levy, and Goelet, all died there on the Fourth. You've heard of Treat, of course. There—"

"Jack Goelet died on the fourth of July? And Corporal Treat?" said Hoyt. "I have not seen a proper casualty list."

"Sorry, I forget—but as I was going to say, about Gordon's sermon . . . " Lake paused to organize his thoughts. "The colonel ended his homily by sharing with us something extraordinary about Colonel Lomax. A strange thing.

"He was speaking of Seven Pines, and, recalling his last words with Colonel Lomax; says, when we first got to Seven Pines, our brigade's colonels met with Hill and Mahone.

"I remember—at the redoubt."

"Exactly. Seems, as we were marching off from there, he (Colonel Lomax) came up to where Gordon was, and he says this to him: 'Shake my hand, Gordon, and let me bid you good-bye.'

"Gordon says the way the colonel put it, it was more than just *hasta la vista*. Lomax told him: 'I am going to be killed in this battle.'

"We all have such thoughts before a fight, right? But then he adds; 'I shall be dead in half an hour.'"

"*He said that?* The morning of Seven Pines?"

"Said it just before we stuck our nose in those damn woods."

"Jemmy . . . "

"Gordon had everyone's attention."

"I imagine he did."

"Said he tried to talk colonel out of it, but Lomax stood fast. No tremor or unease in his voice; said he was smiling throughout, perfectly at ease—that it was 'all right.' Said it was all right. Imagine."

"You believe Gordon? He's not just some drummer wrapped up in the sound of his voice?"

"A lieutenant of the Sixth, was standing next to them *at the time*, and heard Lomax say the same thing; told me the same thing—word for word."

"It is like yesterday, I saw him—he never looked so . . . And half an hour—"

"—from when we left General Hill and the redoubt."

"At the camp on Nine Mile, I was seeing to our wounded. Lord have mercy," said Hoyt, shaking his head.

Going the rest of the way in silence, they reached camp. Hoyt reported-in, then made a point to go around and have a word with each of his Rifles: Aubert, Atkinson, Bryant, Goodloe, Marben, Ryder, Sisemore, Williams. His dwindling band were unusually quiet. Nothing Hoyt could put his finger on, but he sensed a wall had grown between him and his men. Especially Corbet Ryder, who answered him only in monosyllables and avoided his eye.

The eight had been part of the effort to save the life of Easy Mosby. Doc Carter feared Easy would not last long in a field hospital, and in taking Cecil back to the city, promised to take care of Mosby too, if they could get him there. The men carried him by litter to Savage's Station, a hike of nine miles from Willis Church—*at night*. With grapeshot through one lung and both arms, Mosby was put on the first available car to Richmond. Goodloe went with him, to cut the red tape.

The others spent the night at Savages before returning to camp, where Scotty was devastated to learn his friend Jack was dead.

The men did ask Hoyt for news of those in the city, especially Mac and Easy.

"I have not seen either of them," said Hoyt. "They were both alive yesterday morning; I spoke with their mother. They are at their uncle's home, should you find yourself in town." He added, "I. G.'s office also informed me Colonel Battle is heading home—thirty day medical furlough."

\* \* \*

*"Special Requisition:*

*For one Regimental Battle Flag for the use of the 3d Alabama Regt. to supply the place of the one destroyed in the Battle of July 1$^{st}$."*

1LT Thomas. P. Brown,
Acting QM 3d Ala. Regt."

## CHAPTER 45 — *LES MISERABLES*
July 15 – Aug. 7, 1862

IN LEE'S REORGANIZATION, Huger was out; his tardiness at Drewry's Bluff, Seven Pines, and Frayser's Farm, linked to mistakes at Roanoke and Norfolk. Another casualty was Augustus Smith. Under the rubric of ill health, the general was relieved of all field duties. Magruder was also out: his cleverness at Yorktown outweighed by mistakes at Savage's Station and Malvern Hill—plus, his drinking. Plus, that unfortunate lisp. He was sent West.

The ax fell on Northern commanders too: Casey was relieved of command, for the sin of being outnumbered and overwhelmed by Rebels. George McClellan was out, for ignoring The Secretary of War, once too often. Little Mac was brought back to Washington, while his army stayed bottled up at Harrison's Landing. The Army of the Potomac was still formidable, however, and Lee knew he would have to deal with it before he could turn northward.

Longstreet was 'in;' the Texas Brigade assured his name was attached to the victory at Old Cold Harbor. In his reorganization, Lee awarded him command of I Corps, the corps on the right (should it bear repeating): the Position of Honor. Jackson was also in, but with a little tarnish on his reputation—due to his lackluster performance in the Seven Days; Lee assigned him II Corps.

For a time, D.H. Hill appeared to be—if not out, at least sidelined. Longstreet allowed him some credit for Seven Pines, and, he was actually commended for his actions at Malvern Hill. President Davis chose him to negotiate the exchange of prisoners of war and the "scale of equivalents," *viz.* one captured Union officer to be exchanged for X number of Southern enlisted men, etc. Completing this, he was assigned command of the North Carolina Military District. Third Alabama rejoiced to be rid of him but his absence would be brief.

\* \* \*

Lee expected much from his commanders. Never again would the Army's former Chief of Staff accept the excuse of muddled orders, late starts, and faulty maps. As Lee cleared the dead weight from his army, Longstreet was wise to stay silent.

Standards were also raised for the Army of Northern Virginia. Reflecting the will of Congress, the rank and file were now required to be at least eighteen years of age; none older than thirty-five. Third Alabama discharged forty who fell outside the limits.

These matters were resolved in July. In early August, Lee was ready to test the result with a second go at Malvern Hill (since reoccupied by the Federals). Aware that the opposing army was being slowly evacuated, Lee hoped to catch the remainder in a vulnerable position. An assault would, at minimum, speed up the withdrawal.

\* \* \*

On a Richmond sidewalk, three soldiers passed a young civilian. "Master Wise—Johnnie, I say!" the tallest soldier called out. "Johnnie, it's us. You haven't gotten too good to speak to your old friends in the Third, have you?"

The young man turned. Yes, the voice was familiar but the face was all wrong. Johnnie had no recollection of this scarecrow. A sergeant, he noted—but desperately thin and slouched, and unshaven. (Reading his thoughts, the soldier straightened, growing perceptibly taller). Johnnie placed the voice with coon hunts and hounds, bonfires and song, learning cords on a banjo. In carefree times, showing him the sequence to load and fire a cannon, and never to draw to an inside—

"Mister Shanghai! Not for the world! Is it really you? I would not have known you, had you not spoken. Pardon me for saying it, but you are as brown as a—"

"A hard world out there, Johnnie."

"Don't we know: six months, since the fall of Roanoke."

Shanghai winced for his lapse, recalling Johnnie's brother had died there. The boy—Governor Wise's youngest—had grown a couple of inches. Nearly a man, he carried himself like the young gentleman he was.

"Lord—you–don't they feed you?" Wise stopping there, before he blurted out something worse. Their hair was long and their beards unkempt; nails dirty as a field hand. Their uniforms bearing little resemblance to the fine garments he remembered; the trousers now patched; the jackets, greasy and out at the elbows; buttons, once so bright—tarnished, or missing—as was the satin trim from their collars. They carried the musky odors of camp. He was proud to call these men his friends—but still, the shock of seeing them so reduced.

"You remember old Ryder here—'Scotty'? And this old ruffian from the Cadets—"

"Why yes, it is Mister Chigger! *How do you do?* And Mister Scotty—Howdy." Gamely removing his glove, to shake their hands.

Shanghai said, "We are on our way to call on the Mosbys—" Seeing Johnnie react, he added, "Not good. Not good at all. Mac lost an eye and a leg. And he is the lucky one. Malvern Hill." Johnnie nodded.

"What word of Little Joe. And ole Zou?"

Shanghai brightened. "They have both skedaddled—left the regiment. Joseph is with Captain Woodruff—who is lieutenant colonel of the Thirty-Sixth, now, and back in Alabama. Little Joe writes that *he is the Sergeant-Major!* Can you imagine? Says the recruits don't know their left from their right, but that ole Woodruff is having a proper go at 'em."

"Debbel Innerarity, and Sergeant Hoyt, and the tall Stinson boy, Tom?"

"Double-Up was killed at Malvern Hill; Sergeant Hoyt is *Captain* Hoyt, if you please—he's doing finely. Tom Stinson, was a Hornet, you recall—was killed at Seven Pines, where Lonz was taken prisoner. Old Dick is still Old Dick."

The conversation continued in this vein, but the sad news continued to pile up; and it was a relief when Johnnie pleaded the need to keep an appointment.

"Come visit the old bunch. We're down at Poe's Farm. You know it?"

"I do. And I will, *soon*. I will come down this very evening. Give my regards to all the old fellows, won't you? The Mosbys, especially—next chance I get, I will drop by."

\* \* \*

On August 4, Hill's old division (Ripley commanding) marched from Poe's Farm and took a strong position overlooking White Oak Swamp. Seniority was such, Major Sands commanded the Third (with Captain Hoyt, his second in command). Late reports had the Yankees advancing from Malvern Hill. Ripley's Division went out to meet them.

\* \* \*

Casey Witherspoon had been in Mobile more than a month, before Cecil came home. Casey's arm was in a sling, still ached from time to time; but, both it and he, were well on the road to recovery. Cecil's wounds were more serious: his right leg so badly torn, it was whispered, he might never walk again. The odds of his rejoining the regiment, nil.

The Carter home had become part of Casey's appointed rounds, looking-in on Cecil at least twice a week. He rapped on the door.

Cecil's kid sister let him in. As always, her eyes bright and smiling. Before he could say her name, she raised a cautionary finger to her lips. Casey wondered when, exactly, Floy had blossomed into such a beauty. Walking her fingers in a playful gesture, she signaled him to tread lightly, back to the sunroom. There, Cecil was sound asleep in his wheelchair, a blockade-copy of *Cosette,* splayed across his chest. Floy tiptoed out, leaving Casey to wait for his friend to wake.

Curiosity getting the best of him, he attempted to tease the book from off Cecil's chest. His left hand, however, made a clumsy substitute for his injured right, and the patient woke with a start.

"Sorry, old thing. I am caught red-handed. I was just trying to see a few pages. I've heard it is good."

"Hmm—what—what is that? What is?"

"Your book there, I've heard it's good."

"Oh. Oh, hullo, Casey." Cecil stifled a yawn. "Oh, yes, yes, it is. Certainly is—if you read French." Cecil yawned widely, unapologetically. With a shake of his head he brought himself fully awake. He looked at the edition's paper cover. "This is the second part. You know what it is about?"

"Not really."

"Hugo has turned his characters loose upon the France of thirty or forty years ago. Pits a wonderful protagonist—a convict, named Jean Valjean—against a heartless villain: Javert. Although, this part I've just been reading, is a lengthy digression on the Battle of Waterloo, and— " (looking around to assure they would not be overheard) "and on the glorious and varied uses of the word: 'shit,' of all things."

"Good God." Casey was shocked to hear the word uttered indoors.

Cecil smirked. "Well, literally: *'merde'*—but an entire chapter on *'merde,* Casey*;'* the wonders of, facilities of—so on and so forth."

"I should think a sentence would suffice."

"Mmm, you might think that, but you would be wrong. Apparently, Cambronne's famous reply: 'The Old Guard dies, but never surrenders' is not how the natives remember it—and why I suggest you know French. It might be awkward to ask mother Witherspoon, 'Come, Mummy—What do it mean—this word, here?'"

"Well—I'll have you to get me over the rough patches."

"Happy to. But you will be gone soon, no?"

"Yes, actually. Em, in point of fact, I received a message yesterday from Colonel Battle, needing from me a date of expected return. The Cadets are currently under command of Sergeant Ledyard."

*"Ledyard!* What has become of *Señor* Yniestra?"

"He is here in Mobile. I spoke with him the other day. He fears his leg will not stand up to force marches. He goes before the medical board next week, but does not expect to be cleared for service. If they don't, he will have to resign. So—"

"So, your response to Colonel Battle?"

"Haven't yet; I will see what the surgeons say. But I expect I'll be on my way, soon—back to 'ole Virginny.'"

"You up to it?"

"The arm may still need more time, but my legs are fine. I gather something is in the works."

"You mean, an action? Harrison's Landing? Push them into the river?"

"No, I don't think it is that. We don't have enough big guns. And should we, while investing them there, they simply launch a relief force from Fort Monroe. They would catch us in a pincer."

"What, then?"

"The only other thing I can come up with, is we go north."

"Washington City?"

"Not necessarily. The same problem presents itself there—we don't have the siege guns. They are protected by the Potomac on the west, by marshland on the south and, bristling with forts in every other direction. No, Lee's problem is he can't turn his back on McClellan's army—and he can't get too far away from Richmond."

"He could send Jackson's Corps to wreak havoc in Pennsylvania, give *them* a good rogering for a change."

"That is what I think: eye for an eye, tit-for-tat. Old Jack would make them fly! But Lee would lose half his army in the process—communication would be the bugbear."

"Where was Battle when he wired you?"

"Montgomery. Said he would be leaving for Richmond in a few days. He mentioned Phelan is still hobbled, and Chester won't be back anytime soon—I gather the regiment needs every officer it can find."

From down the hallway Floy announced, "Brother? Another visitor come to see you."

"Splendid! Who do we have? A colonel or a general this time? Please show his Lordship in."

Floy escorted Nick Weeks into the room. There followed a reunion of veterans—more bumping of hands than handshakes. Nick's arm was also in a sling—he and Casey had been wounded within minutes of one another. Despite the joy of seeing his comrades, Nick was downcast.

"What is it?" Casey asked.

"I've just come from the Boullemet's—you all know Milton—"

"Is he still on the Missing List?" asked Floy, delaying her exit.

"No, more's the pity. Missing no longer: Milton died of 'wounds received.'"

The chorus of "Oh" was tinged with genuine sadness. Milton was a decent fellow—the Boullemet's eldest child. This sort of news was too common to evince surprise. "Any details you at liberty to share?" asked Casey.

"More than you may wish to know. The letter had just come for the old gentleman, from a Mister Someone, up there. I could tell it was bad news. With shaking hand, he passed it over to me.

"This man wrote that Milton was struck by a ball, just above the hip bone, which, traveling up the spine—paralyzed him from the neck down." Floy made her exit.

"The man said Milton never uttered a word—though his eyes were open when he was found. I imagine he was on the hill a long time—must have been overlooked many times. None of his comrades knew what had become of him. The man went on to say, Milton was carried up to the church, where even the surgeon attending him never learned his name. Before they buried him, our Samaritan went back to where Milton had been found, and discovered his haversack. His bible was inside. The man was very sympathetic; he has a son who is held prisoner. He turned Milton's things over to Simon Bagby."

"This war," said Casey, using the hackneyed phrase. "And more bad news: I have word Easton has died, and Redwood has taken a turn for the worse."

"Marshall only had a scratch on his arm! My father saw him," said Cecil.

"Gangrene. You didn't know? They didn't take it off in time. Now he's too weak to survive the procedure."

"Then it's just a matter of time," said Cecil. *"Merde."* The Redwoods lived just down the street.

To relieve the gloom, Casey said, "It is a long time since we three graced the rail of the *Saint Nick*."

"Ellison and Goldthwaite were there too," Nick reminded him.

"And old Armistead down there, making a hash of the *Manual of Arms*."

The smiles were wistful. "Weren't we all babes in the wood? Well, we are all here still—all of us still in one piece," said Casey. "And look for Goldthwaite and Eliza to tie the knot next year. Hoo-rah for that! A little good news. We must raise a toast."

"Here, here."

Casey presented them an imaginary bottle, which, upon approval of the 'vintage,' he uncorked and poured for each. "Careful, mind the carpet. Don't spill it, don't spill it," cautioned Cecil. "To: Eliza and Goldy." Saluting the couple they tossed off their glasses.

"He has gone with Semple's Battery, Goldthwaite?" asked Nick.

"Yes. Re-enlisted in March," Casey replied. "And you, Cecil—before I forget again—you owe me this: I don't *know* the many times I have been set upon by some wounded man, thirsting for knowledge. Now, what do you think they ask me? How serious their wound is? Or perhaps, do they wish to learn how the battle went? Or, that I might help them write a letter home? No! None of these—they are, to a man, mystified by that *tag* our medicine men have pinned to their collar. The question they ask me, the one of greatest import is: 'Sir: What is the meaning of *Vulnus Scolpeticus?*'

Cecil: "I require more wine—"

"What do I tell them? I tell them, the gist of V.S. is: they are 'going home'—and they should be happy enough at that. (And they are). But it puzzles me too. I have heard a lot of buncombe from this or that know-it-all—so I come to the source."

"The source of all buncombe, you mean?"

"If the shoe fits—"

Cecil was delighted to answer.

"*Vulnus,* as we all recall, is the Latin term for 'wound.' So, I direct your attention to '*Sclopeticus.*' Attend:"

Taking a deep breath, Cecil inflated one cheek. With eyes wide and face turning red, he made a pistol of his thumb and finger. Brandishing the weapon, he placed it against the bulge and pressed. The escaping air, rushing past his sealed lips, created a singular buzz, both comic and rude. Nick and Casey were puzzled.

Savoring the moment, Cecil explained: "In Roman times, the plebs had all sorts of ways of cheering their favorites on—or jeering their rivals—clapping and whistling and so forth, to signal their approval or displeasure. This vulgar sound:" (repeating it) "widely used, would have fallen into the category of displeasure; a particular disdain, known as the '*Sclopus.*' Come the discovery of black powder, somebody (some doctor-scholar—his worthy name lost to history) appropriated the term for the sound of a gunshot. Ergo: *Vulnus Sclopeticus* may be translated as 'gunshot wound.'

"You may thank the good Doctor Jesse for that erudition when next you see him."

After 'sclopeticating' each other a few times, Casey recalled, "That night on the boat: a dream was the subject of much talk, if I am not mistaken. Brother Carter?"

"Oh! The dream! The *dream*—I had forgotten the dream," said Nick. "The Spector of Death, and so on, I believe."

Cecil's playful demeanor, turned somber. "It has rung true, so far as I am concerned."

"'Where Are You?' Has anybody said that to you lately?" Nick teased.

"I 'spect I shall hear that phrase in due course. But I am in no hurry. Let us talk of more pleasant things . . . "

\* \* \*

Rodes' Brigade was arrayed along the crest of Willis Church Hill having completed a pre-dawn march from White Oak Swamp. Along the way, a seemingly endless cavalcade of artillery limbers, caissons, and couriers, had made them jump from the road. Followed by the ambulance train, which they saw again upon reaching the church; the surgeons relaxing in their shirtsleeves, smoking, in the shade. The temperature was rapidly climbing, the humidity keeping pace.

Hoyt had command of First Battalion. Sands passed him word the Yankees were in strength through the woods ahead. From the reek, Hoyt knew they must be near the old battlefield. Lake confirmed this and went on to describe the terrain ahead. Sixth Alabama went forward as skirmishers, their faces set for the worse; Rodes' Brigade would open the ball.

The other regiments, resting on their arms, expected the carnage to commence at any moment. Hoyt noticed the lack of conversations; the difference between here and, say, Seven Pines. Those men had been brassy and talkative, anxious to get into the fight. These were not the same men: alert and watchful, yes, but happy to wait their turn. First Battalion was not much larger than his company of Rifles had been on the first of June. The reduction did not appear to affect the survivors, each man keeping faith in his own luck; still, they missed nothing—if they closed their eyes, their other senses remained alert.

A man came down the line distributing mail. Hoyt received two letters, each in transit about two weeks. One was from his older brother, the second from his mother. He read through both quickly, his mother's twice. Then, tearing them to bits, he let the scrap fall to the ground. Looking up, he saw every man who had received mail, doing the same. A long row of white scraps marked their line.

Orders to advance.

From his position he looked to Lake and his small contingent of Rifles. Maybe twenty. Looking his way, Lake sent him a salute. Another company of artillery arrived ahead of its cloud of dust. Obtrusive and loud, shouting oaths and orders, they deployed to left and right, waiting for the foot soldiers to move off. The ranks shouted right back: "Where were you on the first of July?" and "Welcome to the war."

Lee was a fast learner: every field gun in the arsenal of the Army of Northern Virginia was on hand.

Rodes' Brigade moved through a landscape at peace with their motives. A crow lumbered across the sky, two sparrows on its tail.

Stepping across the creek between the hills, the division appeared to flow onto Malvern's eastern slope like a tide. Shells would soon replace the sparrows and crow. Though riding behind the ranks of his men, Hoyt felt exposed—an elevated target—and wondered how Colonel Lomax remained so calm on that day so long ago. Heart pounding, he never wanted anything so much as to get off this horse. Neither did his horse care to walk towards death. Missing the last elephant did not mean either party was ignorant. The stench increased until it could not be ignored. The enemy deliberately holding its fire, the better to deliver a deadly blow. The lines proceeding through trees now, Hoyt followed, noting the many young pines bent over, or splintered and browning. Hoyt enjoyed the fragrance of pine. It was home; the first smell of spring. Home was not here.

He compared his battalion's lines with the others. No command was necessary; as usual, the Third looked like they were on parade, the color guard escorting their latest battle flag. This one had arrived with the 'SEVEN PINES!' the old one had lacked. To this, 'MALVERN HILL' had also been added. Hoyt wondered if such bona fides would bring them luck, would make this banner last? *What will they call this battle?* Any moment he should be spying the enemy's flags, perhaps they too were emblazoned with 'Malvern Hill.'

Next to appear would be the entrenchments. *Where is the*

*rattle of musketry? The skirmishers must be on top of them by now. The trees, thinning—little cover.*

Open ground ahead, the lines are breaking from the trees. Hoyt braces himself for the sight, that the ranks are first to see . . .

Nothing.

Orders to halt, the brigade stops on the edge of the tree line. Nothing but open hill and blue sky. All eyes on the crest. There, none but their own skirmishers pilfering; a cloud of dust all that marks the abandoned position.

Murmured questions become an infectious cheer, spreading and gaining strength as it washes over the division, running its course of relief and joy. A faint echo arrives from divisions unseen.

Longstreet and his corps arrive from the north, just ahead of McLaws' Division, as beautifully coordinated a rendezvous as any general could order. The Army of Northern Virginia laps the crest of Malvern Hill with no enemy in sight.

Interrogators make their report: The Army of the Potomac has been ordered back to Fortress Monroe. Harrison's Landing is still covered by gunboats but the Federal evacuation is nearly complete.

Lee assembles his generals; their staffs confer and coordinate. The men remain in the ranks looking from one to another—relieved, grinning, speculating, opining; awaiting further orders. Today, they will be no war; there will be no death.

For the Army of Northern Virginia, the time has come.

# Postscript

*"Tonight, 50 years ago . . ."*

Joe Baumer, Drummer
Co K, 3d Alabama Volunteers

# AFTERWORD

THERE IS MUCH more to be said about the Third. Some individuals, however, have seen the last of the regiment; so, a few words about them.

The Rifles' Captain Woodruff and Little Joe Baumer, survived the war. Woodruff became Colonel of the 36th Alabama. The 36th was pronounced: "The finest drilled regiment I ever saw," by none other than the author of *Hardee's Tactics*, Lt. Gen. Wm. J. Hardee. Wounded during the fight at New Hope Church (outside Atlanta), **Louis Woodruff** was eventually retired from active service. After the war, he was elected President of the Mobile Board of Trade. He died in 1869, like Stephen Crane's hero: rushing into a burning building to save others.

**Joe Baumer** was also a fine soldier and, at age seventeen, was appointed sergeant major of the Thirty-sixth. Mentioned in dispatches for the Battle of Chickamauga, he was also at the disastrous Battle of Franklin. He subsequently fought at Spanish Fort (on Mobile Bay). On April 8, 1865, he was knocked unconscious by a shell and evacuated to Citronelle, AL, where, in May, the Confederate forces surrendered.

Coming to Washington in the Cleveland administration, he became Chief Clerk of Naval Affairs for the House of Representatives. He was a proud member of the United Confederate Veterans (UCV), a featured speaker at the 1910 Encampment—the year it came to Mobile. In his address, he laid claim to being "the youngest, *and,* the [longest serving] soldier in the Confederate Army." The facts are hard to dispute: his career began on January 4, 1861, at Mount Vernon Arsenal (at age fifteen), and ended one month after Appomattox. He died in 1924, the patriarch of a large family, his eldest sons named Woodruff and Lomax.

**Winston Hunter**, the frustrated captain of the Metropolitans, resigned from the regiment on October 31, 1861. He was appointed captain with the Second Alabama Cavalry. According to one account, he donated one thousand horses to outfit the command, and was elected colonel shortly after. While on reconnaissance in the Florida panhandle, Col. Hunter was invited to dine by the ladies of Milton. Sometime before dessert his command came under attack. He lost a number of men, and was nearly captured himself. In December 1862, he was cashiered for brawling with a subordinate over a game of cards. Hunter died in 1891.

**Captain William Jelks** (Co L) died on the eve of Seven Pines. Though he played an inconsequential role in the annals of the Third, his life (and death) had enormous impact. His widow and young son were left without support. She remarried, but the new family did not prosper. Jelks' son, Dorsey, came to the attention of some veterans, who gave him a helping hand. He educated himself, became a newspaper editor, got involved in politics and, evolving a platform, ran for office. In 1902, he was elected governor of Alabama. Dorsey Jelks became the first Southern governor to enact "Jim Crow" legislation.

Following the death of Captain Jelks, **Richard Kennon** was promoted captain of the Eagles. The very next day, while leading his company at Malvern Hill, he was felled by shrapnel. "The bursting shell struck Capt. Kennon in the right jaw . . . It came out beneath his chin, broke his left collar bone and went through his left shoulder." He would never again taste solid food. He died at the age of fifty-two.

For others, the trail vanishes. We know nothing of **Jester Simon** (of 'Ole Goober' fame), nor of **James Hunt**, the sentry who shot and killed Lt. Storrs. A little more is known of **William Green Andrews**, Captain of the True Blues. Dropped from Semple's Light Artillery, in 1864, he returned home to his family. He died sometime before 1880.

Major General **Benjamin Huger** never received redress from the Army. Any honest investigation of Seven Pines would have ended Longstreet's career. Huger, relieved of command after Frayser's Farm (where he missed a grand opportunity to split the retreating Union Army), he served the remainder of the war in administrative positions. He remained the scapegoat for Seven Pines long after his death, in 1877.

The body of **Tennent Lomax** was recovered and returned to Montgomery, where it was interred with great ceremony at Oak Hill Cemetery. Lomax House remained the center of Montgomery society for many years, until his widow's death.

**Edmund Fowler** survived his ordeal at Willis Church. The story of the drugs is true. Less one foot, Edmund settled in Montgomery, married, raised a family, and prospered. "Fowler's" became the largest drugstore in town.

Old Zou: Drum Major **William Hartman** transferred out of the regiment following Seven Pines, and re-enlisted as a substitute (in another regiment), where he served honorably. A silk-dyer by trade, he died at Mobile in 1869, receiving an effusive eulogy in the *Mobile Register*. In 1910, Baumer paid tribute to his old mentor, recalling Zou's fondness for cats and moonshine, concluding with this:

> *"On one occasion . . . while the Colonel [Woodruff] was making his rounds, he found Zou alert on his post. The Colonel asked Zou what he would do if a squadron of Federal Cavalry appeared. Zou replied: 'I would form a line.' 'Form a line?' the Colonel questioned, 'What kind of line would you form?' To which Zou replied: 'I form zee bee line for Camp!'"*

\* \* \*

I wish to thank the many descendants (and friends) of the regiment who have been instrumental in reconstructing the events of this book—by the sharing of family letters; tracking down the photographs and memorabilia that shed light not only on their ancestor's career, but also illuminate the lives of many others. In this regard, special thanks to Jimmy Cunningham (a descendant of Troup Randle); Tamara Hamilton, and her uncle, John Hamilton (descendants of Charles Forsyth);

Carol Ginn and Carol Williams (Dick Stinson); Neil McIntyre (Joe Baumer), Deborah Reese and Susan Posey (John Hoyt), Chuck Rand (the Mosby brothers), and especially Frank Chappell, whose wonderful compilation of family letters—discovered in 1991—may be found in *Dear Sister – Civil War Letters to a Sister in Alabama*, the correspondence of the four Branscomb brothers. As rich a collection as Ken Burns never saw.

Also Tim and Lana Dearinger, who first set me on this road; Cheryl DeChristofaro, who helped me locate my first descendants and, through them, the remarkable letters of John Hoyt; Nan Cunningham, who turned up a remarkable manuscript; Sgt. Buck Marsh, for his friendship, inspiration, and his insights of infantry combat in World War II. Lucy Flournoy who corrected my French, and Embry Burris who guided me through the King's English; Michon Trent and Bob Peck, of the Mobile Historical Society, Alice Rutland of the Mt. Vernon [Alabama] Historical Society, Joe Allen Turner of the Wetumpka Museum; Teresa Roane of the Museum of the Confederacy; Norwood Kerr and the excellent staff at the Alabama Department of Archives and History; the William L. Clements Library at the University of Michigan, and the excellent facilities at Army Archives, Carlisle Barracks, PA; Patti Woolery-Price, for her tenacity at the Dolph Briscoe Library, University of Texas. I am leaving out many others who deserve mention—if you ask me, I will gladly sing their praise.

Lastly, I thank my mother, Corella Martin, who was born on her grandfather's land, fifty years after the events of this book. As youngsters, she and her brothers heard Hal Martin's stories. They lived in Macon County, as far removed from the world then, as now, in a small community called Roba, named for Hal's mother. Mom would recite her litany: "Your great-grandfather was seventeen when he volunteered. He was a drummer boy—the youngest in his company. He was in seven major battles, including Gettysburg. I know he was at Seven Pines and in the Seven Days. He was wounded, and when he died, years later, that bullet was still in him. He was a tall man—he looked just like Mark Twain without the moustache."

The Martin home went up in flames in 1950, taking with it nearly every scrap of family history.

Near the end of her life, it occurred to me to ask: What was your granddaddy's regiment? Do you remember the number?" She thought for a moment, but said she did not know. "Why?" she asked. "Is it important?" "Probably not," I answered. "Just another regiment, I suppose. Just curious. But you can find out a lot, if you know where to look."

That afternoon, she emerged from her room, holding a letter in her hand. "This is all I have." A letter Hal had penciled to his wife, 'Pony,' dated "Gettysburg, July 2, 1913."

It reads, in part:

> *"Tonight, 50 years ago, at 2 o'clock we moved to the left and fought on Culps Hill, one of the hottest places I ever was in. The place look just as naturel as it was done a year ago. The trees showes the shots yet."*

The first words my great-grandfather ever spoke to me.

## CHAPTER NOTES

**The Frogs**
[Page 16—Colonel Leadbetter] The Mobile Cadets, Gulf City Guards, Independent Rifles and Mobile Dragoons were in First Battalion under Colonel Todd. Later, all eight militias were united, and designated First Regiment. Elements of this regiment would (temporarily) join other units investing Fort Pickens, at Pensacola. As events continued to unfold, the eight were redistributed to new regiments. Four formed the core of Third Alabama, two others (*Les Gardes* and the Independent Rifles) went to the Twelfth.

[Page 24—following day] Over a period of eight days, Moore authorized the sack of two federal facilities, assaults on federal officers, seizure of federal property, *and* the military incursion into a neighboring state—a *sovereign state,* according to the South's own reading of the Constitution. (All, before his own had declared independence.)

[Page 43—company K] Due to of its similarity to 'I,' there is no Co. J in Civil War regiments.

[Page 44—hodge-podge system] The gauge of Alabama's Montgomery–West Point line was a narrow 4'8½." Georgia used the more common 5-foot gauge (also followed in Tennessee and on up to Lynchburg). North Carolina was mostly narrow gauge, as was the original line from Petersburg to Fredericksburg. In 1861, there was no rail line through the city of Richmond.

[Page 46—hand them down] *"[Joe Eskridge] escorted the little one and I got the taller of the two. Commenced a desperate flirtation with her immediately—but I forgot to tell you their names. They are the Misses Langhorne [Nannie, 19 and Elizabeth, 11]. The tall one was the model of Barbee's celebrated statue the 'Coquette'..."* — John Hoyt

**The Swamp**

[Page 65—the Entrenchment]   Three enslaved men: Frank Baker, Shepard Mallory, and James Townsend, doing similar work at Sewell's Point took a rowboat, the night of May 23, 1861, and escaped to Fortress Monroe. General Butler, in one of the most significant acts of the war, gave them asylum and declared them 'contraband,' establishing the Federal's right to confiscate all 'property' used to aid the rebel cause.

[Page 66—regular army]   Commissions in the regular (i.e. 'national') army outranked those of the same grade at the militia (state) level.

[Page 74—at Saratoga]   The Varner mansion, aka 'Grey Columns,' is today home to the President of Tuskegee University.

[Page 80—Am I clear?]   The men of Company D, were uniquely virtuous: they recorded no cases of venereal disease during the war.

[Page 82—good impression]   Virtually every mess shared the expense of a servant and/or cook, either free, or enslaved, i.e. one hired out for the purpose. Milton Boullemet (Co E) wrote: "We have a very good man cook for our mess whose wife does our washing, and for which we pay 72 cents a day."

[Page 90—all comers]   Paul Morphy (1837-1884) was the chess world's first child prodigy. After the outbreak of war with Mexico in 1846, Winfield Scott was in New Orleans, and asked his host to provide him a competent chess player. Morphy, age nine, was sent for. 'Old Fuss 'n Feathers,' suspecting he was being mocked, had to be mollified before he would sit down with the boy. Morphy took the first two games. There was not a third.

[Page 90—the great comet]   The comet appeared over North America, July 2, 1861.

[Page 95—Pillow, perhaps]  Gideon J. Pillow (1806–1878): lawyer, soldier, blow-hard. One of three generals commanding at Fort Donelson, he was instrumental in snatching defeat from the jaws of victory, include a critical moment in Grant's career.

[Page 96—Randolph and Macon]  Prominent figures in the early republic, John Randolph ascribed to the "Principles of '98," and Nathaniel Macon was called by Jefferson *Ultimas Romanorum*: "the last of the Romans." Macon, GA, and Macon Co., AL are named for him.

[Page 97—Buford and Yancey]  Jefferson Buford (1807–1862) and William Lowndes Yancey (1814–1863): Buford was perhaps the most radical member of the Barbour County Regency, a nationally influential cabal of advocates and propagandists for secession, from Eufaula, AL. They effectively turned the South away from every compromise.

[Page 104—Miss Evans]  Augusta Jane Evans (1835–1909) nationally famous author of *Beulah* (1855), and *Macaria* (1863). Best known after the war for her million-seller: *St Elmo* (1866).

[Page 119—Dress Parade] All regiments were required to have a daily Dress Parade. 3d Alabama held theirs each evening at 6 PM. Newly arriving recruits were mustered into the regiment at the last Dress Parade of the month.

[Page 120—Gracie Manor]  Today, Gracie Manor is the residence of New York City's presiding mayor.

[Page 136—Marrast and Weedon]  Marrast was colonel of his regiment at the time of his death in 1863.

[Page 142—'the ole tar baby']  Stories commonly ascribed to 'Uncle Remus,' of Brer Rabbit et al., predate Joel Chandler

Harris' *Uncle Remus, Legends of the Old Plantation* (1881), and bear a similarity to ancient tales from Africa, India and South America.

[Page 146—John Brown]  John Sergeant Wise (1846–1913) was with the VMI cadets at New Market in 1864. He was a lieutenant at war's end, playing a key role in the last days of the Confederacy. He served in the U.S. Congress and narrowly lost election for governor of Virginia. His insightful *The End of the Era* is one of the classic memoirs of the war.

[Page 150—his business]  The fall of Roanoke resulted in the capture of 2675 officers and men and thirty-two heavy guns. Federal forces captured Elizabeth City on February 10.

[Page 155—news faster]  *Virginia*, aka *Merrimac*, was a sister ship to *Minnesota*—the first class of screw frigates in the U.S. Navy.

[Page 167—tooth puller]  Bonham's appointment to the captaincy of the new Company G (when not re-elected captain of the Beauregard-Lowndes) would cause others to place an asterisk by his commission date.

[Page 168—Armistead]  The same Armistead to gain fame at Pickett's Charge. He is no discernable relation to Robert Armistead, mentioned in earlier chapters.

[Page 173—*CSS Virginia*]  *Virginia*, pride of the Confederate navy was scuttled off Craney Island by these same men, a few days previous, to prevent her capture. Her deep draft kept her from steaming upstream to the defense of Drewry's Bluff.

## King Log
[Page 181—Seven Pines]  There never were 'Seven Pines' at Seven Pines. The name comes from being the seven-mile mark (from Richmond) on the Williamsburg Turnpike.

[Page 184—Old Pete] The nickname 'Pete' or 'Old Pete' was bestowed by his father, who saw his young son as being as dependable as 'the Rock of the Church,' *viz.* Saint Peter.

[Page 185—"I do not."] Huger: letter of August 10, 1862.

[Page 186—Longstreet a major] Of the major generals near Seven Pines, Huger was senior to all but Gustavius Smith, Johnston's second in command. Smith's commission dated from Sept 26, 1861. Huger, Longstreet and John Magruder all attained that rank (in that order) on October 7, 1861; Huger the senior because of 'tie breakers.' Of the other major generals at Seven Pines: D.H. Hill received his commission March 26, 1862, A.P. Hill, on May 26, 1862.

[Page 202—Gillies Creek] The scope of Longstreet's mishandling of Johnston's plan of battle for Seven Pines was not widely known before the release of CSA military communiqués by the federal government in 1881. Many of the Official Reports of Seven Pines submitted by Mahone and others, went missing, and have never been located. Longstreet's report was not made public until 1877.

The Gillies Creek bridge was described by R.E. Colston, one of Longstreet's brigadiers: "A little brook near Richmond was greatly swollen, and a long time wasted crossing it on an improvised bridge made of planks, a wagon mid-stream serving as its trestle. Over this the division passed in single file [. . .] if the division commander [i.e. Longstreet] had given orders for the men to sling their cartridge-boxes, haversacks, etc., on their muskets and wade without breaking formation, they could have crossed by fours at least, with water up to their waists [. . .] hours would have been saved. [. . .] When we got across *we received orders to halt on the roadside until Huger's division passed us."* [Emphasis added]

Colston's remarks were later taken out of context to allege it was Huger who did not want his boys to get wet. To be clear: every soldier on the Charles City Road that morning, was under Longstreet's command.

[Page 209—under maneuver] Just as every company had a precise place to be within the regiment's battle line, so too each soldier. Within the company they were arranged by height, with the tallest men on the right. The captains' position was also on the right; the first lieutenants' position, on the left.

[Page 212—watched them go] John W.H. Porter's *A Record of Events in Norfolk County, VA*,

[Page 212—Notes on seniority] As no officer willingly accepts orders from officers junior in rank, few things illuminate the inner workings of a regiment more than to know who is senior to whom; the dates of commission (DOC) for line officers, especially. At Seven Pines, the seniority of captains (on the line) was: Sands (A); Powell (B); Ready (I); Bonham (New G); Chester (E); Phelan (F); Robinson (H); Mayes (C); Simpson (B); Hoyt (K); Kennon (L). Based on this understanding, 1st Battalion is arranged (left to right): I • B • G • F • L • A (with L in reserve); 2d Battalion is: D • H • K • E • C (E in reserve). At Seven Pines, Sands, as senior captain, is breveted major, so if Lomax, Battle, or Forsyth fall, he will assume command of 2d Battalion.

[Page 216—Stars and Bars] At Seven Pines most regiments went into battle displaying the national flag (the 'Stars and Bars') that so closely resembled the U.S. Flag. The familiar 'rebel' flag—the St Andrew's Cross—was not in general distribution before mid-June.

[Page 237—approving wink] The youth served honorably the remainder of the war. According to Powell, he carried the regimental colors at Appomattox.

[Page 248—railroad car] Powell: *Reminiscences of Army Life*, Chapter XXV.

**King Stork**

[Page 256—*when Whiting moved*] When this letter was eventually made public (in 1881), this phrase gave Gustavius Smith pause. He wrote: "When Longstreet's note, complaining of Johnston's slowness, in moving Whiting, was written, not one of the six brigades in Longstreet's division had been put in action. Eight of the thirteen brigades under Longstreet's control were not put into the fight that day. Yet he would have it believed that before 4 P.M. his ammunition was . . . nearly exhausted." - pg 80, *The Battle of Seven Pines*, by Gen. G. W. Smith, 1891.

[Page 257—James Longstreet] Official Records, Vol. XI, Part III, p. 580. Here, Longstreet was doubling down on his differences with Huger. On June 3, 1862 Longstreet had written to Lee: "The entire division of General Huger was left in advance upon retiring with the forces from the late battle-field. He was absent yesterday [June 2] and not coming to report *after being sent for* [emphasis added], I ordered General Stuart to take command of the division." Official Records, Vol. XI, Part III, p. 570, pub. 1881, and cited in 1891 in Gus Smith's: *The Battle of Seven Pines*, p. 167.

Longstreet's Offical Report was submitted June 11, 1862, but was not made public before 1877. In it, he makes no mention of the issue of seniority with Huger.

Unfortunately, Huger appears to have never submitted an official after-action report for Seven Pines, possibly because to do so, he would be acknowledging Longstreet's errant chain of command. He instead besieged Davis, Lee and Johnston with letters demanding a court martial to clear his name. He never got one.

[Page 276—smaller Confederate batteries] U.S. batteries consisted of six guns, typically; Confederate batteries were four.

[Page 280—command of the regiment] Forsyth did not return to duty until mid-August.

[Page 298—have him whipped]  per D.H. Hill: *Battles and Leaders of the Civil War*, v. 2, p. 391

[Page 298—Do the same]  Jackson to D.H. Hill: Signed by Col. Robt. Chilton, Lee's Chief of Staff, 2PM. Edward Porter Alexander *Military Memoirs of a Confederate*, p. 157.

[Page 301—Miss Guest]  The surname is speculative. "Margar-et," her family, and the encounter in the garden, are faithful to Captain Hoyt's letters.

[page 306—Rate of fire]  At this stage of the war, Berdan's sharpshooters were still allowed to use whatever weapon best suited them, though the Sharps rifle was the standard issue after May 1862. A breech loading, single shot Sharps could be fired accurately 8–10 times per minute.

[Page 326—Balaclava]  Tennyson's *The Charge of the Light Brigade* was as well-known then as now, and 'Balaclava,' a synonym for military blunders.

[Page 328—Chimborazo]  So named for the highest mountain in Ecuador (el. 20564 feet) made famous by the 1802 summit attempt by celebrated scientist-explorer Alexander Von Humbolt.

[Page 336—drop by]  Wise kept his promise: "That evening I rode down to see them, but there was little to cheer [. . . ] There were no more tents, or cooks, or attendant servants [. . . ] or bands or dress parades [. . . ] the men slept on the ground, without any covering. The few camp fires were built along the line, and the soldiers were cooking their own rough fare."

[Page 337—on *merde*]  See: *Mobile Register and Advertiser*, August 19, 1862, concerning the famous chapter from *Les Miserables*.

[Page 341—Gunshot wound] *Leverett's Lexicon of the Latin Language*, 2Ed., (J.P. Lippencott & Co., Philadelphia, 1876)

# APPENDIX A

## Seniority, Captains, 12-31-61:

| Captain | | Militia Co. | DOC |
|---|---|---|---|
| Sands | A | Mobile Cadets | 10-6-46 |
| Woodruff | K | Mobile Rifles | 12-10-46 |
| Powell | D | Southern Rifles | 2-12-60 |
| Swanson | C | Tuskegee L. I. | 12-15-60 |
| Ready | I | Wetumpka L. G. | 2-26-61 |
| Hartwell | B | Gulf City Guards | 3-19-61 |
| Bonham | H | Beauregard-Lowndes | 4-6-61 |
| Chester | E | Washington L. I. | 7-31-61 |
| Andrews | G | Mont. True Blues | 10-18-61 |
| Phelan | F | Metropolitan Guards | 10-31-61 |

## Seniority, Captains, 5-31-62 (Seven Pines):

| | | | |
|---|---|---|---|
| Sands | A | Mobile Cadets | 10-6-46 |
| Powell | D | Southern Rifles | 2-12-60 |
| Ready | I | Wetumpka L. G. | 2-26-61 |
| Bonham | G | Lomax Sharpshooters* | 4-6-61** |
| Chester | E | Washington L. I. | 7-31-61 |
| Phelan | F | Metropolitan Guards | 10-31-61 |
| Robinson | H | Beauregard-Lowndes | 3-29-62 |
| Mayes | C | Tuskegee L. I. | 5-1-62 |
| Simpson | B | Gulf City Guards | 5-1-62 |
| Hoyt | K | Mobile Rifles | 5-15-62 |
| Jelks | L | Dixie Eagles | @5-30-62 |

\* "New G"
\** Bonham's seniority, being based on his Co H DOC (versus New G) is called into question and protested by Phelan

**Comments/Notes**

*Resigns 5-13-62*

*Resigns 5-1-62*

*Resigns 4-22-62*
*Dropped 3-29-62*

*Seniority adjusted downwards, by order; trans. out 2-17-62*
*1LT Elected upon resignation of Hunter*

*Brevet Major*

*1 LT Elected upon resignation of Swanson*

*1 LT Elected upon resignation of Woodruff*
*Absent Seven Pines, illness*